The
Time of
Our Lives

JANE COSTELLO

**SIMON &
SCHUSTER**

London · New York · Sydney · Toronto · New Delhi

A CBS COMPANY

First published in Great Britain by Simon & Schuster UK Ltd, 2014
A CBS COMPANY

1 3 5 7 9 10 8 6 4 2

Simon & Schuster UK Ltd
1st Floor
222 Gray's Inn Road
London WC1X 8HB

www.simonandschuster.co.uk

Simon & Schuster Australia, Sydney
Simon & Schuster India, New Delhi

A CIP catalogue record for this book
is available from the British Library

PB ISBN: 978-1-47112-923-0
EBOOK ISBN: 978-1-47112-925-4
TPB ISBN: 978-1-47112-924-7

Extract from *The Book Thief* by Markus Zusak, published by Bodley Head.
Reprinted by permission of the Random House Group Limited.

Extract from *Captain Corelli's Mandolin* by Louis de Bernières,
published by Secker & Warburg.
Used by permission of the Random House Group Limited.

Typeset by M Rules
Printed and bound by CPI Group (UK) Ltd, Croydon, CR0 4YY

For Isaac

Acknowledgments

Big thanks to the team at Simon & Schuster, especially my brilliant editor Clare Hey, and Suzanne Baboneau, Emma Harrow, Dawn Burnett, Sara-Jade Virtue, Alice Murphy, Ally Grant and Anneka Sandher.

Thanks also to Darley Anderson and his angels, with a special mention for Clare Wallace and Mary Darby.

Love and thanks as ever to my mum and dad, Jean and Phil Wolstenholme, and (Uncle) Colin Wolstenholme, for the number-crunching I'd be lost without.

Finally, lots of love to my children Otis, Lucas and Isaac, and partner Mark, all of whom were put on earth to make sure that there's never a dull moment.

Prologue

There is a universal rule of travel that applies to any holiday destination on the planet: the sunnier the resort you've visited, the more ferociously it will piss down when you land back in the UK.

And Zante was sunny. So sunny that, as my friends and I step onto British tarmac, shivering in the drizzle, it feels as though the only thing in the world that isn't grey is my nose, which is an alarming shade of red. Oh, and possibly my toes, which, courtesy of the flip-flops that seemed like a good idea when I set off, are now as blue and frozen as radioactive ice pops.

Still, I can't complain about the weather, which was the one element of the holiday that was excellent. That qualifies it as a rarity.

'How are your bowels today, Imogen?' enquires Meredith cheerfully as we step onto the travelator.

1

The family of four in front spin round to get a good look at me.

'Better,' I whisper. 'Though that's not saying much.' Twenty-four hours ago, I was gripped by the sort of cramps normally associated with unanaesthetised intestinal surgery, prompted – according to resort gossip – by a recurrent swimming-pool superbug for which our two and a half star hotel was rewarded a modest role on *Watchdog* last year.

Meredith hadn't mentioned that detail when she persuaded Nicola and me to book this two-night trip to celebrate her hen night. That is, her *third* hen night. She and her boyfriend, Nathan, have one of those on-off relationships – one that's so on-off that if you try to keep up it makes your head spin. At the moment it's on, but that guarantees nothing: by the end of the week, she could well have cancelled the 350-seat wedding marquee in Hampshire, fired the string quartet and sent her mother nose-diving to her third nervous breakdown.

'I don't know about you two, but I had a *whale* of a time,' Meredith declares, apparently confident that we'll answer in the affirmative. 'I know it wasn't luxurious, but you got used to those crawly things after a while, don't you think?'

I still have no idea what those 'crawly things' were – David Attenborough would have struggled to identify them – but I do know that I didn't get used to them. Or the shower, with a choice of two heat settings (arctic and lava); or the hair I found in my food every meal (collectively, they'd have produced an entire toupee); or the walls that shook when the couple next door were throwing up, singing or shagging, the latter of which, judging by the speed and noise, involved a variety of moves that could have won them a part in *Riverdance*.

I didn't get used to any of it, and neither, judging by her heavy eyelids, did Nicola. 'It was great, Meredith,' she replies heroically. 'I'm just glad you had a good time. That's the most important thing.'

Neither Nicola or I are flashy types by nature; we didn't grow up surrounded by luxury of any description. In fact, we both grew up in the distinctly unpretentious surroundings of suburban south Liverpool, where we met at secondary school. But even we have standards.

Which is why Meredith, my neighbour in London until recently, is an enigma. Her family appears to own half of the south coast, her father was a major in the British Army and all her other friends have names that belong in a P. G. Wodehouse novel. So my only explanation for her infinite tolerance of the hellhole we've just visited is that she sees it as a novelty.

'You know, if you'd wanted to go somewhere a bit posher, I would've treated you both,' she says merrily, as we arrive at the luggage carousel. 'I really wouldn't have minded.'

'It's very kind of you to offer, but *we* would've minded,' insists Nic. 'We'll just have to save up for next time.'

I look up and, with a sinking heart, realise the bag approaching us ominously on the carousel is mine. Unlike the chic weekend bag I checked in, this heap of canvas looks like an angry hippopotamus has used it as a prop for practising tae kwon do moves: a strap is missing; there is a yawning hole in one side; and my washbag is spilling out, revealing half a pack of Microgynon, enough make-up to put Clinique out of business and a burst tube of athlete's-foot cream that's now smeared on several surfaces.

I haul it off the carousel as two women I recognise from our flight glide past. They look to be in their mid-thirties and are unfeasibly glamorous – all lustrous hair, French-manicured nails and foreheads that, from a certain angle, look as though they've been soaked in formaldehyde. I feel a stab of something unbecoming of me; I fear it may be envy. Not, I hasten to add, because of their appearance, gorgeous as they undeniably are. But because of where I know they were sitting on the flight: in *business class*.

Nicola follows my gaze. 'I'm sure business class is overrated.'

'A ridiculous extravagance,' I concur. 'I'm sure No Frills is just as good.'

Meredith shakes her head. 'You're wrong, you know.'

We head for the gargantuan queue at the customer-services desk to report my luggage as damaged. After ten minutes of the line remaining resolutely static, I find the tattered copy of *Hello!* I bought for the flight and glance through its now-familiar pages.

Flicking through pictures of minor European royals and Jane Seymour posing by the pool in a palace in Kuala Lumpur might not have been a good idea after spending two nights in an establishment with more wildlife than a Tanzanian nature reserve.

'I wouldn't mind a *bit* of luxury next time, I must admit,' I confess, though I'm not sure when the next time will be. It's not that I don't enjoy going away with my friends – their company was the single highlight of an otherwise very challenging trip – but I'm currently in year one of a new job, not exactly rolling in money and, cheap and not-so-cheerful as it was, Zante has eaten into the funds for the main holiday I intend to take with my boyfriend, Roberto.

My heart flutters to my throat at the thought that he's on the other side of the Arrivals-lounge door, waiting for me to slide into his arms.

My friends can't really get their heads around Roberto and me, and the extent to which, after two years together, I still adore him.

I don't wish to sound schmaltzy, not least because I wouldn't want to give you the impression that we're perfect – we've had some positively operatic rows in the past (inevitable, really, when a feisty Italian falls for a girl determined to give as good as she gets) – but, two years on, I've come to realise something about why we were made for each other.

He isn't just the man I love: he's the man who made me

realise that I'm not all that bad myself. Despite the half-stone I've failed to lose over the course of the ten years. Despite my hair permanently refusing to do as it's told. Despite the fact that I couldn't keep a secret to save my life, grind my teeth in my sleep, find it difficult to say 'I'm sorry' and have a tattoo of a spider on my bum, from when I was life-guarding for Camp America, that now looks like a malignant melanoma.

Despite these faults and a million others, he brings out the best in me and, even at my worst, I know he'll still love me.

'Maybe we should start saving up for something more special one day,' suggests Nicola. 'We could put a bit away each month. Then after ... I don't know, three years or so, we could have a proper holiday. A *luxury* one.'

'Nicola, you're a genius. Let's *do* it!' Meredith beams. 'Top flights. Gorgeous hotel. Champagne all the way. It'd be amazing.'

Obviously, she's right. Although after the last two days, somewhere with a flushing toilet would be a bonus.

Chapter 1

Wandsworth, London, July 2012

My make-up bag doesn't look like that of a woman who'll be checking into one of the world's most glamorous hotels the day after tomorrow. Even I know that, with my stunted enthusiasm for these things. There are lots of lipsticks – the only cosmetics I ever seem to buy (intermittently in a bid to 'make an effort') – plus a Rimmel concealer, dehydrated mascara and something called a 'chubby stick' donated by Meredith. That's pretty much it.

It strikes me how bad I've become at the things girls are meant to be good at.

I never used to be. Once upon a time, I was into this sort of thing. But for someone who takes their job as seriously as I do, flaunting your assets is not a good idea. Part of me thinks that if any boss has an issue with glamour and femininity in the workplace, then it should be the patriarchy's look out, but the reality is it rarely works like that. If I turned up at the office all pouty lips and filigree undies, my reputation would never recover – and not just because letting *my* boobs off the leash of their control bra would be such a hideous distraction that I might as well go the whole hog and stick two Mr Whippy cornets on each one.

But, if I'm honest, wanting to be taken seriously at work isn't the whole story. The whole story is a long and complicated one, and can probably be summarised thus: I have other priorities now.

Still, this trip will be good for me, as everyone keeps saying.

Part of me can't believe I've never been on a holiday as luxurious as this. Although, to be fair, I've had hardly *any* holidays in the last four and a half years, unless you count Center Parcs.

'Mummy!' my four-year-old daughter, Florence, cries from her bedroom. 'Something's ... *happened*. But it was only an accident.'

Florence, who was named after her father's birthplace, might have the voice of an angel but there are few sentences capable of making my heart sink faster.

I optimistically interpret her tone as being insufficiently urgent to qualify as a true emergency.

'What *kind* of accident?' I ask lightly, piling my clothes into the bag, deliberately stalling before I face whatever disaster has befallen her.

'Well ... will you be cross?'

I take a deep breath. 'I don't know – what have you done?'

'It wasn't me. And, anyway, it's okay because it was *only an accident.*'

I abandon my packing and head across the hall to her tiny bedroom.

We moved here last year because it's in the catchment area of the exceptionally good state school where Florence will start in September. This monumental date in my daughter's diary unfortunately coincides with our company's most important day of the decade – a headache I have put off tackling because it involves an impossible choice: get my friend and neighbour Debbie to take her to school on her first day there, or face being burned at the stake by my boss – or something like that.

Apart from location, the flat is unsuitable for our circumstances in every conceivable way: it's too small, the garden consists of four potted gerberas, there's an unshakeable smell of damp and it's nowhere near as convenient for work as our old place in Clapham. This means my frenetic daily commute resembles a scene from *Chariots of Fire*, and our regular childminder is permanently threatening me with the sack, apparently unconcerned that it's supposed to be the other way around.

It's also ludicrously expensive, not helped by the fact that the pay rise for which I've been holding out over the last six months has not yet materialised.

Oh yes, and we have a dog. I don't make life easy for myself. But it was only when Spud's owner, Mary – our landlady – died recently that I discovered, to my abject horror, that she'd bequeathed him to Florence in her will. Her son, James – our new landlord – couldn't have him because he's allergic, and has his golfing holidays to consider. Spud's a lovely little thing but, practically speaking, not what I need in my life right now. So I briefly considered packing him off to a rescue home, but didn't have it in me, particularly as if Florence had found out, she'd have held it against me for the rest of her life. Plus, to Mary's infinite credit, she also left us the funds for a dog-walker each day I'm at work for the next five years. Which goes to show what an optimist she was, given that Spud is already knocking on fourteen.

Despite this chaos we do, just about, cope. I can't claim to be mother of the year – there have been one or two low points, the most recent being Florence's nursery's Harvest Festival when, last-minute, the only items I could find in the kitchen cupboards as an offering were a tub of bicarbonate of soda, some cocktail sticks and three bottles of WKD.

That doesn't, of course, stop my mother from telling me every time we speak that things would be much easier if I'd just move back to Liverpool. Which I'll never do – and not only because she lives there.

The fact is, I love Liverpool and I'm proud to call it home – it's the city that made me. But it's London that will forever be the mad, glorious place I can't ever imagine leaving, not when so many memories live here with me.

I push open the door to Florence's room with trepidation.

It is in every way an offence to feminist sensibilities. A haven of pink, it has a glittery dressing table (a present from Grandma), a fairytale bed (also Grandma's work) and more *Disney Princesses* paraphernalia than you'd find in all the store cupboards of the Magic Kingdom.

But she adores it. And, given that I've brought my daughter up to know her own mind, I can hardly complain when she asserts it – even if I wish she'd find something to replace the subject of her current obsession: a pink vacuum cleaner. I refuse to buy it, despite her tearing out a picture of it from an Argos catalogue and sticking it on her wall, like some sort of shrine to domestic servitude.

It's her big eyes I see first. You can't miss them, even when part-hidden behind her wild, dark ringlets. Then I'm diverted.

'I've done my nails. But I smudged a bit,' she declares, holding out her hands.

Courtesy of a bottle of cherry-red polish (again, my mother's work), her fingers look like she's fed them into an office shredder. And, yes, she *has* smudged them. All over her duvet.

'Florence!' I gasp, diving across the room.

It's only when I'm halfway there that I realise my movement has prompted Spud to stir from one of his lengthy snoozes. He bounds towards me to give me a kiss, knocks over the nail

11

polish and proceeds to leap around until there are bright red doggy footprints all over the carpet.

Barely pausing for breath, I grab the bottle and race to my room to locate some nail polish remover, which I proceed to sprinkle about the place in a futile bid to clean up.

'If only I had that pink Hoover to help,' Florence sighs.

Then my phone rings. I press 'Answer' and wedge it under my ear. It's my boss, David.

'Imogen, you asked me to call. Don't you know it's Saturday?'

David is a dream boss on many levels, and I owe him for reasons that go beyond my recent, scarily stratospheric, promotion. He's the chief executive of one of the UK's foremost food-manufacturing companies, Peebles Ltd. You might not recognise the name, but we are an omnipresent force, producing some of the world's best-known brands of biscuits, crackers, breakfast cereals and confectionary. Basically, if there's wheat and sugar in whatever you're eating, it's very likely that we've made it, something we do in no less than twenty-one other countries.

Unfeasible as it might seem for a 29-year-old single mother, I am its UK marketing director. Or, at least, *acting* UK marketing director, which effectively means I've got the job but not the salary, for the moment at least. It's a position for which David plucked me from relative obscurity after my two predecessors went off with stress.

The position is everything I've ever wanted in a job and has come earlier in my career than expected. But that's not the only reason why I love it. It's made me feel as though I'm really going places; it's proved to me that hard work does pay dividends. It's not just the new office, or the fact that I now sit in team meetings important enough for crustless miniature sandwiches (although they are marvellous). I've suddenly become – or at least am on the way to becoming – a woman who can make things happen, who people listen to and respect. Which is a very good feeling, I can't deny it.

On top of that, Peebles is quite simply a nice place to work; an office where camaraderie comes easily. In my pre-Florence days, this manifested itself in impromptu sessions in the Punch & Judy after work. Although these days I have to settle for grabbing a sandwich once in a blue moon with Stacey, Elsa or Roy, my friends on our floor, I still know I'm lucky to work with people I – largely – enjoy being around.

The only downside is that being a high-flyer or, at least, pretending to be one, isn't exactly family-friendly. Although nobody explicitly says so, it's not the done thing to slope off from work to get back in time to eat dinner with your daughter. I constantly feel like I'm slacking, whether or not I'm stuck in front of my computer every night until past midnight. Which I am. Every. Single. Night.

'Sorry, David. I actually left the message last night while I was tying up a few loose ends from home, but thanks for getting back to me. I just wanted to let you know that I've now sent you an email detailing everything you need to know while I'm away.'

'Yes, I got that. And the two earlier ones.'

'Yes. Sorry. I wanted to cover all bases, particularly for anything to do with the merger.'

Eight weeks from now, Peebles will be announcing to its staff, the stock market and the world's media that it is joining forces with Uber-Getreide, which is basically the German equivalent of us. It's all entirely hush-hush at the moment, but the result – the imaginatively entitled Peebles-Getreide Ltd – will create Europe's biggest-ever food-manufacturing giant.

David and his opposite number in Germany will be making the announcement at a press conference on 2 September, but it's my job to get everything ready for him behind the scenes: from liaising with the marketing department at Getreide and appointing a PR specialist here, to determining what colour tie will imbue David with an aura of gravitas on the day.

'That email includes details of everything, from the key contacts at Getreide to the market research results, the PR company we've just appointed, and every contact name and number you might need. Although I'm confident you won't need any of them. They're just in case.'

He sighs extravagantly. 'You know what I think, Imogen?' He pauses. 'I think you need to *relax*.'

I breathe out, only now realising I hadn't done so for several seconds. 'I am. I mean, I *will*. And, anyway, Laura knows absolutely everything and I've told her not to hesitate to call me if anyone needs me. You've got my mobile, but I've also included a number for the hotel, and my friend Nicola's number too, just in case. As I say, none of it should be necessary but—'

'Imogen!'

'Um ... yes?'

'What do I always say at times like this?'

'Oh. Er ...' I am hesitating because there are any number of multiple-choice options to answer this. David is fond of philosophising, although the truth is he's no Aristotle.

'Think long. Think deep. But *think*.' His voice drops an octave, in the same manner employed by Churchill when delivering his war speeches. Then he pauses, reflecting on his thoughts. As do I. Though I haven't the faintest clue what it means.

'I'll do that, David.'

'That's what holidays are for, Imogen. And you must be overdue one. When was the last time you had more than a week off?'

'Hmm ... 2007. After I gave birth.'

'Since then?'

'There hasn't really been a full week, more the odd day here and there. I've had long weekends. I went to Center Parcs in—'

'Then it seems to me you're overdue some time out. We will

15

cope, Imogen! It's not like this place falls to pieces without you.' He laughs. 'And, anyway, it's only three days.'

'A week. Well, a week and a day as far as work is concerned – I'm back at my desk next Tuesday.'

'A week and a day? Holy baloney . . .' My heart skips a beat. 'I JEST! Oh, Imogen, a week's *fine*.'

'A week and a day.'

'Just get some sun on your skin!'

'I will,' I assure him.

'Let your hair down!'

'Will do.'

'Get plastered a few times!'

'Hmm.'

'Sleep with one of the waiters!'

'Oh.'

'Take some drugs! Go skinny dipping! Have a threesome!'

'David, I don't think—'

'I mean it, Imogen. You work too hard. And I promise you this – if that phone of yours rings, it will not be anyone from this company. I'll make sure of it.'

'Well, it's fine if it is.'

'Imogen. Switch it off. I mean it. Switch the damn thing off.'

My palms dampen. 'Really?'

'Really. Now, you run along and have a fabulous time. I don't want to hear from you until Thursday.'

'Tuesday.'

'That's right.'

'Well, that's really kind of you, David—and, thank you.'

'Not a problem. Oh, before you go, did you send me what you've done so far on the presentation I need to deliver to the board next week?'

'Yes.' Twice.

'Okay, good. And the new images I'd requested?'

'Yep.'

'And the additional data?'

'All there.'

'Okay. Hmm.' He hesitates.

'What is it?'

'That phone of yours . . . '

'I'll leave it on, shall I?'

He hesitates again. 'Probably for the best.'

Day One

Chapter 2

There's excited, there's very excited, and then there's Meredith. Nicola and I spot her in Departures in Terminal 5 at Heathrow when we arrive just before 8 a.m. She's flying towards us with her silk Missoni batwings flapping like a designer phoenix poised for lift off.

'This is going to be immense!' Meredith is dressed like a flame-haired version of Paris Hilton – white hot pants, co-ordinating Alice band, and Balenciaga sunglasses perched above her mischievous, cerulean-blue eyes. The other notable thing about Meredith's appearance is that she's pregnant – thirty-three weeks to be precise, which leaves just under two months before she gives birth to Nathan's baby. Meredith has been calling it her 'final fling', which belies the fact that she sees motherhood as the equivalent to a quick but painful death for her social life.

She never did marry Nathan, although we notched up four hen nights before she woke one morning vomiting like a supermodel after twelve chocolate eclairs and, a hasty pregnancy test later, discovered she was to become a mummy. Which isn't something she's entirely taken in yet.

The development has also added an interesting twist to the ebbs and flows of her relationship with Nathan. Once they gave up on the idea of getting married altogether – about three years ago now – the on-off set-up they had had melded into a strange, twilight world in which nobody could work out whether or not they were actually together.

It wasn't an open relationship exactly, not officially. But there is no doubt that a certain amount dabbling went on, albeit fleetingly, and on the unspoken assumption that they'd always end up together again.

Then came the surprise pregnancy, something that changed things all over again – particularly for Nathan. Perhaps he's grown up a little, or maybe it's brought into focus what he feels for Meredith. Either way, he's no longer acting like a man who wants ambiguity between them. And – although all her dabbling has ceased – there's no doubt that these developments scare the living daylights out of my friend.

'I couldn't sleep,' Meredith continues. 'I've been up since two. I don't know what the matter is with me lately – I can't get through the night without peeing at least three times.'

'That's pregnancy, Meredith.' I shrug. 'There's more capacity in the bladder of an incontinent gerbil than yours at the moment.'

'God, that again? Are there any benefits to being this size, apart from a better chance of a seat on the Tube?'

'Well, there *is* the baby,' Nicola teases.

'Obviously,' Meredith replies with mild indignation, as she pushes her overburdened trolley to the check-in desk.

I think back to when Meredith and I first met, properly, on the fourth day after I'd moved to London, into the significantly pokier flat below hers. I'd become intimately acquainted with her musical tastes – largely in the early hours of the morning – from the start, but it was only when my eardrums were still jangling to the tune of various dance anthems several hours after I'd left the house one day that I had decided to bite the bullet and to confront her that evening.

I had prepared myself for the worst, but she couldn't have been more apologetic, erupting with remorse that she'd kept me awake. Then she had turned up on my doorstep that weekend with a bottle of something expensive and bubbly, which we'd demolished with a KFC bargain bucket in front of the newly revamped *Doctor Who*, before heading to Clapham High Street and pulling two short but enthusiastic engineering students from Belize. Our friendship had been sealed. And, soon afterwards, so was that between Meredith and Nicola. Because although they met through me, a few years, copious nights out and a string of personal dramas (the lion's share of which belonged to me), they were good friends with each other too.

The funny thing about Meredith is that, in every way apart

from her money, she is the absolute antithesis of her family. Her sister, Gabriella, is a human rights lawyer, a relentlessly serious type who disapproves of her sister's every move and considers her job as a freelance beauty writer to be so frivolous as to be barely worth mentioning.

Meredith partly has herself to blame for this. Despite loving what she does, and earning a good living – which actually amounts to pocket money compared with the inheritance she received after her father died a few years ago – she's forever repeating the words that could have come straight from the mouth of her mother: 'I'll get a proper job one day.'

My thoughts are interrupted by a little girl – about the same age as Florence – giggling uncontrollably as she heads to the check-in desk with her mum and dad. Since I completed the round trip to Liverpool yesterday – to take Florence and Spud to stay at my mum's, and pick up Nicola – I have been consumed by thoughts of my daughter.

'Everything okay?' Nicola asks me, pulling her dark blonde hair into a loose topknot.

You know how some celebrities claim to love charity-shop chic, but wouldn't actually set foot in Age Concern even if they were escaping a serial killer? Well, Nicola *really* loves it – and pulls off the vintage look beautifully. Today she's wearing a floaty cotton dress adorned with yellow roses, which sets off the warm copper hues of her eyes to perfection.

'Just worried about leaving Flo, that's all.'

Nicola puts her hand on my arm. 'She'll be *fine* with your mum.'

'Oh, I know that,' I reply. 'My only concern is that she'll come back dressed like Kim Kardashian and asking for eyelash extensions for her birthday.'

Nicola laughs. 'Try to relax. This trip must have been five years in the making.'

'Six, isn't it?' asks Meredith.

Nicola thinks for a second. 'You're right. I set up a standing order for my savings account as soon as I got back from Zante. Good job we didn't have to rely on *that*, though – I've pilfered so much of it on the days my rent is due, I'd only saved up enough for a weekend in Pontins.'

She's not the only one to have failed to save successfully – I spent two days before Christmas in Euro Disney with Florence last year, and have similarly depleted resources.

'Good job one of us bothers to enter these competitions, isn't it?' Meredith points out.

Our friend, it seems, is the luckiest woman alive: she's only ever entered two competitions in her life, and won both of them. The first was for a year's supply of incontinence pads, first prize in the raffle at the summer fair run by her great aunt's church. Then, last month, she did one of those giveaways on Facebook that everyone enters but, suspiciously, never seem to win. Well, it turns out that some do – and it couldn't have come at a better time. Only a couple of weekends earlier, when

Meredith had tagged along on a trip home to Liverpool, we'd all bemoaned how we wished we'd taken our pledge six years ago more seriously. I was feeling the strain of my new job, Meredith was desperate for a 'babymoon' – though with us, rather than Nathan – and Nicola, for a reason I couldn't put my finger on, seemed more stressed than I'd seen her in ages.

I don't think it is her job, because she loves that. Nicola is by nature a modest, down-to-earth type who doesn't have a flashy bone in her body, yet she is food and beverage manager of one of the City's hippest venues, Fire and Brimstone. It's a huge, converted warehouse that only the coolest dare enter, and occasionally me if I'm feeling brave. Although Nicola is insistent that the atmosphere is relaxed – they have smoked alfalfa-seed soup on the menu, and regular art fairs to prove it – I can't set foot in the place without feeling as square as a chessboard.

Anyway, the trip Meredith won was billed as a 'romantic getaway for two', but the holiday company who ran the competition agreed to let us pay for a third person, which we did by splitting the cost. So, basically, we've got the most luxurious holiday imaginable, in a hotel that could happily grace the cover of *Condé Nast Traveller*, for a fraction of the cost.

It's so fabulous that Nic's girlfriend, Jessica, was tempted to join us, even though she hasn't come on our previous holidays. But she had to attend a medical conference: something there's been a lot of since she qualified as a junior doctor at Liverpool's Cardiothoracic Centre. I like Jess a lot, and she's good for Nicola: funny, feisty and loyal, the first person my best friend has ever got really serious about. That was nine years ago – ages after she'd confided in me, aged sixteen, that she was gay (I hadn't had the heart to break it to her that I'd already worked that out).

Despite it being an almost-freebie, I didn't immediately jump at the trip. Although I'm owed tons of holiday at work, I knew I'd miss Florence too much. But, one evening, after a horrible day when I was one of only two people who'd remembered it was 'Wear Your Pyjamas To Work Day' for Comic Relief (the other being our 84-year-old security guard, Graham), I mentioned the possibility of the trip to my mother on the phone.

I should have known better. Having grumbled constantly since the day Flo was born about how deprived she is of opportunities to look after her, the decision was virtually made for me.

'So, the bit I didn't tell you,' Meredith says, grinning the way she did when she last had a cold and combined one too many doses of Benylin with a heavy night out, 'is that our luxury treat starts now. Not when we get to Spain, but now.'

'What do you mean?' I ask.

'Follow me!' She winks. So we do, bewildered, all the way to the sign marked, BUSINESS-CLASS PASSENGERS.

Nic shivers. 'You're not going to try and get us a free upgrade again, are you?'

27

Meredith once claimed that she had a guaranteed technique for securing this, the details of which I won't bore you with, except to say that it involved flashing more than her passport.

'It's all part of the prize,' she says. 'I only found out a week ago when the marketing woman from Elegant Vacations phoned me to check everything was in order.'

'You've kept this a secret for a week?' I ask.

'Nice surprise, eh?' Meredith smiles and marches straight to the business-class desk as every head in the economy queue turns to look at her.

The woman behind the check-in desk flashes us a gleaming smile. 'Hello ladies, where are you travelling to?'

'Barcelona,' replies Meredith.

'And you're in business class?'

I glance at Nicola incredulously then turn back. 'It looks that way,' I reply coolly, suppressing a sudden urge to cheer.

Chapter 3

I unclasp my necklace to go through airport security and feel a shiver of unease that doesn't evaporate until it's safely back in place around my neck. I know I have friends who think I shouldn't still be wearing jewellery given to me by a man who everyone knows isn't coming back. But, despite the fact that I've reluctantly accepted that I'll never see him again – just about – something still stops me from taking off the necklace permanently. It's not just that it seems to complement every item in my wardrobe, or that I fell in love with its delicate, blossom-shaped pendant the second I saw it. It's because whatever misery I went through when Roberto had gone, it was given to me during times I still consider to be the best of my life. It's a reminder that once, albeit in the distant past, he and I had something undeniably, uniquely *good*.

As we arrive at the business-class lounge, these thoughts evaporate.

For those who have not experienced the unbridled joy of

this oasis – and that included me until three and a half seconds ago – allow me to let you into a secret: if ever there was proof that life's not fair, this is it. I would be overcome with a sense of injustice if I wasn't already overcome with the complimentary croissants and Buck's Fizz.

As we find a seat with a view of the runway, I note the sublime peacefulness, the subdued lighting, the chairs of infinite plushness. There are no kids running about. There are no students, sweaty from travelling and asleep on their rucksacks. Everyone is sharply dressed, tapping away meaningfully at laptops and – the sign of a true world-class traveller – managing to restrain themselves from stuffing their faces with the free food.

I, on the other hand, am happy to concede that I am not a true world-class traveller. I am a mere pretender, a fleeting visitor to this world. And I am starving.

'Do you think you'll be able to leave work behind on this trip?' Nicola asks me.

I can't help but smile. She knows me, and my job, only too well. This might be the first holiday I've had in years where I actually relax the way normal people do – with no phone ringing, no work distractions. And I'm going to read a book. A proper one, not *The Gruffalo*.

'You always have had a wild streak,' she says, grinning. 'Well, I'm impressed. Meredith and I have been worried about you lately.'

'Me? Why?'

'You have so much on your plate. You've taken the term "juggling" to a new level, Imogen – it's like watching a circus act sometimes.'

Nicola has always looked out for me. She is an only child, just like me, but she's been my surrogate sister since we met. My formative years were spent combating chronic shyness (once, aged five, I got locked in a downstairs toilet at a birthday party, and rather than pipe up and make a fuss, opted to sit there for two hours until my mum came and my absence was discovered). So starting secondary school had been a hell that had no equal. But about five days after the beginning of term, Nicola had sat down next to me and introduced herself with a quiet smile. It was all it had taken for me to know that everything would be okay.

And it was. We were never members of the popular, pretty – and spectacularly bitchy – clique at school (most of whom are working on the checkout at Poundland these days). Despite repeated efforts with Nic's mum's false tan, we were plain and unassuming, the type of girls people nobody really fancied and (until my breasts grew ... and grew) hardly even noticed. Nicola was the one whose shoulder I cried on when, aged thirteen, a pack of Tampax fell out of my bag and cascaded across the school canteen; and again, when James Dickinson nearly burst his appendix laughing at the Valentine's card I'd taken three weeks of inner turmoil to muster the courage to send; and indeed, in 2007, when I fell into the black hole that opened up when Roberto wasn't there any more. I've done a lot of crying on Nicola's shoulder, there's no doubt about it.

'Why don't you do something really crazy and turn off your phone?' she suggests.

'That's a step too far. I've disabled my email and Internet settings, but I've got to keep the phone on, and not just for work emergencies. I'd never relax with Florence on the other side of the continent. I need to know that if anything goes wrong, I can be easily reached.'

'Nothing will go wrong.'

'Well, *I'm* severely tempted to turn off my phone,' Meredith breaks in, glaring at hers. 'Nathan is driving me up the wall. He's already phoned three times this morning to check I'm doing my pelvic-floor exercises. Oh, and of course to bring up, again, the fact that I'm going away in "my condition". I hate that term. You'd think I was a used car, not a 28-year-old woman.'

'He's not happy about this trip, then?' Nicola asks.

Meredith shakes her head. 'He hasn't said that but it's fairly clear that's the case. I know he's only worried, but even his books say that it's fine to fly at this stage in pregnancy. Besides, it's not like we had a choice – it was the holiday company, not us, who chose the dates.'

I'd never have had Nathan down as an obsessive future parent. He's a DJ by trade and former wild-child by disposition yet, these days, he seems more concerned with memorising Gina Ford's newborn routines than any of the dubious escapades he regularly got up to a couple of years ago.

'He's just concerned and excited about being a dad, Meredith. It's nice that he's so interested,' I point out.

'Lots of men aren't,' Nicola adds.

Meredith grunts and changes the subject. 'Are you going to turn off that phone or not?'

'I can't. And it's a moot point anyway, because everyone's promised not to phone, unless it's a real emergency.'

'Even your mother?'

I nod. 'Even my m—'

My phone interrupts me. It's my mother.

'So sorry to phone so soon after you've left.' Her enunciation is near perfect, despite growing up with a debilitating childhood lisp for which she received regular hidings from her authoritarian father. She eventually got rid of it using a self-help book and an hour of tongue exercises every night, something she says taught her that anything is possible in life if you put your mind to it.

'I know I said I'd keep calls to a minimum, but your father's taken Florence and Spud for a walk so I wanted to check on a few things. First is the itinerary for this week. Tomorrow we're taking Florence to *Princess Wishes* at the Arena. On Tuesday we're going shopping for dresses. On Wednesday she's coming with me to get a pedicure. On—'

'What?'

'Shopping,' she repeats.

'No – the one after that.'

'Oh, the pedicure. Well, obviously it'll be *me* having that, but they won't mind letting her have a go. She'll love it.'

'I don't doubt that, but she's only four. What next, a full leg wax?'

'I thought you said it was up to me where to take her?' she points out.

I hesitate. 'Yes. Yes, I did. Take her where you like. I ... trust you.' Which is true if we're simply talking about my daughter's general wellbeing and safety; whether I trust her not to return Florence dressed like one of those children on *Big Fat Gypsy Weddings* is another matter. She was exactly the same when I was little: obsessed with cultivating my inner-girliness – losing battle that that was.

My mother is PA to the boss of a private bank that manages the money of 'ultra high-net-worth individuals' ('rich buggers' to you and me), but I get the impression she runs the place, a bit like the way Rasputin did Tsarist Russia. This, her job for the last fifteen years, represents the least glamorous of her professions since she ran away from home aged sixteen. The only thing not on her CV is 'Bond Girl', although she apparently did once serve falafel to Roger Moore during a brief stint as a restaurant hostess in Abu Dhabi.

My parents met in their early thirties when my dad, who's

an engineer, was working for a company in the Middle East. They only moved back to Liverpool, his home city, after they had me, an event my mother describes charmingly as the worst experience of her life – I was born nine weeks early and weighed the equivalent of two of the ubiquitous bags of sugar. The fact that Mum was convinced she was going to lose me could be one of the reasons why she barely leaves me alone today.

She and Dad have one of those she-wears-the-trousers relationships and it seems to suit them both because, more than twenty years later, they're still together. That's despite the fact Dad is a *Guardian*-reading, bespectacled liberal, and in all honesty you wouldn't automatically put them together.

I look up and note with panic that there is a surge of interest in the breakfast bar. Meredith's plate is piled high with croissants, crudités and Marmite – a psychopathic combination even accounting for the fact that she's pregnant – and she's been joined by several others tucking into the dwindling supplies. My stomach growls like a werewolf during a full moon.

'I'd better go, Mum. Thanks again for looking after Florence for me, it really is appreciated. Can I phone you when we get to Barcelona so I can speak to her?'

'Before you go, have you got that special bag with you?'

I hesitate. 'Yes,' I lie.

Unfortunately, my voice always rises an octave when I'm

not telling the truth – an oral version of Pinocchio's nose. This does not escape my mother's notice.

'You haven't brought it, have you?'

It's been years since my mother has been to Barcelona and, following some Internet research, she's concluded that there is now a grave pickpocketing problem there.

You would never believe that someone so worldly wise could be this neurotic about her daughter, but Mum still treats me like I've barely learned to tie my own shoelaces. As a result, she purchased on my behalf a bag that looks like the sort of thing Securicor would use to transport gold bullion. Its proportions are preposterous – I tried carrying it briefly, and decided I'd have returned home in traction had I persevered.

I will, reluctantly, admit that there's an inkling of truth behind the pickpocketing stories. After the holiday had been arranged, I read an article about tried-and-tested tricks used by street robbers. In one, a woman on the metro stands up to announce that she has just been pick-pocketed, and suggests that everyone checks their wallets. At which point, all the men pat the pocket they keep those wallets in, and this gives her accomplices a clear indication of their whereabouts. In another con, fake bird-poo is squirted on an unsuspecting tourist's shoulder before someone leaps to their aid to wipe it off – and help themselves to the contents of their handbag.

Even in the light of this dazzling array of anecdotes, of which the Internet is awash, I still wouldn't bring the bag. It's so big and so ugly that even if you'd told me if I was destined to be marooned on a desert island and my only possible chance of escape was using it as a makeshift kayak, I'd prefer to take my chances with the breaststroke.

I clear my throat and deliberately lower my voice before answering her. 'Of course I have.' It comes out like Barry White on steroids.

'What about the Acidophilus I gave you? You know, to cope with digesting the shellfish.'

'Yes, I've taken lots of those,' I reply, meaning none. My mum loves health supplements. It's never occurred to her that the human body could possibly function without the existence of Holland & Barrett.

Nicola returns to her seat with a plate full of rye bread, cheese and other goodies, the sight of which makes me feel as though I'll fall into a coma if I don't eat.

'Mum, I have to go.'

'But I haven't mentioned the glucosamine sulphate!'

'Flight's being called. Speak soon! Love you!' I press 'End'.

'Haven't you got some nosh yet?' Meredith asks. 'We're going to have to go to the gate soon. You'd better get in there quick.'

I race to the brunch bar, and a cloud of wanton gluttony descends on me. It's not merely that I'm hungry and that before me is an array of goodies that could rival one of Henry VIII's feasts. It's that it's *free*.

I tell myself not to be such a pleb about this, but then I reason that I *am* on holiday and therefore, hungry or not, I'm allowed to pile up my plate.

There's only one large dinner plate left and, as I reach to pick it up, a bony hand gets there first. Its owner is an anatomical skeleton dressed head to toe in Prada; a woman so skinny that she'd surely need three weeks to make her way through one of these platefuls. She pouts. I narrow my eyes. But she's obviously used to this sort of stand-off so, wimp that I am, I back off. I'm then left with the choice of looking like an insufferable greedy guts and *asking* for a big plate, or settling for an infuriatingly modest one.

I sniff and opt for the latter.

I start with a croissant. Which looks lovely, so I have two. Then I spot some little madeleine-type things and add those, then a dollop of honey. If I was sensible, I'd stop there. But there's something in my Irish-Liverpool ancestry that means I'm genetically programmed to behave like the best I'm used to is half a rancid potato, so I add a little coconut cake and a pot of jam. Then I realise I have two handily empty pockets and so add two more pots – they're so cute! – leaving plate-space free for a couple more items.

By now I'm in almost a hypnotic state, as if having an out-of-body experience as my hand frenziedly reaches out and grabs item after item. It's only when I've paused for breath that I realise I've created a culinary version of Buckaroo on my plate – it's piled so high, it's now difficult to move without the entire thing collapsing. I'm still considering my options when I note that my neighbour, the skeleton, has allowed herself to go wild with three slices of melon, which sit in solitary confinement on her oversized plate.

I decide it is time to return to my seat. I do so as carefully as I can, holding my breath, with the stealth of a tightrope walker, baby-step by baby-step, glancing cautiously from my plate to my destination ... as an announcement is made: 'British Airways would like to apologise for a delay to flight BA—'

At which point my ears fail me. 'Was that ours?' I holler to Nicola, increasing my speed. At least, I attempt to: instead, a human-shaped brick wall suddenly appears from nowhere, upending my pastry goodies and spilling lavish amounts of Bucks Fizz down my front.

'Oh God!' I shriek, temporarily immobile as a wave of embarrassment overcomes me and I glare, crimson-faced, at the food I've firebombed over the pristine carpet. I then become hyper-aware that the tapping of keyboards has ceased and dozens of eyes are now peering over their laptops at the source of the commotion.

'Let me help,' a male voice says, its owner grabbing my plate and piling debris back onto it.

When he's finished, he reaches for a new plate and hands it to me. 'You may have to start again.'

I open my mouth to reply but nothing comes out.

His features are more sexy than classically handsome, with midnight blue eyes and shamelessly full lips: when he smiles, they produce a kind of half-smirk, an unsettling look that gives the clear impression that he's probably slept with far more women than is good for anyone.

I know, simply know, that by the time I've returned to my seat, Meredith will have spotted him, given him the once-over, and be working out how she can chat him up: although I doubt even she'd cheat on Nathan in current circumstances, she's not let the small matter of pregnancy stop a bit of harmless flirting. And he's exactly her type: big, broad, slightly unshaven and, in her demented head, the sort of bloke you *just know* will be a fantastic shag – a quote I've heard more times than I can tell you over the years.

'That'll teach us both to look where we're going,' he adds, reaching to grab some napkins. It's only then that I realise my Buck's Fizz is all over his shirt too. He begins mopping it up, before handing a napkin to me.

'Us *both*?' I ask, wiping my T-shirt. 'I thought I was, to be honest.' I say this politely, sweetly almost. But I've taken enough management-course assertiveness modules to know that it must be said.

He pauses and looks at me, smirking again, which really gets up my nose. 'Well, let's not worry about it. Just one of those things.'

I go to reply, but his expression stops me in my tracks. It strikes me that he probably thinks I did this on purpose, because I fancy him, like Meg Ryan in a 1990s romcom. I suddenly want to get out of there. 'I'd better go. Thanks for the napkin,' I add, to show there are no hard feelings, except as I wave said napkin in front of his nose, I manage to drop it.

So I bend over to pick it up, at which point the two pots of jam in my pockets plop onto the floor, next to a smattering of chocolate muffin. He picks them up and adds them to my plate with another hint of a smile.

There is an awkward silence and, as ever (despite the obviously useless assertiveness modules), I am engulfed by the hideous need to fill it. 'I collect jam jars,' I announce, as if such a hobby would be any less embarrassing than having the appetite of a ravenous water buffalo.

He blinks, clearly unable to think of a reply to that one. 'Right. Well. Have a nice flight.'

I nod and force a smile, then head back to the girls, thanking the Lord that I never have to see him again.

Chapter 4

He's on the flight. Of course he is. I'm rifling through my complimentary bag of up-market toiletries when I register someone walking past and realise it's him. He's removed his shirt and is down to a grey marl T-shirt. I take a deep breath and pray that he doesn't sit next to me.

He pauses, surveying the seats as he glances at his ticket, before sailing past to sit two seats in front. I exhale with genuine relief.

Nic and Meredith are together in two seats by the window, while I'm in the middle, adjacent. It matters not that we're separated by an aisle – in this utopia of aviation *nothing* matters.

Meredith leans over to me, wide-eyed. 'There's that guy!' she hisses.

'Hmm?' I say vaguely, as if I hadn't noticed.

'The GUY! The one you threw your drink over.' Meredith jabs her finger at him as if providing driving directions to a half-blind simpleton, and Nicola, torn between amusement and feeling my pain, nudges her and tells her to shush.

Meredith lowers her voice – slightly. 'Oh, come off it, Nicola Harris. Tell me you're not thinking exactly what I'm thinking?'

Nicola raises her eyebrows innocently, with a half-smirk. 'What would that be?'

'That we need to stop neglecting our duties and get Imogen off with a gorgeous bloke like that.'

'I'm saying nothing,' replies Nicola diplomatically, going back to her book.

'That sounds like an excellent idea, Meredith,' I hiss sarcastically, drawing a finger across my neck just as Hot Guy spins round, prompting me to slump in my seat, pretend I've never met this woman before in my life and do everything in my power to concentrate instead on enjoying my first ever business-class flight.

It's already amazing, and we're not even off the tarmac. Oh, the luxury, the sophistication . . . the prospect of not sitting for two and a half hours with my knees in the optimum position for a triple pike. The air hostesses are smiling angels – attentive, but not overly so – offering to cater to our every whim, with the possible exception of supplying Ryan Gosling and several tubs of whipped cream (this isn't exactly on the menu, but you get the picture). Plus, the majority of passengers are seated and ready for take-off, and it's looking like the three seats next to me are going to be free. If I was in economy, my heart would leap at this prospect – I could stretch out! – but here, no encroaching on an area other than mine is required; my own legroom is so vast, I could probably undertake an entire Pilates session in it.

'What are you reading, Imogen?' Nic asks, leaning across Meredith as I take my book out of my bag.

'*The Book Thief.* I've been trying to get this started for a while, but life's got in the way. This time it's going to be different.'

I used to read constantly – everything from chick lit to classics such as *Great Expectations* and, my all-time favourite, *Captain Corelli's Mandolin*. These days, reading represents a luxury that I don't have enough time for. Consequently, I first opened *The Book Thief* in 2010 and got to chapter three. I tried again that September, then in January 2011, then March this year. Those first three chapters were bloody good, so this time I am absolutely determined to get through it.

I open the first page and re-acquaint myself with the haunting words of its opening passage. '*Here is a small fact: You are going to die.*'

This might not be an optimal reminder just before take-off, but I persevere. I get to the third line before I am abruptly interrupted by a sound similar in volume to that of a Cape Canaveral rocket launch.

'*WAHHHHHHHHH!*'

The piercing screech of the small boy who has suddenly appeared in the seat next to mine is discernable only nano-seconds before his foot lands with a violent thud on my chin.

Neither of my friends witness this; indeed, it's only when Meredith breaks her momentary gaze at Hot Guy in front that she does a double take. 'Have you got a nosebleed?' she asks me.

'Oh . . . bugger!' I grab the complimentary lemon and berg-amot wipe from my cosmetics bag, rip it in half and shove it up each nostril as the captain announces we're ready for take-off.

'Anisha. Now. NOW!' The source of these frenzied pleas is the chubby little boy's mother. She looks like an Arabian supermodel, with perfect eyeliner, glossy hair and a figure so tiny it's impossible to believe that belly ever contained not one but two children. Despite the cabin crew's repeated requests for the little boy to fasten his seatbelt, it's his older sister who is being shrieked at by their mum for refusing to hand over her iPad.

'NOOOOOOOOWWWWWW!' she adds, just to be absolutely clear.

'Um . . . can I help?' I offer, but she doesn't even hear me and the dispute between mother and daughter escalates until it is less a familial tussle and more something you'd expect to see on WWE's *SmackDown*: hair is pulled, eyes are scratched but, even-tually, the iPad is ripped from the little girl's hands and she's thrust into her seat, a lollipop produced from somewhere and shoved in her mouth. I have no idea what's in it – Valium, judging by its effects – but it certainly calms her down.

'Madam, I'm so sorry, but you really need to take your seat,' the air hostess pleads.

'I'm *attempting to!*' growls the woman, flicking hair back from her now perspiring forehead, grabbing her little boy's legs and – as I dive out of the way – flipping him over with the skill of a Chinese gymnastics instructor. The lollipop trick is employed on him too and, finally, the woman flings herself down and clicks on her seat belt. Seconds later, we take off.

I her offer a sympathetic smile. 'Flights can be a bit of a challenge with kids, can't they?'

She responds with a flaccid look and picks up the in-flight magazine.

Over the next two hours and twenty minutes, it's evident that the flight would have been more peaceful seated next to a hyperactive goat. The only saving grace is that I'm not seated in front of the Demon Child – that seat is kicked, stamped and head-butted to such an extent that I'm surprised the passenger sitting there isn't in need of emergency spinal surgery.

Their mother, or perhaps she's their probation officer, has the right idea: she flips on her headphones, orders two large gins and tonic, and reclines her seat, clearly hoping to shut out the last five years. It's only when she throws a pill down her neck and pops on her eye mask that I consider getting a bit cross – particularly as it coincides with her son trampolining on his seat, launching into a rousing rendition of 'Food, Glorious Food' and spilling my champagne all over my copy of *The Book Thief*.

'Are you okay?' Meredith asks, an hour from landing. She's been asleep and the whole episode, nosebleed apart, has passed her by.

'This is fantastic, Meredith.' I dredge up a genuine smile. 'Honestly, it's incredibly kind of you to have shared your prize with us.'

At which point, a bumper bag of M&Ms spills exuberantly all over my lap and the little boy attempts to retrieve them by shoving his podgy hands under my bum.

The children's lunch menu has a choice of dishes, including spaghetti Bolognese: a genius addition given that no under-five ever manages to get more than about 25 per cent of it in their mouth. Sure enough, my neighbour's sauce ends up in the seat pocket in front of him, the seat pocket in front of *me*, in his hair, in *my* hair – everywhere, in fact, except his stomach. He concludes this dining experience by picking his nose with a bright red-sauce-coated finger, wiping it on the arm rest between us, and burping voluminously. At which point, Hot Guy two seats in front turns around, clearly believing it to have been me.

I sink even more deeply into my seat as the two children

47

put their complimentary flight socks on both hands and proceed to have a 'puppet show'– which may be better described as a GBH spree.

The air hostesses are aware of all this, of course, and make up for my misery by pushing as much champagne as possible on me, presumably to dull the pain. Other than that, there's little they can do given that there are no spare seats to move me to. The children's mother remains in a near coma until the very end of the flight, when she wakes up with a start, rushes to the toilet, and begins throwing up loudly, a process that continues right until we're on *terra firma*, when she emerges, wiping her mouth, her eyeliner only slightly smudged.

By that stage, I am filthy, drunk, and have read only ten words of *The Book Thief*. It's fair to conclude the experience wasn't entirely as I'd envisaged.

Chapter 5

At least I can look forward to our first treat on Spanish soil: the limo that Elegant Vacations promised would be picking us up. It's not a proper limo, according to Meredith that's the sort of thing in which a rap star snorts coke off a Page 3 Girl's bum cheeks, it's really just a plush taxi. At least ... it *was*.

After a fifteen-minute wait and a long phone call by Meredith, it becomes evident that the plush taxi company that was supposed to be picking us up is, in fact, the figment of someone's fraudulent imagination.

'The woman from Elegant Vacations is beside herself with apologies,' Meredith says, shaking her head when she comes off the phone. 'I felt a little sorry for her.'

'Oh, tell her not to worry – we're hardly in a position to complain,' I reassure her.

We take the metro instead, a transport system that, in common with most major cities in the world, does not showcase the best of Barcelona. Within minutes, two descriptions spring to mind: oppressively hot and grotesquely grubby. And that's just me.

I rest my head on the window and close my eyes, slipping into a familiar dream: a flashback to the day I met Roberto.

It was when Peebles was about to sign a deal for its brands to become one of the official sponsors of the Commonwealth Games. I was a junior marketing executive at the time, but as my boss was off sick it was down to me to brief the PR company so they could produce a press release.

I was slightly late after my previous meeting had overrun, and I arrived in the boardroom distracted and self-conscious. David was already introducing the members of the legal team employed to work on the contract, of which Roberto was one.

The only available seat was next to him and, as I sank into it, I singularly failed to register how gorgeous he was – at least, at first. Maybe it was because I'd recently come out of a relationship that, although not serious, had lasted a year, so the furthest thing on my mind was another man, but, with hindsight, it wasn't only that.

Roberto wasn't the sort of man who walked into a room and made everyone look twice. He was handsome but understated, with a slight build, modest smile and dark, glossy eyes framed by unfeasibly long lashes. His attractiveness was the type that started small but grew and grew on you until you could do nothing but be dazzled by his beauty. In fact, the first thing that grabbed my attention that day was his smell: a sublime combination of soap and Grigioperla. One minute I was taking notes about the deal, the next I was struggling to concentrate on anything but the heat coming from the person next to me.

When the meeting broke for coffee, I was unable to resist any longer. And so I took my first glimpse of the man with whom I would fall irreversibly in love; the future father of my child.

'I'm Roberto D'Annucio.'

I could never resist the way Roberto spoke – his accent would make bingo-calling sound like a sonnet. In those early months of his time in the UK, he relished picking up quintessentially English phrases, everything from, 'I've eaten like a horse', to 'Sleep tight', the latter of which he would soon whisper to me every night, between kisses.

That day, as we shook hands, the dry warmth from his fingers radiated through me and, though I've never believed in love at first sight, it stirred every inch of me.

He sent an email the following day about the press release. I sent one back. Those first few were infuriatingly perfunctory, achingly business-like. Although I would soon become very acquainted with the fire in his belly, at the start Roberto was nothing but reserved. It was therefore to my surprise that the emails continued after the press release was sent out, appeared in the media, and the deal was well and truly completed. They become friendlier, sweeter and with a tantalising hint of flirtation. But, after eight weeks of lying in bed each night, unable to expel thoughts of him from my head, I became convinced that my growing obsession was futile.

Then a note containing two simple, perfect sentences arrived in my inbox.

Imogen, I'd like to take you for drink. Would you agree?

Our first date – because it *was* a date, as foggy as that definition felt in the run-up to it – was at my favourite pub in Clapham, the Windmill.

It was on the best type of winter afternoon, with a vivid blue sky dotted with storybook clouds and a marshmallow layer of snow on the rooftops. We settled by a window and hours disappeared in minutes as I lost myself in his eyes and a blanket of darkness fell upon the day.

We didn't just have things in common: meeting Roberto was like discovering a male version of me. He'd overplayed that *Razorlight* album as much as I had, laughed at the same bits in *Meet the Fockers*. We even worked out that he'd arrived in London for the first time in exactly the same week that I had.

'Do you think Fate is telling us something?' He smiled and I laughed and blushed. And silently prayed that he wasn't joking.

The Roberto I discovered that afternoon was a man I'd never realised could exist: as sweet and funny as he was clever and kind (although, admittedly, at the time the sole basis I had to conclude the latter was the £1.50 he gave to a *Big Issue* seller). And, despite being convinced that a man who'd taken nearly two months to ask me out surely wouldn't kiss me at the end of the date, he proved to be deliciously bold. On that heavenly, snow-laced London afternoon, we stood beneath a blackberry sky and his lips met mine.

What started off slowly, with that mouth-watering wait for him to ask me out, became rocket-propelled. We saw each other three times a week, then every night. He came to Liverpool to meet my family (prompting my mother to fall immediately in love with him); I flew to Florence to meet his. Before I knew it, he had moved into my flat and we were filling it with knickknacks bought together at flea markets, eating like kings – he was an incredible cook – and spending lazy weekends getting drunk on each other.

Oh, those days. Days when we had a *serious* amount of sex. Hot sex. Slow sex. Frantic sex. Every type of sex you could think of, in fact, with the exception of bad sex, which I naïvely convinced myself was a chemical impossibility between us.

I become vaguely conscious that this thought, of those long-gone days when Roberto and I couldn't keep our hands off each other, is making me squirm with pleasure ... At which point, I am violently awoken.

It isn't that the accordion player's rendition of 'The Girl From Ipanema' is all that bad – not if you're comparing its musical qualities to, say, fingernails screeching across a blackboard. What it is, though, is loud. Devastatingly, flatulently loud. The musician in question is clearly either completely deaf or under the impression he's performing at a venue comparable in size to the Camp Nou football stadium, rather than the small, confined baked-bean tin that is this carriage.

I look away and slump in my seat, trying to pretend it's not happening, but to my alarm he reads my body language and perceives this as a challenge.

He begins to Dad-dance towards me with an enthusiastic grin, stomping his feet in a deranged, tuneless serenade. I glare at my friends, who snigger in wide-eyed disbelief as he throws in a little jig to this display, which he clearly considers jaunty despite his generosity of body fat.

Just as I am close to expiring from embarrassment, he spins around, pausing briefly to encourage people in the carriage to start clapping. Fortunately, the only person he succeeds in persuading to join in is an elderly man with a Brillo-pad beard who, until now, has been sucking on an electric cigarette like he's trying to vacuum it directly into his lungs.

As other passengers look on, I root around in my bag and produce a couple of euros, foisting it on the guy in the hope that it will get rid of him. Sadly, as my cheeks inflame almost as much as my ears, I realise that he has interpreted this move as an indication that I'm impressed with his work and want more. So he continues. And continues. Until, finally, we reach our stop and I drag my sorry self off the train in the certainty that my ears will be throbbing until at least this time tomorrow.

Chapter 6

The B Hotel rises majestically out of Barceloneta's platinum sand beach like a gargantuan, glistening spaceship. It has all the attributes of a super-cool urban hotel, but its location at the end of a boardwalk sprinkled with relaxed tapas bars and over-looking the tumbling, ultramarine waters of the Mediterranean also gives it the feel of a holiday resort.

Inside, there is absolutely no evidence of the troubles that have hit Spain's economy in the last few years. The decor couldn't be more impressive if it'd been the brainchild of a design guru called Flashy McSwanky. A vast foyer leads to a pool area of knee-trembling tranquillity, an oasis of polished tiles and palm trees arranged in a swaying phalanx around an elegant infinity pool. Ambient tunes drift across the deck of rich, dark wood, accompanying the chatter of beautiful people as they sip rainbow-coloured cocktails and massage suncream into their already well-moisturised thighs.

I cannot *wait* to join them, even if I've failed to find time to moisturise my thighs in weeks.

Back at the reception desk, it's the most popular time to check in, judging by the crowds in the foyer, all of whom own the sort of luggage that makes mine look as though I bought it from the seconds stall at the world's worst jumble sale.

'Have you seen the limo that's just pulled up outside?' Nicola says, craning her neck to see past me. 'I've seen shorter National Express coaches.'

'I wonder if it's someone famous?' hoots Meredith as she shamelessly heads off to get a good look. Nic and I coolly hang back, attempting to generate the illusion that we encounter this sort of thing every day.

I don't recognise the woman who steps out of the car, followed by a troupe of hangers-on and a stack of luggage the size of a modest Hebridean island. But, from the proportions of her bouncers, height of her heels and the obligatory aviator glasses, she must be famous.

'She does look vaguely familiar,' says Nicola. 'Although she wasn't in the *Heat* I read on the plane.'

The hotel staff have acquired the air of a team of Victorian domestic servants, scurrying around her before she's whisked away, no doubt to a room of palatial dimensions.

'That was Spain's hottest new movie star, Calandria Benevente,' Meredith informs us triumphantly, having quizzed the doorman. 'She's tipped to be the next Penelope Cruz.'

While we're waiting to check in, Meredith nips off to the loo – again – and I take the opportunity to have a brief conversation with Florence for no other reason than to hear her voice.

When we eventually reach the front desk, we're greeted by a young concierge who's as groomed as a championship dressage horse.

'Hello, ladies. May I take your passports?' He's Spanish, but with perfect English pronunciation and a manner clearly honed at a succession of customer-service tutorials in grovelling.

Nicola hands over her passport, while I give him mine and Meredith's.

He taps at a keyboard, pausing as his smile disintegrates. 'I'm terribly sorry about this . . . it seems that your rooms aren't quite ready yet.'

'But it's 2 p.m.,' I wail. I'm coated in a putrid concoction of Bolognese sauce and small child's snot, and I am desperate for a shower. 'I thought we could check in now?'

He looks profoundly disturbed, as if this is the stuff of nightmares from which you awake in a tepid sweat screaming for your mother. 'I'm so sorry. It's extremely unusual, but we've experienced a staffing shortage among our cleaning team that we're trying to resolve as soon as possible. It's the first time it's ever happened. We can hold your bags while you take a walk on the beach, or perhaps a cocktail at the bar? On us, of course.'

The truth is, I'm quietly rat-arsed from the flight and the novelty of free drinks has worn off.

'It's no problem,' I reply, not wanting to make a fuss. 'Will someone come and let me know when it's ready?'

'Of course! Leave your mobile number with us and I'll phone you when it's done.'

Meredith returns from the toilet and I break the news to her about the rooms. Meredith and I will be sharing the one that was part of the prize. It felt a bit *Mallory Towers* at first, but she said she'd prefer it that way, adding ominously that it would be 'just like a girlie sleepover!'

The three of us head through the gleaming granite lobby, towards two enormous glass doors that lead to the hotel's private beach. It is so perfect even the sand looks as if it's been sieved.

In the light of the fact that I look as though I have waded through a swamp to get here and really don't feel ready to take on the glamorous clientele around the pool just yet, I persuade the girls to head a little further afield so that we can stretch our legs.

The main beach is in every way what you'd expect from Spain on a sunny day – hot, packed and full of people in various stages of undress. Having been to Spain before, it's no surprise that plenty of people are sunbathing in the Continental (i.e. topless) fashion; what I hadn't expected, as we slowly make our way along the boardwalk looking for a suitable spot, was that some people are not just topless. In fact, some people are significantly more than topless.

'HAS HE GOT HIS CROWN JEWELS OUT?' Meredith whoops, at the sort of volume Amazonian Indians might employ to communicate with people in neighbouring villages.

'*Sshhhhh!*' I hiss.

Nicola suppresses a laugh. 'It was mentioned in the guidebook I bought at the airport. Apparently, for years before our hotel was built, this was one of Barcelona's nudist beaches. The powers-that-be assumed that would stop when the hotel opened, and it largely has. But some of the older generation keep the tradition alive.'

This history lesson explains another curious phenomenon: the only people brave enough to have whipped off everything are those who clearly got here on a free bus pass. Part of me admires these game over-sixties: their lack of inhibition, their *joie de vivre*, the fact that they're sticking two fingers up at society's obsession with youth. That's the part of me that doesn't get an eyeful of drooping, leathery buttock every way I turn.

Anyone our age is significantly more prudish, with the exception of a smattering of topless girls. Oh, and one other exception:

'Come on!' Meredith's top and maternity bra are off faster than you can say 'tandem Space Hoppers', followed by her shorts.

Nicola raises her eyebrows in despair.

'When in Rome!' Meredith grins, casting off her Mamas and Papas knickers and skipping towards the water. She plunges in like a newborn hippo enthusiastically attempting to learn the breaststroke.

'My pants are staying where they are,' Nicola tells me.

'Don't worry – mine, too.'

Nic and I find a spot in which to sit and I remove a pair of shades from my bag and put them on, only to discover that my hurried packing has left me with the 3D glasses I bought at the Odeon when I took Florence to *Ice Age 4* last weekend.

'Cool.' Nicola smirks.

'Oh God! Still' – I gesture to four old gents with bellies bigger than Meredith's playing a lively game of naked *boules* – 'their saving grace is they make everything look nice and blurry.'

I lie on my side, attempting to look entirely relaxed about the fact that I'm surrounded by gentlemen's unmentionables, and take out my book. It might have been an eventful journey, but *this* is when it starts: my peace and quiet. My opportunity to relax. My first proper holiday in years . . .

'*Here is a small fact . . .*'

'IMOGEN COPELAND!'

I don't recognise the voice, but it's very clearly British with a hint of Scouse. 'Imogen Copeland and Nicola Harris. Well. I. *Never!*'

We gaze up at the figure addressing us, squinting as the sun streams into our eyes. Nicola scrambles to a standing position and I follow suit ... immediately wishing I hadn't.

'Mr Brayfield! What a ... *surprise*,' Nic manages, in the same way you'd greet a severe bout of cystitis. 'My mum mentioned she'd seen you in Sainsbury's the other week.'

Mr Brayfield was our geography teacher at school; our one-legged geography teacher, to be precise. He was very good at his job – I got an A in my GCSE – and was known for his boundless energy. The precise nature of how he lost his leg was the subject of endless speculation and theories abounded, ranging from a shark attack, to getting it stuck in the lift in John Lewis. He deliberately refused to tell us the real story, preferring to retain a sense of mystery – an approach I sincerely wish he'd extended into all other areas in his life. For, the notable thing about Mr Brayfield right now is not his singular leg, nor his crutches – famously carved with the initials of every sixth former he's ever taught. It's that he's not wearing anything. He's as devoid of strides as the day he was born.

Of all the views I expected on holiday, I can think of none for which I could have wished less.

'Yes, your mum and I had a good old natter,' he says with a grin. Nicola's eyes are darting to the sky, then the sand, then at the rollerbladers zigzagging past on the boardwalk. Anywhere, in fact, that isn't Mr Brayfield's nethers. 'She mentioned you'd found yourself a new man, Nicola. Well done you!'

'A new . . . man?' I ask, to check I've heard right.

'Don't tell me she hasn't told you about her new fellow!' Mr Brayfield guffaws. 'Your mum seemed to approve of him, anyway.'

I glance at Nicola, who squirms uncomfortably.

'So, what are you two doing here?' he continues.

'Oh . . . erm, we won a competition. We're only here for a few days,' I mumble.

'Lucky old you two. Barcelona's got everything!' he declares, swinging out his arms triumphantly. We take a step back. 'Dot and I have been coming for years, haven't we?'

He spins round and registers his wife coming up twenty feet behind, clearly unable to keep up with his considerable pace.

Mrs Brayfield is a large, glistening woman, her pale pink flesh flushed to a violent russet from the neck up, who wheezes her way to us wearing only (and I mean, only) a large camping rucksack.

'Keep up, old girl,' chuckles Mr Brayfield. 'I was telling Nicola and Imogen here that we come to Barcelona all the time, don't we?'

She's puffing and panting like a steam train under threat of decommission as she joins us. 'Hello, yes, we . . . love it. It's a splendid place. I'm Dot.' She holds out a hand, which we tentatively shake while maintaining firm eye contact. 'So!' she hoots, as I pretend to be distracted by an enthralling game of Frisbee. 'Are you ex-pupils?'

We nod awkwardly and she bursts into laughter. 'Bry-*an*! You shouldn't be giving these two an eyeful of your ding-a-long! They'll be embarrassed, won't you?'

Nicola and I shift from one foot to another, trying to think of an answer.

'Not that you should be – once you've seen one, you've seen them all,' philosophises Mrs B, pulling the rucksack off her back with a hearty huff. 'And there's nothing offensive about Bryan's, is there?'

We stand mute as the horrifying possibility dawns on us that she's inviting us to examine, and possibly compliment, the genitalia of the man who taught us the difference between erosional and depositional landforms.

I glance at Nicola, who is green. 'I'm sorry,' she announces suddenly. 'We need to go and check in now.'

'Yes, we do,' I reinforce. 'We very much do. We need to go and get our friend, then go.'

'Where are you staying?' asks Mr Brayfield.

'Madrid,' Nicola replies.

But, having made themselves comfortable on a tartan blanket, they're now too busy rummaging around in the backpack to hear.

'Sure you don't want to stay and have a picnic?' offers Mrs Brayfield, as she picks damp pieces of paper napkin off some soggy breakfast buns clearly appropriated from a hotel buffet.

'Ah, we could have a chat about old times!' Mr Brayfield

adds, but Nicola is now backing away as though she is being threatened with a pump-action shotgun.

'Thank you, but no,' she says. 'Enjoy the rest of your day.'

'Oh, we will,' Mr Brayfield assures us. 'And be careful with the suncream. Muggins here missed a few bits last time – ouch!' He grins, pointing downwards.

At which point Nicola looks like she might faint.

Chapter 7

We finally get to our room around 5 p.m. I'm not sure why but, judging by the anxiety etched into the concierge's forehead, it isn't something that happens often.

The room is a miracle of modern hospitality: an ambiently lit, orgasmically appointed homage to interior design. Silk curtains fall heavily on a carpet of intense depth and softness, while state-of-the-art gadgets sit in subtle juxtaposition to a view of amaranthine loveliness across the sea.

I am running my fingers over the crisp white sheets of one of the two enormous twin beds, imagining how it will feel to sink into the whispering softness of its pillows, when Meredith bursts out of the toilet.

'There's a LOO-ROLL LIGHT! Isn't that *awesome*?'

'What's a loo-roll light?'

'Well ... it lights up your loo roll,' she replies, an ask-a-silly-question response if ever I've heard one.

There's no doubt about it – it couldn't be more perfect.

All I need now is to clean myself up and enjoy this properly.

As Meredith settles down with Spanish *Vogue*, I go to take a shower, a prospect I've never relished more as I peel off my Bolognese-coated T-shirt.

I reach out to turn the chrome tap, closing my eyes as I anticipate warm suds sweeping down my body. Instead, I am assaulted by water colder than the deep end of Tooting Bec Lido in January. Shrieking, I leap out, and spend the next five minutes hopping about, turning blue and wrestling with the temperature knob as Meredith provides what she clearly believes to be helpful instructions, formed solely on the basis of watching one episode of *DIY SOS*.

I reluctantly reach the conclusion that nothing I do is going to work, a fact I struggle to compute – that my five-star hotel, the likes of which I'm never likely to see the inside of again, has failed to provide me with hot, running water.

I grab a dressing gown and tiptoe into the bedroom to discover cards next to the phone advertising the hotel's 'Whatever your whim' service, which apparently caters for every tiny request imaginable. I phone the number and explain that my only whim is for a shower. A simple, straightforward shower.

After apologising profusely, they send up a man. He proceeds to fiddle with the shower until, to the soundtrack of his frenzied cries, it sends water spewing all over him, our room and our carpet of intense depth and softness.

So another man comes along and – apologising profusely – tells us we need to move rooms. At which point a woman appears and – apologising profusely – marches us to another room on the floor above. She reassures me that I can keep hold of the dressing gown until I get there, as if I'd considered the alternative.

Meredith can't resist a bit of a grumble, however, although that's partly because she's received a text from Nathan telling her he loves her and enquiring if she's massaging her perineum regularly.

But, all in all, I think we're remarkably stoic – something that can partly be attributed to the profuse apologies, which are so relentless I'm not sure how many more I can take.

We finally settle in our new room with a working shower, and it is every bit as exquisite as I'd hoped. The result is that I am now bathed, relaxed, swaddled in a robe so fluffy you could wear it while husky-sledging across an Alaskan glacier, and intending to spend a few blissful minutes on the balcony reading before I get ready for dinner.

'*Here is a small fact . . .*'

My phone rings. I pick it up and glance at its screen, noting the words 'Private number'.

If I were a better woman, I'd leave it, confident in the knowledge that 99 per cent of calls from an anonymous number are from somebody to whom you don't want to speak.

But it rings and rings until I do what I always do – huff demonstratively, then answer.

'Hello, Imogen Copeland.'

'Hello, Ms Copeland. I'm SO sorry to bother you. It's Laura Greenwood here.'

Laura, our new office administrator, is a sweet but smart Geordie in her early twenties who is so vastly overqualified for the job I literally blush when I ask her to order new pencils.

'You really don't have to call me "Ms Copeland", you know.' I think of Laura as the sort of woman who, a few years ago, I'd have been drinking with in a student union bar, yet she addresses me like I'm about to send her to sit outside the head teacher's office.

'Sorry,' she replies.

'It's fine! Look, Laura, I'm actually away on holiday at the moment,' I tell her.

'I know. I'm so, so sorry. But Diana told me that there was no alternative to phoning you.'

Diana, David's secretary, is a strikingly attractive divorcée in her mid-forties with an MA in Business Studies, and a PhD in calling the management wankers. She despises her job and is incapable of engaging in conversation with David, our esteemed leader, without rolling her eyes theatrically. I suspect he's secretly terrified of her, which is probably why she's still there – I don't think Stalin would have had the balls to sack her.

'Did she not tell you that Roy's deputising for me?'

'She did. Well, I already knew. The problem is, he's nowhere to be found.'

It's been brilliant having Roy as a deputy, partly because I've known him for ever. Despite the fact that his gentle personality means he has a tendency to blend into the background, he's actually good fun. Unlike me, he seems to have the balance of work–family life exactly right, judging by the fact that he's been happily married since the age of twenty-one and has more pictures of his three kids around his desk than I have Post-it notes (and that's A LOT).

I worried when I first got this job – given that he's six years older than I am and has worked at Peebles for longer than I have – that he had every right to resent my luck. But he's been great to work with and, although I fretted about leaving him in charge while I was away, I know that is about my inability to let go rather than his competence.

'Is he in a meeting?' I ask.

'I've no idea where he is, but this is urgent. So he said anyway.'

'So who said?'

'The journalist from the *Daily Sun*.'

'What?'

'I don't know how to tell you this, but ... they're working on a front-page story about us.'

My heart skips a beat. The last thing I did before I left was to authorise a press release from our PR agency about a new breakfast cereal we're launching, aimed at the teenage market. I hadn't thought it overly newsworthy, so the idea that they might be considering it for the front is unbelievable.

'The *Daily Sun*? As in, one of the UK's biggest newspapers? Are you sure?'

'That's what the journalist said. I sent him to Ace Communications, obviously,' she says eagerly.

'Oh, that should be that then,' I reply. 'Julia, our account manager, will be on the case already. She's very good. All you need to do now is fill Roy in when he gets back from his meeting.'

'The problem is, Ms Cope—Imogen . . . he phoned back to say that there was no answer at Ace and that he wanted to speak to someone urgently. And there just isn't anyone. No one at all. I'm so sorry.'

'This *is* about the press release we sent out on Friday, isn't it?'

'Oh . . . I actually didn't ask that. Oh God, I should've found out . . .'

'Laura, it doesn't matter. Roy's been briefed to handle any matters like this in my absence. All it needs is for him to get on the PR company's case and make sure Julia follows up the call.'

'Ms Co—Imogen, I don't think you understand. I even got Graham to try and track him down on the office CCTV, but he spotted nothing except a potentially hazardous fire hydrant on the fourth floor.'

'Well, I presume he'll be back soon,' I reply, getting a little exasperated.

She takes a deep breath, clearly unconvinced. 'I'll keep trying him on his mobile then, shall I?'

'I'd appreciate that. Thanks, Laura.'

'No problem at all. I won't rest till I've found him.'

'And . . . oh, it doesn't matter—'

'Anything at all.'

'Well, could you phone the journalist back and reassure him we'll be happy to help? It's a straightforward press release. I'm sure all they want is some freebies for a taste test.'

'Consider it done,' she says, as I open my book, realize it's time to get ready for dinner, and close it yet again.

That night we banquet on tapas at a buzzy little beach bar. A warm breeze dances through the air, and couples stroll along the boardwalk arm in arm.

I love this sort of food. It's not just that picking at tiny plates lulls you into the completely false idea that you're eating modestly; there's also something deliciously unpretentious about it. Not that I mind the opposite now and then – on our last night we're booked in, as part of our prize, to the hotel's Michelin-starred restaurant, where I'll expect as much pretentiousness as possible, thanks very much.

Meredith spends the evening flirting with our waiter, but manages to resist his thinly veiled invitation for a 'walk' along the shore, while Nicola rolls her eyes extravagantly. After hearing nothing back from Laura and leaving my own (unreturned) messages for both the PR agency and Roy, the only thing for me to resist is the wine. And I can't, as my large, consecutive gulps make plain to everyone.

'Is something the matter, Imogen?' Nicola asks.

'Oh, nothing. Well, work stuff,' I reply, tapping my fingers on the tablecloth.

Meredith frowns. 'That's so wrong. You're on holiday!'

'I know,' I reply. 'I'm sure it's nothing to worry about. Not that that tends to stop me.'

'In which case, the wine is probably a good idea. I suggest you carry on.' Nicola smiles, sympathetically.

I do as instructed, so much so that, as we weave our way back to the hotel, I'm overcome by a desire to hit my bed. Thankfully I'm not the only one.

'Pregnancy is *exhausting*,' Meredith declares, as she links arms with me.

'It is the way *you* do it,' I point out.

'I've got to hand it to you, Meredith,' Nicola says. 'There are rabbits on heat that don't manage to pull as fast as you. And when you're heavily pregnant, too. Amazing.'

Meredith shrugs. 'I thought I was remarkably restrained. Did you see that waiter's bum?'

72

'Wasn't he a bit young?' Nicola asks.

'Yep.' Meredith grins. 'Anyway, I know you were worried I'd spend every night wanting to talk, Imogen, but I'm absolutely shattered. I'll be dead to the world before you've even finished brushing your teeth.'

We get into the hotel room and I quickly perform my ablutions, emerging to see that Meredith's prediction was accurate. She's lying fast asleep on her back with her mouth wide open, so I gently remove her flip-flops, pull the sheet over her and roll her onto her side. She's not the type to read the pregnancy manuals that warn against lying on your back, but I pored over them so enthusiastically when I was expecting Florence I could've passed a degree in obstetrics.

I pull on my pyjamas and am about to climb into bed when I spot a notepad and pen on the desk. Addressing a sudden urge to put them to use, I pick them up before returning to sink into bed.

'*Amore mio . . .*'

It was Roberto who first used the Italian for 'My darling', in a text exchange we had soon after we moved in together:

While you're at the supermarket, could you pick up some bin bags? *xxx* I promise my next text will be more romantic!!

I should hope so! xxx

And some toilet paper xxx

Er . . . what happened to romantic?! xxx

Apologies. And some toilet paper, AMORE MIO xxx

Ho bloody ho!

Somehow, despite previously considering pet names the preserve of half-wits and the stars of 1970s sitcoms, it stuck.

I don't write to Roberto regularly but, sometimes, usually when I'm drunk, the need engulfs me. I know it's stupid – it's not as though it makes me feel any better about what happened. And I try not to think about the fact that I never actually send them.

'I'm writing while on my first full week's holiday since the last time you and I went away with each other. It hasn't exactly got off to a relaxing start.

I must admit it feels odd being away without you. It's so different from our last trip together. You have to admit that the Greek Islands were blissful, even if you were initially pissed off that my burgeoning overdraft prevented us from going long haul. I'd just assumed that Thailand could wait until the following year – which goes to show how presumptuous I was, even until the end. When I fell pregnant I knew things would change, but I had hoped that we would simply go on family holidays from then on – you, me and Florence, together. Clearly, that wasn't meant to be.

I sound bitter, don't I? I know I do. It doesn't matter how long it's been since I last saw you; I can't shake the feeling that you should still be in our lives, bringing up Florence with me.

I never wanted to be a single mum, Roberto. Not because I can't cope on my own, but because, quite simply, everything would've been better if I was doing it with you. Is it totally pointless for me to say that I'm certain we could have had an amazing life together? Probably.

My hand hesitates over the page as I contemplate my next words. He's never going to read them, so what does it matter?

I still love you, Roberto. Rightly or wrongly, I always will.
Imogen xxxxxxxxxx

I swallow back a lump in my throat and fold away the letter. Then I glide between my beautiful sheets, desperate to submit myself to slumber.

'GNNGH–*herrr*–GNNGHHH–*herrr* . . .!'

My eyes ping open as Meredith's snores reverberate around the bedroom with such force that the cocktail shaker vibrates.

I close them again and try to block out the sound.

'GNNGH–*herrr*–GNNGHHH–*herrr* . . .'

I get out of bed, pad over and gently nudge her until she makes a few gerbil-like noises before stopping.

I get back into bed. I close my eyes. A minute passes.

Tension drifts away from me as I descend into a rapid, deep and blissful sleep.

'G N N G H – *h e r r r* – G N N G H H H – *h e r r r* GNNGH–*herrr*–GNNGHHH–*herrr* . . .'

It suddenly feels like it's going to be a long night.

Day Two

Chapter 8

I finally stumble into sleep some time after 5 a.m., having spent most of the night attempting to block out Meredith's snores by lagging my ears with two torn-up panty liners.

In the process, my mind drifts to the issue of the *Daily Sun* and those unreturned phone calls. Having relaxed about it while I was tipping red wine down my throat, by the early hours of the morning I have whipped myself into a mild panic.

What if they've found out about the merger and want to run a story about it before anyone's ready?

The irony of my failure to drift off while lying in the world's most comfortable bed is not lost on me. In fact, it irritates the hell out of me. Which only keeps me awake longer. Worse, I know full well that neither Roy, the PR agency nor a phone call from a journalist qualifies as matters that should be vexing me so badly. The most that should tax my overworked brain on this holiday is deciding between a Cosmopolitan or a sangria.

I wake up just after ten, having missed the hotel breakfast. Meredith is still asleep and, for the first time in ten hours, not emitting the sort of snores you'd expect from an 18-stone truck-driver after a binge-drinking competition. I am briefly contemplating attempting to go back to sleep when my phone rings.

ROY!

I sit bolt upright and maniacally scrabble around my bedside table until I find something phone-shaped. I start jabbing at buttons, desperate to finally make contact, at which point I am assaulted by a pyrotechnical array of activity: the curtains fly open, then close; the television bursts into a medley of flamenco music; Meredith's bedside light flashes on and off.

She leaps up in wild-eyed bewilderment, her hands to her bird's nest head. 'Answer the bloody phone!'

I glance at my hand and register that I'm holding a remote control that seems so omnipotent, I'm half wondering if I've inadvertently launched a missile somewhere in the mid-Atlantic.

I chuck it onto the quilt before locating my phone under the bed and hitting 'Answer'.

'Ms Imogen! Copeland! I mean . . . Imogen!'

Groggily, I wipe my eyes and clear my throat. 'Oh, Laura.'

'That reporter's been on the phone again,' she says breathlessly. 'He left a message first thing. No one got back to him yesterday from the PR company.'

My blood runs cold. 'What about Roy?'

'He said not. I'm so sorry to be bothering you with this – I feel awful. It's just that they said that the story's going in tomorrow, at least they think so, and they need a quote from us.'

'Right. And it's about Teeny Pops?'

'He didn't mention them.'

'What did he say it was about, then?'

'I don't know quite how to put this. It's . . . kind of X-rated.'

I check my ears for residue from the panty liners, but they remain disturbingly clear. 'What did you say? X-rated? In what way?'

She swallows. I can hear the mortification in her voice as she speaks. 'I'll read to you my verbatim note of what he said.' She clears her throat. '"We're running a story that's been picked up by one of our agencies about a senior Peebles executive being thrown off a flight from Stuttgart after getting frisky in first class with the woman next to him, another executive."'

'"Getting frisky"? Tell me they mean he was doing aerobics.'

'"Fellow passengers reported witnessing the executives drink copious amounts of champagne in the first-class lounge two hours before the flight. Then, on the plane, laugh and flirt hysterically before reclining their seats to the lie-flat position and disappearing under their complimentary blankets."'

'How do you "flirt hysterically"?'

'"A series of loud and inappropriate noises was heard to come from their direction and, when questioned by an air hostess, it was discovered that the female executive had at some point during the course of events become topless."'

'This has got to be a joke.'

'"They were both asked to refrain, but seemed to consider the whole thing to be extremely funny, until the plane landed and they were arrested and charged with being drunk and disorderly and indecent exposure offences." Then the reporter asked if he could have a comment. So, without putting too fine a point on it . . . can we?'

'Shit a brick.'

'Wow. I'm not sure what they'll make of that.'

'That's not my comment!'

'God, of course. So sorry.' My head spins as I contemplate the consequences of a front-page story like that. We'd be the laughing stock of the industry. All our nice, reassuring adverts featuring wholesome families with 2.4 children would be mocked mercilessly. And with plenty of time left for Getreide to put the brakes on the merger, who would blame them for wanting to disassociate themselves from a company whose reputation has become suddenly and dramatically sleaze-ridden?

'I need to think about this,' I mutter, hyperventilating. 'I need to look into this. I need to find out if this is true. What am I saying? It *can't* be true. It sounds like a load of nonsense. What on earth made them think it was anyone to do with Peebles?'

'One of the passengers heard him bragging that he was a big cheese in this company.'

'Did this journalist have the name of whoever he thinks was involved?'

'I don't think so because he asked us for it. He said we'd be doing him a big favour, although I don't know why he thought we'd be inclined to do him any favours. You don't think it was Gaz Silverman, do you?' Gaz Silverman is our deputy accounts director, though I have no idea why Laura would think it was him.

'I honestly don't know,' I reply. 'Is Roy not in the office yet?'

'Well, I've just noticed that his coat's here, so he must be in a meeting.'

'At least he's in the building then. Please try and track him down, Laura. And the PR agency. Let's both of us get on to them.'

'Okay, Ms—boss.'

I'm about to insist she calls me Imogen when I realise 'boss' doesn't sound too bad at all.

Chapter 9

I know I should be enjoying our day trip to Las Ramblas; it's my sort of place: a majestic, tree-lined pedestrian avenue that's abundantly atmospheric and flanked with bustling shops and restaurants.

It's one of Barcelona's biggest tourist attractions and visiting was one of my top priorities. So why is it currently playing second fiddle to my preoccupation with work? That, and the fact that my new flip-flops appear to have an integrated cheese grater between the toes.

'Imogen, why do you look so worried?' Nicola asks, linking my arm with hers as an intense sun beats down on our shoulders.

'I don't,' I protest. 'I mean, I'm not worried.' I pause. 'Okay, maybe I am. I can't deny I'll feel happier when I've got hold of Roy or the PR agency. Unless I hear from them soon I'm going to have to tell David what's going on, a prospect I am not relishing. I can't understand why neither of them are returning my calls.'

'Isn't that someone else's problem while you're on holiday?' Meredith asks. She's in Daisy Duke cut-offs and from behind she doesn't even look pregnant, a phenomenon I've noticed is particularly unsettling for those with aspirations to chat her up.

'You'd think so—' I am halted mid-sentence by a hot, damp sensation that splashes onto my shoulder with an ominous plop. I do a double take, realising to my horror that a bird has 'done its business' on me. Though a description of such benign modesty hardly suffices – whatever creature emptied its bowels as it passed overhead has clearly been feasting on the same grub as King Kong. 'Oh, noooo!' I shriek as the offending pulp trickles down my arm with all the resistance of a Cornetto in front of a three-bar fire.

Meredith's eyes grow to three times their usual size. 'What the *hell* is that?'

'What does it look like?' Nicola mutters as she roots around in her bag for a tissue. But someone beats her to it.

'*Déjeme ayudarle.*' The voice is gruff but barely audible, even if I could speak Spanish. Its origin is a tall, craggy-jowled man with eyebrows that could remove rust from a haddock trawler. To my alarm, he begins wiping my shoulder with a tea towel, attempting to get rid of the debris.

I smile awkwardly, not wishing to appear ungrateful, but uncomfortable with physical contact from a complete stranger. '*Gracias! Gracias!*' I announce, nodding in that British way we reserve for pronouncing languages we know we're crap at.

I am about to direct the girls away when an array of recently learned facts click into place, and I freeze.

I can't believe I fell for this. *IT'S THE BIRD-POO DUPE!*

I quickly scrutinise the 'poo' again, and from its consistency and colossal volume deduce that there's absolutely no way it's real. And am I seriously expected to believe some bloke would happen to be strolling along Las Ramblas with a tea towel at the ready, prepared to leap to the rescue of recently shat-on maidens?

As these thoughts flood my brain, I open my bag and register that my purse is gone. I glare at the man.

He freezes and glares back, the eyebrows twitching nervously. He knows that I know.

'I'd like my purse back, please,' I hear myself saying.

'*Que?*'

'I said I'd like my purse back.'

He shrugs and puts on a flimsy display of bewilderment as Nicola starts spluttering. 'Imogen! What makes you think he's got your purse?'

'Oh, he's got it,' I reply, coming over all Cagney and Lacey.

'Are you sure?' Meredith scrunches up her nose as she looks at me.

'I've read all about this,' I snarl, refusing to break eye contact. 'This is a tried and tested trick, isn't it?'

The man shakes his head and backs away.

'You've messed with the wrong tourist. Give me my purse back. *Now.*'

'Imogen, you're being hasty,' Nicola protests.

At which point, the guy turns on his heel and attempts to make his getaway. But I'm too fast for him – before he's taken four steps, a queasy wash of adrenalin races through me and I leap through the air like a novice long-jumper, landing on him in a demented piggy-back. He attempts to push me off, but I squeeze my legs around his waist and tug at his neck, grappling him to the ground. We are a violent jumble of legs and arms as he attempts to wrestle me away but, despite his size, I manage to grip on, hard.

'*POLICIA! POLICIA!*' I bellow, as he finally pushes me off and I land on my backside on the pavement. Miraculously, two police officers appear almost instantly. But the man doesn't get up and run away.

'Officers, arrest this man,' I chuff, as I brush myself down and step aside so they can spring into action. Except they don't spring: they barely even twitch. On the contrary, they actually help him up and allow him to straighten his clothes while he delivers a frenzied rant in Spanish that appears to be directed at me.

When he's finished they turn to me. 'Why did you assault this man?' one asks, in a robust Spanish accent.

'*This* man robbed *me*,' I reply, open mouthed at his audacity.

The two police officers frown simultaneously before putting my allegation to him. It prompts a series of wild gesticulations that make it a wonder he doesn't dislocate something. I don't precisely know what he's saying, but when he starts whirling his hand around his head then jabbing his finger at me, it's clear I'm not coming out overly well from the description.

I feel I need to speak up for myself. 'He put fake bird ... *doo-doo* ... on my shoulder, and used it as a diversion to pinch my purse.'

The officer looks at me sternly. 'Doo-doo?'

I squirm. 'You know. Poo.'

He looks at me blankly, at which point I am forced to perform an elaborate game of Charades that involves simulating how a large bird might look while excreting its lunch mid-flight. There's no dignity involved, but I think I make my point.

'You believe this man covered you in shit?' the policeman asks, poetically.

'*Fake* shit,' I clarify.

'*Señora—*'

'*Señorita.*' I correct him, indignantly.

'*Señorita*, I do not believe you are right.'

'I *am* right. My purse is gone! This is one of the oldest tricks in the book, according to ... Google! This is egg white – you can instantly see that,' I say, dipping my finger in the offending substance. 'This is how confident I am,' I add, poised to lick my finger.

'DON'T!' Nicola shrieks. 'Imogen, that does not look like something you'd use to make a meringue.'

I hesitate and sniff it instead.

A horrible realisation occurs to me: she might be right. It smells distinctly natural, and not in a good way. The implications of this seize me as the police officer addresses me again.

'*Señora—ita* ... Eduardo is one of the most respected café owners in Las Ramblas. He saw what happened and stepped out to help you.'

'Then where's my purse?'

'In your hotel room? In your pocket? I don't know, and that is not my concern. Why don't you look again?' he suggests.

I swallow, really hoping it isn't in my bag. I open it up and put my hand inside. Then freeze.

'Um ... sorry about that,' I whisper, as Eduardo shakes his head. 'Crazy bloody Eenglish.'

'You certainly know how to make an impression abroad,' Nicola says, suppressing a smile.

'Oh, please don't,' I reply, emerging from a chemist with a bumper pack of baby wipes. 'I'm covered in this stuff. Meredith, don't come near me – it's dangerous for pregnant women.'

'Huh? Is it?'

I am midway though giving myself a walking bed-bath when my phone rings. 'This could be Roy,' I gasp, thrusting the wipes at Nicola. I grapple with my phone – still covered in bird poo and baby wipe slime, before pressing 'Answer'.

'So sorry to phone again ...'

'Hello, Mum,' I sigh, grabbing at more wipes.

' . . . but I'm certain you'd want to hear about this.'

I freeze. 'Has something happened to Florence?'

'Of course not. Good Lord!'

'Sorry. Can I speak to her?'

'Yes, but first . . .' Her words trail off and I wonder if she's attempting to instil a sense of suspense.

'What?'

'Sorry, I was just getting it. The article in *Woman & Home*.'

I throw my mountain of filthy baby wipes into a bin. 'You phoned me about an article in *Woman & Home*?'

'It's about urinary-tract infections,' she continues. 'I had to give you a ring because I know how you suffer.'

I frown. 'I've had two in ten years.'

'It's more than that, Imogen.'

'It isn't.'

'Definitely.'

If my hand wasn't now covered in bird poo, I would be biting my fist. 'Okay, Mum,' I manage instead.

'Well, I've got the solution. You've got to take an antibiotic every time you've had sex. Lesley Garrett swears by it.'

I am too stunned to answer this point on so many levels, I barely know where to start. Not least of what on earth makes her think I'm having sex.

'You've phoned me to tell me Lesley Garrett's tips for getting rid of UTIs?'

There is a small silence. 'Imogen,' she says, in her I'm-only-trying-to-help voice, 'you've got a tone.'

I close my eyes and breathe in. 'I'm sorry. I'm very grateful. I'm just a bit tied up.' Realising my necklace is caked in bird poo, I wedge the phone between my chin and shoulder and release the clasp. 'Can I speak to Florence, please?'

I examine the necklace as I wait for Florence, trying my best to expunge the offending substance. Finally, I hear a rustle at the other end, followed by her voice. 'Hi, Mummy.'

'Hello, darli—'

The necklace is ripped from my hand before I can work out what's happened, and in the second or two it takes to realise that it's no longer between my fingers, all I can do is look up and witness the outline of a young, teenaged boy sprinting through the crowds.

'I've got to go!'

There is no strategy or logic behind my decision to race after him. Instinct, quite simply, takes over, and I find myself sprinting behind the dark, swishing hair of a boy who has significantly more natural athleticism than me.

I push on frantically, feeling my face turn heart-attack red as the gap widens between us. I realise my prospects of catching up are getting slimmer by the moment.

He is about to dart down a side street when he trips and stumbles to the ground. He turns and looks back at me and I realise with a jolt that he can't be older than twelve.

I also know this is my moment.

'Give me that necklace!' I shout, and am about to pounce when someone grabs my arm.

'What's going on?'

One of the police officers from earlier is glaring at me in breathless disbelief, as if he's walked in on a puppy chewing his slippers. Again.

'He's got my necklace!' I tell him, but when I spin round to point to him, he's gone. And so is my last remaining memory of Roberto's love.

Chapter 10

It is the first full day of my five-star dream holiday and several hours of it have been spent in a police station with nothing to do except fill out forms, reason with the staff and count the blisters between my toes, which currently look as though they're padded with bubble wrap.

It's not even a very nice police station – not that I was expecting Laura Ashley curtains and a chic Chesterfield sofa, of course. The only positive thing to say about this experience is that I'm *not* here because I've been arrested, although it was a close thing.

You wouldn't believe how difficult it is to persuade a foreign police officer that you're totally innocent when he's personally witnessed you hunting down two separate people and attempting to grapple them to the ground. Fortunately, though, he believed my story as there have been similar reports about a boy fitting the description of the one who stole my necklace.

Not that that prompted him to run, Jason Bourne-style, after the perpetrator. He just gave me directions to the police station, where I have to report the necklace stolen for insurance purposes. Which I can't help thinking means they're not likely to throw all available resources at this case. I pointed this out to the girls, before insisting that Nicola took Meredith back to the hotel before her ankles swelled up to the size of beach balls in the heat.

So here I am, having waited long enough for my bum cheeks to fossilise, passing the time by making more useless phone calls to try to get to the bottom of my company's unfolding PR disaster.

'You've been robbed too, then?'

At first I barely register the question, let alone the person asking it. Having abandoned all attempts to reactivate my Internet connection on my mobile – which refuses to do what it's told – I'm now busy trying to make contact with Florence again. But my mother, while good at phoning *me*, is less keen to answer when it doesn't suit her. She's probably teaching my daughter how to pluck her eyebrows.

'I have, yes,' I reply distractedly, pressing 'Send' on my sixth text to Roy. Then I look up and nearly swallow my tongue in shock.

It's *him*. The guy from the plane. The one with the eyes and the smirk and the shameless lips. Only this time he's wearing glasses, ones that should make him look geeky, but simply serve to exacerbate his sexiness.

My cheeks flame to a colour reminiscent of Santa's trousers, and I try to think of something clever to say.

'Oh,' is all I manage.

He laughs. 'I'm not stalking you, I promise.'

He's wearing combat shorts, with flip-flops on his tanned feet and a T-shirt that even someone in head-to-toe Per Una can recognise as cool. It's white, with geometric shapes and 'Calif' scrawled underneath. T-shirts like this intimidate me. If someone tasked me with purchasing clothing that featured geometric shapes, the best I'd manage would be a crocheted jumper covered in Christmas trees. There's no getting away from it: this man has style. Just being around him makes me feel like a gawky 15-year-old and, when you're twenty-nine, that's not a good thing at all.

'Oh, I never thought that,' I reply, realising that it actually sounds like I did.

He smiles again. I wonder how many women have dropped their knickers at that smile.

'My wallet was taken in Las Ramblas,' he explains. 'Fortunately, I was carrying cash rather than all my cards.'

He also has exceptionally good legs, I notice: all tanned contours and muscular knees. I wish he'd put them away, but they're just there, right in my face. Well, not *right* in my face – that would be strange – but they're close enough. I shift my chair away.

'Wise move,' I mutter, peering at my phone. My mother hasn't phoned back. Neither has Roy, nor the PR company, nor David, to whom I hadn't really wanted to break this news before I could assure him that the former two were on the case. Now I'm going to have to.

That thought, and my desire to not be sitting next to some-one who makes me feel like I need a bag over my head, prompts an urgent need to address at least one of those issues.

'Excuse me,' I say politely, standing and moving away from him as I press 'Call'.

I try David first, then Roy again, then my mother. This time, she answers.

'Hi, Mum. Can I speak to Florence?' I look up and note that he's watching me. I turn away as my mum launches into the UTI conversation again. 'Mum, I'm a bit short of time, could you just get Florence?' She huffs.

I look up again and he smiles. I return it awkwardly.

'Hello, Mummy!'

'Hello, sweetie!' I reply, my voice bursting with relief. 'How are you enjoying things at Grandma's house?'

'Good.'

'So what have you done so far today?'

'I can't remember.'

'Have you been out anywhere?'

'Yes.'

'To where?'

'I can't remember.'

'Um . . . are you missing me?'

'What?'

'Are you missing me?'

'Yes,' she says unconvincingly.

'Okay, well, I love you, Florence.'

'Okay.'

'I really, really love you.' I pause, waiting for her to respond. 'Do you love me?'

'I'm watching *The Little Mermaid*.'

At least it's not *Sex and The City*, I suppose.

'And how is it?'

'Good.' Things are either 'good' or 'bad' in Florence's world, there's no in between. So the likelihood of her giving me a review worthy of *Empire* magazine was never high.

'Right, well, I'm going to put the phone down now, so we'll speak tomorrow. I love you.' I wait for her response, but there's a stony silence. 'I love you, Florence.'

A series of muffled noises ensue, which sound as though she's dropped the phone in a handbag and is swinging it around the room like a shot putter.

'Florence? Florence?'

'Grandma wants to speak to you,' she replies.

'Oh, okay, byyeeee!' I respond, hastily cutting off the call.

I look up and see that Hot Guy is smiling. 'How old is your little girl?'

'Four.'

'Not the greatest conversationalists at that age, are they?'

'Not when I'm competing with Disney.'

'My nephew turned five last week, and things haven't improved much.'

I smile, uncomfortable at the fact that he's looking at me again. First because, although I don't think he's *looking* looking at me – you know, in an interested kind of way – he is still ... well, looking. And if I'd walked out of the hotel room this morning knowing I was going to be looked at by a man, I'd have made a bit more effort. Or would I? I can't remember the last time I even worried about that.

It brings home a rather unpleasant reality: I look a bit of show. No, I'm overstating it. Possibly.

The principal quality of my shorts-and-vest-top combo when I bought them was inoffensiveness. Suddenly, that's exactly the problem. They're not just inoffensive. They're bland. Insipid. *Prematurely middle-aged.* I'm going to have to face this: I am dressed like a vicar's wife with a Bon Marché loyalty card.

I never used to be like this. There was a time when I *liked* fashion; when buying clothes was a source of pleasure, not something I didn't bother with because there was nobody around to look nice for any longer.

'I'm Harry.' He holds out his hand, waiting for me to shake it, but my phone rings and instead I pull a weird, semi-apologetic face as I leave him hanging.

'Imogen!' David shrieks down my handset. 'I had a message to phone you. Aren't you supposed to be away?'

'Yes, but ... well, it's kind of an emergency.'

He sighs. 'You know what I always say about emergencies.'

I hesitate. 'Hmm. Remind me.'

'Emergencies are challenges in a more challenging form.'

'Ah.'

'So, what's the problem?'

I consider thinking of a way to sugar-coat this. But David sugar-coats everything anyway, so you have to give it to him straight – straighter than straight – for him to ever understand the significance of something.

'The *Daily Sun* have been on to us and they're running a story about a senior Peebles executive caught feeling-up a top-less fellow executive on a first-class flight from Stuttgart.'

He pauses momentarily, before spluttering his response with a throaty cough. 'SON of a Belgian BUN!'

Maybe there's such a thing as too straight.

'*Whh . . . aaat?*' he continues.

'Yes, it *is* something of a shocker,' I concede.

I look up and realise that Hot Guy – Harry – is at the front desk, completing his paperwork and speaking to the police officer there in what appears to be fluent Spanish.

'Do they know who it was? The executive, that is?'

'Apparently not. Who's been to Stuttgart recently?' I ask.

'The whole of the senior team have been several times in the last six months since work on the merger began.' Not me, I note, although now probably isn't the time to raise this. 'You know, I bet I know who it is!' he exclaims.

'Who?'

'Gaz Silverman. He's rogered everything that moves. His

latest was the woman who came in to clean the telephones last week.'

'Really? Gareth Silverman has always struck me as fairly unassuming.'

'Oh, Imogen, I don't think there's a single woman in the office he hasn't tried it on with. Not one!'

'He hasn't tried it on with me,' I point out.

'Hasn't he?' David huffs. 'Well, it's never been your sort of thing that, has it?'

'What do you mean?'

'Well, you know. Men.'

It occurs to me what he's implying. 'I'm not a lesbian, David.'

His voice softens. 'You needn't worry, Imogen. We are a *totally* inclusive company.'

'David, I've got a daughter!'

'We're fine with it, I promise.'

'David, you're not listening to me.'

'I'd never really thought about it until you brought that *friend* to the corporate tennis last year . . . '

'David,' I begin calmly. 'Let me repeat this. I am not a lesbian. I have no problem with lesbians – indeed, as you say, one of my best friends is a lesbian. But I am not. I am a red-blooded, heterosexual female and I've had as much of the opposite SEX in my life as the next woman!'

The word 'sex' reverberates around the room at three times my usual volume.

Someone taps me on the shoulder and I spin round. It's Harry. I have a sudden desire to run down platform nine and three quarters and jump on a train to another world.

He points at the desk, indicating that it's my turn to be seen.

'David, I need to go. I'll phone you back to fill you in properly about the *Daily Sun* when I can.'

'Don't – I'm in meetings all day. Just tell me you're going to get rid of this. Make it disappear.'

I open my mouth, but it takes a second to formulate a response that isn't, 'Who do you think I am? David bloody Blaine?'

'David ... I'm not sure I can do that.'

'Well, we can't have this, Imogen. Not when so much is at stake with Getreide,' he laments. 'MOTHER OF THE BRIDE! This *would* happen the week you're away.'

'I know ... there was just no way I could've known anything like this would happen.'

He pauses long enough to pull himself together. 'Of course you couldn't. I'm sorry, Imogen. Everyone needs a break. I'm shocked about the story, that's all.'

'Well, we've got one of the best PR agencies in London looking after us and I'm sure they'll manage the situation brilliantly,' I say, reassuringly. 'Plus, Roy is there on the ground – I know that he'll want to grasp this issue with both hands and deal with it. As soon as I can get hold of him.'

'You haven't even spoken to him about it?'

'I'm on the case. I promise you, David, I'm on the case.'

Chapter 11

There's a long walk back to the hotel. I know that much, without looking at my map.

I step out of the police station, wincing every time my shredded feet make contact with the ground, and work out the direction of Las Ramblas. That leads to the harbour, then the boardwalk, which in turn stretches out endlessly to our hotel.

I text Nic to tell her I'm on my way, then set off, determined to be philosophical. After five minutes, I become vaguely aware of someone adjacent to me, ten or so feet away. I look up. It's Harry.

'Hi,' he says, with a grin.

'Hi,' I reply awkwardly, stepping up my pace.

A few seconds later, he's still there.

So I stop. Then *he* stops. 'Can I help? I ask.

'Don't think so. I'm walking back to my hotel. It's in Barceloneta.'

'Oh.' I carry on walking.

'Where are you staying?'

I wonder why he makes me so uneasy. 'I'm in that direction too.'

'Oh, great – where? I'm at the B Hotel.'

I swallow. 'Great.' I'm not going to tell him I'm there as well. No way. Except, if I don't tell him, what happens if we bump into each other at breakfast? Oh, bollocks. 'I'm there, too.'

'Really? That's a coincidence! I'll walk with you.'

'Great,' I repeat. Only I don't feel great. And not just because my toes are starting to bleed.

'There's a chemist up here if you want to get some plasters.' He gestures to my feet and I redden furiously. 'I can come in and get you some antiseptic cream if you like. I speak Spanish.'

'No! I can manage. Why don't you go on ahead?' I suggest.

'It's all right, I'll wait.'

Oh, *must* you? I take a deep breath, nod and push through the pharmacy door.

For someone whose previous experience of speaking Spanish has been limited to ordering drinks, my efforts to communicate are pretty good, if I say so myself. The assistant understands perfectly what I'm attempting to enunciate with only the help of a English–Spanish mini-dictionary, and hands over the cream with a courteous smile.

When I emerge, Harry's still there, as promised. I start walking.

'Aren't you going to put those plasters on? There's quite a way to go.'

I hesitate, before taking a seat on a bench, removing the antiseptic cream from the paper bag and lavishing it between my toes. I find myself resorting to small talk to cover my embarrassment.

'I wish I knew more Spanish, but you get by when you have a knowledge of other Latin-based languages. I can speak fluent French and a bit of German,' I witter, in a spectacular display of embellishment. 'It was actually very straightforward in that chemist – surprisingly so. I suppose it's all about confidence ... sorry, did you want to say something?'

'That stuff you're putting on your feet—'

'Yes?'

'It's denture cream.'

By the time I've returned to the pharmacy, purchased then applied the correct cream and set off on my way, I'd rather hoped to have shaken him off. But apparently not.

Added to this, the entire forty-five minutes it takes for us to walk along the boardwalk to the hotel involves a repeated and increasingly uncomfortable scenario: we are being checked out. People are looking at us as if we're a couple, and not in a good way. I keep getting knowing looks from fellow females that say, 'Good on you, girl, for punching so far above your weight!'

There's something else that's odd, too. After learning that Harry's originally from Aberdeen, lives in London and is here for work, our conversation skips to the sort of banter you'd have with a friend after too much sangria. Given that I haven't *had* any sangria, it's a mystery how he sucks me into it.

'Favourite character in a book or film?'

'Hmm. Offred in *The Handmaid's Tale*, Jo in *Little Women* or Princess Leia.'

He nods slowly, turning this over in his mind. 'Excellent choices. Okay – best feature?'

'Whose?'

'Yours, of course.'

I frown and contemplate the possibilities, those bits and pieces of me that my friends compliment: 1) Eyes – which are in fact blue and boring; 2) Boobs – far too big, despite efforts to minimise with bras capable of restraining a subsiding building; 3) Waist – which is not in fact small. It only *looks* small compared with 2 . . .

'My wrists,' I conclude.

He laughs.

'What's wrong with my wrists?'

'Nothing. But they're not your best feature.'

This comment, accompanied by his distractingly handsome face, prompts a sudden and vivid insight into the kind of guy he is. Fun, yes. Flirtatious, undoubtedly. And someone who likes women just a little too much.

105

That glint in his eyes reminds me of the cocky, conceited types at university, the ones who might as well have been holding up a sign saying: 'I am gorgeous. I have a huge penis. I will show you a fabulous 24 hours then never, ever phone.'

I could never work out how even the brightest of my friends fell for such dubious charms. Personally, I decided on the first day of Freshers' Week to date only the sensitive, respectful, corduroy-wearing types, even if that wore thin on occasions. It's difficult to fancy a man who thinks they know what it's like to own a womb.

'What's *your* favourite fictional character?' I ask.

'Hmm. That's a tricky one.'

'But it's your quiz!'

'True, although I hadn't finished with yours yet.'

I sigh. 'You've already asked me everything except my shoe size – what can you possibly need to know?'

'It's not a question of *need*. I'm just interested in anyone who holds Princess Leia in the same esteem as I do. And if you really want to disclose your shoe size, I'm not going to stop you.'

I throw him a look. 'Do I seriously come across as the kind of woman who'd discuss such a thing with a stranger she'd met for the first time today?'

'We met yesterday when you threw your breakfast all over me, remember.'

'Not *quite* all over you – I tried my best to get some cereal down the collar of your shirt, but failed miserably.'

He laughs. 'Well, if you're not going to give me your shoe size, I'd better settle for your name.'

'I . . . oh.' I'd forgotten I hadn't introduced myself. 'Imogen.'

'Pleased to meet you.' He stops walking and we shake hands.

The physical contact makes me feel uneasy. I pull away and start walking again as I think of a way to change the subject.

'Do you often get to stay in places like the B Hotel?' I ask.

'I'm more used to a £39 Travelodge.'

I'm about to ask if he won a competition too, when his phone rings.

I try not to listen, but can't fail to notice that he appears to be talking to his boss. He seems keen to get rid of him; glancing over from time to time as if he's worried I might overhear. I haven't the heart to break it to him that I'm not remotely interested in anyone's work issues other than my own.

When he ends the call, he turns to me. 'So, is your little girl with her dad while you're here?'

'No, he's not . . . no,' I reply as I reach for the necklace.

And feel a punch of dismay when it's not there.

'You know, I hate to say it,' he says, as we enter the lobby of the hotel, 'but you probably need to forget about that necklace.'

I freeze. 'I can't *forget* about the necklace.'

'I'm simply saying,' he continues, failing to notice my irritation, 'I don't get the impression they're leaping to try and solve the crime.'

'Well, I might phone them tomorrow to see how they're getting on. You never know.'

'Hmm. Good luck.'

I suddenly despise him and his flippancy. As a dry, burning heat erupts in my throat, I want to be as far away from him as possible. 'This isn't just some *wallet*, you know. This isn't something I'm going to fill out a form for, claim on the insurance, then go and buy a new one. Some things are more important.'

He slows down, realisation and regret sweeping across his face. 'I'm sorry.'

My jaw twitches. 'Don't worry about it,' I reply, and hurtle up the granite stairs before he can see the tears in my eyes.

Chapter 12

'When are you going to put down that bloody phone, Imogen?'

Meredith thrusts a large glass of sangria at me as we lounge by the pool, as if this is going to solve all my problems. I am deeply, inconsolably upset about the necklace. In fact, if it wasn't for what's going on at work, I'd barely be able to think about anything else. So I don't know if the fact that I've just sent my tenth text to Roy is a good thing or not.

He's having the Caps Lock treatment on this one – that's how pissed off I am with him.

Dear Roy, phone me soon or the first item on my to-do
list when I return is to *SET FIRE TO YOUR DESK*. Lots
of love, Imogen x

I compose myself and instead focus on my surroundings. The wanton glitziness of the pool deck never ceases to amaze me. Tanned cocktail waiters in shorts of dazzling whiteness weave past canopied sun beds, while guests flick through copies of *Harper's Bazaar* and dip their expensively painted toes into the infinity pool.

I've been here a day and have yet to see someone actually swimming in it. Occasionally, someone slips in to hover temporarily at the side, refusing to remove their shades or, indeed, put down their champagne glass.

This is a people-watching extravaganza, a recession-proof bubble where wealth fuses with glamour to produce smooth-skinned heiresses gliding around in a waft of Hermès, and buff forty-something men who are never off their phones.

We are reclining opposite Yellow Bikini Lady (as christened by Meredith): a stick-thin woman who is smoking energetically, tanning herself to the shade of a conker and who appears to have had two Fisher Price play balls surgically implanted into her chest.

Next to her is Meatloaf. Not *the* Meatloaf, obviously – this is his hairier, richer cousin – a man who's ordered enough Cristal in the last half hour to fill his Jacuzzi.

Then there are The Wankers, an undetectable-accented threesome of young, overtanned blokes who clearly believe themselves to be the most ravishing creatures to walk the earth and whose conversation hasn't deviated from two subjects: their fitness regimes, and how many women they've bedded.

And, as I look up from my phone – yes, my bloody phone – suddenly there is Harry.

The first thing I notice is that he isn't wearing the geek glasses he had on at the police station, and for some reason that makes me slightly disappointed.

He strolls through the glass doors from the bar area and heads for the only free sun bed, before sitting on its edge and idly selecting a magazine from a nearby table. Yellow Bikini Lady perks up considerably, as does the woman to his right. And his left.

I quickly turn onto my front and wonder if I should text David to check if he's heard anything.

'Have you been listening to a word I've said?' Meredith asks. She puts down her copy of *Company*, holds a tube of factor 25 over her belly and squirts it like you'd adorn a hot dog with mustard.

'Believe me, Meredith, I would love to put my phone away. But there's a full-blown crisis going on at work and, whether I'm here or not, the buck stops with me.'

'Do you know where *my* phone is, Imogen?' she asks.

'No, where?'

'My phone is in the safe in our bedroom which, I discovered, is entirely soundproof.'

'But you won't be able to play Scrabble,' I point out. It's her obsession and she's absolutely brilliant at it, the only person I've ever met who can batter her opponents in one move using only two obscure consonants and a vowel.

'A small price to pay to get some respite from Nathan's texts.'

111

'Oh, dear.' Nicola bites her lip.

Meredith sighs. 'The frustrating thing is that when we spoke this morning and he told me about his gig last night, I could only think how much I fancy him, even after all these years. I'll give him this – he's still hot stuff.' She pauses, then grimaces. 'It was all going well until he told me he'd bought me some nipple cream – and I'm talking about the stuff from Mothercare, not Ann Summers. I dread to think what he'll be like when the baby's born. As if things aren't going to be horrendous enough.'

I laugh. 'Horrendous?'

She looks at me, failing to join in. 'All I hear from other mothers is sleepless nights, stretch marks and urinary incontinence. Sounds fairly horrendous to me.'

'All a small price to pay,' I reassure her.

She rolls her eyes and looks entirely unconvinced.

A waiter dressed like a Wimbledon finalist appears at our side clutching a small, round tray. 'Anything more to drink, ladies?'

'Yes, keep supplying sangrias until this woman becomes so inebriated that she loses her phone,' Meredith instructs. He looks perplexed.

'I think we're okay for now,' Nicola reassures him.

Meredith shakes her head. 'You're being very restrained considering you're allowed as much booze as you want – unlike me, who can't touch a drop.'

I suddenly wonder if I am being a bit over the top about this work issue. The *Daily Sun* hasn't phoned back. Surely, if they were serious about the story, they'd have been on this non-stop, but when I spoke to Laura half an hour ago, they hadn't been in touch today. Maybe they've lost interest. Or been put off the scent. Then there's always the possibility, heaven forbid, that I'm being neurotic ...

I sit up to take a sip of sangria and notice that Harry has company. The woman standing above him is holding a clip-board. She has a pretty, heart-shaped face and defiant eyes that hint at a feisty streak, a combination that makes her both beautiful and interesting. Her hair has that dark, glossy swish unique to women of Mediterranean origin, while her heavenly curves appear to have been poured into her slick, white pencil dress.

It's clear from her body language that she's attracted to him – the liberal use of laughter, the tossing back of hair, the tilt of her perfect chin. Then she does something I'd never have had the balls to do: clicks her fingers at a waiter. I didn't know people did that in real life. He arrives seconds later with a bottle of champagne and a glass for Harry, which he at least has the good grace to look embarrassed about accepting.

It's as Harry engages the waiter in conversation that I register the effect he has on men and women alike. They linger on his every word, are generous with their smiles and obviously, quite simply, enjoy being around him.

I pull down the straw hat I grabbed hastily from Debenhams last Tuesday lunchtime and try not to look.

'Isn't that the guy you crashed into at Heathrow?' Nicola asks, propping herself up on her elbows as she lowers her sunglasses.

'It IS!' Meredith hoots. 'Did you know he was here?' She turns to Nic.

Nicola shakes her head. I say nothing. Then they both look at me.

'Did *you* know he was here?' Meredith demands.

'He was at the police station.' I shrug, nonchalantly. 'We walked back together.'

They exchange glances. 'And you chose *not* to mention this?'

'What's the big deal?' I open the first page of *The Book Thief*. '*Here is a small fact . . .*'

'So what did you find out? Spill the beans!' Meredith demands.

'Nothing much. He's from Aberdeen, lives in London.'

'Is he loaded? I'll bet he is – lots of people here are. Oh, Imogen, I bet he's a billionaire playboy like Christian Grey. He'd be perfect for you!'

'Because he's like Christian Grey? I haven't had sex for five years, Meredith. I think a butt plug on my first go might be a little ambitious.' I open my book. '*Here is a small fact . . .*'

'He has the air of a millionaire about him. I can spot it a mile off.'

'He said he was more used to a £39 Travelodge than here,' I point out. 'That's a direct quote.'

'Haven't you ever read a Mills and Boon?' Meredith continues, unconcerned. 'At the beginning, the heroines are convinced that the hero is a taxi driver, then they turn out to be running a multi-million pound empire and appear in *Tatler* every other month. Why don't you go and have a chat with him?'

I lower my book momentarily. 'I'm not going to do that.'

'Why wouldn't you?'

'More to the point, why *would* I?' I retort.

'Because he's GORGEOUS,' Meredith splutters.

I humour her in the only language she comprehends. 'He's not my type.'

'Imogen, you haven't had a type for nearly five years,' Nicola pipes up.

I frown at her. 'Don't *you* join in.' Trying to bully me into getting a man is normally Meredith's domain; Nicola has always understood.

Only, now, she bites her lip, hesitating. 'Well, I can't help it. I agree with Meredith. It's *time*, Imogen. Don't you think?'

'Look, I'm just here for a relaxing holiday,' I say, feeling the need to defend myself. 'My first in as long as I can remember. Yet between the robbery, work and almost freezing to death in my shower, it's been about as relaxing as having my toenails surgically removed. The last thing I want now is to add "Chasing a bloke" to that list. That's not what I came here for.'

'We just think you need to, you know ... *move on*,' Meredith says.

'I hate that phrase,' I reply.

'I know, but I happen to think it's true.'

'He's not my type,' I repeat, clearly losing the argument.

Nicola hesitates. 'You mean he's not Roberto.'

I glare at her. 'Well, no, he's not. He's just some bloke I bumped into in a police station.'

I don't even bother to mention the small matter that he'd never be interested in me and my M&S shorts in a million years.

'You need to stop comparing people to Roberto,' Nicola continues. I must admit, this is starting to irritate me a little now. 'It's not healthy, Imogen.'

'What sort of idiot goes looking for a holiday romance? It's pointless and it's tacky,' I argue, at the exact moment I realise Meredith is slinking to the bar to chat up one of The Wankers.

Chapter 13

Meredith has guaranteed no snoring tonight, a claim so bold I wonder how she can make it.

'*Pineapple?*' I repeat, as a waiter produces a plate piled so high you'd think he was serving the Man From Del Monte.

We've dined on tapas again and, before we head out to sample Barcelona's nightlife, Meredith is experimenting with ways to open up her airways naturally, that she read about on the Internet. 'I'd usually have a Pot Noodle over a piece of fruit any day, but this is my sixth portion today,' she announces, thrusting a piece into her mouth.

'That isn't a portion, that's half the export trade of South East Asia,' I point out.

'It has an enzyme that suppresses unwanted goings-on in your nasal passages,' she continues, not sounding overly scientific. 'You wait. You'll have the best sleep of your life tonight.'

After dinner, we try out several establishments before ending up in a lively bar playing jazz funk to an eclectic crowd. For a brief few hours, as we perch on bar stools, reminiscing and shrieking with laughter, I feel a pang of nostalgia for the days when life was always like this; when holidays – even the awful ones – involved unshackling myself entirely from work and responsibility, something I seem entirely unable to do these days.

As Meredith and Nicola excuse themselves and head to the Ladies', I'm about to order the next round of drinks when I become aware of someone standing next to me.

I look round and am confronted by a short, sweating man who, if it wasn't for the polyester suit, would bear an uncanny resemblance to Barney Rubble. He's a good fifteen years older than anyone else in here and is attempting, I think, to dance – his moves could easily be mistaken for the onset of a gastrointestinal emergency.

'Hello!' He grins, planting his elbow on the bar. At this point I feel slightly alarmed. Because while it's a possibility that the movement is to stop him falling over – such is his level of intoxication – I'm concerned that he might have what my mother refers to as . . . *ideas*.

'Hello,' I reply uneasily, scanning the room for my friends.

'You're English, aren't you?' As he edges closer, I get a waft of stale perspiration so potent I'm momentarily convinced I will black out.

'Um, yes,' I mumble, shifting away.

'*MOI AUSSI!*' he announces energetically, as if this

118

coincidence is akin to discovering we were born in adjacent hospital beds.

I smile politely but say nothing, praying he will go away. Instead, he inches closer, so close that I can see each strand of hair protruding from his nostrils and the pools of sweat gathered in the wild tufts of his eyebrows.

'How about a dance?' he demands, grabbing me by the hand and forcing me to slip off my stool.

'Er, no – thank you,' I insist, disentangling myself. 'I'm here with my friends. And I don't dance.'

'Oh, go *on*,' he blusters. 'Let's face it … you and I aren't going to pull anyone else in here, are we?'

I open my mouth. 'What?'

'All these young whippersnappers … might as well accept that none of them is going to be interested in anyone our age.'

'I … I'm twenty-nine,' I protest.

He steps back, tips back his head and scrutinises me as if he's determining the freshness of a side of salmon. 'Really?'

'Yes!' I growl, as Meredith and Nicola arrive at my side.

'Sorr-ee!' he cringes, backing away. 'I always thought I was good with ages, too.'

We don't stay long after that.

'How bad *was* he, exactly? I didn't get a proper look,' Meredith says as we attempt to flag down a taxi. 'I only ask because I'd never discount a man just for being ugly. Ugly men try harder and are more grateful.'

'He was a slimeball,' I reply. 'Do I look middle aged?'

'No,' Nicola insists. There's an ominous silence.

'Although, you probably don't dress with the same ... *joie de vivre* you once did.' This is Meredith's best attempt at diplomacy.

'Which is understandable, because you've got other priorities,' Nicola adds, hastily. 'Besides, you still look lovely. End of story.'

'I can't believe that *he's* the best I could do,' I say, dejectedly.

'He's not!' Meredith protests. 'He was just some pissed-up letch in a bar. You already know we think you could do better because we've *attempted* to set you up with dozens of men, all of whom were a significant improvement on him.'

To be fair, this is true. And while I've only ever been out with one, once, to get them (temporarily) off my back – a good-looking but self-important cookery writer from one of Meredith's magazines – I trust them enough to know that the others wouldn't have been hideous either.

'I should stress that I don't actually *want* to pull while I'm here. I just hate the thought that, if I did, that's the standard I should expect.'

Nicola and Meredith dutifully continue to protest but, by the time we reach the hotel and I'm back in our room, I've ceased to care about how unfabulous I look. Largely because I'm utterly exhausted. And praying that Meredith's efforts with the pineapple might have worked.

As I crash into bed and open my book, Meredith has already plunged into a deep and, to my amazement, silent sleep.

'*Here is a small fact . . .*'

I roll over, idly reaching for my necklace, then freezing as one issue I'd managed to push to the back of my mind for a few hours swamps my thoughts.

Oh God, Imogen. How could you have lost your necklace?

Roberto gave me the necklace on one of the most unexpectedly romantic days of my life. 'Unexpectedly', because it was only three months after we'd met and the day until that point had been nothing less than disastrous.

It wasn't just the plumbing emergency I'd woken up to; the bank card that had been swallowed four hours earlier; or the fact that my mother had announced she was coming to stay for a week. We'd also been viewing our dream flat, a small but perfectly formed pad near Hampstead Heath. Our appointment was at ten thirty and we'd taken a picnic to eat in the park later. I'd assumed the area was beyond our budget, until an estate agent with whom I'd ingratiated myself ('Call me Julie') tipped me off that the flat was coming on the market.

It was tiny; I can't deny it – I've been in more spacious rooms while trying on jeans in Monsoon. But we fell in love with it. It was directly above one of those chic, quintessentially London cafés, the kind that serves artichoke teas, hangs dried chillies from the ceiling and has a sous-chef called Ollivander. I stood in the tiny bedroom, clutching Roberto's hand as I breathed in the scent of designer coffee wafting through the windows, and knew that this was The One.

I'd expected to have serious competition. But Call Me Julie said it was ours if we wanted, and that she could have the paperwork done within the hour.

So we sat in the chic little café, our heads swollen with dreams as we awaited her call. Only she didn't call. Call Me Julie texted instead, clearly unable to summon sufficient levels of bottle to talk to us personally.

Whoops! Sorry, Imogen – turns out the flat's gone! Got a
nice pad in Brixton you might like tho! J x

I was fuming so hard as we walked across the heath that ducks were diving for cover. 'That flat had our name on it. Only now someone else has got it. Someone else is going to be living in *our* flat!'

'Imogen.' Roberto gently took me by the arm and spun me round. He put his hand behind my neck and I relaxed into his kiss. Even now, thinking of his kisses, the soft pillows of his lips sinking into mine, warms my belly like hot chocolate on a cold day.

'It doesn't matter,' he breathed into my hair.

'But it does. I could see us coming home after a hard day at work and snuggling up on the sofa in that gorgeous living room.'

'That very *small* living room.'

I opened my mouth to protest.

'And don't say "bijou",' he added. I managed a smile as he ran his fingertips across the skin of my jaw, lifting up my chin. 'There will be other living rooms. You don't need that one to snuggle up to me.'

He was right (annoyingly, he often was) – after an extensive search, he ended up simply moving into my place in Clapham, where we were blissfully happy. But that afternoon, of course, I didn't know this, so the fact that he lifted my mood so drastically, so quickly, is testament to the effect Roberto had on me in those days.

That afternoon, we lay on our picnic blanket above the curves of the London skyline, exchanging slow kisses as we grazed on ripe peaches and Prosecco. It was close to perfection.

Then we had our first conversation about having children.

I have no idea who brought it up; it could well have been me, because there was nothing I couldn't share with him, even that early on.

And it didn't surprise me that he was so determined that he never wanted a baby.

His childhood, while not troubled in a way that would vex social services, had not been the source of fond nostalgia that mine had. My memories were dominated by lavish, sausageson-sticks birthday parties organised by Mum (who still throws better parties than anyone I know), and wobbly bike rides along the prom with my dad.

Roberto's were all about the aching fear of a cold, unaffectionate mother and the near-permanent absence of his philandering father.

So when he told me in no uncertain terms that babies would never be on the agenda, I reassured him: 'That's fine, because I have no desire to have kids, either.'

It was the truth at the time. I was obsessively focused on my career and had never been gripped by the maternal twinges my cousins had (I'm a godmother five times over – my extended family could win Olympic medals in breeding).

'Imogen, are you only saying that because you think it's what I want to hear?' he asked, clearly worried.

'I'm saying it because I mean it.'

His anxiety visibly slipped away. 'When you're this in love with someone, it's hard to understand how there could be room for another person.'

I was about to lean in and kiss him, when he reached into his pocket. 'I have something for you.'

My insides surged as he placed a small, blue box in my hand.

'It's not a ring,' he said self-consciously, as I gently pulled on its ribbon. 'Although one day I'd like to give you one of those, too.'

'What is it?'

'Open it.' And I did.

Inside was the most exquisite piece of jewellery I'd ever seen: a delicate, blossom-shaped pendant with a slender, silver chain that glittered in the sunlight. It confirmed – as if I'd needed it – that he sometimes knew me better than I knew myself. Its gorgeousness was in its simplicity.

'Roberto, you can't give me this . . .'

'Of course I can.'

'How on earth did you afford it?'

'A little light company embezzlement. You've got a yacht coming next week.'

'Very funny.'

He placed the chain around my neck and fumbled with the clasp until it was fastened. Then he brushed his lips gently against the back of my neck, making my entire body tingle.

'Wear it for ever.'

When I responded, it was with a giddy, half-blind certainty that nothing was ever going to go wrong.

'I will,' I told him. 'I'll never take it off.'

My eyes spring open and I know I'll never get to sleep now. The clock reads 3 a.m. and I'm wide awake.

It takes at least another hour before I've calmed down enough to feel my eyelids flutter closed . . . and it's just as I'm submitting to slumber that I am jolted awake by a sound vibrating through the room that almost convinces me that Meredith has rolled onto a whoopee cushion.

'PWTTTHHHHHHHHHT!'

I frown at her, stunned at the sheer volume, and seriously hoping that it's a one-off.

'PWTTTTTTTTTHHHHHHHHHHHHHT!'

And so I have my answer. Meredith's pineapple might have cured her snoring, but it's also produced the sort of wind power that could supply half the National Grid.

Day Three

Chapter 14

I am woken at 7.04 a.m., after two and a half hours of sleep, by the piercing jangle of my phone.

I vault out of bed, taking care not to launch anything untoward with the remote, be it the television, the curtains or the flush toilet on the International Space Station.

'Is that my sodding phone?' Meredith sits bolt upright, like Christopher Lee emerging from a coffin. 'Or is that *your* sodding phone? Either way, ANSWER THE SODDING PHONE!'

I am now prancing about the room like a decapitated chicken, but totally fail to locate it before the ring dies.

Meredith flops down with an emphatic groan and buries her head under her quilt.

'You're not meant to lie on your back after the first trimester . . .'

'PWTTHHHHT!'

There's not a lot I can say to that.

The super-grade curtains on the windows allow absolutely no sunlight to sneak into the room, so I tiptoe around trying to find my phone with only the loo-roll light to illuminate my path.

It proves an ineffective surveillance aid, however, as proved by my resulting trip on the hairdryer cord and dive, which could have kicked off an 800-metres swimming final. I just see the corner of the luggage rack in an all-too-impressive close-up before I make contact, landing with a sharp thud directly on my eye socket.

My resulting shriek is loud enough to convince those working out in the basement gym that there is a wild boar being slaughtered on the sixth floor.

'Ehh— Whaaa—' Meredith manages, before instantly falling asleep again.

I make great efforts to suppress my overwhelming desire to scream as pain throbs through my frontal cortex and down into my neck. I crawl on my hands and knees to the mirror and switch on the smallest, most modest light I can find, which only succeeds in floodlighting the entire room.

'IMOGEN! WHAT IS GOING ON?' Meredith cries, rearing up again as she shields her eyes.

'Sorry! I'm sorry!' I mumble, dimming the lights. She thuds down as I peer into the mirror to examine my left eye. I'm seeing triple, so there are three of them but, apart from that, it could be worse. It's swollen and starting to go purplish, like a rotting beetroot that's been boiled for several days. You know – exactly the sort of look you want on holiday.

Meredith cocoons herself again in her duvet as I hear a beep from the bathroom, and discover my phone in the pocket of one of the two dressing gowns.

David has left a voice message.

'Imogen!' He sounds breathless and echoey, like he's running inside a biscuit tin, and his voice has a quality that is rare in my boss: urgency. 'I need to speak to you. It's about this *Daily Sun* thing. We need to get rid of it, Imogen. Now. It could be catastrophic, not just for the merger, but the company per se. I'm still trying to track down the ... the *bottom wipe* who got us into this mess. Although I've come to the conclusion that ultimately it doesn't matter who it is – all that matters is that we stop this happening. Can you phone me asap? That's ASAP. Thanks.'

Attempting to quell my alarm, I phone him back. It goes to voicemail, but I want to speak to David directly, so I end the call and try again. And again. I reluctantly leave a message telling him, in the calmest voice I can muster, to phone me back so we can update each other. Which I realise gives the impression I have something to update him on, but never mind.

Two hours later, as I wait to meet Nicola for breakfast, having left Meredith to lie in, I've heard nothing from him.

And he's not the only one. I've made three calls to the police station about my necklace, but managed only to connect with a non-English speaker who listened intently before putting down the phone on me.

I sigh and adjust the sunglasses Meredith threw at me from her bedside table before I left the room. They are the size of two small dessert plates and dark enough to stop me walking in a straight line, but they're an improvement on the black eye, I can't deny it.

Nicola arrives looking refreshed and relaxed. 'Morning! So, did the pineapple work?'

'Yes.' Then, 'No.'

She laughs. 'Eh?'

I lift up my sunglasses to read the breakfast menu and she gasps. 'Why do you look like *Million Dollar Baby?*'

'Oh. Thanks. I had a fight with a luggage rack and lost.' My morning's struggles have left me hungry, and I look around eagerly. 'Where's our waiter? I've been here for twenty minutes and haven't been approached yet.' While whomever is serving us appears to have gone to Seville for their fag break, the rest of the staff are treating everyone else as though they have a Masters in sucking up.

'Excuse me!' I cough politely. 'Could we possibly—'

A waitress marches past carrying a coffee jug to attend to a couple who've already drunk so much they'll be awake until a week on Tuesday.

'She'll be over soon enough. Maybe we should go and get something from the buffet,' Nicola suggests.

We wander into the adjacent room and gaze upon the most spectacular feast I've ever seen.

'Maybe we can live without the coffee,' I say.

Nicola nods. 'You could be right.'

Despite the bountiful nature of the food, I resolve to show some restraint this time and not fall into the same trap as at the airport. I take only those items I *really* want: a modest slice of melon, a boiled egg, a piece of coconut cake and some dried prunes. Admittedly, I'd win no prizes for menu co-ordination.

I'm just reaching over a big, silver bowl of chilled fruit yoghurt when my phone bursts into life from the back pocket of my shorts. With nowhere to put down my plate, I hastily balance it on one hand and attempt to retrieve my phone, but I'm so hell-bent on swiping the green button before it rings off this time that I promptly drop my phone into a cut-glass bowl of fruit salad.

'SHIT!'

'What have you done?' hisses Nicola, appearing at my side.

'Imogen? IMOGEN?' echoes David's voice from between a cluster of cherries and a chunk of mango.

'You need to get that out quickly,' says a voice.

Before I can argue, my phone is being fished out of the bowl and I watch with a throbbing heart as Harry begins wiping it off with a napkin with his big, tanned hands. I am momentarily mesmerised, before grabbing the phone and shoving it against my ear, only then realising how sticky it is. 'David? David?'

The line's dead. Harry looks slightly taken aback.

'Sorry. I didn't mean to snatch,' I say, providing the requisite response I expect from Florence in similar situations.

'Don't worry about it,' he says. 'That looked like one hell of an important call.'

'You could say that.'

'Worth marinating your mobile for, I hope?'

I frown down at my phone as I hold it gingerly between thumb and forefinger. 'Oh God, look at it!'

He picks up some more napkins. 'Turn the phone off and lay it on these while you open it up and get the battery out. That's the most important bit.'

'How are you such an expert? I ask, frantically dismantling the phone.

'I did something similar once. Only worse.'

'Not the loo—'

'Fortunately not,' he replies with a laugh. 'Just a muddy puddle. I spent the night Googling solutions on my computer, none of which worked. But they might on yours. You got it out pretty quickly.'

'You mean *you* did.'

'Yeah, well, don't call me a hero until you've got that melon juice off your sim card. Any news on your necklace, by the way?'

It's then that I realise that he's striking up a conversation with me. Just like the first time, it unsettles me.

'Not a word. So you can be satisfied that you were probably completely right.'

'I take no satisfaction in that. Sorry if I gave the impression otherwise.'

'You didn't. The necklace is just a big deal to me, that's all.'

Harry looks at me. 'You don't seem to be having much luck on this holiday.'

'You don't know the half of it,' I reply, lifting my sunglasses onto my head to get a better look at the phone as I start to put it back together.

He tries to play down how startled he looks. 'Oh ... dear.'

I put the glasses back on, self-conscious. 'Hmm. Not a good look really, is it?'

'Are you okay?' He looks genuinely concerned, which only makes me feel like dying inside.

'I'm fine. Hardly hurts at all, really,' I lie. 'So what are you up to today?'

'I believe I'm off to the Picasso museum, then tonight I'm going to some big party here at the hotel.'

'I thought you were here working?'

The click of stylish heels interrupts our conversation and, as I look up, the woman Harry was with yesterday appears at his side. She looks even better close up, with flawless skin and a spectacular smile.

''Arry Pfeiffer!'

If I spoke at that volume, I'd sound about as dulcet-toned as Dot Cotton mid-meltdown. *Her* voice, on the other hand, is forceful but melting, like she's performing the final scene in *Carmen.*

'We need to go!' She grabs him by the arm.

'Sorry. I'm in demand, apparently.' He shrugs playfully as he's whisked to the exit by Clipboard Barbie, before he's been able to pick up so much as a croissant.

I gaze after them, at her slender arm linked through his and, for a fleeting moment, wonder what it must be like to be one of the Beautiful People.

People with whom I have nothing in common.

I've gone back to rescuing my phone when I see Harry unravel himself from the woman and weave back past two tables, before grabbing something from the surface of one. Then he makes his way back, catching my eye en route.

'See you later,' he says smiling, as I notice a copy of *The Book Thief* in his hand.

Chapter 15

The plan today is to visit La Sagrada Família, one of Barcelona's most celebrated landmarks. I've read a lot about it in the guidebooks and it's the place I've been keenest to see, given the monumental hype it attracts.

According to what I've read, construction for Gaudí's giant basilica started at the end of the nineteenth century and it still isn't finished (which will be little comfort to the blokes overseeing my mum's kitchen extension, who threaten delay at their peril).

The building, I'm told, is stunning, and I can't wait. At least, I *couldn't* wait, but, just as we're walking through the hotel lobby, my phone springs into life. I finally manage to answer it without injuring myself, someone else, or dropping it in the healthy option on the breakfast buffet.

It's David. 'Imogen – they've phoned me,' he splutters. 'The swines PHONED me.'

'You mean the *Daily Sun?*'

'Yes! YES!'

I frown, registering that his voice has the same tinny quality as earlier. 'David, where *are* you?'

'Fourth-floor gents lavs. It was the only place I could get some privacy. Imogen, what am I going to DO?'

'Okay, don't panic,' I say, as if I'm not doing so myself. 'What did they say, exactly?'

'They said they know who it is, Imogen. They *know*. FOR THE LOVE OF PETER, PAUL AND MARY! I tried to play it cool, I tried to bluff it out ... but I think they might not be lying.'

'Who is it, then? Did they tell you?'

'No,' he croaks.

'Then they're probably just calling your bluff. They must be. I'm *sure* they are,' I say, in a supernova of wishful thinking.

'Do you *really* think so? Oh, I hope so.'

I'm suddenly not only furious with Roy and the PR agency for failing to respond, but genuinely, overwhelmingly concerned. It's been two days since I first tried to get hold of them and the deathly, unprecedented silence can only mean something's very wrong.

'This could be the undoing of us, Imogen,' David begins again, breathlessly. 'All my hard work. Everything I've strived for. Oh, SPHERICAL OBJECTS!'

'David, calm down!' I snap, then bite my tongue. 'I'm sorry. I didn't mean to ... the point is, this is bad, yes. But, it's *one* executive. We, as a company, can't be responsible for that. We simply have to take action. Announce an internal inquiry, promise to come down on him like a ton of bricks.' I can feel a plan coming together. 'David, we're going to be okay, so don't be afraid of the *Daily Sun*. We just have to act like a responsible company and make sure heads roll.'

'You mean sack someone, don't you?'

'I don't know, I suppose so.' I can't actually believe I'm advocating making someone lose their job, but I'm struggling to see an alternative. 'Look, we're getting ahead of ourselves. I bet it's someone fairly junior, whatever the journalist said. Nobody senior would be stupid enough; in fact, the more I think about this, the more convinced I am that we'll be fine. As long as it's not you, of course,' I joke.

He doesn't respond.

'David?' I sit on the sofa, waiting for him to speak. 'David? Are you there?'

Meredith looks at her watch. Nicola mouths, 'Are you ready?'

I shake my head apologetically.

'David, why are you not saying anything? Please tell me you're not saying anything because you've dropped your mobile in the urinal and not because ... because ...'

'Because what?'

'Because ... it's you—'

He starts making a noise like he's woken up from an

anaesthetic while having his tonsils removed. 'My phone isn't in the toilet.'

My mouth opens, but I am completely devoid of thoughts about how to respond. It's *him*. David. My boss and mentor is The First-Class Fondler.

'Oh, David,' I mumble, numbly. 'Oh … David. Oh … *David*.'

'If you say "Oh, David" one more time, Imogen, I may have to cry.'

'I'm sorry. I don't know what else to say.'

'It was a momentary indiscretion,' he whimpers.

'I thought it was a two-hour flight?' I splutter.

'Okay, it was a two-hour indiscretion. I've never been unfaithful to Carmel before. Well, not since … there was a woman in Johannesburg once, but she knows about that. And Cape Town, but that was years ago.' He's beginning to ramble now.

'Do you specialise in the Southern African sub-continent?'

He is silenced, and I remind myself that a) he's my boss and b) whatever he's done, he's still been my greatest advocate at work in the last few years.

'I'd come back from a terrible meeting – it had gone catastrophically badly. I was stressed out. And I found myself sitting next to an accountant who I swear looked like Nicole Kidman. And I've always loved Nicole Kidman.'

'But *why*, David?' I urge.

'It was ever since *Days of Thunder*.'

'I mean, *why* did you get it on with this woman?'

'Oh, I don't know!' he howls. 'I was stupid. She was sexy. We got through three bottles of champagne and, before I knew it, we were under the complimentary blanket. Her top had gone the way of Shergar and she was experimenting with the recline button.'

I'm glad he can't see me wincing.

'The *thought* of the kids finding out about this! Michael will be distraught,' he continues.

This is another reason to help David: his teenage son and daughter, God help them. Not that that brings me any closer to a solution.

'Okay, David, you're going to have to leave this with me. Just give me the journalist's number and I'll sort it.'

'Will you, Imogen?'

'Yes,' I reply, hastily. 'One way or another, I'll sort it.'

Our PR company is DEAD. When I finally get hold of them, I intend to tell them exactly that. But I haven't got hold of them so, instead, I send Meredith and Nicola on their way and sit in the bar, making a series of phone calls, determined that, one way or another, I will not be ignored.

I am half convinced that the pure fury I'm radiating down the phone is one of the reasons that eventually, miraculously, I get through to Roy.

'Where *are* you? Oh my God, I'm so relieved to have got hold of you,' I say, suddenly feeling guilty about my last text. 'Roy, you've got SO much to do!'

'What? Eh?' His voice is drowned out by an almighty cacophony of screaming, which is very different from our usual office soundtrack, even after the half-day budget meetings.

'DAD! Come on … it's GO-INNNG!'

'Really sorry, Imogen, I can't stop and talk,' Roy tells me.

'Roy. You CAN stop. You MUST stop. Please, Roy, just STOP.'

'I can't,' he replies, as the screams get louder and are joined by a strange clanking sound.

'Didn't you get my messages?' I demand.

'Messages? No, Janine hits the roof if I keep my phone on while we're away. I only turned it on to check the cricket.'

'What do you mean? Where are you?'

'I'm on the Tower of Terror.'

'What?'

'I'm in Euro Disney.'

'What the hell are you doing there? You're meant to be deputising for me!'

'Well, I know, but Janine's brother's kids got severe gastroenteritis and, rather than their entire family holiday going to waste, they gave it to us. I know the timing wasn't ideal, but I went to David to ask if he'd mind. The last thing I wanted to do was let you down, but David said that we haven't got much on at the moment – apart from some top-secret thing that you personally are working on. So he said it's fine and— WAAAAAHHHHHHHHHHHH!'

At which point my eardrums come close to shattering, and the line goes dead.

Which is marvellous. Just *marvellous*.

Chapter 16

I take a seat in the lobby again and try to make sense of my muddled mess of thoughts. At which point, a gargantuan limousine pulls up outside as the concierge bursts into life to open the door.

Meatloaf and Yellow Bikini Lady emerge in a billowing cloud of cigar smoke, like the dry ice in a Kate Bush video.

Another besuited staff member sprints over to attend to them. 'Mr Venedictov! How is your stay so far?'

Mr Venedictov manages a lackadaisical grunt before heading in the direction of the pool deck.

This strikes me as a very good idea. If I've got a major PR crisis to tackle from just under a thousand miles away, I might as well do it while basking in sunshine. So I grab my belongings, follow him outside and find a sun lounger, before ordering a cranberry and orange juice and spreading out the series of notes I've made this morning.

I probably don't need to spell out the fact that nobody else is doing this – every other guest is sunbathing, reading, relaxing . . . activities that are all within my grasp if only I can box off this issue and then try to forget about it.

With a tightening chest, I pull up the PR agency's number on my phone. I go to press 'Call' at the exact moment that the handset rings and 'Mum' flashes up on the screen. I let out a spontaneous groan.

'*So* sorry to phone, Imogen. Bit of an emergency,' she announces wearily, sounding very unlike someone about to put out an SOS call.

'Oh, dear. What happened?'

'It's Spud. There's something wrong with him. Very wrong.'

My eyes widen. 'Don't tell me he's been run over?'

'It's impossible to explain on the phone, Imogen. I need to *show* you,' she replies ominously. 'Why don't we do Skype?'

'Mum, I'm worried now,' I say. 'What's happened to my dog?'

'This is a visual matter, Imogen – you need to *see* it. It's a full-scale, multi-sensory issue, if the truth be told . . .'

I sigh as inaudibly as possible. 'Give me ten minutes, and I'll find the business centre here so that we can Skype. Is Florence around, too?'

'Yes, yes, I'll put her on when you Skype us. At the moment, all I'm concerned with is Spud. This dog needs help. And so do the rest of us, frankly.'

I end the call and head into the lobby, passing models, businessmen and a sheikh with an entourage bigger than the Red

Army during the Battle of Kursk. It strikes me that I'll never feel anything but out of place here, although obviously the black eye doesn't help.

A sign next to the lift tells me that the business centre is on the second floor, so I press the button and am poised to step in when my phone rings again. This time, it isn't my mother's number. It is Madeleine Bowers. *The* Madeline Bowers. My PR hell is *over*! I abandon the lift and answer the phone.

'Imogen Copeland,' I simper, hearing the relief in my voice.

'Imogen, sweetie,' Madeleine drawls.

It's difficult to describe how pleased I am to hear her voice, except to say that I suppress an urge to cartwheel across the lobby, flick-flack onto the pool deck and finish with a reverse dive into the infinity pool.

Madeleine is a director of Ace Communications, a PR giant who has been in the business for at least thirty years. She's one of those women whose oversized personality and sheer presence silences people simply by walking into a room. Although perhaps that's just her dress sense – nobody rocks a peacock-feather-trimmed trilby and gingham ra-ra skirt quite like she does.

On a day-to-day level it's always been Julia, a junior account executive, with whom I've dealt, and I'd been impressed with her until she decided to disappear off the face of the earth.

Still, in Madeleine, the PR company has brought out the biggest of their big guns. Although I suppose when you've got the *Daily Sun* threatening ruination, nothing short of her phenomenal power will do.

'I had a message you rang,' she continues. I can picture her in her vast office, clicking her fingers to summon her army of PR lackeys, poised to spring into action.

'I did. Thank you *so* much for phoning back. You've probably worked out from my messages that we've got a major crisis on our hands. I've got the phone number of the journalist who's on our trail and, well ... Madeleine, I'm just so grateful that you're now on the case. I was hoping you'd assign someone senior to this but never dreamt—'

'Imogen, let me stop you there. Please.' It's then that I realise she doesn't sound quite the powerhouse I'd come to know. Au contraire. She sounds as though she's had the weepy bits in *Marley And Me* on repeat all morning. 'You've obviously not heard that at Ace Communications, we have some issues of our own.'

'Oh,' I say. I have no idea why I feel chastised, but I do.

'Imogen ... I don't know what I'm going to do!' she bleats, before exploding into an asthmatic splutter.

'Madeleine, what's the matter?' I ask, as if we're both fifteen and she's about to tell me she's been dumped by a sixth former for not having big enough boobs.

'We've gone bust!' she howls.

'What?'

'It's so unfair, this is all Adrian's fault,' she wails. 'He was

147

supposed to be in charge of all the financial do-dahs. That wasn't *my* job. But he buried his head in the sand and went on spending. You wouldn't believe where we've taken our big clients in the last year. Wimbledon ... Royal Ascot ... we even took our top-paying clients to Monte Carlo for a weekend.'

'Really?'

'Yes, but you must have experienced this – Peebles were one of our biggest. Didn't Julia take you anywhere nice?'

'We did Starbucks in Charing Cross once, bu—'

'Oh, it's all irrelevant!' she interrupts. 'Now it's all gone, gone in a puff of smoke.'

'Are you telling me that the company is *completely* no more?'

'It's as dead as a dodo. A dodo that's been run over by an articulated lorry, fallen off a cliff and then been cremated.'

'I don't mean to be insensitive but ... does this mean we have *no* PR representation?'

'Oh, Imogen, it's okay for you,' she continues, as if she hasn't heard me. 'You're young, at the height of your career, so full of spunk it's almost coming out of your nose. Me, I'm a washed-up old PR in her mid-f—orties.'

I raise an eyebrow.

'If you could see me now, Imogen. I'm sitting here in my dressing gown, weeping, watching Jeremy Kyle and drinking oolong tea spiked with Gordon's. I don't know what I'm going to do!'

'I'm really sorry, Madeleine, but I'm sure you'll find something. You're an absolute legend in this business.'

'Not after this!'

I frown. 'Look, can I make a suggestion? I have a major PR problem with the *Daily Sun* at the moment and I need someone to deal with it for me. Why don't you take this on as a freelance job?' It strikes me as the perfect solution. It'd be helping Madeleine *and* Peebles. 'All isn't lost, and we need someone of your calibre.'

'Oh, I couldn't!' she says theatrically, and I'm pretty sure I can hear the chink of glass bottle on teacup. 'I'm in mourning for my career. I'm too stressed, I'm too tired, I'm too . . .'

'Yes?'

'Sorry, I've just thought of how you *can* help,' she says, perking up. 'It's the ideal solution.'

'Which is?'

'We'll get Peterhouse Deevy to deal with it for you. I *adore* Mike Peterhouse. Gorgeous brown eyes and a smile like Donny Osmond. And maybe, just maybe, if I can hand over some of my old clients to them, they'll think about giving me a job.'

'Hmm. I'm not sure,' I say.

'I'd really prefer to deal with just you. Wouldn't you consider it Madeleine?'

'Imogen, it's out of the question. Peterhouse Deevy are your answer. I promise you. They're one of the top ten PR companies in London!'

'I know, but I was talking to one of their former clients at a networking event last month and they described them as lacklustre. She said she felt they were trading on their past reputation, without putting in a great deal of effort today.' I could remember her words almost verbatim, as I'd been quietly congratulating myself on being with Ace. Oh, the irony.

'Imogen, don't listen to gossip. This is perfect. Besides, you're not exactly overflowing with options at the moment, are you?'

Chapter 17

The business centre is so slick I'm convinced someone could feasibly run Microsoft from here.

It's a vast, semicircular room, with state-of-the-art computers lining the curved window above the sea. Despite boasting more technology than the command deck of the Starship Enterprise, absolutely nobody is in here, which I'm very glad about. If I'm going to consider taking on Peterhouse Deevy – because Madeleine's right about my options being limited – it will mean briefing them about David's indiscretion, something I'd rather not make any more public than it already is.

I fire up a computer, torn between gratitude and unease about Madeleine's suggestion that we go with her recommended PR agency. It's obviously nice of her to propose an alternative, although the fact that we've got to go with someone new and unfamiliar during the biggest publicity crisis in our history is not good news. There's no doubt that Peterhouse Deevy are a big, respectable company – I'm just hoping that what that woman told me at the networking event was off the mark.

I'm about to log on to Skype when a text arrives from Mum:

Are you nearly ready?!

I take a deep breath and check the webcam is on as I connect to my mum's account.

We've used Skype a lot since Florence came along. Or, if the truth be told, we have since Mum discovered that Roberto's mother was doing it once a week – to talk to her in Italian in a bid to make her bilingual (which hasn't been overly successful, judging by Florence's glazed expression).

When she finally appears on the screen, it's in a state of profound disequilibrium.

'I can't live with this,' she sighs, blowing hair away from her eyes in one long breath.

'Mum, what is it?'

'His *bottom*,' she says with a sigh.

I frown. 'What?'

'Imogen, I have never smelled anything like it. Your father and I were attempting to watch *Driving Miss Daisy* last night as he dragged himself along the floor creating the stench of a flatulent camel. It's not natural, Imogen. Can dogs get cancer of the bottom?'

'Mum, it's not cancer, it's—'

'I don't think the air quality in this house will ever recover. I've been Shake n' Vac-ing all morning, and it's still making my eyes stream. Imogen, you need to see this.'

'But, Mum—' I'm trying to tell her that this is nothing that a routine trip to the vet and sturdy pair of latex gloves can't fix.

'I can't work out if it's normal or not,' she continues, before picking up the laptop and carrying it shakily across the living room floor as she pursues Spud.

'Mum, I don't . . . this isn't necessary . . . it isn't . . .'

But she's a woman possessed, hunting him down like something in *The Hunger Games*. She finally gets him to stand still with the aid of a chew bar and, as Spud blithely chomps his way through it, oblivious, she lifts his tail and positions the webcam to provide such an amplified view of the problem it could get me put on some sort of register.

'Bloody hell, Mother,' I mutter, turning to shield my eyes . . . as I come face to face with quite another vision.

Harry is mesmerised as he stands in the doorway, staring at the screen, drained of the ability to speak. I spin back, praying the picture has disappeared, to be confronted by the continuing sight of my pooch's bum in glorious, gargantuan techicolour.

'This is not what it looks like,' I mumble, my face blanching as I examine the screen. Except, it is. It's a giant, inflated view of a dog's arsehole. Simple as that.

I start hammering keys to try to shut it down as he walks

towards me, but am rewarded solely with one of those twirling icons that denote the computer's frozen. I make a split-second, desperate decision to try to shield the screen from view, so cross my arms and plonk myself over the keyboard. It protests with a loud, angry beep.

'I stumbled on this website,' I blurt out, wondering whether lying actually is the better option here. 'I'm trying to get rid of it so I can do some work.'

'No problem,' he says, taking his sunglasses off his head and placing them on the desk. 'What was it?'

'I'm not sure. I really have no idea. It looked dodgy, that's for sure.'

He's about to speak again when a voice comes loud and clear through the computer's speakers. 'Imogen! You're not looking! He's in a perfect position here. Hurry up so you can get a good look.'

Thinking on my feet, I hoot, 'OOH, look at that!' as I point out of the window. As Harry turns to look, I hit the button on the monitor, killing the power. Then I sit, breathlessly, on the edge of the desk, as his eyes return to me.

'What am I looking at?'

'Oh, didn't you see that bird?' I say casually. 'It was amazing.'

'Really?'

'Hmmmm.'

'What was it like?'

'I'm not sure what species, but I guess it was a type of . . .

of' – I'm no ornithologist, but I scan my brain to try to think of a bird, any bird, that might find its natural habitat around a Mediterranean beach – 'owl.'

He looks at me as though I'm completely demented.

'An . . . owl?'

'Maybe I'm mistaken,' I say hastily. As a thought suddenly strikes me.

In the midst of this mortifying moment, I find my blood pounding through my veins for another reason. My face is flushed. And I'm feeling something I haven't felt for a long, long time.

I can't. I surely can't.

Do I *fancy* this man?

'Do you need this room in private, Imogen?'

I freeze at his use of my name, at the effect the overfamiliarity has on me.

'I do, to be honest.'

It might be true, but so is something else that I'm only now recognising: I don't want him to go. I want him to stay. I actually want to be around this man.

'Not a problem, I can come back later.' He starts backing away.

'Oh . . . you don't need to. I mean, it's hardly fair. This is a public part of the hotel. I couldn't keep it to myself.'

'I'd only popped in to send an email that's too long to write on my phone. I can come back later – it's no big deal.'

Then he smiles a devastating smile – one that reduces my insides to marshmallow – and disappears out of the door. Leaving me with only my mother, the dog's backside and a long, difficult call to a PR company to think about.

Chapter 18

I spend the next half hour pacing around the business centre on the phone to Cosimo Usborne, the account manager assigned to us by Peterhouse Deevy.

He is twenty-two, has worked in PR for less than a year, and his other clients include Grill-O-Bloo, a company that makes oven cleaners; and Smoovie, who make smoothies. Presumably for people with speech disorders.

'You're in good hands,' he assures me fervantly. 'I've got *loads* of experience in this sort of thing. I'm carving out a speciality in foodstuffs. I've done two launches since March, and the clients were delighted. I got Grill-O-Bloo in *Take A Break*.'

'Yes, but this is a crisis-management job. You understand that, don't you? It's completely different from promotional work. We need someone to liaise with this journalist and minimise the negative messages surrounding Peebles. Keep our name out of it if at all possible. Are you sure you'll be okay?'

'There is nothing I don't know about handling publicity for popular snacks,' he announces huffily. 'I was born to do this. It's my vocation.'

'Yes, but it's not the same as putting out a press release.' I'm starting to feel – and sound – quite desperate. 'We've got a crisis on our hands here. This is very serious.'

'You can rely on me.'

I don't want to undermine him. Equally, I don't want the company where I've built my career to implode because David can't handle himself after a bottle of fizz. Or three. 'Have you . . . have you got someone senior supporting you on this one?'

'Of course! Our account director, Ben, is always on hand.'

'Can I speak to him?'

'He's at his place in the Grenadines.'

'Ohhhhhhhh . . .' Now I'm whimpering. I can't help it.

'Ginny . . . can I call you Ginny? I think that's short for Imogen, isn't it? Look, please leave it with me. I'll speak to the journalist, see what they've got on the story and take it from there. I'm confident I've got something that'll put him off the scent.'

'Really?' I leap on this nugget of hope.

'One of the techniques I learned on my PR course was to knock a potential bad story off the front page with a good one.'

'And you've got a good one?'

'Grill-O-Bloo are launching a new pan scourer that's so

effective I'm hoping to get a quote from NASA endorsing it. *Prima* won't be happy, but I'll give it to the *Daily Sun* as an exclusive.'

When I finally put down the phone, I have never felt less relaxed in my entire life: less than the hour before I did my driving test; less than the minute before my A levels; less than the time I bungee jumped when Roberto and I were on holiday in the Dordogne.

At which point, a fundamental issue hits me. This *cannot* go on, not while I'm supposed to be on the holiday of my life.

I close my eyes, take some deep, yogic breaths and try to think positively. Peterhouse Deevy is an experienced, established company whose reputation at stake – albeit not as much as ours – if things go wrong. Maybe it's just the control freak in me that's worried about Cosimo? I need something to take my mind off this.

I drum my fingers on the desk, trying to think of something, anything, that isn't work. Two words pop into my head.

Harry Pfeiffer.

It's an appealing name I think, a name that's solid but exotic at the same time. I hesitate before slinking to the door and opening it briefly to check the coast is clear. Then I dive back to the computer and type in his name. There's a Harry Pfeiffer, miner; Harry Pfeiffer, High Court judge; Harry Pfeiffer, ballet dancer; and Harry Pfeiffer, journalist.

I click on 'Images' to scan through and see if I can see *my* Harry Pfeiffer, but am confronted by row upon row of mug shots, promotional images and one piece of abstract art by Harry Pfeiffer, artist, that looks like something vomited up by a hyperglycaemic cat.

I'm on page four of the search engine's results and about to give up when one face leaps out at me. It's *him*.

It's an official portrait, although for what, I don't know. But the sight of his face, bespectacled and beautiful, does odd things to my insides. I click on the image as a sentence escapes from my mouth: 'Well, hello, Harry.'

'Hello, Imogen.'

I gasp like a vacuum cleaner stuck on the surface of a cushion, before leaping at the computer and reaching round to pull out the plug. The computer fizzles and dies.

I would quite like to do the same myself.

'I left my glasses here.' He walks to the computer next to mine, and the sunglasses hiding at the side.

'Silly you,' I splutter, in a similar way to which I addressed Florence when she was two.

He laughs, apparently unconcerned. 'Yep. Silly me.'

Chapter 19

The sun deck is quiet again when I next go outside. It seems everyone has followed Meredith and Nicola's lead and gone sightseeing. I try not to seethe too much at my confinement to the hotel, aware that there are worse maximum-security units. Besides, at least I can try to get a bit of a tan.

If I was thinking straight, I would remember that tanning is one of the most pointless exercises invented, and one to which I should *never* succumb given that UV rays have a similar effect on my skin as a wire brush and Cillit Bang. I have one of those 'English Rose' complexions, which basically means it's as pasty as a tray of uncooked sausage rolls and all it takes to fire up my prickly heat is a flimsy display of sunshine breaking through the clouds.

You'd think I'd learn. But, every holiday, I fall into the same trap and compare my pale blue legs with everyone else's bronzed beauties, convincing myself I'd benefit from some rays.

The worst instance of this I ever experienced was when

Roberto and I spent ten days in his aunt's farmhouse in Tuscany. Fed up of remaining as white as a sheet with my factor 50 (which had the consistency of lard and smelled slightly less appealing), I'd misjudged the effect that dropping down a factor or two might have and ended up with legs on which you could've barbequed kebabs.

Roberto could barely suppress his amusement, although he did treat me to dinner that night, in a beautiful hilltop restaurant nestled inside the medieval walls of San Gimignano. He had a knack of knowing all the best places; the back-street restaurants with al-fresco tables, flickering tea lights and views from heaven.

It was a people-watching paradise, from the backpacking American students to the head-over-heels-in-love elderly couple on the next table, who, we discovered, after Roberto got chatting with them, had made the journey from Rome.

I'd been mildly bewitched by those two and the idea that, one day, after a lifetime together, Roberto and I would still be like that, holding hands, laughing at each other's jokes, comfortable in our own skin with each other in every way.

'They're getting married next year,' Roberto revealed as we made our way down the steep, cobbled hill towards home. 'They only met in December, after his wife passed away last year.'

'What?' I wailed. 'How disappointing.'

Roberto laughed. 'What's wrong with that?'

'Oh, nothing – it's nice, I suppose. I just liked the idea of them acting like newly weds when they'd been together for sixty-odd years, that's all. I feel robbed.'

'Obviously, *we*'ll be like that after sixty or so years.' He grinned. 'Although, if I go first, for the record, you can go and marry who you want. No point in being unhappy.'

'I'll have to say the same now, or I'll look churlish,' I replied, with a mock pout. 'Fine then. If we both reach our nineties, then I go, you have my full permission to go bungee jumping with someone else.'

He laughed. 'That's very good of you.'

I breathed in. 'What *is* that gorgeous smell?' It had been everywhere since we'd arrived in Tuscany, but I only seemed to register it at that moment.

'You mean, apart from me?'

'It's herbier than you.'

'Ah . . . that's the sage. Lovely, isn't it? It's associated with a long and happy life, according to legends, anyway. That, and treating mouth ulcers.'

I know that my second excursion to the sun deck today won't be much better than the first, as now I'm simply lying down and stressing about when Cosimo's going to ring. Not that I can really do much until he does.

I find a spot on the edge of the sun deck and order a drink from a passing waiter. Ideal as it isn't that I've got to work, I can't deny this beats sitting at my desk in London. I pull out a pad from my beach bag and start jotting down a potential quote for Cosimo to supply to the *Daily Sun*. But I scrub it out, and come up with something else, before repeating the exercise, then ripping off the page and dumping it in the bottom of my bag, deciding it's better if we can suss out what they're going to run first. I pick up my book. Perhaps distraction is the best tactic after all.

'*Here is a small fact . . .*'

I glance up and spot the gorgeous woman with the clipboard, fussing over a group of people by the pool. A bit like me, none of them looks like they quite belong here. Though I'd struggle to define why this is beyond the Next T-shirt worn by the young guy with Einstein hair, and the fact that the girl with the streaky red lipstick keeps her suncream wrapped in a plastic Boots bag.

I lower my eyes again to my book.

'*Here is a small fact . . .*'

A soft breeze whispers past and lifts up my chin. My skin prickles with interest. Because Harry's joined the group. And he hasn't got a top on.

I feel an increasing sense of agitation as I peer over my book at him. Unthinkingly, I reach up to touch my necklace and when I register its absence, experience a swell of unease, abhorrence almost, at what I'm feeling. Because there's no doubt I'm feeling *something*.

I focus hard on my page, looking at the words without actually reading, until I become aware of Harry engaging in conversation with another new member of the group – an older guy with a walking stick, and knees that clearly haven't seen sunlight since the mid-1980s.

Clipboard Barbie is finding it impossible to quell her heaving bosom and, nauseating as it is, it's easy to see what's motivating her. Men with muscles have never held much appeal to me on the basis that their owners usually spend so long admiring themselves, they haven't got time for anyone else. So I can only think that I'm struggling to keep my eyes off Harry's torso because, after five years of singledom, it's natural to find some fascination with the male form.

I realise that these new, or rediscovered, stirrings feel like the return of a long-lost, slightly mucky friend one half of me is glad to see, even if the other doesn't like her that much. Of course, I'm not saying I haven't felt hot and bothered once in the last five years. But those moments have been rare, and prompted by old favourites such as the rainy day bit in *Dirty Dancing*, or an especially diverting scene in *True Blood*, rather than by a real-life human being.

Yet, as each time I catch a glimpse of Harry's body, all I can think of is how gratifying its strong lines are, how distracting its masculinity. He has an honest-to-goodness six-pack. And I know that if I closed my eyes, I could so vividly imagine kissing it I can almost taste the sunshine on his skin. So I don't close my eyes. I open them wide, trying to think of a way to halt the cloudburst rising in my pelvis.

'Well, you missed a treat!' Nic's smiling face appears above me.

Meredith's generous shadow suddenly eclipses the sun. 'We're going to have to go again – it'd be right up your street, Imogen.'

'Really?' I cough, pulling myself together as I take a sip of my drink to cool down.

'Undoubtedly.' Meredith takes a seat next to me. 'Big place, lots of history, very photogenic. Of course, the hunky tour guide helped.'

'It's a church – you're not supposed to be drooling over the tour guide,' I point out.

'God won't mind,' she says confidently. 'He wouldn't put men like that on earth if he didn't want women to drool over them.'

I glance up as Yellow Bikini Lady arrives at a sun bed on the other side of the pool, this time sporting a blue rhinestone swimsuit that's even smaller than her previous efforts. 'You should've seen the car she arrived in earlier,' I whisper.

'Oh, that waiter I got chatting to the other day mentioned them – they're regulars. Russian, apparently.'

'I heard the concierge mention his name,' I say. 'Venedictov or something.'

Meredith Googles him on her phone. Her eyes widen. 'Alexander Venedictov.' She looks up.

'Is he a movie star, too?' asks Nicola, stretching out on the sun bed next to mine.

'No, he's one of the world's most infamous crime lords,' Meredith replies casually. 'Can I have a sip of your sangria?'

My eyes widen. 'You're kidding? We didn't have that at the Hotel Sunshine in Zante.'

'Exciting, eh?' says Meredith.

Nicola suppresses a smile and picks up her phone as a text arrives. 'My mum says hi to you both.'

'Aw . . . say hi back,' Meredith replies.

Nicola's still close to her parents, who always struck me as jolly, salt-of-the-earth sorts with a door that was forever open and a kitchen that smelled of freshly baked scones. They adore Nicola with the peculiar intensity that some parents feel when they have an only child; it's no exaggeration to say that when she was growing up, they'd have preferred not to eat for a week than fail to fulfil any wish on her Christmas list.

'So, Imogen . . . how's our man?' Nicola asks, with a nod towards Harry that's heavy with implication.

I frown, mock-menacingly. 'I don't like this new, pushy Nicola.'

'I'm not pushy,' she laughs. 'I just get the impression he likes you.'

I start spluttering. I don't say anything in particular, simply forcing out a series of derisive grunts, before adding insouciantly, 'What makes you say that, as a matter of interest?'

'I can see it a mile off. He's looking over now.' She nudges me.

I tentatively lift up my eyes. Harry waves. I almost fall off my sun bed.

'Wave back,' Meredith hisses from between a fixed smile.

I lift up my hand and wave, unable to sustain it for longer than a couple of seconds before hastily peering at my book to catch my breath.

'*Here is a small fact . . .*'

Meredith shakes her head before waddling off in the direction of the Ladies, and I take the opportunity to raise a subject with Nic that I've been meaning to since our first day on the beach.

'So, what was the deal with Mr Brayfield and the conversation with your mum in Sainsbury's? Last time I looked, you didn't have a boyfriend, and weren't in the market for one, either.'

She groans. 'Please never mention that to Jess, whatever you do. She'd go ballistic.'

'Has your mum ever made up an imaginary boyfriend for you before?'

She shakes her head. 'This is the first I know about.'

Nicola adores her parents and she adores Jessica. Sadly, the two parties do not adore each other. In fact, despite she and Jess having been together for years, they still haven't even met.

I would never have predicted this peculiar set-up. It's not as if Nicola's mum and dad are right-wing loonies or overzealous religious nuts. They've always seemed normal and nice; old-fashioned maybe, but no more excessively strait-laced than anyone else's parents.

Even Nicola was surprised by their reaction when she finally came out to them. They didn't hit the roof. There was no shouting or threats. Her mum simply sat with her hands clasped and head bent, weeping gently, as her dad tensed his jaw and failed to utter anything fitting.

Nicola was convinced that they were simply in shock and that if she gave it time, things would be ironed out. Nine years on, she's still waiting for that to happen.

Her parents' approach – to pretend it isn't happening – is a policy to which they've stuck resolutely over the years. Even when Nicola failed to ever turn up at home with a boyfriend; even when, as a student, she was spotted by her dad leaving her flat holding another woman's hand. And even when, nine years ago, she attempted to introduce them to the only significant other she's ever had: Jessica.

It was then that they had their first big row – a voices-raised, doors-slammed kind of conflagration; the sort that peppered my teenage years when I lived with my parents but which had, for some reason, eluded Nicola's family.

Weeks went by, then years and, despite the issue continually rearing its head between Jessica and Nicola, they still haven't met.

Whether they think that this strategy will magically transform their daughter into a card-carrying hetero and make her marry the next handsome prince that comes along, I have no idea.

'Anyway,' says Nicola, clearly wanting to change the subject. 'Why wouldn't you go and talk to Harry, Imogen? What is it you're afraid of?'

It's suddenly a question I don't know how to answer. 'Nothing,' I reply, defensively.

The truth is closer to *everything*.

She raises an eyebrow. Nobody is immune to Nicola's eyebrows. All she needs to do is lift one slightly and you're ready to confess anything.

'Okay, fine.' I exhale. 'I'm afraid of making a fool of myself with someone who's out of my league. I couldn't stand next to him without people thinking I was his ugly sister.' Nicola tuts. 'I'm afraid I've forgotten how to speak to a member of the opposite sex about anything other than work or what my gas meter reading is. And I'm afraid of being attracted to someone I don't know, I've hardly spoken to, is quite clearly a ladies' man and whom I'm never going to see again after this week.'

There's one more thing to add to the list, however; I know it, and I'm pretty sure Nicola knows it, too.

She looks at me. 'He might be attractive, but that doesn't automatically mean he's a ladies' man, and that wasn't a conclusion I came to. Besides, even if he was ... Imogen, can I speak candidly?'

'Of course.'

'You need to chill out about Harry, about being scared and about what this is really about – Roberto.'

I look down at my hands.

'This isn't a big deal,' she implores. 'This is something very simple – chatting to a man and seeing where it goes. Which may be nowhere. Or you may get a snog out of him.' She smirks.

'Who says I want a snog out of him?'

She throws me a look. 'I'm simply saying it'd be no bad thing if you had one. Don't think too hard about this, Imogen.'

I look over to where he's reclining on a sun bed. 'There is no way that man and I are ever going to snog.'

'Why not? What have you got against him?' Meredith asks, as she reappears and sits on the edge of my bed.

'It's just not going to happen for a multitude of reasons, not least that he's so far out of my league we're in different time zones.'

'Imogen, I assure you – he's not.'

I need to say at this point that I haven't got body dysmorphia, I'm not fishing for compliments and I'm not trying to claim that I have a face like a dropped pie. At some indefinable point in the distant past, you might have put Harry and me together. But not now. I have let myself go, gradually and willingly.

'Ladies, I am not asking you to contradict this to try and

make me feel better but, for the last couple of years, I've looked like a "Before" photograph on *This Morning*. And that's before we even get to the black eye and chewed-up feet I've accumulated in the last day or two.'

Meredith takes a deep breath. 'Okay. I'll admit it, then. You haven't done yourself any favours on that front in the last few years, it's true. But it's nothing that isn't easily rectified. Imogen, you have natural assets in abundance,' she continues. 'And I'm not just talking about those boobs of yours.'

I cross my arms.

'Is it such a bad thing that you're attractive?

'Don't try and bully me, Meredith, it'll never work,' I mutter.

'Hey, I've got an idea!' She grins.

And that's when I know I should be really worried.

Chapter 20

Meredith has clearly seen *Pretty Woman* one too many times, a fact that becomes apparent when she strides along Passeig de Gràcia, a boulevard whose sole *raison d'etre* appears to be sucking up unspeakable amounts of people's salaries. This is haute couture heaven: row upon row of understatedly poncy designer shops, with prices capable of melting your brain.

'I can't afford any of these shops, Meredith,' I say, even if being here underlines how serious an overhaul my wardrobe requires.

'I'm paying,' she insists, pushing open a heavy, glass door to lead me to my fate.

'No, Meredith, you're not,' I begin, but before I can finish my sentence, the shop assistants are all over her like an acne flare-up. She might be wearing Mamas and Papas' finest, and have a penchant for junk food, but the Prada piranhas have a sixth sense that Meredith knows how to spend money when she wants to.

I can't deny the clothes are beautiful: there's everything from Alexander McQueen to Vivienne Westwood, Givenchy to Sonia Rykiel. But I won't be moved: as Meredith whips out her credit card, I snatch it away. 'Meredith, thank you for offering, but let's just go to H&M. Please?'

She frowns, takes back the card and reluctantly slips it back in her purse. 'Have it your way.'

We leave the shop, turning our backs on the three assistants, who look like they may just cry.

Outside, the city's beautiful crowd strut along in Versace dresses and sunglasses that cost more than my car as we head for somewhere more suited to my budget: the Plaça de Catalunya.

There's an eclectic mix of styles here: Grecian-haired beauties in high heels rub shoulders with tattooed counterculture hipsters in baggy pants. All of whom look good, in their own unique way. By which I mean cool, chic, effortless. Harry would look at home here, I know it. I'm starting to think Harry would look at home anywhere.

I look down at my own ensemble – another ubiquitous pastel vest top, khaki shorts and flip-flops – and sigh. 'Where am I going to start?'

Meredith leads us into a shop that's eye-wateringly on trend. Obviously, I *want* to look fashionable – why wouldn't you? – but I've never felt more old-fartish than now, surrounded by shoppers with that elusive Catalan ability to wear *anything* and look cool.

Nicola homes in on a black top that is revealing to a stupefying degree, the sort of thing Rihanna might throw on when in a particularly fruity mood. 'That's nice, don't you think?'

Meredith contemplates it. 'Ooh, yes. But a little safe, maybe.' Nicola, to my astonishment, agrees.

'Hang on a minute,' I protest. '*That's* safe? What sort of evening of debauched Bacchanalia do you think I'm about to have if *that's* safe?'

Nicola laughs, clearly under the mistaken impression that I'm joking as they head for another rack.

Over the next half hour, my two best friends, commandeered largely by Meredith, stride around gathering up armfuls of garments and thrusting them in the direction of the assistants, while I scuttle around in an increasing state of disquiet. I am eventually led to a spacious changing room and confronted by an array of clothing as vast as it is, in all cases, disturbing.

Despite Meredith's vehement reassurances, they're *really* not me. She tries negotiating gently with me on this subject, arguing that I need to try something new and keep an open mind. I make the mistake of arguing back, to which she responds. 'So, what IS really you, Imogen? *This?*' She gestures to my outfit, without apology, and I'm forced to concede the point.

'Just humour her,' Nicola whispers, grinning.

'I don't appear to have much choice.'

She links my arm reassuringly as Meredith strides ahead. 'If it means anything, I think she knows what she's talking about. Fashion-wise, I mean.'

'There's no doubt she always looks amazing, no matter what she wears,' I agree. 'The same does not apply to me.'

Nicola shakes her head. 'Stop doing yourself down, for God's sake. Besides, you don't know anybody here apart from us. Why not do as she suggests and wear something a bit more daring?'

I end up agreeing to buy more of the items than I'd have predicted. And while I take Nicola's comments about being daring to heart, it's the pink camisole Meredith is intent on teaming with skinny jeans that causes the most controversy. The trousers are so tight around the backside you couldn't risk breaking wind in them without doing yourself an injury. And as for the top . . .

'That looks like underwear,' I say. I can't deny it's beautiful, but there's simply no way I'd wear it outside the privacy of my own bedroom.

'It's not underwear, it's a top,' she replies.

'Meredith, I'm not wearing that. Not by itself.'

She frowns. 'Just try it.'

'I'll look like a slut.'

'You say that as if it's a bad thing.' She sees my expression. 'Oh, I'm joking. Come on, give it a go. If it doesn't work, I'll find you something else.'

The top is designed for one thing only: displaying a cleavage. Which is fine for most women. Unfortunately, in my case, *everything* shows off my cleavage – I've got Arran jumpers that manage the job. So when I pull on a top that's deliberately designed to look *sexy*, it has an alarmingly magnifying effect.

I look in the mirror and tell myself that it takes a certain type of woman to pull off this look; a woman I'm not and never will be. And yet, something makes me take it to the till and pay for it, even if the likelihood of me actually wearing it tonight, or indeed ever, is negligible.

Despite the shopping trip leaving me undeniably exhilarated, I return to the hotel full of trepidation about Meredith and the sinister toolbox of beautifying products she can't wait to unleash on me.

I hate the idea of makeovers. The last one I undertook was in 1988 on a Girls' World styling head whose bonce I painted blue, then styled with my dad's Remington nasal hair trimmer. So when the tables are turned on *me*, it's not an experience I enjoy. I am waxed. I am plucked. I am manicured. I am concealed (at least, my black eye is). I am fake-tanned (required, because all today's hour in the sun achieved was to puff up my ankles). My hair is blow dried, then curled, then sprayed with so much Elnett I'm tempted to don a gas mask and commando crawl to the loo under the cover of its toxic clouds to escape. Meredith has a travel version of *everything*: miniature beauty gadgets that, despite the candy colours and glossy images on their boxes, have but one objective: attack, attack, attack.

Just when I think my hair follicles might be about to shrivel up and beg for mercy, Nicola knocks on the door.

'Wow, you look amazing,' she says almost convincingly.

She's been investigating the event Harry was talking about at breakfast and it turns out it's some big VIP night on the sun deck to celebrate the hotel's first birthday.

'That's that, then – we're not VIPs,' I say.

'Of course we are, we're residents,' Meredith tells me.

'Everyone looks extremely glammed up,' Nicola adds, uneasily. 'And there's a rumour that James Franco's going to be there.'

Meredith's eyes light up like the headlights on a 1985 Audi Quattro. 'This gets better and better.'

'But we won't be allowed in!' I argue.

'Oh, Imogen, we just need to look the part,' Meredith says. 'Believe me, I've done this loads of times, it won't be a problem. Especially in that pink top.'

She picks it up and throws it to me.

As it flies through the air, I'm overcome by a quasi-superstitious notion and it's this: if I catch it, I *have* to wear it. I have absolutely no choice in the matter.

The next thing I know, I'm clutching the top.

'Why do you look so worried?' Nicola asks.

'No reason,' I reply, heading to the bathroom to pull it on.

A minute of so later, I take several deep breaths as I check my appearance, turning side on and running my hands down my jeans.

The top isn't *really* slutty. Just a little sassier, more revealing than I'd usually go for.

Who am I kidding? I am completely out of my comfort zone. Which brings me to one conclusion: Meredith could be right, it's probably perfect.

Chapter 21

When we arrive downstairs in the lobby, my stomach is swirling with nervous energy and Harry is at the front of my thoughts.

The whole of Barcelona – at least anyone who's anyone – appears to have turned up here tonight.

'You look *gorgeous*,' Meredith enthuses, taking my hand and tugging me on.

I'm not entirely sure I believe her, but the reassurance is welcome given how uneasy I feel about every single item on my body. There are the jeans, giving me that classic finishing-school walk, a bit like I have osteoarthritis. Then there are the shoes – borrowed from Meredith – so high they virtually qualify as gymnastics apparatus. And that's before we get onto the top. Which is definitely, unquestionably, a mistake.

'I know what you're thinking, but you're wrong,' Nicola says. 'That top might not be what you're used to, but you look really elegant and sexy.'

'I would tell you if you looked tarty,' adds Meredith, with her usual sledgehammer candour. 'And you don't. Just do as Anastasia Steele in *Fifty Shades* would, and unleash your inner goddess.'

I only got forty pages into that book, and wanted to spank her inner goddess myself, for entirely different reasons than the hero.

We approach the glass doors as Meredith releases my hand and flicks back her hair. My heart clenches.

It's the start of the evening, but this already represents the hottest ticket in town. Endless-legged girls in glittering dresses flirt and laugh as expensively dressed men with dark eyes sip martinis like twenty-first-century Gatsbys. Music throbs in the dying heat of the day as fairy lights begin to shimmer on the infinity pool, and the deck fizzes with potential.

Meredith's eyes are glinting with mischief. 'Let's go and have an amazing night,' she announces, placing a firm hand on the glass door to step out.

At least that's the theory. A theory brought to an abrupt halt as an arm falls across her path. It belongs to a bouncer who could have a Saturday job as a double-decker bus.

Meredith responds with a saccharine pout. 'Excuse me,' she says politely, at which point, his arm grows rigid.

'*Recepción privada*,' he announces, granite-faced.

Nicola and I slink into the background.

'No, no, no.' Meredith smiles patiently. 'We are *hotel residents*.' Her tone is a blend of benevolence and threat, implying that if he doesn't drop this matter, she'll personally see to it that his balls appear on the hotel menu served deep-fried with a complementary coulis.

'It is not important that you are residents,' says a female voice behind us. 'Zis is a private party.'

Clipboard Barbie hasn't lost her clipboard, but that's the only hint that she's still on duty, judging by the fact that she appears to have been dressed by whomever looks after Beyoncé. Her hair cascades over her shoulders in silken waves and her bronzed legs spill out of hot pants so small and tight they almost qualify as a sex toy.

She smiles smoulderingly at the bouncer and says something in rapid-fire Spanish before turning and beckoning over the same group that Harry was with yesterday.

The girl with the wonky red lipstick is first, followed by the other two. Then, trailing behind them, with them but not, is Harry.

My heart reacts instantly to the sight of him, swishing between fear and excitement as he approaches. He's on his phone, distracted, but pauses when he sees me. His mouth turns up into a smile that reminds me that I should be far too sensible to be attracted to this clear breaker of hearts. 'One minute, Ken,' he mutters into his handset. Then he asks me, 'Are you coming here tonight?'

The question leaves me flustered. 'Not sure yet,' I reply, just as he is swept away in a flurry of hot pants and dark glossy hair, onto the sun deck, where he disappears from view.

Meredith puts her hands on her hips. 'That's settled it. We've *got* to go in.'

The bouncer has other ideas. He starts telling Meredith something in Spanish as she gazes at him blankly, pretending not to notice it doesn't sound at all like, 'Come on in and make yourself at home.' When she doesn't move, he begins gesturing for her to move back, in a manner that's one step short of physically throwing her onto the street.

'Wait,' Meredith says, wrestling him away. 'Let me speak.' She grabs him by the arm and walks him to a corner, before quickly scanning our surroundings. 'Would you accept . . . this?' she says, removing a note from her back pocket and handing it over seductively.

He looks at it and starts shooing her away again.

'WAIT!' she says again. He frowns. 'How about . . . *this?*' she murmurs, lowering the zip on her top.

'Get out, crazy English,' he says, and this time Meredith is forced to accept that her charms are lost.

'That's never failed before,' she huffs, as we move off.

'You *are* more than seven months pregnant,' Nicola points out.

'So?' Meredith shrugs. 'I can't believe he didn't accept the money either,' she says, pulling out the note.

Nicola and I narrow our eyes.

'You do realise you've just tried to bribe the bouncer with a prescription for thrush cream?' Nic points out.

'Oh,' Meredith replies flatly. 'I was wondering where that went.'

Chapter 22

'Meredith, this is a bad idea. A terrible idea. You have never had a worse idea in your entire life.' And this is a woman who once tried to perm her own eyelashes.

I glance at Nicola, who appears even more uncertain than I am. Meredith is poised by the kitchen door, waiting to pounce. She fixes her cleavage and checks her strappy platforms are secure, before scanning the immediate area with *Bravo Two Zero* eyes.

A waitress carrying a mountain of expensive crockery marches past and studies us suspiciously, before a glass threatens to topple from its zenith and she is forced to push open the swing door into the kitchen.

Meredith takes the opportunity to pop up her head and peer through the door's porthole.

'Ready,' she hisses, holding up her arm. The arm flies down: 'GO, GO, GO!'

'Yes, all right, Private Benjami—' But before Nicola can

finish her sentence, Meredith has her by the elbow, I'm stumbling behind and we're all in the kitchen, squatting behind an oversized steel work surface.

All is relatively quiet on this side of the kitchen, in sharp contrast to events two workstations away, where three chefs are having a colourful disagreement over a batch of tempura. It is volcanically hot in here and beads of sweat prickle my skin as I nudge Meredith.

'You're not meant to be overheating,' I whisper.

She purses her lips. 'There'll be plenty of opportunities to rehydrate once we're in that bar. All we need now is for that chef on the right to disappear for a minute and ...' She gasps. 'NOW!'

Before Nicola and I even get a chance to exchange an eye roll, Meredith is crawling on her hands and knees across the kitchen, displaying about as much stealth as you might expect from a woman in the third trimester of pregnancy.

'She's a bloody lunatic,' Nicola murmurs.

'Yes, but she's *our* bloody lunatic,' I reply, and we head off after her.

The distance between the work surface and door to the sun deck feels like a mile, and traversing every inch of it in this position has the equivalent effect on my kneecaps as a claw hammer. But, incredibly, we reach the door, sticky with sweat but undetected, bursting onto the far corner of the sun deck in a heap onto its boards.

It isn't the grandest of entrances, but at least we're in.

'What happened to your shoe?' Nicola asks.

I glance down and note that I appear to only be wearing one of them. 'Oh, bugger. I'm not sure.'

Meredith looks at me incredulously. 'Do you know how long it took me to find a pair of snakeskin sandals with that exact heel?'

'I'm sorry! I'll find it,' I reply, although as I push open the door again, the kitchen is now buzzing. 'Oh God . . .'

'Do it later. We have another priority now – mingling.' She grabs me by the arm and I follow, with a pronounced limp.

As the sun sets over the sea, the sky is a breathtaking swirl of oranges and reds, yet there's nothing peaceful about the sun deck. The crowd has expanded since we tried to get in legitimately, and a DJ rises above it on a massive podium at one end of the infinity pool as music thuds across the evening air.

Being among such a glamorous crowd is not an entirely positive experience. Having minutes ago convinced myself I looked tarty enough to make a living grinding my hips against a pole, I now feel like I'm on my way to man the cake stand at a summer fête. I lower my neckline slightly.

Nicola offers to buy the first round, but returns from the bar three minutes later. 'These are free,' she whispers with wide eyes, as she hands them to us.

'What?'

'It's a complimentary bar. For VIPs like ourselves, of course.'
She winks.

I take a sip and allow myself to be dazzled by my surroundings. For the first time since I left UK soil, I'm starting to
believe that I'm *finally* getting the holiday I'd hoped for.

My phone beeps. It's a text from David:

FOR THE LOVE OF PETER, PAUL AND MARY. WHEN
are you going to tell me you vE got rid of this story?! God
DAM Daily Sun ☹"@" (and yes I am drunk**)

My stomach plummets as I begin composing a reply:

David, new PR firm is fully briefed and on the case. Will let
you know when I know more. Hope you are okay. Imogen

The tone, I hope, is polite but confident, despite the fact that
I'm feeling neither.

When Cosimo and I last spoke, he'd only managed to leave
a message with the *Daily Sun* journalist, who had apparently
been pulled off the story – temporarily – to work on an exposé
involving a senior politician and a 72-year-old masseuse from
Burnley.

'Maybe they'll just go off the story,' Cosimo said, dragging
my confidence in his ability even closer to the gutter.

'You're not on that thing again, are you?' Nicola asks.

I shove the phone in my bag. 'It's going away now,' I promise.

'Seriously?'

'Seriously. In fact' – I take a slug of my cocktail and feel a heady rush of impulsiveness as I hand my phone over to her – 'you look after it.'

'Are you sure?'

I nod. 'I'm ... sure. Listen out for it, though, won't you? I don't like being totally inaccessible when I'm this far from Florence.'

'Done,' she says, as her gaze drifts upwards. 'Oh God ...'

I follow her look across the deck and to some dancers on a podium. When we walked in (okay, *fell* in), there were four lithe women on it, wearing sequin handkerchiefs and strappy heels, swirling their hips around as if in complete control of invisible hula hoops. Now, however, they have been joined by Meredith.

The one thing you can say about her J-Lo-style choreography is that she moves with surprisingly agility given that she has a girth like Henry VIII's right now. A small crowd gathers, joining in tentatively, as if trying to work out whether the krumping pregnant lady represents some hip new trend in upscale entertainment.

Nicola and I stand shiftily at the back of the crowd as a smattering of others start to clap, and one or two even begin to cheer. When Nicola begins wiggling her hips, I know the only thing left to do is for me to join in.

I've barely managed to shuffle into place when things take an unseemly turn for the worse.

Nicola spots the bouncer first, pushing his way through the crowd until he's standing before Meredith, eyeing her like it's a bomb rather than a baby under her swing top.

She's oblivious to him as he's almost at her feet, but then she does a double take that nearly makes her head fall off. Before she can argue, she's led down the steps onto terra firma.

As the bouncer ignores her loud protestations and leads her towards us, I feel as though my heart is about to burst out of my chest. I have never been one of life's rebels – the closest I ever got to teenage insurgence involved a two-minute experiment behind the school bike sheds with a nicotine patch.

The bouncer is in the process of bundling us all through the glass doors – not something you can be a part of while retaining any dignity – when a voice rings out.

'Wait!'

We all stop and look round. It's Harry. He's wearing his glasses. Clipboard Barbie is behind him.

'They're with us,' he announces.

Clipboard Barbie glares at him indignantly. He turns to her and, as they lock eyes, he has this remarkable look that's part sheepish, part sexy – and 100 per cent effective.

'Would you mind?' He shrugs. 'They're good friends of mine. I'd really appreciate it.'

She unclenches her teeth and visibly melts before turning

to the bouncer and firing a few words of Spanish at him, at which point Meredith, Nicola and I are released from his grip.

'You're a gem. Much appreciated,' Harry says with a smile as she totters away, glancing back once.

My friends are beside themselves, gushing thanks like a pair of defective taps until he actually looks uncomfortable. 'Seriously, don't worry about it. I couldn't watch a group of fellow Brits be thrown out of somewhere with a free bar.'

We follow him back to the party as my friends both link arms with me.

Meredith leans in to whisper in my ear: 'He. Is. *Gorgeous.*'

I open my mouth to respond, and suddenly find her very difficult to argue with.

Chapter 23

You know those moments in *Scooby Doo* where Shaggy and the other meddling kids are all together, then he turns around to discover they've disappeared? That's exactly what happens to me, only I know they haven't fallen through a trap door, and hopefully I look slightly better than Shaggy, even with one shoe. Although, believe me, trying to balance on one foot at the exact height of the other to mask this problem is not easy.

Harry either doesn't notice, is polite enough not to point it out, or is distracted by my cleavage, which wouldn't be hard in this top.

Whatever the case, my friends have disappeared with negligible subtlety. They didn't even make excuses, simply grinned and proclaimed 'We're leaving you two to it.' Which raises one question: to *what* exactly are they leaving us? The thought makes me horribly nervous. Obviously, there's only one solution to that.

'Finished that already? Let me get you another,' says Harry as I drain my cocktail. He reaches to a passing waiter to take another from his tray. It's only then that I realise that I haven't eaten a proper meal since breakfast, not unless you count a handful of posh spiced nuts and the chocolate the maid left on my pillow last night.

'Who do you work for, Imogen? Each time I look in your direction you're on your phone. I was starting to wonder if it was surgically attached.' Every so often when he says something – just small talk like this – it sounds flirtatious. But it strikes me that it's possible this might not be deliberate.

'I work for a big-food production company, Peebles. I'm their UK marketing director. Well, *acting* UK marketing director.'

'Sounds important. Do you enjoy it?'

'Most of the time I absolutely love it, although it can be full on. I'm not one of those superwoman working mothers who can keep a dozen plates spinning at once.'

'I'm sure you're being hard on yourself. I'll bet your plates are perfectly intact.'

'Believe me, my plates are cracking up. A bit like me.'

He laughs a big, natural laugh, the sound of which warms my belly. I feel suddenly and dramatically good about myself. I want to make him do it again.

'What do *you* do for a living?'

'I'm a journalist,' he replies.

'Oh ...' So that *was* him on the search engine. Harry Pfeiffer – journalist.

'Do you still live in Liverpool?' he asks.

'You recognised the accent then?'

'Of course.'

'No, I've lived in London for years.'

'Oh, whereabouts? I'm in Putney.'

I feel a smile creeping to my lips, happier about this than I should be. 'Not far from me. I'm in Wandsworth.'

'Nice.' His smile prompts a flush of heat to creep around my neck.

'You wouldn't say that if you saw my flat.' I wonder tipsily what it would be like to be friends with him, to replay this conversation in years to come. ('You were such a flirt!' 'You were the one who invited me to your flat!' 'It was not an invitation!' 'Yeah, right!')

'Well, I would've loved to see your flat, but London and I are parting ways very soon.'

My fantasy disintegrates. 'Really?'

'I'm moving home to Aberdeen to be with my mum. In fact, I'm flying directly there after this trip.'

'Oh ... how come?' I hope the dismay isn't showing on my face as much as it's revealed by my voice.

'It's a bit complicated.' He sighs a little. 'I left home when I was twenty-two and made a promise to her that I'd be back in ten years. She brought up me and my sister single-handedly after my dad left, so I always told myself I'd stick to it. Of course, when I was twenty-two I felt like that day would never come. Only now it's here.'

'Wow. And she's holding you to your word?'

'Well, she used to remind me every time I saw her. Now I've actually handed in my notice on the flat and am due to move there in less than a week, she's gone quiet. Basically, she feels guilty. But I don't want her to. Aberdeen's great – and I owe this to her. Besides, she needs me right now, put it that way,' he says.

'What about your sister?'

'She lives in Australia. They come back to visit once a year, but that's it.'

I take this in. 'It's incredibly … noble of you.'

'Not really,' he replies with a laugh. '"Noble" isn't a word I've ever thought about applying to myself, to be honest.'

As the night progresses, there are moments when I'm so nervous that I actually want this to be over. I think constantly about making an excuse and heading back to my room to get my breath back, to go back to the world to which I'm used. But then he laughs at something I say, or asks questions about my job – detailed, genuinely interested questions – and everything changes. I start to feel amazing around this man: witty, warm, interesting and – at those moments when he allows his smile to linger just a little too long – attractive.

There are few quiet corners of the party, but we manage to

find one – an enclave of soft sofas and twinkling candlelight overlooking the sea. And we talk. *Really* talk. About the Barcelona sights I'm still determined to see; about Florence; about his reading material (it's the second time he's read *The Book Thief*); about where else he's been in the world that he loves. I even get some things off my chest about the PR hell I've been dumped in – and discover that he's a fantastic listener.

I'm enjoying the whole thing so much that, when I receive several (increasingly hysterical) texts from David, I resist replying all but once, when I write:

D – relax! I'm not AT ALL worried xxx

Which is true. God, I love Piña Coladas.

And, suddenly, I love Harry Pfeiffer's mouth. I can't keep my eyes off it, its delicious curves that, when he smiles, make my insides swirl with pleasure.

'You *don't* believe in thunderbolts?' he asks. I don't even know how the conversation meandered here, except that it started with the 1990s, then moved on to Hugh Grant, then *Four Weddings and a Funeral*, then … well, here we are.

'Of course not.' I'm very drunk by now. Very, very drunk. My lips are moving but I have virtually no control over them.

'Haven't you read *Sense and Sensibility*? Or *Catch-22*? Or *Cinderella*?' Harry's enthusiasm lights up his eyes.

'You're telling me to base life decisions on fairy stories now?'

'I can't believe you're knocking *Cinderella*.'

'Actually, I've modelled myself on her for some time now. Right down to losing my shoe.' I untuck my bare foot – which I've been hiding – and hold it out to him.

'Oh, dear.' He bursts out laughing. 'Where on earth have you left that?'

'Don't ask. I'm not even thinking about it until the morning. When, no doubt, Meredith will attempt to kill me.'

He raises his brow.

'They're not mine,' I explain.

Then he looks into my eyes, suddenly serious. And, as the light from the moon casts shadows on his beautiful features, I wonder what on earth he's going to ask me.

'Can you still dance with only one shoe?'

I swallow. 'I can't dance with one shoe, two shoes or no shoes.'

'Oh, come on! Stop with the false modesty!' He grins.

'It's true! I don't dance. Honestly, I don't. I have absolutely zero coordination.'

I'm about to protest again when I look up and see something that brings me down to earth with an unpleasant bump: Clipboard Barbie is sashaying towards us. *And she has no clipboard.* In fact, she has a glint in her eye that very clearly means business.

''Arry, I wondered if—'

'Okay,' I splutter, standing up and kicking off my singular shoe. They both look at me. 'Let's dance.'

Harry smiles. 'Was it urgent?' he asks Clipboard Barbie.

'Well ...' She pouts, but is forced to shake her head.

So Harry takes me by the hand and leads me to the dance floor next to the infinity pool.

My heart is racing as the heat from his touch creeps up my arm. I look at the men and women around me. They all look so unbelievably agile, sexy, stylish. I hesitate, unable to move. Because, I just don't *do* dancing like this ... I don't know how.

Harry starts moving his hips effortlessly as I stand, immobile, like an overgrown toddler playing a game of Musical Statues. He senses my unease and does something that makes my breath hover in my throat, unable to escape: he reaches out for my hand, clasping my fingers as he pulls me towards him.

My head moves into his chest and I breathe in the salty, clean scent of his skin as we sway silently, ignoring the tempo of the music. It doesn't matter that the air is throbbing with staccato beats; we are dancing the slowest of slow dances, our bodies touching in places that make me feel indecent if I think about them.

But I'm not thinking. Not really. I'm completely swept up in the moment. All I can concentrate on is the feel of his chest against me, his hands on the small of my back. My skin tingles with longing. And, suddenly, I am overcome by an urge to do something I haven't done for a very long time.

I lift my head slightly, pulling back at an angle that invites him to look at me. He obliges. Our eyes lock and my lips part inexplicably. I am trembling as I urge him to move closer. I want to feel his lips on mine. His pupils dilate.

'Imogen!'

I leap away from him like I've been caught reading someone's diary.

Nicola is out of breath, holding out my phone. The first thing that flashes into my mind makes me feel sick with fear.

'Florence?'

'No,' she hisses, covering the handset. 'I didn't know what to do. It's the *Daily Sun*. They want to speak to you. Now.'

Chapter 24

The journalist's voice sounds unexpectedly affable. Not that that makes him any less likely to stitch me up. I stand listening to him repeat himself, trying to focus as I sway like a grass skirt in a force nine hurricane.

'Hello? Hi – are you there?'

Nausea rises into my throat. 'Yesh,' I croak. 'Yesh, I am. But I can't hear you over the music.'

'Can you go somewhere quiet? This is quite important.'

I mouth something probably completely unintelligible to Nicola and Harry and stumble off towards the doors, into the lobby, where it's slightly less ear-splitting. I lean on the wall and focus on the floor with a vivid sense of déjà vu from when I was last in a fairground crazy house.

'This is Jeremy Morgan,' he announces. 'I'm a freelance journalist working on a story for the *Daily Sun* about Peebles. Is this Imogen Copeland?'

I gaze woozily at myself in the mirror behind the bar. 'Yes. No. I mean . . . I'm not available.'

He pauses. 'Er ... right. Well, I think we're going to have to run with our story, anyway. We've gone to great lengths to get a quote, and haven't even had our calls returned from Ace Communications. We'll just have to go with what we've got and say a spokesman was unavailable.'

'NOOOO!' I shriek, causing the bartender, who's spent the last few minutes demonstrating perfect Tom Cruise-style cocktail acrobatics, to drop his shaker. 'It's ... hang on – I'll get her for you.'

I thrust my phone inside my bag and rustle it around among the tissues and make-up, before shoving it against my ear and taking a deep breath.

'Imogen speaking,' I say, two octaves higher.

'Ah – at last.'

'I believe this is a pressh call,' I continue, as professionally as possible, 'and for that you need to be speaking to our new PR agency, Peterhouse Deevy. They have something for you. A really good ... scoop. In fact, someone left a message for you, I understand.'

'From Peterhouse Deevy? I did have something from them, but not about this. It was some dippy bloke called Cosmic or something. He said he was phoning about pan scourers.'

I suddenly feel more desperate and drunk than ever before.

'To be honest, the story is nearly there,' he continues. 'All we need is a quote from you, then I'm sending it to the news desk.'

'You know who it was, then?' I croak.

He hesitates. 'I … might. Do you?'

'I … might.'

'Really?'

'No. I meant no.'

'Hmm.'

I have a moment of brilliance. 'You show me yours and I'll tell you … I mean, you tell me mine and I'll … eurgh. Who do you think it is, exactly?'

I hear a few clicks, as if he's tapping something into a computer keyboard. 'J. Meyer,' he announces.

Our gay operations director? 'No,' I reply, bewildered.

'Okay … G. Basterfield,' he tries, as I hear several more taps on the keyboard.

I narrow my eyes. 'Wrong.'

'I. Copeland.'

'That's me!' I protest, as it dawns on me foggily that he's simply scrolling through the names on our company website. 'And it's not, just for the record,' I add, huffily.

'Look, let me level with you,' he continues. 'It's a game, this. You help me and I'll help you. Give me the name of whoever it is and I'll make sure Peebles's statement is right up there at the top of the story. You'll come out smelling of roses.'

I'm drunk, but I'm not drunk enough to believe this. 'I need to get my PR firm on the case.'

'You don't mean Cosmic?'

'It's Cosmo. Cosimodo. Cos—oh, look, he'll phone you back.'

'I already tried phoning him as he'd been in touch about a Peebles story – although not this one. I'd thought he might be a way forward, only I got a message saying he's on holiday until a week on Tuesday.'

'*What?*'

'Seriously. Try him yourself.'

Panic floods through me. 'Okay. Please just bear with me. Please. I'll do anything to make sure Peebles gets through this. It's such a cock-up, the whole thing. Frankly, I feel like crying.'

'I take it this conversation is on the record?'

'NO! No! Look, just say this instead . . .'

He hesitates, clearly poised with his pen. 'Yes?'

I open my mouth, ready to give him his quote. Then something happens as if I'm having an out-of-body experience: someone ends the call.

It appears to be me.

I collapse on the floor in a heap, wondering how I'm going to get out of this one.

I spend twenty inebriated minutes phoning Cosimo's mobile number, only to get the same message the journalist did: he's on holiday.

Emotion has just begun to overcome me when my phone rings again. It's David. He's devastatingly pissed and, for that reason, strangely easy to communicate with, compared to everyone else.

'Tell me you have good newzz!'

'Errr ...'

'Before you answer, I have this friend at my golf club, Charles Blackman. He runs a PR agency. I know you said you're confident in the people you've got but—'

'Get him on board!'

'Who? Eh?'

'Your pal. Get him on the case. That'd be great! Just fantastic,' I gabble.

'Right. Okay ... good ... AMAZEBALLS! Glad you've said that, I'll get him to give you a ring as soon as I've put the phone down. Oh, Imogen, it'sh terrible. I can't *shleep*. I've got through half a bottle of cooking sherry tonight.'

'Why cooking sherry?'

'I'm meant to be on the Atkinssh Diet and I don't want to give the game away to Carmel. Still ... I alwaysh have been good at holding my drink.'

Charles Blackman is having a peculiar affect on my head. The more noise he makes, the blurrier, spinier and more generally confusing everything gets.

'Details! I need details. Fill me in on *everything* you know.'

So I do. Everything. And by the end of our thirty-minute phone call, I'm feeling almost sober. He sounds like he knows what he's doing and, for the first time since this whole debacle began, I feel a small sense of relief as I end the call.

I lean on the wall while I compose myself and my thoughts

turn immediately to Harry. Will he still be at the party? Will he be waiting for me? I think about how close I came to kissing him, and the thought is like a cattle prod in my behind.

I straighten my back, fluff up my hair, breathe deeply and attempt to pout as I head towards the doors, consumed by the thought of how his skin felt next to mine. I have my hand against the door when Meredith and Nicola appear.

'You're not heading to bed, are you?' I ask, glancing over Meredith's shoulder to search out Harry.

'Oh ... I'm bushed!' replies Meredith, grabbing me by the shoulder and spinning me round. 'And there's absolutely zero sign of James Franco. Lots of footballers and that film star that arrived when we did, and various models, but no James.'

'Can't we just stay for one more drink?' I suggest. 'I was hoping to speak to—'

'Harry's gone to bed.' Nicola interrupts me, but there's something about the way she looks at me as she says this that makes me uneasy.

'Let me check.' I push past her.

I only have to go through the door to see him. With Clipboard Barbie. In the corner. The quiet corner. *Our* corner. I can only see his legs: the rest of him is shielded by her as she crosses her ankle seductively over his.

They couldn't be any closer. And I couldn't feel more like vomiting.

Chapter 25

Meredith doesn't snore all night. Nor break wind. Yet do I enjoy a peaceful night's sleep? I do not. And all because of a little-discussed pregnancy side-effect, caused by the Molotov cocktail of hormones swimming around her body.

'The bigger my bump gets, the hornier I am,' she once confessed to me airily, adding that she couldn't get enough of Nathan even on the days when she'd happily stab him with a dessert fork.

That was about five months ago. The bump is now BIG and, judging by her sleeptalking, she wasn't wrong about the correlation.

'There . . . YES! . . . Oooh!' she groans exuberantly.

I shove a pillow over my head and close my eyes, attempting to force more palatable thoughts into my mind. They instantly drift to Harry and the delicious and impossible feelings he stirred in me tonight.

I'm partly glad he went off with Clipboard Barbie, for a

multitude of reasons. I remove my pillow from my face in an attempt to draw breath and immediately regret it.

'Where's the paddle, Christian? Ooooowww ... *YES!*'

I don't remember feeling that frisky when I was pregnant. Although I wouldn't have done under the circumstances ... Not when Roberto was there one minute and gone the next. Not when the pregnancy itself set off a chain of events that ultimately meant I wouldn't get to spend the rest of my life with him, as I'd always assumed I would.

Conceiving Florence hadn't been planned, obviously. It was a surprise in every sense of the word and, right up until the moment I saw the results of the test, I'd hardly given the possibility a second thought.

Aware that I may have been a few days late, I'd idly thrown a Clearblue pack into my trolley at Tesco earlier in the week, before it sat in my bedside drawer for three days. I'd stumbled across it on Saturday morning after I'd returned from the gym and Roberto was out buying ingredients for dinner.

I opened the packet and took the test feeling certain it wouldn't be positive, because although my period seemed late, my cycle has never run like clockwork. My complacency was such that I'd cleaned the windows, paid a gas bill and was dancing around the kitchen to Scissor Sisters when I remembered it. I high-kicked my way into the bathroom, pirouetted to the loo and there it was.

I screamed. A proper, throat-splitting squawk, capable of breaking the shaving mirror.

I pulled myself together and ventured to the chemist to buy four more tests, before downing two litres of water and taking them all, one after the other.

I don't know how long I stood in the bathroom, staring at them as they lay in a fan on the loo cistern.

'Hello!' The door slammed and I scooped them up in a panic. 'Imogen?'

I didn't answer, so Roberto tried to open the bathroom door and, finding it locked, gave three sharp knocks. 'Is everything all right, *amore mio*?'

'Yeesss!' I croaked.

He didn't buy it. 'What's the matter?' I didn't answer. 'Imogen, seriously, you're worrying me.'

Tentatively, I opened the door.

He told me afterwards that my skin had been candlewax white, colourless from shock, as I produced five pregnancy tests from behind my back like I was doing a card trick.

He walked in silently and perched on the edge of the bath while I flung them into the bin and washed my hands.

'Imogen . . . does this mean . . .?'

I turned off the tap and dried my hands, barely able to bring myself to turn around. When I did, I simply nodded as tears pushed their way into my eyes.

Roberto's views on this issue had been crystal clear, views

I'd said I agreed with. Technically, we were both responsible; we instantly knew that. Just as we knew when it had happened: a few weeks earlier, when my Pill had run out and I was waiting for a repeat prescription. In the heat of the moment we'd ignored the risks and resorted to a contraception method as old as sex itself: you know, the one that involves jumping off the train before it's reached its final destination. The one all the magazines tell you doesn't really work, a fact that's sometimes too inconvenient to believe.

Well, it turned out *Cosmo* was right. Roberto's sperm had reached its destination, alighted, and had made itself at home in the waiting room drinking a nice cappuccino, unbeknownst to both of us.

While we were both technically at fault, I blamed myself. I'd been the one who'd grabbed his backside and pushed him inside me, overcome with desire. There was really only one thing to say. 'I'm so sorry.'

His eyes fluttered closed as he pulled me into his arms and squeezed me tight.

At that moment, I felt things would never be the same between us again. And I was right.

Day Four

Chapter 26

Harry is in my bed. The heat of his hands penetrates my bare skin as he kisses and caresses me, lavishing attention on every inch of my pulsating body.

That I'm vaguely aware this is a dream does nothing to slow my racing heart. It's the closest I've had to sex, either in slumber or in reality, for so long my endorphins can't know what's hit them. His kisses tingle on the skin behind my ear, before I pull him in front of me and look into his eyes. Lust shimmers in his pupils.

'You're beautiful, Imogen,' he whispers, smoothing hair away from my face. 'I want you like I've never wanted anyone before.'

'Me?' I laugh coquettishly.

'Yes, you.' He kisses me again.

'But why me? You don't only want me for my body, do you?' I purr, gazing down at myself. It's a magnificent sight. I have the slenderest of thighs and flattest of stomachs, both so firm they wouldn't wobble at the seismic peak of an earthquake. Even more impressive are my breasts: so small, pert and delightfully manageable I could get a job modelling training bras. Oh God, I love them! And so, apparently, does he.

'I want your body, I want your brain, I want every little bit of you,' he murmurs, and begins devouring every inch of my skin as I writhe in the 400-thread-count sheets, noting how I suddenly appear to have been upgraded to a room with a plunge pool.

I gaze at the ceiling as he peels off my knickers, smiles seductively, and parts my legs. I gasp as he disappears between my thighs, carnal waves rising inside me. Then he says something. It's kind of muffled, so I prop myself up on my elbows. 'Sorry to interrupt, when you're ... you know' – I nod in his direction – 'but did you say something?'

He pauses and looks up. 'I'm a journalist,' he repeats, before plunging down to re-acquaint himself with my leisure areas.

I flop down and try to get back in the zone. But this isn't a mere passion killer, it's a mass murderer. I push up on my elbows again and cough politely. 'Ahem ... one other thing, if you don't mind?' He pops up his head and grins. 'When you say you're a journalist, could you clarify who it is you work for?'

'The *Daily Sun*, of course. This is my little thank-you for helping me with my enquiries. This story is going to make my career.'

My jaw drops. 'You don't mean ... you're not working on

the story about Peebles? Is this why you were asking so many questions last night—'

My voice trails off as dark thoughts assault my brain and I see that the smile I once thought devastatingly gorgeous has developed a sinister, demented quality, his eyes seeming to boggle like those old film posters advertising *The Shining*.

He is poised to dive down again, but I have other ideas.

I lift up my leg and welly him hard on the chin, then watch with cartoon eyes as he soars across the room, crashes through the window and plunges twelve floors down until he explodes into the sea.

Then I wake up. Or rather, I spring up panting like I've been left in a car on a hot day with the windows closed. My brain is throbbing as I glance around the room. I haven't been upgraded, there is no plunge pool and the window is mercifully intact.

But the question remains of why I dreamt that Harry is a *Daily Sun* journalist. I replay the events of last night and recall in hazy detail our conversation veering not just once, but several times, to my job, to David, to my PR crisis. I have a hideous feeling that I basically told him everything . . . and he was only too happy to listen intently.

I look over at Meredith, who is sleeping silently for the first time in about eight hours, just as my phone rings. I answer it immediately, mercifully without incident.

'Imogen Copeland,' I manage.

'Charles Blackman here.'

I have never met an army colonel, but decide that Charles Blackman sounds exactly as I'd expect one to be: brusque, efficient, domineering and slightly intimidating. All of which make me feel as though we're in significantly better hands than with Cosimo, who was about as domineering as Peppa Pig.

However, my newfound happiness turns out to be short-lived.

'Do you have any news?' I leap out of bed and tug on a dressing gown as I head into the bathroom. The contrast between my businesslike manner and my hair, which looks like something you'd feed to a Shetland pony, is acute.

'I've spoken to the *Daily Sun*,' he announces. 'It's all under control. I've drafted a response from a company spokesperson, which I'll be emailing now.'

I swallow. 'They're running the story then, for definite?'

'No getting out of that, I'm afraid. What is unclear is whether they'll be naming David.'

'Does the journalist know it's him?'

'I think so, but he hasn't got enough hard proof to get their lawyers off his back. They're trying their level best to get that proof and, from what I can tell, the paper is throwing serious resources at this story. Don't be surprised if they phone you again to try and get it out of you. Or, indeed, if you're approached by a stringer out there.'

'A stringer?'

'A freelance journalist.'

'You mean *in person*? They'd try to track me down out *here*?'

'You're the one contact they've managed to speak to from inside the company. They'd much rather deal with you direct than a PR like me.' His voice hardens. 'Why? Have you had any approaches from a journalist while you've been there?'

'Yes. No. I mean, I don't think so. Not about this, anyway.'

'Let's hope it stays that way. They're tricky buggers, sometimes.'

Nausea swells in my stomach. 'Are they?'

'We'll just have to keep our fingers crossed, keep our heads down, and manage the situation.'

'I think David was rather hoping the story wouldn't appear at all.'

'Not an option, at this stage. This is now about damage limitation. Which is why I'm trying to get hold of the ... ahem, lady in question. If she talks, we've had it.'

'I understand,' I reply, although I'm not sure David will. 'Well, hopefully the story will appear tomorrow, we'll take the temporary pain and embarrassment, then all move on with our lives the day after,' I say optimistically.

'Hmm, it won't be quite that simple. I've had a call from *News Morning*.'

My heart sinks to my stomach. *News Morning* is Britain's hardest-hitting radio programme. 'Please tell me it was about our new flavour of Teeny Pops.'

'They're on to the story too, and they want a spokesperson to appear on the show.'

'I take it you said no?'

'Of course not. The story's out there – it would be disastrous to look like we're hiding under a stone now.'

'But I'd *like* to hide under a stone,' I whimper.

'Not an option.'

'Oh, poor David ... I mean, he's in such a state already, going on the radio would be a nightmare for him.'

Charles snorts. 'We can't possibly put David on the radio. At the moment, there's still a chance nobody will find out he's at the heart of the story. Putting him on *News Morning* would be like throwing him to the lions.'

I flop down onto the bed. 'Who are you putting on then?'

He chortles.

'Why are you making that noise?' I ask.

'Sorry. Did you really want me to answer that question?'

'Yes,' I manage.

'It'll have to be you, of course.'

Chapter 27

Today we are visiting the magnificent, world-renowned Park Güell. Or rather, we're supposed to be visiting the magnificent, world-renowned Park Güell. But having been instructed by Charles to stay near a landline because *News Morning* wants to talk to me in advance of the programme tomorrow, I'm again stuck here at the hotel while the others go off and enjoy themselves.

'Imogen, this is so unlike you,' Nicola says, as we head out of the restaurant after breakfast. 'You've read that guidebook from start to finish. I thought you'd be the first to want to explore the city.'

'Believe me, this is not how I imagined this holiday,' I mumble, grabbing an extra pastry for later when my sugar cravings take hold, as they always do when I'm stressed. 'I haven't had a week at work this horrendous since I started . . . and I'm not even there.'

Nicola frowns and tries to change the subject. 'Any news

about your necklace?' She realises her error as soon as the words are out of her mouth.

'There's been a stony silence about that. Oh, this is so depressing!' I wail, taking a massive bite out of the pastry.

'On the plus side, you can relax about my shoe,' Meredith tells me, reaching into her beach bag and pulling out a snakeskin heel. 'I grabbed one of the waiters earlier and he was more than happy to go looking for me.'

As I look up guiltily to thank Meredith – I had completely forgotten about her shoe – I see Harry on the phone at the far end of the lobby. When he spots me, he stops talking, and I experience a rush that's very different from last night.

This isn't desire. This is danger. He might as well be covered in flashing red lights.

'What's the matter?' Nicola asks.

Harry narrows his eyes, ends his call and starts walking towards us as panic ripples through me. I need to get out of here. But it turns out that moving with any speed when you've stuffed three-quarters of a pastry into your cheeks isn't a good idea. Rather than darting off like a gazelle, I am brought to a devastating halt by a choking fit that forces me to bend forwards, then back, then forwards again. With bulging eyes, the blood vessels in my cheeks pulsating, I try to dislodge the offending blobs of pastry from my windpipe. I succeed only in catapulting crumbs across an unfeasibly wide radius.

It's only as I'm a florid shade of magenta that something hits me, literally – the thump on my back is delivered with the force of a battering ram attempting to break through the door of a fortified citadel. 'Don't worry! I can do the Heinrich manoeuvre!' shrieks Meredith and, although I note hazily that she hasn't got the term quite right, certainly delivers it like a psychopathic Nazi. It's only as she has her arms tightly around my ribcage, bump pressed into my back that by some miracle of godly intervention I manage to stop choking.

'Works every time!' she says with a grin, as I woozily check for dislodged pieces of cartilage in my spine.

'Are you okay?' Nicola asks me, as Harry stops in front of us.

'I was about to ask the same.' He sounds concerned, but I refuse to be taken in while so much is unclear. 'Why don't you come and take a seat?'

'I'm fine,' I reply, still feeling an urgent need to get away from him. I turn to the girls. 'I need to speak to you both. Bye!'

I fling a wonky smile at Harry before grabbing my friends by their elbows and striding to the lift. I push the call button, cross my arms and wait for it to arrive with spontaneously tapping fingertips.

Nicola leans over. 'What are we doing?' she whispers.

'Just get in the lift with me,' I reply through clenched teeth.

'But we're going to Park Güell, aren't we?' Meredith asks.

Unable to suppress an urge to see if Harry has gone, I glance behind me. He is still there, immobile and looking a bit perplexed. He starts walking towards us as I slam my hand on the button again.

When the lift arrives, with Harry still approaching, we fall into it and I press the button for our floor. It refuses to spring into life, so I repeat the exercise. Then again and again, augmenting speed and force until I'm mildly berserk, sweat beading on my brow.

'You need your key card to make the lift work!' Meredith urges, equally frantic but clearly not knowing entirely why.

'Oh, bloody hell!' I rifle around in my bag, pulling out lip balms, nail files, a shower cap I appropriated from our bathroom on the first day and a whole raft of up-market miniature toiletries I brought with me from the plane.

'HERE!' Meredith leaps in, producing her card.

The door closes just as Harry is steps away and I hit a button – any button, as long as it gets me out of here.

I sigh with relief and flop back on the wall of the lift.

'What the *hell* is going on?' asks Nicola as the lift starts its ascent.

'Harry is a *journalist*,' I tell them both.

They look at each other, bewildered.

'And the thing I've been dealing with ... you know – the crisis at work ... a journalist is trying to get hold of me.'

Nicola frowns. 'So? The journalist who phoned last night was in London, wasn't he?'

'Yes, but I've been told they're probably using a stringer and last night ... oh God, I blabbed. *Seriously* blabbed. He convinced me he was just being a good listener. What a f—'

A loud ping interrupts me as the lift comes to a halt on the top floor. Meredith goes to step out.

'What are we doing here?' I ask.

'You were the one who pressed the button,' Nicola points out.

'Did I—'

'Oh, come on, can't we have a look at the view now we're here?' says Meredith enthusiastically, but I grab her by the sleeve and yank her back.

'I'm terrified of heights,' I remind her. 'Besides, Harry told me last night he was up on one of these top floors. I'm *trying* to escape him.'

I press the button and the doors close.

'You're not seriously suggesting he's working on that story? Wouldn't that be a bit of a coincidence?' Meredith asks.

'It's not a coincidence,' I reply, as we reach the third floor. I press the button again. 'It's anything *but* a coincidence.'

'You think he's following you?'

'At the risk of sounding paranoid ... yes. Although ... maybe no. Oh, I don't know!'

'Why can't you just accept that he fancies you and that's why he's interested in talking to you?'

I hesitate. For a flicker of a moment, I want it to be true. Then I remember how much of the conversation last night was dominated by my work, how much I ended up telling him, and how suspiciously interested he was. 'I don't think so.'

'Well, I do!' Meredith says staunchly. And, after a circular conversation that goes on for another sixteen floors – both up and down – I realise I'm getting nowhere, and have to send them on their way.

I spend four hours incarcerated in my room. Four hours of praying for my phone to ring . . . and praying it won't.

I try reading my book to relax, but typically fail to get beyond the first line. I scan the room service menu and cogitate on what I'd eat if calories were not a consideration and my state of intense hypertension wasn't now so bad that it's killed my appetite anyway. I watch a Spanish version of *Bargain Hunt* and conclude that daytime telly is the fastest route to brain rot the world over. Then I lie on my bed, staring at the silky blankness of the ceiling, before deciding enough's enough. I am supposed to be on *holiday*, not in Wormwood Scrubs.

I throw on my bikini, pack my beach bag, pull on my oversized glasses, and head out, torn between anxiety that I'll bump into Harry and a certainty that I'll lose my mind if I stay in the room any longer.

I convince myself there's every chance he won't be around today; I have a hazy recollection that he said last night he'd be out on an excursion. And, even if I'm wrong, all I need to do is avoid him.

Easy enough, surely?

Chapter 28

I head for the private stretch of beach right outside the hotel, after sending Charles a text to tell him that if he or *News Morning* wants to reach me, they should try my mobile first and I can be back in my room in three minutes.

As I cross the lobby towards the door that leads to the beach, a woman in front of me is heading in the same direction. She is wearing a see-through sarong, a microscopic cropped top and bikini bottoms that are more bottom than bikini.

The contrast with own approach to beachwear today couldn't be more acute: there's my massive glasses, my massive hat and a kaftan thingy my mum bought me six years ago that is only slightly more revealing than a burkha. I look horrendous, but this combo has at least one benefit: I am in disguise. As a tent.

I step out of the double doors edgily and scan the beach.

It's quieter than the sun deck, with only one or two couples lying out under huge, white beach umbrellas. I am greeted by a beach butler, who escorts me to a secluded spot beneath a gently swaying palm. He produces a towel as thick as a 15-tog quilt and flips it onto a lounger like a matador's cape. He offers me a drink, then something to eat, then enquires if he can adjust my umbrella, followed by a plethora of other suggestions that eventually forces me to thrust a tip into his hand just to get shot of him.

I settle on my front anxiously, pull out my book and tell myself to relax. I *have* to relax. Relaxing is now an absolute MUST-DO.

'*Here is a small fact . . .*'

'Helloo!'

I place my hand above my eyes and squint up into the silhouette of a man. 'Um, hi,' I reply, adjusting my position to avoid the blinding sunshine.

He appears to be in his early twenties and slim, bronzed to the colour of turkey gravy and with teeth so bright they must be visible from space.

'I think . . . zis . . . I think you drop.' He holds out the shower cap, the one from the room.

'Oh . . . thank you,' I say, hastily shoving it in my bag and making a mental note to stop collecting hotel toiletries, particularly since I've never used a shower cap in my life.

I smile and settle down again.

'*Here is a small fact . . .*'

'Do you mind eef . . .' I look up and he's gesturing shyly to the sun bed next to mine. My heart sinks, followed by a rapid feeling of guilt at being so antisocial, even if it *is* difficult to be gregarious when you're near psychotic with anxiety.

But am I going to tell him I'd prefer to be alone, even if that's true? Of course not. I'm British.

'Not at all.' I smile enthusiastically as he gestures to a beach butler, who appears with a towel.

He makes himself comfortable and stretches out, which makes him appear even more toned, in a reedy kind of way. Not that I'm looking. He's far too young for me, even if there weren't a million other issues at play.

'Here is a small fact . . .'

'Are you Eeenglish?'

'Yes. Where are you from?' I desperately want to go back to my book but have always suffered from this reverse type of Tourette's, where I have no control over the polite words spilling out of my mouth.

'Italy,' he replies. 'Firenze.'

Florence. He's from Florence. He's just become 1,000 per cent more interesting.

'I know Florence well.'

'Really?' he says softly.

I prop myself up on my elbows and study him, only then realising that he reminds me of Roberto in more than just the obvious ways. He's got that good-looking-but-unassuming vibe going on. Despite that, he looks almost intimidated by me, despite ploughing on with the conversation. I decide to show more enthusiasm.

'That's where my boyfriend was born,' I tell him.

'Oh,' he replies, looking disappointed. 'Are you 'ere with your boyfriend?'

'Oh, he's not ... we're not ... sorry – I'm single these days.'

He perks up. 'I 'ave never been to Barcelona before, 'ave you?'

'It's my first time. I haven't seen much of it yet, though. Your English is very good,' I add politely.

He looks ecstatic. 'Reeally? You theenk? That means so much to me. It make me feel *so* horny to know that.'

I do a double take. 'You mean ... *happy?*'

'Happy, happy – yes! I so happy.'

I smile. Then I return to my book.

'*Here is a small fact . . .*'

''Ave you been on the entire of the beach?'

I look up. 'You mean have I walked along the whole board-walk? Not yet, but I might try it at some point.'

He smiles. He has a sweet smile, wide and amiable. 'I would like to. It is my first day only here. But I love wanking. Wanking is my passion.'

'Walking,' I correct him.

'Yes, *wanking*,' he agrees. 'My father always say, wanking is

226

the best possible exercise. Wank *everywhere* if you can ... in the summer, in the winter, in the sunshine, in the night.'

'WALKING is very good exercise,' I reply, stressing the pronunciation.

'*You* like wanking, too?'

I suppress a smile. 'Oh, at least once or twice a week.'

When he grins, I realise how much his dark eyes look like Roberto's. It makes my stomach flip.

'You look sad,' he says. 'You not have a nice time on holiday?'

'I'm having a lovely time,' I reply, slightly defensively.

'Good. Is very good.'

I smile and am about to try reading again, when my phone rings. I sit up in a cold sweat when I hear Charles's voice. 'Imogen, there's been a change of plan. You're on in fifteen minutes.'

After a brief conversation with my PR guru, it turns out a producer from the *Afternoon* programme, *News Morning*'s sister show, is phoning me in ten minutes and counting. With *News Morning* threatening to scoop the *Daily Sun*, *Afternoon* somehow picked up the story too, and its reporters are determined to get in first. Which means they want me live on the show. Not tomorrow morning. Not at some unspecified point in the future. But in *ten minutes*.

Charles fills me in on a few questions they might throw at

me. I write his suggested answers on the back page of *The Book Thief*, barely taking in anything beyond, 'I'm here to be as open and honest as possible,' a line he suggests I fall back on if I feel flustered at any point. He thinks I'm joking when I tell him that might be the only thing I say.

With my heart thumping like the bass on a Motörhead album, I rip the page from the book, leap up, throw on my kaftan and grab my belongings.

'Sorry, but I've got to run,' I announce to my neighbour. 'It's been lovely to meet you.'

'Yes,' he smiles, sitting up to shake my hand. 'I am erotic to meet you, too.'

Chapter 29

I am racing to the lifts in the lobby, attempting to prevent beach paraphernalia tumbling from my arms, when I spot Harry again. WHY can't I get rid of this man? He's by the lift, blocking the fastest route back to my room, which I have precisely nine minutes to reach.

I've homed in on the door to the stairs – my next best option – when he starts to turn around. At which point I plunge into the Ladies' as they are the nearest available room in which to take momentary refuge.

At least, I'd thought they were the Ladies'. But, as I glance around, the presence of five gleaming urinals would indicate otherwise.

'Shit!' I mutter, prising open the door a crack to see if Harry's in the lift yet.

To my alarm he is walking in this direction. Even the man's bladder is conspiring against me.

I stumble back and head for the nearest cubicle. I'm almost

inside when my sunglasses clatter to the floor, but there's no time to collect them. Instead, I stumble inside, lock the door and, conscious that if my toes are visible underneath the door I'm busted, leap onto the rim of the toilet in an ungainly squat, while attempting to keep the hem of my kaftan out of the bowl.

I hold my breath as he enters the room, walks directly to my cubicle and attempts to push open the door. It rattles threateningly . . . but stays shut. I cover my mouth with my hand and try to silence my breathing.

'Sorry,' he mutters, and tries the adjacent cubicle.

I squirm with discomfort, and not just because my calf muscles are physically shaking in this position. This was the man who, whether I liked it or not, set my pulse racing. Am I really going to have to listen to him *on the toilet*?

On the plus side, if he's locked in for a prolonged period, I can at least make my getaway. Unable to sustain the squat any longer, I shift my position a little on the loo, believing I've been successful until I watch the last page of *The Book Thief* floating down into the toilet pan, complete with the sum total of my media briefing from Charles.

Harry blows his nose briefly, and I realise he'd obviously just popped in for some loo roll. Then the main door squeaks open and I breathe out silently, relieved that he's about to leave. But he is halted in his tracks by a ringing phone.

'Harry Pfeiffer here. Hello, Ken, how are you?' There's a pause, then Harry continues. 'I managed to get her by herself last night and think we're nearly there. If I can just pin her down on the details about the flight, I should have everything over to you earlier than deadline. Yeah, really.' He laughs. 'Of course I'm confident! It's fair to say this is one of the less demanding jobs I've been sent on.'

Less demanding? Well, we'll see about that!

I've just put my feet on the floor as he's ending the call, when something horrendous happens: something far worse than losing my media briefing on the last page of *The Book Thief* down the loo; something that makes that look like no big deal at all.

I drop my phone in the toilet.

It lands with an uncompromising plop, then sinks, bubbling to the bottom, the final ingredient in my cauldron of misery.

'Arrrrgghhh!' I don't care if Harry hears me; the priority now is resuscitating it. And I know there's only one way, if his advice after I dropped it in the fruit salad was correct.

I hold my breath and shove in my hand, a process indescribable in its repugnance. I successfully fish out the phone and frantically begin dismantling it, removing the battery, then the sim card, then shaking every bit of water out.

'Oh ... please!' I say to no one in particular as I wipe it on my kaftan.

'Everything all right in there?' Harry knocks on the door.

I take a deep breath and, shoving my spare belongings into my bag, I unlock the door.

'Yes!' I hiss, pushing past him, not caring now if he's a member of the press, the paparazzi or the bloody Mob.

'What happened to your phone?'

'I had such fun dropping it into the fruit salad yesterday, I thought I'd try it in here this time.'

He frowns. 'Can I help? Maybe if you put it under the hand dryer . . .? What are you doing in here, anyway?'

I sniff. 'I took a wrong turn. I was looking for the . . . oh, it doesn't matter.'

'Hey, while I've got you . . . are you around tonight?' He smiles at me easily. 'It'd be good to have a drink together if you are. It'd be nice to have more of a chat. I find your job really interesting.'

That's it. Fury bubbles upside in me. 'Interesting? Tell me . . . why would a journalist find *my* boring old job interesting?'

He looks taken aback. Clearly, the last thing he's expecting was for me to catch him in the act – actually talking about the Peebles story with his news desk.

'I just . . . well, we don't have to talk about—'

'Let me stop you there.' I interrupt with a surge of inner strength. 'I am on *holiday*. If you people want to interview me, or find out anything you like about David Hartnett and his . . . misdemeanour, then please do as everyone else has done and phone my PR company.'

'I didn't want to interview you,' he replies.

'Of course you didn't,' I snap. 'You wanted to get a scoop –

you wanted an "off the record" chat. Well, fine, here's something very much ON the record – keep away from me.'

He is momentarily silenced. 'Fine. If that's the way you'd like it,' he says eventually.

'I would.' Then I gasp. 'Shit! What time is it?'

'Twenty past one—' But he hasn't even finished his sentence before I hurtle through the door to meet my fate. My first-ever radio broadcast, going out live across the UK.

No pressure then.

Chapter 30

I arrive at the hotel room as the landline is ringing and am inches from the handset when it stops.

'SORREEY!'

I turn and glare at the toilet door. It's one of those trendy frosted ones – beautiful to look at but, given that with the door closed you can still see the outline of the user, only truly appropriate for use when you're bunking in with very close family members or the visually impaired.

'What are you doing here?' I ask Meredith, averting my eyes.

'Dodgy stomach,' she shouts through the door. 'We came back early. Didn't you see Nic? She went looking for you – we assumed you'd be on the sun deck.'

'I was on the beach. Look, are you going to be long? I'm expecting an important phone call ... or maybe not, actually,' I add, gazing at the phone hopefully. 'Maybe they've given up on me.'

It rings.

'What did you say?' Meredith shouts through.

'I said this is an *important* . . . Look, it doesn't matter – can you just be as quiet as possible?'

'I didn't catch that,' Meredith replies, as I pick up the phone. 'Hello?'

'Is that Imogen Copeland?'

'Yes,' I squeak.

'Donna Sollenberger from the *Afternoon* programme. I've been trying to get hold of you.'

'Sorry – I was held up.'

'Well, it's okay, we've got you now. But we're on air in about thirty seconds, so Jim Bryson will be with you then, okay?'

'I . . . suppose so.' Jim Bryson is the programme's lead presenter and is known for being the journalistic equivalent of a Rottweiler. I take several deep breaths and tell myself I can do this; I *can* muster up a masterful performance, no doubt about it.

'Good luck,' she says nonchalantly, and flicks a switch so I can hear the programme being broadcast.

'We move on to the remarkable story that Afternoon *brought to you* FIRST *in the one o'clock headlines – that of a senior executive from one of the UK's most prominent companies, who was arrested after allegedly engaging in sexual intercourse on a first-class flight from Stuttgart.'*

I gasp. It wasn't full sex! But before I can gather my thoughts, there's a knock on the door. I consider leaving it, but it becomes more insistent as I catch snippets of the programme in the background.

> *'Peebles, the confectionary and cereals giants, are holding an internal inquiry about the incident, which allegedly took place on a flight between Heathrow and Stuttgart last month.'*

I open the door tentatively, the phone glued to my ear. *'Servicio de habitaciones . . .* room service,' declares a waiter. Before I can protest, he pushes through a hostess trolley, complete with silver-service tray. What the hell has Meredith been ordering?

> *'Joining me now is Imogen Copeland, spokeswoman from Peebles.'*

My stomach goes into freefall as I realise I'm now on air. I need to get rid of this waiter. Only, he won't move. He just stands there, waiting for his tip. I frantically survey the room for spare change, flinging items around the room until, in desperation, I locate a 10 cents coin and thrust it in his palm.

> *'Ms Copeland . . . what has the chap in question had to say for himself?'*

My mouth goes dry and my lip starts to wobble. The waiter is immobile, glaring at the tip like I've just put a snotty tissue in his hand. But all I can concentrate on is that that was *not* one of Charles's predicted questions. Even with my media briefing now floating around a Catalan sewerage system, I know that much.

I usher the waiter out of the room, almost engaging a size-six espadrille against his arse as he refuses to move with any speed, then I start talking. I barely process what I'm saying, but I am at least talking.

'Um ... well, like you said, the internal inquiry will happen shortly so we will have to discuss this matter with ... with the ... individual in question then. I wouldn't like to pre-empt that.'

'I see. And—'

'Can I clarify something, though,' I add, knowing that if I don't correct this now, I may never get the chance. 'They didn't have ... sexual intercourse.' The thermostat on my cheeks is turned up several degrees as I say the words. 'Not ... you know, *completely*.'

'Not completely?'

'No.'

'So there was no sex? The police got this wrong?'

'No, I'm not saying that ... there was some, you know ...'

My mind is suddenly blank. There is a deafening silence on the line as he waits for me to continue. I open my mouth but nothing comes out of it.

'*IMOGEN!*' Meredith suddenly hollers, shattering the quiet. Oh God, I need to keep talking!

'There was some, um … *funny business*,' I begin, as if my broadcast training was delivered by Benny Hill.

'Funny. Business?' Bryson says the two words as if he's got something stuck in his teeth.

For some reason, dabbing sweat from my forehead, I feel as if my only option is to expand on the description. 'He got to … well, he got to third base.' I wince.

'*IMOGEN, CAN YOU PASS ME SOME LOO ROLL?*'

I sprint to the bathroom cupboard, rifling around in it until I locate the toilet paper.

'I … see,' says Bryson uncertainly. 'For those of us unfamiliar with American baseball terms, perhaps you could expand?'

I bite my fist. 'What … *really?*'

'Well, what else have you come on here for?' he asks snarkily. '*IMOGEN … ARE YOU THERE? IMOGEN? I'M STUCK ON THE BOG HERE – DO ME A FAVOUR, WON'T YOU?*'

'I … I'm here to be as open and honest as possible.'

I grab the loo roll and race out into the main room, chucking it over the top of the cubicle.

'Well, perhaps you could explain then.'

I feel like saying: '*How* can you never have heard of the term "third base"? Where have you been all your life?' But I don't. In fact, I don't say anything. I *can't* say anything. I can only mouth silently into the phone for a few seconds, before the unbearable silence is broken by the flush of the toilet.

It sounds as if we're standing at the base of Niagara Falls during a tropical cyclone. Loud. Gushing. Relentless. I frenziedly spin around the room, desperate to escape the thunderous noise.

'Boobs!' I splutter in desperation, just as there's a knock on the door and it opens. It's the cleaning lady. She trundles in with a vacuum cleaner the size of a Sinclair C5. I attempt to wave her out. 'He . . . he . . . copped a feel, that's all,' I splutter, as she shrugs her shoulders, bewildered. 'That's all it means.'

Did I really just say that? Really? *Live on air?*

Either way, Bryson clearly wishes he hadn't asked. 'I . . . um . . . perhaps we could move on to the ramifications of this incident.' I frantically push the cleaning lady out of the door and she finally backs off, disgruntlement etched on her forehead. 'Peebles shareholders aren't likely to be impressed, are they, Ms Copeland?' he continues, as I shut the door and focus on the question.

To say they won't be impressed is putting it mildly. And that's without them even knowing the half of it.

'Well, the actions of one individual don't necessarily reflect that of the company as a whole,' I reply.

'But surely if the person in question is senior, it reflects extremely poorly on the judgment of those in charge of the company?'

I take a deep breath and summon some inner strength. I cannot allow my sole contribution to defending the company's honour be blurting out the word 'boobs' on national radio.

'Peebles is one of Britain's most successful businesses, a real UK success story,' I say firmly, straightening my back. 'It's done tremendously well throughout a recession, when everyone else in this sector has really struggled. We've given an enormous amount to charity and—'

'Thank you, Ms Copeland. That's all we have time for.'

At which point, I hear a click, and the producer comes back on the phone. 'That was great, cheers,' she says breezily.

Given that my heart appears to want to leap out of my mouth and go for a swim in the Med right now, the contrast between her demeanour and mine couldn't be greater.

I put down the phone and lie on the bed as I fumble my mobile back together. It springs into life immediately.

It's a text from Mum:

So sorry to bother you. Florence has swallowed half a lipstick. She seems okay, but am wondering if you think I should phone an ambulance?

'Sorry, I didn't realise you were on the phone,' says Meredith, drying her hands as she emerges from the bathroom and examining the feast she's ordered from room service. 'Anyone interesting?'

'You could say that,' I reply, before burying my head in a pillow and yearning for a quick, painless death.

Chapter 31

It quickly becomes apparently that 'half a lipstick' actually means a fragment so microscopic you couldn't complete a makeover on a budgie with it. I set about persuading Mum that Florence's mishap does not constitute a full-scale medical emergency, that airlifting her to hospital will not be necessary, and that if she really meant the 'So sorry to bother you' bit in the text, then perhaps she might consider simply . . . not.

I don't actually say the last bit; I just think it, though her telepathic powers clearly start picking up on something.

'You don't sound very relaxed considering you're on holiday,' she notes.

'No,' I reply dully.

'I never used to get stressed when I was a young woman,' she continues. 'If I was feeling like things were getting on top of me, I'd simply visit the masseur, twice or three times a week sometimes. The sheik used to pay for them for all the girls. All he wanted in return was a nice smile and a pleasant word. Well, mainly.'

'Can I speak to Florence?'

Mum hands the phone to my daughter.

'Hi, Mummy.'

Hearing her voice somehow makes everything vastly better. 'Hello, sweetheart!' I gush. 'Gosh, I miss you. Lots and lots. I *love* you!'

'I'm busy,' she replies.

'Oh,' I say, wondering when my four-year-old's schedule became too tight to fit me in. 'Well, what are you up to?'

'Trying on Grandma's high heels. She's going to buy me some of my own. And I've decided what I want to be when I grow up.'

'Oh, what's that?' I ask, hoping she's going to say astrophysicist.

'A princess.' She announces it in an I-can't-believe-I-hadn't-thought-of-this-earlier! voice.

'Oh,' I reply flatly. 'Well, the only way to become a princess would be to marry a prince. And it'd be far better to do a really exciting job you'd got all by yourself – by being clever and working hard. Don't you think?'

She doesn't even ponder this for a second. 'Not really.'

I frown. 'But what if you fall in love with someone who *isn't* a prince? You couldn't still then marry someone else, even if he was a prince.'

'I would,' she replies defiantly. 'Princes are the handsomest.'

I grit my teeth. 'Being handsome isn't everything, Florence.'

'No. They're rich too,' she replies.

I decide to move on. 'So, how did you end up eating Grandma's lipstick?'

'I don't know. It tasted of cherries at first. Then it didn't taste nice. Mummy?'

'Yes?'

'Do you know yet if you can take me to school on my first day?'

I squirm. 'I'll know soon,' I reply. Frankly, after my performance on national radio, I'm in no position to rock the boat work-wise.

'*When* will you know?'

'I'm working on it, I promise. But, you know, it'll be absolutely fine if Debbie has to take you. She'll hold your hand. And I can pick you up that day, definitely.'

'It's not the same.' Her little voice wobbles.

'I know, sweetie. I'll do my best. I'll do my very, very best. I love you, Flor—' The line goes dead.

I glance at my phone and realise that a message has been left while I was talking, from someone at the police station. It's in an odd, Spanglish-type language, but I work out this much: there's bugger-all news on the necklace, and they'd like me to desist from phoning them.

I perch on the end of my bed, utterly dejected. I'm in this

243

beautiful hotel room, supposedly miles from my troubles and with everything I could wish for, yet the simplest of things – relaxation – eludes me.

Part of me wants to pack my bags and go home. Although that would involve showing my face at work and, after the performance I've just managed, it's not a prospect I relish.

Instead, all I can do is lie back on the bed, gaze at the ceiling and remind myself how lucky I am to have Florence, even if she is too busy with her grandma's shoes to do anything other than grunt at my pathetic pleas for affection.

It strikes me that Florence's assertion of her personality seems to accelerate by the day, judging by her recent declarations that she's now too sophisticated for most things, from *Dora the Explorer* to holding hands when we cross the road – she seems to think of the Green Cross Code as a quaint but entirely optional custom. I have no doubt that more surprises are in store, which is exactly how things have been from the beginning.

When Roberto pulled me into his arms in the bathroom after I'd taken my five pregnancy tests, I was convinced it was the prelude to him saying goodbye. That, or trying to persuade me to get rid of the baby. He had a forceful personality – not in a sinister way; he was simply someone who knew his mind and wasn't afraid to express it. And he'd made his views perfectly clear.

The thing I've since discovered about having children, however, but didn't know then, is that they force you to change. You think you know yourself, but until there's a tiny person in your life, totally dependent on you alone, you have no real idea of your capabilities, your potential, the depths of darkness and the highs of light you have within you.

And, even before Florence was born, when she was no more than a few cells making magic inside me, she managed to effect the most fundamental turnaround in a human being possible.

'I'm sorry,' I repeated, over and over again, through numb lips. I've never been one for saying that word. My terminal reluctance to admit I'm wrong is one of my worst flaws, something Roberto could've complained bitterly about. But not that day. That day, I couldn't say it enough.

We didn't discuss it for hours. We carried on as if nothing had happened – went out for a walk, then came back and curled up on the sofa in front of back-to-back movies. But that whole time, throughout that enforced, unnatural silence, a storm was building inside me. Inside both of us.

Roberto cooked his signature dish that night, *risotto ai carciofi*, but I could hardly touch it. And when I went to clear up the dishes, he gently took hold of my wrist.

'Imogen.' I was convinced his eyes said everything. 'This baby . . .'

I didn't want him to say the words I knew he was going to, the ones he had every right to say: *We can't keep it.*

Only he didn't say that.

'I want us to have it.'

My stomach twisted in shock. '*Really?*'

'I know what I said. I know what I told you. But now it's happened, I feel different.' He picked up my hand and weaved his fingers between mine. 'I want us to have a family together.'

And that was it. The day everything changed. The day we thought our lives together – me, Roberto and our child – were mapped out.

Which goes to show that nobody ever has any idea what the future holds.

Chapter 32

'Imogen, relax. The interview can't have been as bad as you think,' Nicola says, picking at a bowl of *patatas bravas*.

We're at a tapas bar at the end of the beach where, despite the warm swish of evening breeze and mouth-watering food, I feel queasy for reasons that can't be blamed on a dodgy scallop.

'Nicola, I said the word "boobs" on national radio. How could it possibly have been worse?'

'Tits?' offers Meredith.

'What?'

'You could've said "tits",' she repeats. 'Or arsehole, or fanny or—'

'Thank you,' I interrupt. 'The point is, it was so bad that I couldn't even bear to go to the business centre to look at the newspaper websites this afternoon.'

'I can get them on my phone if yours still can't get online,' Meredith offers.

'No,' I shake my head determinedly. Then, 'Oh ... go on then.'

'NO!' Nicola interrupts. 'There's nothing you can do about it now anyway, so please just try and relax.'

I put my head in my hands. Stacey texted from work earlier to tell me that everyone in the office had heard the interview and they all wanted to offer me their support. When I replied asking if that meant it wasn't as bad as I thought it was, there was a half-hour delay while she thought of a diplomatic response, before I received another:

Well, we all just think it was really unfair for you to have been put in that position without having had the proper training. P.S. Keep your chin up – I will bring cake in on your first day back! :) Hugs xx

Another text then arrived seconds later, which read:

P.P.S. I take it you are coming back?

'You're probably tired too,' Meredith says. 'I know I haven't helped with that. Did I snore again last night?'

'Hmm, kind of.' I quickly change the subject. 'I dread to think what the newspapers' full editions will say in the morning.'

'Why don't we shuffle around tonight? You and I can share,' Nicola suggests to Meredith. 'At least then Imogen's guaranteed a half-decent night's sleep.'

'Oh, it doesn't matter,' I say dismissively.

'No, I insist,' Meredith replies.

'Well, thank you. But, honestly, don't worry about me. In fact, let's not *talk* about me. I'm sick of even thinking about my catastrophes. Can't we discuss your problems instead?'

'We're meant to be on the holiday to end all holidays,' Meredith points out. 'I'd hoped we'd labour under the delicious falsehood that none of us had any.'

'Fine. Let's talk about things that are going well, then.'

Meredith thinks for a second. 'Nicola, how's Jessica?'

Nicola looks up. 'Jessica's great. Jealous as hell that we're sunning ourselves while she's having to work, but apart from that, wonderful. I spoke to her just before we left the hotel.'

'You two are so good together,' Meredith says. 'I'm in awe.'

'We're not perfect.'

'You never argue.' Meredith widens her eyes without having to spell out that you couldn't apply this description to her and Nathan.

'Not often,' Nicola concedes.

'Do you think you'll ever get married? Oh, go on, do! I love a good wedding. I haven't been to one for ages.'

Nicola shrugs. 'Things are still tricky with Mum and Dad, to be honest.'

'Do you think they'll ever agree to meet Jessica?' Meredith looks at her sympathetically.

Nicola bites her lip. 'I'd like to think one day they'll thaw enough to do so. But at the moment, I can't see it.'

'How does Jessica feel about it?' Meredith asks.

Nicola takes a deep breath. I know at that moment that Jessica couldn't be more pissed off about this bundle of issues if they came tied up with barbed wire and were delivered by a man with dog poo on his shoes.

'We had an argument about it just before I came out here,' Nicola confesses. 'I feel terrible about it. Even though my mum and dad are wrong, they're still my parents and I love them. But I know this whole thing makes Jess unhappy. And me, for that matter.'

'Maybe you should try talking to them about it again?'

'Yeah, maybe.' Nic shrugs. 'The thought of it brings me out in a cold sweat, but you're probably right.'

That night my room is so silent I have to cough every so often to check I haven't gone inexplicably deaf. I pull the duvet around my shoulders, turn off the lights and prepare to sleep. With only the faint amber glow of the loo-roll light to subtly illuminate the designer surfaces of the room, it couldn't be more relaxing.

All, in fact, would be perfect, if an explosion of thoughts hadn't infiltrated my mind about Florence, her school, my job, Harry, my radio performance ... oh, and what tomorrow's papers are going to make of their latest big scoop.

Day Five

Chapter 33

I have my answer at 6.40 a.m., when I wake after four fragmented hours' sleep, tug on my dressing gown, grab a key card and lope groggily to the business centre to view the online versions of the papers.

The first story I stumble across is about a tragedy somewhere in South East Asia in which hundreds of office block workers were killed in a fire. It's a dreadful piece, one that makes me count my blessings as I read it. All those poor people ... this must be more newsworthy than our predicament surely? Then I spot the first article about David.

It isn't good. It couldn't be further from good if it'd taken a one-way ticket to Bad, changed its identity and vowed to never come back.

PEEBLES CHIEF IN MID-AIR SCANDAL

That, it turns out, is one of the tamer headlines.

FIRST-CLASS BOOB: CEO arrested after he 'copped a feel' of topless woman on flight

MILE-HIGH MAESTRO: Police step in after Peebles boss gets frisky on flight

David is identified in all but one of them. He's thoroughly, one million per cent busted, as is the woman – a sinewy redhead with inflatable lips who works for a small-sized clothing company. As she's nothing like as high profile as David, she gets off fairly lightly.

I scan through article after article in a desperate attempt to unearth *some* redeeming feature – my quote about our charity work for example, or a mention of our exceptional performance throughout the recession. But they're nowhere. Instead, in every tabloid and broadsheet is a line that goes something like this:

> Imogen Copeland, a spokeswoman for Peebles, confirmed that a senior executive at the company had been involved in what she termed, 'funny business', adding, 'He got to third base.'

Did I *really* say that?

> Ms Copeland confirmed that the executive had – in her words – 'copped a feel' of the woman in question's 'boobs'.

I am overcome by an urgent desire to fall to my hands and knees and cry until my eyeballs have shrivelled up.

As I stare out of the window across the vast blue of the sea, I tug my dressing gown tighter with one hand while a question pounds through my brain: how did they find out it was David? I didn't mention him in the interview, and the subsequent official quotes provided by Charles certainly didn't. Someone as slick as him wouldn't have blurted it out . . .

I pause. I think. And another hideous wave of recognition sweeps over me. I might not have blurted it out on national radio, but I blurted it out somewhere. My last conversation with Harry comes back to me in blood-curdling technicolour.

'*I am on* holiday. *If you people want to interview me, or find out anything you like about David Hartnett and his . . . misdemeanour, then please do as everyone else has done and phone my PR company.*'

Oh God. I've been completely stitched up.

As Meredith scrutinises the breakfast menu, Nicola seems to be failing to grasp the gravity of the situation.

'I'm simply saying it sounds far-fetched that they'd put up some journalist in this hotel just to try to get the inside scoop. Is the story really that big?'

'Nicola, it's in every single paper in the UK this morning. On the front pages of half of them.'

She almost chokes on her orange juice. 'Including the serious ones?'

'Absolutely. They're *loving* it. And there's only one person I've revealed David's name to – Harry.'

'But he hasn't confessed to all this?'

'He was never going to do that, was he?'

She raises her hand to try to get the attention of the waitress, clearly exhausted by this conversation. And the fact that we're being ignored again.

'I thought competition winners were supposed to get special treatment?' I grumble, feeling that if I don't get my coffee this morning I might start banging my head against the table until I get my own way, like Animal from the Muppets. 'This is the second time this has happened. If she doesn't hurry up, I'll snitch on her to Elegant Vacations.'

'I'll speak to them if need be,' Meredith offers.

'I wasn't serious.'

'Oh. Well, anyway, *I* think it's outrageous,' Meredith continues. 'About Harry, not the waitress and the coffee, I mean. I don't blame you for being annoyed.'

'Perhaps you should have it out with him, before you come to any more conclusions,' Nicola suggests. 'In the meantime, one thing I am certain of is that you need to switch off. It's beyond a joke. I'm getting wound up just looking at you.'

'Me too,' Meredith adds.

'Don't do that, it'll stress the baby.' I say. 'From seventeen weeks onwards, their neuro-behavioural development is affected by your moods.'

She shakes her head in despair. 'How the *hell* do you remember this stuff?'

I lie on the sun bed next to Meredith in the full knowledge that relaxation, at least for today, is once more out of the question. By 11 a.m. I've already had twelve phone calls from, among others: David (who's now in hiding in his Great Aunt Janice's caravan in Stornoway); Charles (who was infuriatingly calm under the circumstances); Roy (in a lacklustre attempt to 'check in', as he dashed to Buzz Lightyear's Laser Blast before his Fast Pass expired); and my dentist (who I apparently short-changed to the tune of 36p last week, despite paying more than £200 for my treatment). Cosimo also sent me a text from Buenos Aires, where he's backpacking, saying he hoped I was well, sorry he forgot to mention he was off discovering himself, and he'd have the press release about Grill-O-Bloo ready to unleash on the world's press as soon as he was back, to try to take the heat away from Peebles.

'I might take a break from the heat and go inside for a juice,' I eventually tell Meredith.

She looks up from her mobile, on which she's been playing Scrabble all morning. 'I'll come with you. I'm totally stumped at the moment. I refuse to believe it's baby brain.'

'Baby brain's a fallacy, it's been scientifically proven,' I tell her, deciding not to reveal one notable incident when I was pregnant involving a lost mobile phone, which I subsequently discovered in the freezer.

We gather our belongings, I help her up from the sun bed and we start walking towards the bar area by the lobby.

'Where did Nicola go after breakfast?' I ask.

'No idea. She was talking earlier about popping to that convenience store down the road, but she's been gone ages,' she replies.

We head towards one of the sofas directly underneath a pleasingly arctic air-conditioning system, at exactly the same time as a waiter arrives from the bar area.

Just as I'm ordering two orange juices, I'm interrupted by the distinctive sound of a tiny baby's cries coming from a table in the bar area.

The little girl can't be more than eight weeks old, yet, tender age or not, she produces a phenomenal level of noise. Her father, a young Spanish man with world-weary eyes, picks her up from her pram and begins walking up and down in an attempt to pacify her, while her mother frantically roots through a changing bag the size of a small caravan, emerging eventually with a bottle of milk.

Their efforts to calm her down meet with mixed success; the cries die down every so often, only to resume soon afterwards. She doesn't want the bottle offered by her mum; she doesn't want a dummy. Eventually, Daddy – with a generous sweat on his brow – decides to bundle her past us for a walk outside, which, judging by the continuing if distant cries, is about as successful as his previous attempts to cheer her up.

'I remember Florence doing that once in Costa Coffee,' I say. 'I was mortified. Still, they're so gorgeous at that age. So tiny . . . and that lovely soft skin.'

I glance at Meredith, who is looking at me like I'm talking in some strange, obscure dialect that her ears can't process. 'Do you really think that?' she asks.

I shrug. 'Of course.'

Meredith shakes her head, still staring at me. 'But it's making SO. MUCH. NOISE.' I notice her voice is laced with panic. 'I mean, that poor man! I bet he was good-looking once, but now he's got purple bags under his eyes and his beard is grey. And that's before we get on to him pounding up and down outside instead of sitting here having a nice coffee. And as for his wife' – we glance over as subtly as possible – 'she looks broken.'

The woman is now slumped at the table, reading the wine list longingly.

'It won't always be that hard,' I assure her. 'It's no walk in the park – I won't insult your intelligence by claiming otherwise. But it does get easier. And even at its most challenging, it's still worth every minute. You'll see.'

'Will I?' she says sarcastically.

I laugh at first, convinced it's a joke. Until I really look at Meredith's face, the tension in her jaw.

'Are you okay?' I ask, squeezing her hand as the father returns with a – mercifully – quiet baby.

Meredith sniffs and forces a smile. 'Course. Sorry. Oh God, look . . . there's your arch enemy.'

She nods in the direction of the double doors we came through a few minutes ago. Behind them is Harry. Just looking at him makes fury sizzle up in me, something Meredith senses.

'Are you going to say something?'

'Absolutely.'

'Who'd have thought he'd be to blame for all this? He had such potential too.'

'The truth is, my ludicrous boss is to blame for being too liberal with the term "in-flight entertainment",' I tell her, 'and my deputy is to blame for disappearing to Euro Disney when he was supposed to be covering for me. Various PR companies are also to blame for being about as useful as a steak and kidney pie at a vegetarian dinner party.' I'm really working myself up now. 'And then there's me, for using the term "third base" and "boobs" on national radio, in the press and – Charles informed me earlier – on TV this morning.'

Meredith's eyes widen. 'TV?'

'Apparently my quote was read out on every "what the papers say" round-up in Britain,' I explain. 'I was trending on Twitter at one point, until I was knocked off by Harry Styles announcing he's squeezed a spot or something.'

'Oh, sweetheart,' she says, rubbing my arm. 'Maybe you do need to get this off your chest.' She nods over towards Harry. 'Be careful what you say, though. He might be taking notes.'

'There'll be few printable words,' I reply, steeling myself as I stand up and start to march in his direction.

I barely realise Nicola is coming up behind me until she grabs my elbow, just before I push my way through the door.

'Imogen! You need to see this.' She's out of breath and carrying a stack of A4 paper.

'What's this?'

She diverts me back to the sofa next to Meredith, where she hands it over. I start flicking through the pages.

'Harry's writing. Imogen, he doesn't appear to have written a single tabloid article in his entire career. He's not even what I think you'd class as a news reporter.'

I open my mouth to say something, but shut it again. 'What is he then?'

'He writes for various newspapers. It's all very serious stuff. He's a science correspondent.'

'What?'

She nods. 'There are features here covering everything from genetics to space travel, IVF to climate change. And absolutely none about groping chief executives.'

My head throbs. 'But I heard him talking about *me*, about this story. He said he was filing it before the deadline. I heard it all when I was hiding in the Gents.'

She looks at me as if I'm unhinged. 'Why were you hiding in the Gents'?'

'Because – oh, it doesn't matter.'

'I don't think he's your man, Imogen.'

I glance in his direction. 'But he must be.'

'I don't think so.'

I look down at the papers again. Suddenly, none of it makes sense any more. I have no idea how to explain the conversation I overheard in the toilets but, equally, judging by Nicola's evidence, writing a sleazy story for the *Daily Sun* doesn't seem to be Harry's style.

'Just because he doesn't usually write for the *Daily Sun* doesn't mean he never would. Why else would he have been talking about me and the Peebles story in the toilets?'

'No idea. You clearly need to ask him. But, Imogen?' Nic puts her hand on my arm warningly. 'This time be nice.'

Chapter 34

Harry is with the same group of people I saw yesterday, who appear to have gathered in preparation for an excursion. Which, when I think about it, probably isn't what you'd expect a roving reporter to do when they're hot on the heels of a major scoop.

I feel ridiculous marching up to him when there are spectators, particularly Clipboard Barbie, who is today wearing chic, wide-legged trousers and a simple vest: masculine-looking items which have the converse effect of accentuating her soft, slender curves. But there seems to be no other option.

I straighten my back and walk towards him casually but with conviction, determined that nobody could be left with the impression that there's anything untoward about this conversation.

I clear my throat meaningfully. He doesn't look overly pleased to see me, which could be attributed to the mouthful of abuse with which I rewarded him the last time we spoke.

'Um ... have you got a sec—minute?'

Clipboard Barbie lowers her sunglasses and glares at me as if she's just trodden in something gelatinous that's washed up on the beach.

'A sec-*minute*?'

'It's somewhere between a second and a minute. About thirty seconds, to be precise.'

Clipboard Barbie sighs. 'We are going to Camp Nou. We need to get on the bus.'

I turn to Harry, who responds with an apologetic-but-not-really shrug at me. 'You heard the lady.'

'Okay,' I reply, aware that the entire group is watching me, anticipating my next move. I'm going to have to do this – in public, it now turns out – so I might as well get it over with. 'Well, I wanted to say that I *may* have got the wrong end of the stick about something yesterday. About what we discussed in the' – I glance at the others and steel myself – 'in the toilets. If that's the case, and frankly I just don't know what to think any more, then, clearly, I'm sorry. Although I still don't know why you were talking about me and David and the flight. So if it was because you were writing for the *Daily Sun*, then in that case I don't apologise. Absolutely not. My original comments stand. But if you weren't, then they don't.'

Harry looks utterly lost. 'Hmm. Glad we've cleared that up,' he deadpans.

'The point is, when I'm wrong, I say so,' I clarify, whilst

injecting a noble tone to my speech (even if it isn't true). 'And, I may be. Though I'm not sure. So ... I am doing ... At least I think so. By which I mean, I say sorry when I am. And ... *I am* I think.'

The group now stares at me as if I've just added a racy twist to a Neighbourhood Watch meeting by throwing my car keys onto the table. I feel an urgent need to get out of here, despite being no closer to solving the mystery.

'I'll leave you to it!' I announce, spinning on my heel and torpedoing myself towards the door. Anything to escape the looks of utter bafflement on everyone's faces.

Outside, I quicken my speed towards the beach, for which I am not remotely dressed, but that's the least of my worries. A tidal wave of thoughts is rushing through my head as I try to estimate when the coast might be sufficiently clear to be able to return to the girls, when a voice calls out.

'Imogen, wait!' My heart swoops as I turn round and see Harry running towards me. My legs begin to tremble spontaneously. Only, there's nowhere to hide now.

I can't look in his eyes long enough to work out whether he's cross at me or not, but I suspect I know the answer to that. I stand up straight to give an entirely flimsy illusion of composure.

But it's not only the thought of confrontation that makes me uneasy. I'm getting that sensation again that makes my insides feel wrong, the one I got last time I was around Harry, and the time before that. But I know his effect is fairly universal, judging by the female attention his smiles attract; I don't know when I got so predictable, but I seriously dislike it.

'I wanted to say,' he begins, 'that I have no idea what you were talking about – either then, or in the loos. But, apology accepted. If of course that is what it was. I realise you are still in two minds about that.'

I burst out laughing. 'Thank you. Perhaps I need to explain.'

'Why don't we go for a walk?'

'Don't you need to go to the Camp Nou stadium?'

'I've made my excuses. It's not really the done thing on these sorts of trips, so I might as well make the most of it.'

We find space on a couple of sun loungers and Harry puts up the parasol.

'When you say "these sorts of trips", what do you mean, exactly?' I ask.

'I'm on a press trip. Basically, a PR company invites journalists from a variety of publications to review a hotel. That's who the others are in the group you've seen me with. There's Darren from the *Daily Mirror*, Jill from the *Manchester Evening News* and Bob from the *Herald*. It's supposed to be work, but I can't pretend it's too taxing. All you have to do is turn up, allow them to treat you like a king for a few days, go on the odd, all-expenses-paid tour, then write a travel piece. It's hell, as you can imagine.' He smiles. 'I'm a freelance science writer normally, so this is far from my day job. These sorts of trips only come along once in a blue moon, and only if the features editor is in a good mood and none of the staff writers is available.'

'So . . . you're not working on the story about my boss?'

He ponders for a moment. 'The guy who got frisky in first class? Why would you think that?'

I shift awkwardly. 'I was told by my PR advisor that I might be approached by a journalist. Then you were asking lots of questions about my job the other night. And . . . then when I heard you talking about getting details out of me about the flight . . .'

'The only flight details I needed were from Delfina.'

'Delfina?'

'The Spanish lady with the clipboard. She's organised the whole trip, including a flight upgrade, so I needed details about the cost and schedules from the airline so I can include it in the piece.'

I swallow. 'Oh.'

'And I didn't mean to give you the third degree about your job. I was only making conversation. I was genuinely . . . interested.'

The word makes my temperature soar.

'I feel like an idiot.'

'Well, there's no need to on my account. And I should confess that I have done *some* work for a tabloid,' he says.

'Oh?'

'Work experience for one of the red-tops when I was seventeen. It involved sitting outside Delia Smith's house for three days, until someone pointed out that she was on a publicity tour of Scotland and had already been interviewed by the chief feature writer that morning.'

'Oh dear.'

'It was never really for me. Although I do have friends who work for some of the tabloids and I promise you, they're very nice people. Though I can see why you wouldn't want to meet them in a professional capacity.'

We spend the next few hours on the beach, chatting, sunbathing and soaking up the atmosphere.

Meredith and Nicola don't reappear and, for the first time since I arrived, I'm not in a rush to go after them. Or indeed anywhere. Because, and I can barely say this without squirming, being around Harry is an unmitigated pleasure.

Not just because he's funny, sweet and intelligent. Not just because he has hidden depths ranging from a passion for judo to a job that's seen him writing for everyone from *Vanity Fair* to *The Economist*. It's because the way he made me feel the other night – witty, warm, generally wonderful – wasn't a one-off. He's gone from intimidating me wildly to making me feel entirely comfortable in my own skin.

And everything I learn about him endears him to me. He was raised by a single mother after his father disappeared with another woman when he was seven, moved to Canada and has not shown the slightest interest in his son since. His mum never met anyone else – 'and never will, she's too set in her ways' – which is clearly why he's felt an increasing sense of responsibility towards her as he's grown older.

He is certain he wants to be a parent himself – 'partly to prove I'd do everything differently from my own dad' – but hasn't met the right woman.

'Nobody's ever come close?'

He thinks for a second. 'It's been a long time since I felt close to being in love.'

'Who was she?'

'There were two people. Samia Wallace, a fiery, clever psychotherapy student who introduced me to Moroccan food, F. Scott Fitzgerald and generally rocked my world. She was an older woman – nineteen when I was seventeen.'

'Hardly Mrs Robinson,' I say with a smile. 'What happened to her?'

'We had this intense, nine-month relationship, then I went to university in London, while she stayed in Aberdeen to continue studying.'

'So you met lots of attractive and clever bright young things and no longer had eyes for her?'

'No, I pined pitifully, wrote to her three times a day, then returned home to discover that she'd dumped me for her lecturer.'

'Oh, no!'

'A tale of woe, I know. And the second one, when I was twenty-two, isn't much better. Her name was Naomi Gillespie. She was without question the most beautiful woman I've ever been out with, if not set eyes on, before or since. We were together for three years before she left me for a Portuguese photographer and moved to Lisbon. They have two children now, and are sickeningly happy.'

'Shit.'

'I know. Still, I'm over it now. It's only taken ten years.' He grins.

'It's her loss. You're lovely,' I blurt out, regretting it instantly. 'Sorry, but I felt obliged to say that.'

He laughs. 'Well, it means a lot that you think so, so thank you. Although you don't really know me. I could be a brute.'

'True.' I mock-sigh. 'Are you?'

'No, you were right first time – I *am* lovely. My girlfriends just don't seem to realise it.'

'So, nobody since then?'

'I've dated lots of people but never had anyone serious. I have this ... problem.'

'Do I want to know this?' I mutter.

He laughs. 'It's nothing contagious, don't worry. I just mean ... I would absolutely love to meet someone and fall head over heels love. Someone I can't stop thinking about, someone who could blow my mind like when I was a teenager.

I smile. 'Have you ever read *Captain Corelli's Mandolin?*' I ask.

'Oh, that's a great book,' he says.

'There's a line in it, something like: "love is a temporary madness that erupts like volcanoes then subsides . . . and when it subsides you have to work out whether your roots are so entwined that it is inconceivable that you should ever part."'

'Now that is a brilliant quote,' he says. 'And it perfectly sums up my problem.'

'Your volcano won't erupt?'

He bursts out laughing again. 'I wouldn't have put it quite like that, but that's essentially it. And we're not talking about a *physical* malfunction here, incidentally. Just to be clear.'

'Of course not. I'm sure that's all functioning perfectly.'

'It is. Can we please end this metaphor now?' He grins. 'The point I'm making is this – any fool is supposed to be able to fall in love, it's *staying* in love that's meant to be the hard part. Well, I can't even manage the bit that any fool can. As much as I want that to happen, it never does. I'm starting to think I've become incapable of it.'

'How old are you again?'

'Thirty-two.'

'If you were ninety-two I might not argue with you, but come on. I'm sure you're totally capable. Perhaps you just want it so badly that it's affecting your judgment.'

'What do you mean?'

'Well, maybe every time you meet someone you're not just asking yourself, "Do I like this person enough to go out with her on another date?", so that you then simply relax and see where it goes. Instead, you're asking yourself, "Do I like this person enough to spend the rest of my life with her?" Nobody's ever that good. Falling in love instantly is just not possible. You have to let someone grow on you.'

'I'm not totally unrealistic. I agree that love at first sight is "just not possible".' He flashes me a look. 'But, fair enough, maybe there's something in the idea that I'm expecting too much, too soon. When did you become good at this stuff? Relationships, I mean?'

'Ironic, really,' I reply.

'Oh? What's the deal with your daughter's dad? Are you still together?'

'Oh, he and I …' I'm about to come out with my usual vague stuff that negates the requirement to reveal the complicated and hideous truth. Only I stop. And hear myself saying something that I've never confessed to a stranger before. 'No, we're not. Although I was completely in love with him.'

'So what happened?'

I close my eyes and in that split second of darkness, it comes back to me in a nauseating flash. The day that's a constant battle not to think about, a battle I usually lose.

*

I'd never seen Roberto in such a sharp state of excitement and anticipation. In all the time we'd been together, there was no gig we'd attended or football match he'd shouted at that had brought alive his face so much.

'You're sure you want to find out if it's a girl or boy?' he asked.

'Yes. No. Maybe. Oh ... sod it, yes. If I walk out of here without knowing, I'll be kicking myself for the next four and a half months.'

'Good. Because I need to know – yesterday.' He grinned, clutching my hand as we arrived at the hospital for my 20-week antenatal scan.

By the halfway point, my pregnancy had been going like a dream. I'd had minimal morning sickness, with little more than mild heartburn at the end of the day, and, despite Roberto and I trying to put a lid on our excitement until further along, we'd already procured sufficient amounts of baby paraphernalia to open a branch of Mothercare.

There was the traditional sleigh cot, the coordinating wardrobe and the urban 4x4 pram, the one with the suspension of a Lamborghini. That's before we got on to the bath, the thermometer, the bath thermometer ... and the endless other bits and bobs I'd never dreamt a tiny human being could require.

Roberto had even splashed out on a car – nothing fancy, just a runabout – on the grounds that, even in London, life with a newborn wouldn't be practical without one. The only thing we hadn't done was to decorate the nursery. We'd had the go-ahead from the landlord, but had reserved that job for after the scan.

My pregnancy had cemented my love for Roberto in ways I'd never predicted. I'd worried about whether he'd fancy me with a swollen belly, but he answered those fears by lavishing me with love and attention. Barely a week went by without him turning up with flowers and another gift for our growing baby.

He rubbed my feet when they were sore. He put me to bed when I was tired. He kissed my bump with such tenderness it sometimes made my heart want to burst out of my chest.

In those momentous twenty weeks, we'd gone from a state of elated shock to the most excited future parents possible. We made plans together. We dreamt together. Our future as a little family was all mapped out, and it couldn't have been brighter.

'How much did you have to drink before this scan?' he asked as I waddled in extreme discomfort towards the ante-natal department.

'A litre of water. It helps them get a clear view of the baby. They won't keep us waiting for too long,' I said, as they proceeded to keep us waiting for forty-five minutes, during which time my bladder expanded to the size of a blue whale, I came desperately close to peeing myself and had to hobble into the appointment room like a woman who'd taken a gunshot wound to both kneecaps. At which point I was informed that it was only the twelve-week scan for which I needed to drink that much and that, actually, my bladder was way too full to see anything anyway.

After I'd relieved myself and returned, the midwife got down to business. I'll never forget that ominous silence as the scanner slid across my belly and Roberto and I exchanged looks.

Her face gave away nothing as she scrutinised the image, examining every millimetre of our baby.

Eventually, Roberto couldn't stop himself from clearing his throat. 'Is everything all right?'

'Oh! Sorry, yes ... everything's fine,' said the midwife. 'I was concentrating on these measurements. Sorry if I went quiet. We have to get it exactly right, that's all. But, from this scan it appears you have a beautifully healthy baby.'

I didn't need to know what we were having after that. I'd forgotten all about that issue. All that mattered was that our child was okay.

'Do you want to know what the sex is?' she asked.

Roberto nodded. 'Yes, please.'

She looked up and smiled. 'We can never be one hundred per cent sure, but from what I can see, you're having a baby girl.'

I did a double take at Roberto as a small tear swam down his cheek. I'd never seen him crying before and the sight was as strange as it was beautiful.

As we walked to the car he repeated the same sentence, laughing, about five times. 'We're having a girl. We're having a little girl!'

The theme continued in the car as we drove home. I remember that much. The rest, however, is fuzzy.

They say shock can do that to you: you recall snippets of information about what happened immediately before, but lots of pieces of the jigsaw don't fit together.

The snippets I have retained are these: Norah Jones on the radio. Sunshine streaming through the clouds. A dog barking on the pavement. Two teenagers kissing at the bus stop. Roberto's fingers reaching for mine. A motorbike. A lorry. Screams.

Then nothing.

I've learned not to dwell *incessantly* on that day, simply because it slows everything down and makes life near-impossible; something I can't afford with a job, daughter and endless other responsibilities. It's still there all the time, of course, hovering in the background and ready to leap out on me every so often. But, most of the time, it's vaguely under control.

In the early days, though, I couldn't get it out of my head *at all*. It was all I thought about – to the detriment of everything else – all day, all night, while I was awake, and in my dreams.

My immediate priority when I woke in hospital was the

baby. Because, as my eyes flickered open, I immediately knew something was wrong.

It was dark outside. The bright lights above me made my head throb. My right leg was twisted – fractured in three places as I was informed later – my skin stung, and pain penetrated deep into my bones. I was battered and broken and I panicked.

In a clammy sweat, I tried and failed to sit up as I registered that Dad was next to me – I discovered later that Mum had popped out to get some tea. He looked pale and shaky and older than usual, but seeing me stir sent a wave of relief across his face.

My hands shot to my bump. 'The baby . . .'

'It's okay, sweetheart,' he told me, through trembling lips. 'Your baby's fine. The doctors checked while you were asleep. The baby's fine. You're fine.'

I didn't bloody feel fine, that was for sure.

He swallowed slowly and reached for my hand. 'Do you remember what happened?'

My head rushed with broken thoughts. 'I . . . I think so . . . I don't know. There was a lorry – it swerved to avoid a motor-bike. I . . . don't know.'

'It overturned,' he told me.

'Was the driver hurt?'

Dad nodded. 'The motorbike rider died.'

I filtered this fact, just about. 'God. We're lucky to be alive then.'

He nodded again. I looked around the room. 'Is Roberto on a different ward? I need to see him. Does he know the baby's okay? He'll be worried sick.'

I continued to talk. And talk. You know, sometimes, when you carry on talking even though you can tell from the look on someone's face that they're not listening and none of it matters anyway? Suddenly I could tell.

When I stopped speaking I realised I was crying, and so was Dad.

I struggle to describe the feeling I experienced in that moment, except to say that it was as if a great, big fist plunged into my chest and ripped out every tiny part of my heart.

'He's gone, isn't he?'

Dad looked down at his hands and it took all his strength to answer. 'He is.' He paused, trying to find the right words. 'It happened straight away. He didn't suffer.'

Later, in the months after Roberto's death, I would grieve quietly, but at that moment something primeval overtook me. My lungs expelled a sound that was terrible in every way: pure, loud *pain*; pain that was worse than anything physical I've experienced before or since.

Just thinking about it now, that raw disbelief and despair, makes my insides burn. I think it always will, whether it's five years on or fifty years on. Forgetting doesn't seem to be an option. And I don't think I want it to be.

Harry realises he's asked a difficult question – he knows it the second I lower my eyes. Yet, for some rare reason, I *want* to tell him about Roberto. I don't want to brush it under the carpet, not this time. 'He died.'

'Oh God,' he whispers. Only he doesn't do what other people do in this situation, the thing that's always made me reluctant to reveal this too quickly. He doesn't fall to pieces and start rabbiting about something else and make his excuses to leave. He doesn't squirm and bring up the weather and pray that I'll oblige by agreeing wholeheartedly that it's way too hot. He simply touches my arm. His hand feels nice there, and I'm glad of its presence. 'I'm so sorry, Imogen.'

I wonder for a second if he's going to ask any questions, then it strikes me that I don't actually need him to. 'It happened when I was pregnant with Florence. It was a car crash.'

'I can't imagine what that was like for you.'

'I've never got used to losing him.' I glance up, wondering if I should feel self-conscious. 'I'm sorry. Here's you making small talk, and I'm filling you in on the great tragedy of my life.'

'Don't be silly. I'd rather hoped we were beyond small talk by now.'

A smile flickers to my lips. 'I suppose we are.'

'So talk. If you want to.'

And I do.

It doesn't feel uncomfortable; it feels good, solid and

cathartic. I feel proud to tell him about Roberto and absolutely no need to hold back.

'He sounds like an incredible man,' he says finally.

'He was,' I reply. Then my phone rings. I look at the screen and my heart plummets. 'Excuse me, Harry. I'd better take this.'

After a day littered with phone calls, I feel numb while talking to Charles. In fact, I feel numb to this entire situation. I step away from the sun bed and go through the motions of updating him, and vice versa.

He has a quote ready for the follow-up pieces in tomorrow's press. I can't see how anything can be worse than those in today's press so authorise them, and end the call with a sigh before returning to Harry.

'I need to go to the business centre to look over a media statement,' I tell him.

'Aren't you supposed to be off-duty when you're on holiday?' he replies, helping me gather my things. 'Or is yours one of those companies where you have to sign your name in blood on your first day?'

'It's not usually the latter, although I'm beginning to wonder this week. I'm totally out of my depth at the moment.'

He starts walking me to the door of the hotel. 'Everyone feels like that in a new job. I don't know how you cope on your own, with a young daughter on top of it all. Most people's stress levels would be sky high. And living in London can't help.'

'It's not London's fault,' I say quickly, used to defending the place against my mother's views. 'I love the place. I could never live anywhere else.'

'Hmm,' he says.

'You don't agree?'

'Actually, I love the place too. I'm just in denial.'

'Because of your move?'

He nods as he holds the door to the lobby open for me. 'But it's the right thing to do, even if my mum's now feeling so bad about me moving back that she virtually begged me not to when I spoke to her last night.'

'You sure she actually wants you?'

He laughs. 'Quite sure. She just doesn't want to feel like she's making me do something that isn't right for me. But it is right, I know it is. She's had a tough time lately and she needs me whether she's trying to hide it or not.'

'What happened, if you don't mind my asking?'

'She was made redundant from her job as a care home manager. She'd been there for years and it really hit her hard – she became quite depressed and was struggling for money. She then got a new job but was overcome by anxiety about starting it. She hadn't started a new job in twenty-five years.'

'Has it got any better?'

'So she says.'

'You think she's just putting on a front?'

He nods.

'So you just want to be there for support, really?'

'I think it's the least I can do. Still, shame we can't meet up after this trip, eh?' he adds, with uncharacteristic hesitancy.

I don't manage to find an answer as we arrive at the lift and the doors open.

'Well, hopefully I'll see you later,' he says.

And for a short, misguided moment, I want him to kiss me. Like at the end of a date. Because in a small way, that's what today felt like. Despite the interruptions. Despite the circumstances. Despite everything.

I allow myself to look fleetingly into his eyes as I consider the vague possibility that he might be thinking the same. But he simply smiles and starts backing away. Disappointment rises in my throat.

'Oh ... Imogen?' he says.

'Yes?'

'Are you around later?'

'Yes, I guess so.'

'Why don't we meet for a drink?'

I nod, not feeling as nonchalant as I hope I look. 'That'd be nice.'

'How's 8.30 at that little beach bar opposite the sailing club?'

'Great. See you then.' I smile, turn to the lift and step in.

The doors are about to close when someone slams on the button and they spring open again.

'I meant to say . . .' Harry begins.

'Yes?'

'I think you're lovely too.'

Chapter 35

Under normal circumstances I wouldn't be able to stop thinking about 8.30 p.m. But these are not normal circumstances, because this is my life and nothing in my life is normal. Even on holiday, when I'm trying to switch off.

Determined to get out and about to see more of Barcelona, Meredith, Nicola and I head to the Museu Nacional d'Art de Catalunya. It's described in my guidebook as 'a one-stop immersion course on the world of Catalan art, from medieval church frescoes to chairs designed by Gaudí.'

Nobody could ever accuse me of being an art enthusiast. I realise I run the risk of being seen as a philistine by saying that, but quite often when something is supposed to stir every corner of one's soul, I'm left completely cold.

I do books. I do music. I've even been to two operas, although admittedly that was in a fruitless attempt to impress Roberto's mum. But when I hear people enthusing about works of art – even proper ones that don't involve unmade beds – I never quite *get* it. Which obviously never stops me nodding sagely in fervant appreciation. I don't want to look completely thick.

Still, I need to do some sightseeing, or I'll leave Barcelona having experienced only the same level of culture as if I'd spent the week in a high street establishment called Tanerife.

The experience, however, is far from the promised 'immersion course', as the only thing in which I'm immersed is other people's problems.

'Imogen, I am beside myself after yesterday,' Carmel, David's wife, tells me on the phone as I peer at something I'm reliably informed is Romanesque. It's very agreeable, although I wouldn't have one at home. 'You don't mind me phoning, do you?' she continues, failing to pause for me to respond.

I've never considered us friends before: our acquaintance stems solely from the manifold social functions at which I've been seated next to her. But that doesn't stop her now.

'I am *furious* with David. *Fucking* furious. And, by the way, I *never* use the f-word, so this gives you a measure of how furious I am. I've just said it to the postman too. He dropped his bag in a puddle.'

I don't doubt that Carmel has never used the f-word. Everything about her is refined and sophisticated, from her cashmere wardrobe to the dinner parties accomplished enough to make Marco Pierre White hang up his apron. She was a midwife at an exclusive, private hospital before she met and married David, although it's impossible to imagine her ever doing a job that involves quite so much mess. I saw her at 4.30 a.m. a couple of months ago, having picked her and David up from the airport to accompany him straight to a board meeting. Unlike the heap of a human being I represented at that ungodly hour, she was fragrant and angelic, with not so much as a crease in her Jaeger slacks.

'It was a ridiculous mistake. I think David would be the first to admit that,' I say, trying to be diplomatic, but conscious that my first loyalty has to be to my boss, arse that he is.

'Ridiculous is one word. Treacherous. Reckless. Idiotic. *Fucking* idiotic. There. He's made me say it again. Dear God, he's turning me into Billy Connolly,' she laments.

'How are the children?' I venture. I don't know why I still refer to Michael and Lydia as 'the children' – as if I'm about to give them 50p for an ice cream – when one is sixteen and the other has just finished her A levels.

'Oh, don't ask.' She exhales.

'Okay, well—'

'Lydia has gone out and spent a fortune on new shoes in case she's "papped", whatever that means, and Michael has been sitting in front of the television, refusing to move, for almost twenty-four hours now.'

'He does that quite a lot anyway, doesn't he?'

'Yes, but there's an insidious glaze in his eyes now. And he's watching *This Morning*. It's extremely unsettling.'

I open my mouth to speak, but she's on a roll. 'David has jeopardised his career for this, Imogen. And it's not like he can claim his requirements weren't being fulfilled at home. The man is *unstoppable* in the bedroom, a fact for which I've had to make considerable sacrifices, let me tell you.'

I urgently want her to stop talking now.

'He's *bent,*' she reveals. 'You know, *down there*. Like Bill Clinton. And I'd probably have preferred to service *him* for the last thirty-four years rather than David, let me tell you. At least I'd have got a decent wardrobe and some world travel out of it.'

Nicola taps me on the shoulder in an attempt to point out some wondrous piece of work, but I simply nod and press on with the call.

'Have the media tried to get hold of you?' I ask.

'They're camped outside here now.'

'God, *really?*' My hand flies to my mouth. 'Are you trapped in there? Have you said anything to them?'

'Of course! I offered them bacon sandwiches and told them if they were expecting us to come out and do the loyal-wife-and-husband bit, they would be inordinately disappointed.'

'You said that?' I groan inwardly and make a mental note to warn Charles Blackman of this new source of angst.

'I did, but they don't believe me that he's not here. They obviously think I'm hiding him in the airing cupboard. Not that I'd let him near my bed linen these days, the grubby . . .

fucker.' The last word bungee jumps out of her mouth as if it's the most liberating thing she's ever uttered.

I move through to the next room, trying to keep up with Nic and Meredith as they weave through the crowds. 'Dare I ask if you've spoken to him recently?'

'No, that's what I'm phoning you for.'

'Me?'

'Yes. There's no reception at Great Aunt Janice's caravan. I've tried texting him, but he's obviously either ignoring me or there isn't a signal.'

'How do I fit in?'

'I need you to pass on an extremely important message to him next time he phones you. Because I know he'll phone you. He phones you more than he phones me.'

My head starts to throb again. 'Okay.'

'It's very important that you pass this on word for word, direct from me.'

'Er . . . okay, let me get a bit of paper. I want to make sure I get everything down right.'

I open my purse and remove an old receipt as I squeeze past the elderly German tour group in front of me and find the one and only free spot in the gallery.

'Okay. Fire away.'

She clears her throat extravagantly. 'David. *Fuck* you.'

Chapter 36

My phone does not stop for the rest of the afternoon and into the evening. The only respite I get is on the metro, where there's no reception. So joyous is the experience that, if it weren't for the raging heat in here, I'd consider staying on it and looping the city until morning.

When we emerge up the escalator into blinding sunshine, more talks follow with Charles, who is trying to find out what the press is intending to quote Carmel as saying in tomorrow's papers. He also tells me that they got David's name from a police press officer.

There are calls from a variety of radio stations, who seem to have acquired my number from the *Afternoon* programme, and who are phoning to see if I have anything to add. I direct them to Charles, who is at least capable of opening his mouth without some anatomical colloquialism spilling out.

There's a call from Elsa at work, begging me to think of some way she can help me. God love her, it's an offer I'd love to take her up on if she didn't work in Accounts and would be the first to admit she wouldn't recognise a crisis management strategy if it hit her in the face.

And finally there's David, who phones as I'm traipsing wearily back to the hotel, resigned to the fact that, while I can technically tick the Museu Nacional d'Art de Catalunya off my sightseeing list, I'm not convinced I actually *saw* much of it.

'I'm in a phone box,' he announces. 'The reception here is terrible but, on the plus side, I'm very isolated. I think the only way to handle this is to pretend it's not happening.'

'How are you feeling?'

He draws in a long breath. 'I feel like I'm in that film *The Road*. You know, post-apocalyptic, but with a certain weary dignity.'

'You haven't seen the papers then?'

'I'm not even looking. I'm just going to stay here, keep my head down and emerge when the new parliament opens.'

'The new parliament?'

'Charles tells me that August is silly season for the news industry. The press has nothing to write about because all the politicians are away in Carcassonne or wherever for the summer, so all I need to do is wait until next week when Cameron and his crew are back. They're bound to do something stupid enough to knock me off the pages of the tabloids.'

I note the use of the word 'me'.

'You know they've printed your name, then?'

'It was inevitable.'

'Have you had any contact with anyone from Getreide about this yet? I ask.

'Yes, and it's safe to say they're re-considering their position.'

'You mean the whole merger could be off?' I ask.

'It wouldn't surprise me. The point is ... The point is I don't care any more,' he wheezes. 'Clearly I'm not saying that to the board, but it's true. You know what I always say in situations like this, don't you, Imogen? Be real. Be cool. *Be yourself.*'

'Hmm,' I manage.

'Why aren't you saying anything? Oh God, is it the papers? Tell me! Are they awful?'

'No! I mean ... I heard from Carmel earlier,' I prattle.

'I don't think she's very happy with me,' he says dolefully. 'I'm getting that distinct impression.'

'She might come around.'

'The last text she sent instructed me to trap my knob in the caravan door. I haven't responded. What did she say to you?'

'Um ... it was a similar theme.'

'I'm hoping she'll come around. I think she needs a good holiday, if I'm entirely honest. I suspect we all do, eh?' He laughs.

I end the call before I say something I might regret.

Chapter 37

I start to get ready as soon as Meredith and Nicola leave for dinner, an hour before I'm due to meet Harry. I'm confident that that'll be plenty of time. But, shortly after stepping into the shower, there's a call from my gas supplier asking me if I've considered having my loft insulated; as I'm curling my hair, someone else phones asking if I've been mis-sold PPI; as I slip on my dress, the dry cleaner phones, threatening to incinerate a skirt I dropped off in 2011 and forgot to pick up. This, of course, is apart from Charles and David, both of whom seem incapable of allowing an hour to pass without hearing the sound of my voice.

It'd be sweet if I wasn't teetering on the verge of a nervous breakdown.

In short, as the time slips by and I make strenuous efforts to glam up without the aid of Meredith and her beauty emporium, my phone seems determined to scupper every tiny step, from applying foundation to spraying on perfume and applying my now well-worn concealer stick to my eye.

Some of the calls are quick (Wi-Fi provider call-centre worker: 'Is that Imogen Copeland?' Me: 'No.'); others, such as that from Charles, are not. And as I'm pacing around, performing a veritable circus act of multitasking – inserting earrings and applying mascara with my phone wedged in my shoulder – I'm aware that the clock is ticking without needing to actually look at it.

Finally, when I am 85 per cent ready and therefore as ready as I'll ever be, and I'm about to throw my bloody phone into the bin, it rings again.

My hand hesitates over it, willing myself to leave it. Except it's Mum and, therefore, while I'm 99.9 per cent certain it won't be a genuine emergency involving Florence, the 0.1 per cent possibility wins the day.

'You won't be aware of this because you're away,' she begins, 'but your company has been all over the news.'

'Really?' I drawl, frantically surveying the room for my key card.

'Well, you told me to only phone you when it was an emergency. I don't suppose there's anything you can do about it from there, but I thought you'd want to know. That boss of yours is an absolute pervert.'

'He's not a . . . yes, I suppose he is.'

'You've not done something like that on one of your business trips, have you?' she adds.

'Mum, it's not company policy.'

'Because, old-fashioned as it sounds, Imogen, a girl has to keep her reputation. It doesn't matter what you're up to behind the scenes, but you can't do that sort of thing *publicly*.'

'I'm not doing that sort of thing privately or publicly!'

'You know I'm no prude, but you've got to have some class about these things. If there was one thing my time in the Moulin Rouge taught me, it was that.'

I sigh. 'Is this what you've phoned to tell me, Mum?'

'I thought you'd want to know about the papers, that's all.'

'Thank you. Seriously.' I always add that word when I'm in danger of sounding disingenuous. Mum gets it a lot. 'If that's all, I've got to go.'

'Oh, did you—'

I put down the phone, grab my key card and am about to leave the room, when for the first time since I entered it, I get a proper look at the clock.

My breath feels as though it's being sucked out of my lungs. I'd realised I was under pressure for time, but I'd been oblivious to the extent.

It's 9.15 p.m.

I've stood him up. I've actually gone and stood him up.

Running in 31-degree heat is difficult. So is running in Meredith's shoes, the ones that never actually fitted me in the first place. This cocktail of challenges becomes even trickier when you're dodging a group of lackadaisical pensioners, a rollerblader with a death wish and three blokes carrying canoes that are each the length of an Orient-Express carriage.

'Excuse me!' I pipe up, to no avail.

I pull up from my frantic dash right behind them. 'Excuse me! *Con permiso!*' I try, and they turn round simultaneously, at which point I realise my error.

I attempt to dart as if dodging a bullet, but fail to move with sufficient speed to avoid being thumped on the temple with the hard edge of the vessel. I am propelled off the boardwalk and land face-down on the beach, marinating my tonsils in sand.

'Sorry! Sorry!' The owner of the canoe, who looks to be in his fifties, drops his boat and rushes to my aid.

'It's fine!' I spit dirt out of my mouth as I spot my opportunity and leap up, pull off my shoes and attempt to sprint across the sand, a surface that proves about as suitable for the task as a tray of freshly made toffee.

With sweat snaking down my face and the wind howling into my meticulously tousled hair, I turn the corner to the beach bar with a racing heart and scan the tables.

There are couples, families, groups of friends. But not Harry.

I crumple with disappointment as several facts become apparent. I actually liked this man. I fancied him. I enjoyed his company. *I wanted something to happen between us.*

For most women this would be no a big deal, these commonplace bubbles of attraction that, with no opportunity to grow, will simply float away and be forgotten. But for me there's nothing commonplace about meeting someone I like. Until this week, I believed 100 per cent that when Roberto died, a light bulb shattered inside me that could never be pieced together.

Only, it appears that it has been. And I appear to have stood up the man who made that happen.

I gaze out to sea, wondering what Harry must make of this. I am unable to decide whether he'll be in his hotel room weeping into his sangria, or sticking pins in a voodoo doll. Both scenarios make me feel horrible.

But not quite as horrible, it turns out, as the reality.

As I'm turning to leave I spot them, on the beach together, looking like something from a late 1990s Davidoff advert.

It's Harry and Clipboard Barbie. They're in each other's arms.

Chapter 38

A small part of me tries to look on the bright side. My hair is matted with sand and sweat and, I discover, when I catch a glimpse of my reflection in the window of a Seat Ibiza, I've managed to rub mascara down my cheek, enhancing the jaundice-yellow effect of my black eye.

I slump back to the hotel, desperate to talk this through with the girls, only to discover texts saying that Nicola has gone to bed with a migraine and Meredith, having had another exchange with Nathan about coming away in her third trimester, is sampling some local hotspot with the waiter she met on the first night.

The thought of being in the hotel room with a ringing phone all night is too much to bear, so I do what seems to work for all dejected women in the movies and order a Scotch on the rocks while I perch at the bar, wondering if a friendly-and-wise bar-tender will invite me to share my troubles.

In fact, it's a woman who serves me, and she doesn't seem

inclined to stretch her job description beyond slapping my glass down on a coaster in front of me.

'It is you! The very beautiful Eenglish lady! May I join you?'

It's the guy from Florence – he who is fond of wanking.

I muster up a smile. 'Why not?'

'Are you having a stimulating time so far?' he asks, climbing onto the stool next to me.

He's sweet, if a little lacking in the English department. Not that my Italian's great (and as someone who lived with an Italian, I've got absolutely no excuse).

'Very stimulating, thank you,' I say, suddenly horribly aware of my appearance. I rake through my hair with my fingers, but it's like trying to groom an Old English Sheepdog with a dessert fork. 'Are you?'

'Yes, although I am looking forward to going to Firenze again. I miss the pussy,' he explains mournfully.

I blink. 'Oh.'

'Yes, everywhere I look here, there is beautiful pussy, wanking in the street, or the beach. It reminds me of my baby at home. You want to see?'

He holds out his mobile phone and shows me a picture of a ginger cat.

'That *is* a beautiful pussy,' I agree.

'I know,' he replies. Then his eyes soften. He leans towards me and whispers something in my ear. I can't quite hear it.

'What did you say?' I say with a smile, pulling back.

'I say, you are beautiful, too.'

I suddenly feel quite hot.

My increase in body temperature isn't because I'm attracted to this person. I'm fairly certain I'm not. He's far too young for me, the language barrier is disastrous and, although he's got all his bits in the right places, I find him oddly unsexy. Yet, as he leans forward to kiss me, I consider not moving away.

I can't pinpoint why, beyond an unsettling neediness after I'd finally got my head around the idea of fancying a man, only to have him snatched away into the arms of Clipboard Barbie. And so, some deep, dark part of my brain thinks about closing my eyes, just to see what happens. I contemplate each of these thoughts as I sit, otherwise immobile, fixated on the Italian's nose as it inches so close I am almost cross-eyed.

Then something – Fate, providence, a jolt of uncertainty about whether I brushed my teeth – makes me glance up.

Harry is standing at the door, looking right at me.

Our eyes meet briefly.

As he turns on his heel and marches away, all these feelings fall away. I spill my untouched Scotch as I pull away from the Italian and run after him.

Chapter 39

Harry steps into the lift before I reach him and the doors close quickly. I stand and watch in dismay as it ascends to the eighteenth floor before the adjacent lift arrives and I press the 'Up' button.

When it arrives at my destination, I step out tentatively into an empty corridor. Vertigo hits me in a wave as I creep along the carpet past a window so high up I feel suffocated by the clouds. Nor is this the only problem. There are ten doors stretching in front of me, and therefore ten possible places into which Harry has disappeared.

I knock on the first door and wait with my heart pounding in my throat, until it becomes evident that nobody's going to answer. I edge towards the one next to it and do the same.

It swings open and I am confronted by Yellow Bikini Lady, wearing an unfeasibly short neon-pink kimono and a lavish strip of bleach on her upper lip.

I back away apologetically before I knock on the third door, which is opened by a man who'd make such a perfect James Bond villain I half expect to peer around him and see sharks swimming under a see-through floor.

I mumble apologies before crossing the corridor to the fourth door. I knock. And . . . it's him.

I take in the indecipherable look his eyes and experience a surge of attraction that nearly knocks me off my feet, followed by the realisation of how hurt I am. How bewildered. Feelings I honestly don't know how to react to, not when I'm catastrophically out of practice.

I cross my arms. 'You went off with Clipboard Barbie!'

He crosses *his* arms. 'You stood me up!'

'I – I didn't,' I stammer. 'I was running late!'

'By forty-five minutes? How long did you expect me to wait?'

'So if I'd been there twenty minutes sooner, you wouldn't have had your tongue down Clipboard Barbie's throat?' I realise I am shaking so hard I tighten my knotted arms in a bid to disguise it.

'*Who* is Clipboard Barbie? And I didn't have my tongue down *anyone's* throat.'

I'm about to answer when Yellow Bikini Lady's man emerges from their room and pelts us with a stream of machine-gun Russian that would appear to indicate he's not overly happy about being a party to this conversation.

I freeze and apologise, imagining that I'm now on some list

that his gang of mafia chums use to regularly replenish their fish-food collection.

'Look, why don't you come in,' Harry says to me grudgingly.

I don't need to be asked twice. I dive in, shut the door behind me and thrust my back against it.

I look around and am lost for words.

The similarities to my room start and finish with the contemporary furniture, plush carpets and massive mirrors. Other than that, I could be on a different planet. It is four times the size of mine. There is a Jacuzzi, 180-degree views of Barcelona and the Mediterranean and a *champagne bar*. A great big thing, bang in the middle of the wall, stocked with enough fizz to supply a royal wedding.

'Is this what I think it is?' I pick up a bottle and peer at the label.

'Can you answer my question?'

'You've got a champagne bar and you didn't even pay for this yourself? And there we were, getting all of a quiver about a loo-roll light . . .'

He frowns at me, then his face softens.

And I suddenly wish I wasn't here in this room in these circumstances. I wish I was here at the end of our date, if it ever was one.

I realise that what I'd been hoping for was to flirt all night, dance a bit, then smooch on the beach before rolling up here a bit tipsy and touchy-feely and . . . oh God.

Do I want to have sex with this man?

I remind myself what I've just witnessed. 'I'm referring to the woman organising your tour,' I say.

'Delfina?'

'I went to meet you where we arranged and saw you on the beach. In each other's arms.'

'It wasn't what you think,' he says calmly.

'Oh?' I purse my lips to underline my indignation.

'She's lost her job.'

My lips unpurse. 'Oh.'

'Despite appearances, the recession has hit this place hard and they're cutting back on their marketing spend next year. So this is her last assignment. You know how fragile Spain's economy is at the moment – and she's the only one in her family with a job.'

I bite my lip.

'At least she was. Her brother is a shop assistant and has been made redundant …' I bite a nail. 'And her elderly mother – who has cancer – can't afford the rent on her apartment so is about to be thrown out.'

My jaw is now open. 'Oh God, please tell me there's no more.'

'Well, her other brother has cerebral palsy, her fiancé recently dumped her and …'

'STOP! Please stop.'

'… and she broke her toe at the Camp Nou stadium.'

I look in the direction of the window. It's not the altitude that's making my head do the breaststroke now. It strikes me that not only do I have no evidence that he's a philanderer, but everything points instead to him simply being a nice man.

'She just needed someone to talk to, that's all,' he adds.

I sigh. 'I am the worst person in the world.'

'I doubt that. But you did jump to conclusions.'

This sentence hits me like a tidal wave. I remind myself that all he did was ask me for a drink, yet I've walked in here throwing accusations at him as though we're betrothed.

Mortification overwhelms me. He must think I'm a bunny boiler, whereas the plain truth is that I'm so hopelessly unused to dealing with this sort of thing I feel like some dippy work-experience girl who can't manage a bit of light stapling without falling to pieces.

'You're totally right,' I mumble. 'I think I'd better go.'

He hesitates, as if he's about to say something, but simply nods. 'I understand.'

I'd rather hoped he'd protest, grab me gently by the arm and tell me that he really, really wanted me to stay. I turn to leave.

'I did see that you'd found someone else.' He shrugs as I turn back. 'These things happen. Enjoy the rest of your evening.'

His words filter through my brain and I realise what he's talking about. 'Oh ... the Italian? No. He's not for me. Honestly.' I consider telling him he's a self-confessed wanker, but I stop myself. 'The thing is ...'

I don't even know how I'm going to finish the sentence when my phone rings. I realise I've had the sound turned on low, so it's only quiet, but once I'm aware of the noise, it's all I can hear.

I stand immobile, telling myself I'm not going to answer it. I *can* ignore this phone, I absolutely can. It's my choice, after all!

And if I don't, then maybe, just maybe, Harry will reach out and pull me into a *Casablanca*-style embrace, gifting me that kiss I'm only now realising how desperately I want.

The problem is, it keeps ringing. And ringing. And ringing.

I grab it from my bag and answer it with the sort of force you'd use to poke your worst enemy in the eye.

'David's sent me a text message,' begins Carmel, as my heart sinks.

I pace in small circles as she tells me she's consulted a divorce lawyer who's informed her she's entitled to the house, the yacht, the two dogs and obviously the children. She's decided she'll let him have the rabbit.

I try desperately to get rid of her, but it takes a good five minutes and only then because I tell her there's a bomb scare and I'm off to take cover in the wet room.

I end the call and look at Harry through anxious eyes. 'As I was saying ...'

My phone rings again which, judging by the calls I've missed, it's been doing for a while. I hesitate, ignoring it for an infinitesimal moment before caving in.

It's David. He tells me he's still refusing to buy the papers but has heard an outlandish rumour about a quote I gave on the radio, but I'm not to worry as he knows I'd never say such a thing.

The next call is from Cosimo, who's still in Buenos Aires but has heard that the story's out because a friend of his 'Liked' a link to it on Facebook.

There follows another message from my mother, this time to inform me that when she tucked Florence into bed, she noticed she's burping a lot and feels I should insist the GP refers her to a gastrointestinal specialist as soon as I'm home.

I pause for breath during a momentary ceasefire in the calls and realise Harry is looking at me, torn between astonishment and pity. 'Is this what your life is always like?'

'Not all the time,' I mumble, then wonder why I'm lying. 'Yes.'

'Even on holiday?'

I plonk down on the edge of the bed and put my head in my hands as blood rushes to my face. 'Yes.'

I am vaguely aware of him crossing the room to the champagne bar. I hear the pop before he turns round and, even without confirmation of its source, it's the most wonderful of sounds – crisp and resonant, full of promise . . . I look up and he's pouring two glasses.

'Is this all paid for?' I'm not sure I could accept it after doing Delfina such a disservice.

'No, this one's on me. It's absolutely necessary. Medicinal, in fact.'

He sits next to me and places a glass into my hand as I find myself looking at his knees again, just the outline of them through his stone-coloured trousers. I can't remember ever being quite so taken with a man's knees before. 'This is no way to live,' he tells me.

'I know. I've actually started to hate my phone. I mean properly *hate* it. I'm no technophobe, but part of me misses the world before texts and 4G and all that malarkey. It doesn't seem to have enhanced much, not in my life, anyway.'

He shrugs. 'I actually love my phone, and my tablet, and my MacBook and all those other things. I do miss letters, though. Proper ones, on paper.'

'Oh God, so do I! Nobody writes letters these days, do they?'

He shakes his head. 'There was something in *The Times* the other week saying that the love letter has been virtually obliterated by text and instant messaging.'

I tut. 'Both have their place, but it hardly compares. There is nothing like a bona-fide, bells-and-whistles love letter.'

He grins. 'All this technology wouldn't have done for Lord Byron, that's for sure.'

I take a sip of the champagne, feeling its tiny, exquisite bubbles disintegrate on my tongue.

His closeness feels intoxicating and I experience a surge of pleasure just looking at him. I am bursting with lust, every bit of me wanting this man to lean over and kiss me.

His face moves towards mine and I realise that *this is it*. The first man I'm going to kiss in five years. My pulse thunders in my ears as I feel the softness of his breath against my skin and I lower my glass onto my lap to stop my hand trembling.

My phone rings. The spell is broken.

I go to answer it when Harry grabs my hand, preventing me from reaching it. The grip of his fingers on my skin makes my heart race again.

'What would happen if you turned it off?' he asks, his expression serious.

'I . . . I couldn't.'

'Why not?'

'I . . . because, honestly, Harry . . .' I squirm. 'There's so much going on at the moment and—'

'But you're on *holiday*. Being good at your job, or being a good mother or daughter . . . it doesn't mean you can't have a life.'

The phone's ring seems to become louder and more urgent.

'Seriously,' he says, 'what would happen if you turned it off? For . . . I don't know – let's say twelve hours. That's all.'

I blush at the question, wondering if he's suggesting I could spend the next twelve hours with him. 'I . . . I don't know.'

'You do know. You know that *nothing* would happen. They'd all just have to get on with things all by themselves. To stop relying on you constantly, and use their own brains. It'd do them all good.'

I pause for a second. I actually *don't* think he's right. Then I do. Then I suddenly don't care if he is or isn't. I decide to stop thinking. Because all I want in my head is not work, or my mother, or the dentist or any other bloody thing except the thought of kissing this man.

I pick up the phone and recognise Elsa's number as it rings off. Then, clutching it between both my hands, for the very first time since I got here, I press 'Off'.

I inhale woozily and take a large mouthful of champagne. 'What now?'

He doesn't answer with words. He takes my glass from me and puts it on the table beside us, before cupping my face in his hands and kissing me as the world around us tumbles into silence.

Chapter 40

I am having sex! I AM HAVING SEX!

Those four words flutter through my head, over and over again, until I'm cheering internally so loudly I can barely think.

It is quite simply a mind-blowing and monumental thought that I (yes, me, *me*, ME!) am doing what everyone all around the world does, but I haven't for so long that it wouldn't have been a shock if my lady bits had rusted up.

Strictly speaking, we're still at the foreplay bit, despite hours having passed since my first item of clothing slipped to the floor but, as you can imagine, that's nothing to complain about. Not when I'm busy contemplating the swell of his buttocks against the palm of my hand; his mouth on my breasts as I arch my back, alive with desire.

Desire. I'd almost forgotten its existence, considered it virtually extinct. But, here it is, exploding into my life in the form of this man, naked and godlike, whose hand is buried between my legs as I groan with pleasure and part them without hesitation. I am drunk on passion as much as the champagne, which I've downed enthusiastically all night, although not so much that I can't enjoy every second of this.

I have never felt so bad in such a joyful way. Not for a moment am I embarrassed to be naked. I wanted him to peel off my underwear and bury his head into my neck as his hands went on a voyage of discovery over my skin. And I wanted him naked too, even if heat shot up my neck when I saw him towering above me as he kicked off his underwear and rolled me into the bed, our legs entwining and his lips meeting mine.

His kisses have been interspersed with the sweetest whispers, odes to my gorgeousness that sound beautifully dirty when applied to the bits of me to which he's referring. I feel worshipped and I feel wonderful. And, as his kisses become more passionate, I hear myself vocalising the need I've had since the first moment our lips met – a need that hasn't abated despite the fact that I've come twice already.

'Have you got a condom?' I whisper.

He gazes into my eyes and nods, pressing his lips against mine before he gets up. I try not to gawp. I lie back and pull the smooth, cotton sheets over my body as he finds his wallet and rips open the packet.

I am tingling as he approaches, my insides aching for him. He begins by kissing me again as he moves to be on top, caressing me as I nuzzle my face into his neck, so breathless and hot that it's almost to my own surprise that I take matters into my own hands.

My fingers trace the small of his back as I wriggle closer to him. He gazes into my eyes as I push him slowly inside me and groan with intense pleasure.

Afterwards, I feel like I've taken a happy pill, tiptoed through fairy dust and pranced across meadows singing 'The Hills Are Alive'.

'I don't know what's come over me.' I shake my head as I loll in the Jacuzzi, fuzzy from champagne and post-coital delirium. 'I never do this sort of thing.'

He laughs and leans in to kiss me on the cheek. 'You mean you haven't got a Jacuzzi in that flat of yours in Wandsworth?'

'No, but I think I'm going to have to get one.' I grin, feeling more smug than I'd thought possible. 'I'm now convinced that these things are the main reason celebrities get into so much trouble.'

'What, Jacuzzis? As opposed to appalling judgment and reckless levels of testosterone?'

'Absolutely. You simply can't have a Jacuzzi in a bedroom and *not* get it on with someone.'

He smirks. 'Though as I recall, you didn't need the Jacuzzi for encouragement.'

'No,' I splutter with laughter, 'I didn't, did I?'

He puts down his glass and edges towards me, putting his

big arms around me. His naked skin is slippery against mine and sends a rush of heat through me. 'I'm glad you enjoyed it.' He swallows, looking momentarily vulnerable. Then he reaches over and brushes a hair out of my face, decisive again. 'I think you're amazing, Imogen,' he says simply.

'Oh, give over,' I reply, rolling my eyes. The more I've got to know Harry this week, the more my view that he must be a raging lothario has shifted. But I refuse to believe this is anything other than Instagram Eyes, caused by the sex, the alcohol, and him wanting a bit more of both.

'I'm serious.'

For a fleeting moment, I believe him. But I do so in the realisation that it's only because I *want* to believe him.

I look down at my glass. 'You know, this has been the first time since . . .' I can't bring myself to finish the sentence.

'Since Roberto?'

I nod.

'That must have felt strange.'

I shrug.

'Well,' he begins, formulating his thoughts. 'I want you to know that I'm honoured that I was the one you chose.'

I reply with a smile, but it's a forced one this time. Because the reminder about why it's been such a long time since I did this intimate, intense thing chills the blood in my veins.

Suddenly, I feel as though everything's changed. I look down and try to push various unpleasant thoughts out of my head. Then I throw back the last of the champagne and wonder what to say.

'I'd better get out. My fingers are shrivelling up.'

It's gone 3 a.m. and I plummet into sleep surprisingly quickly, my final thoughts registering only how strange it feels to have a man's arms around me in bed. I'm so used to sprawling out in the middle, alone and unfettered, that it takes a moment to get used to the protective warmth of human contact.

But that's not the whole story. Although exhaustion drags me towards dreams, they're unsettled from the beginning. I wake several times during the night, before registering where I am and pushing away consciousness again.

As dawn creeps into the room, the events being played out in my head become increasingly distressing. I drift in and out of thoughts about Roberto until, finally, as sunlight shears through the cracks of the hastily drawn curtains, they turn to his funeral.

The last time I'd been on a plane to Florence, Roberto had been sitting in the seat next to mine. This time, I was buffered either side by my mum and dad.

'Do you want some Bach's Rescue Remedy?' Mum leant over and asked, scrunching up her nose. 'I think you could do with some.'

I shook my head without looking at her. I couldn't. I hadn't been able to look at anyone for days because every time I did I crumpled into a heap of tears. I wasn't crying now, but was simply in the grip of a sharp, acute grief, one that tore up my stomach and wouldn't allow my hands to stop trembling.

I closed my eyes and cradled my bump as I felt the soft thuds of our baby's first kicks under my palms. It should've been a moment of unrestrained joy; instead, I was swamped with the ugly realisation that Roberto would never feel those kicks, surely the most fundamental of paternal rights.

In truth, that was the least of it. Roberto would never be able to do *anything*. Swim in the Indian Ocean. Climb Kilimanjaro. Kiss me in the morning as he stepped out to work.

We only stayed in Florence for two days, partly because I knew I wouldn't be able to bear any longer than that. The funeral, I'm sorry to say, provided no comfort at all. You know how some funerals are beautiful, a celebration of someone's life? Roberto's wasn't. It was organised by his mother, and was a very obvious reflection of the fact that she didn't know her son very well at all.

It took place in a small, dark church in a remote village outside the city. The music was turgid. And, although three of his friends from London had flown over – the others sent cards and flowers in their dozens – I got the impression the ceremony was largely full of people he'd barely known.

He'd have hated it.

Its one saving grace was that, after days of torment about whether or not to read a eulogy, I actually managed it. His cousin translated. I hadn't thought I'd be able to, but it's amazing what the human spirit is capable of when you're determined enough. And I felt I owed it to Roberto: it was up to me to remember the real him and, as arrogant as it sounds, there was no doubt in my mind that I knew him better than anyone else there.

'Roberto once told me that when our baby was old enough, he was going to buy a boat. Nothing flashy, just a little wooden rowing boat, the simpler the better. He wanted to while away sunny afternoons with our child, exactly as he'd done as a little boy.

The long, hot summers he spent in Lombardy with his grandfather, who he adored, were the source of his happiest and most vivid childhood memories, the ones he talked about most.

The two of them would splash about for hours on the lake, throwing stones and catching fish. It was there, Roberto told me, that he learned from his grandfather how to become the man he wanted to be.

I never got to meet Roberto's grandfather, as he died the year before he moved to London. But I feel certain that he would've been proud of Roberto. A successful lawyer. A loyal son. A man who adored books and films, who could cook a delicious dinner out of seemingly nothing and who loved a good debate, as I discovered myself, often.

Roberto had endless amounts of love to give. And I will forever thank God that I was the one to whom he chose to give it, even if it was for a far shorter time than any of us imagined.

I can't think of many people who'd have made a better parent than Roberto. I can think of few men more capable, patient and loving. And I know that, of all Roberto's skill in his job – something we all know he was unbelievably good at – his true vocation was one he'll never get to fulfil: a daddy.'

I'd got through the whole speech remarkably well until that point, but that word had crashed into my head, opening the floodgates for my tears. The last sentence was almost impossible to say – I still don't know how I managed it.

'But today isn't a day to dwell on what Roberto was denied. Today is a day to remember him . . . how he was. And how lucky we all were to have him in our lives.'

I didn't stay long at the wake. I couldn't stand the looks from his family as they gazed into my sunken eyes and told me I really must start eating again. Which of course I knew was true – I was carrying a baby – but was easier said than done. Every mouthful felt like I was trying to digest a rock.

The following day, we were due at a lunch hosted by his family. It felt wrong being with his parents when he wasn't there, as if someone had forgotten to invite the most important guest. But of course I went; I did my duty and my parents did theirs. It wasn't their fault I couldn't stand being around any of them.

I made my excuses and walked aimlessly, numbly, across the Ponte Vecchio as tourists and locals weaved around me. I stood and gazed at the sunset over the Arno River, contemplating briefly if the child I was carrying was the only thing that was stopping me from jumping in.

I scolded myself for being so melodramatic, but I made myself a promise. Or rather, something I simply knew would be the case. For ever.

Living or dead, Roberto would always be the only man for me.

Day Six

Chapter 41

I wake up with a forehead damp with sweat. I reach automatically for my necklace and remember that it's not there. I turn and look at Harry with a sharp sense of disconnection from the events of the night before.

I know what I did. I know what I felt. And as I gaze at his parted lips as he snores lightly as he dreams, I'm aware that were he a lesser man – someone less sweet or kind – I'd probably be recoiling in horror right now.

So I don't do that. Not quite. Instead, I'm struggling to process what happened, or indeed to recognise the woman I became last night.

Had I been someone else, I probably wouldn't have thought anything of sleeping with someone I'd only just met, not when he's single, I'm single, we used protection and had an undeniably good time.

But I'm not someone else. I'm me.

And I don't think I'm being too hard on myself for the

growing repugnance I'm feeling. Not because I acted like a slut, but because I'd acted like I'd *forgotten*.

I peel myself out of bed and creep around the room, picking up clothes in the dim morning light as I try desperately not to wake Harry. I quietly wrestle with my clothes until I'm dressed – at least in a fashion. My dress is dish-cloth soggy from spilt champagne and, after discovering my knickers in the Jacuzzi, my only option is to stuff them in my handbag and go commando.

I spot my phone on the bedside table and the recollection of turning it off propels me into a cold panic. I press 'On' with a heavy sense of dread, convincing myself as it springs to life that I'm being neurotic. I wriggle into my shoes as the phone checks for messages, repeating to myself that turning it off for twelve hours was absolutely the right thing to do and, in fact, could've done me the world of good.

That's before the first text appears. Then the second, third and fourth, pinging onto my home screen like coins dropping from a slot machine. The arrival of several voicemail messages coincides with Harry stirring.

My instinct to get out of there before he can speak to me is halted as I glance at my phone, registering the final tally of missed calls: sixteen. Then I open the last text message that David sent:

Imogen: YOU'RE FIRED.

Chapter 42

Harry wants me to stay. I have never wanted to leave anywhere faster.

'You don't understand. I need to … look, I'm sorry,' I mumble. 'You're a really nice person. But this was a mistake.'

A veil of hurt sweeps over his face, but I have other things on my mind. I glance again at my phone and go to dive out of the door.

'Wait!'

I pause as he stands up, clutching the sheets to his midriff. He might technically be covering his modesty, but the sight of his half-naked body feels indecent this morning, and I tear away my eyes to avoid looking at what stirred me last night.

'Look, I … thank you for the champagne.' He looks offended, and I briefly consider adding, 'And the orgasms.'

'That's fine,' he says awkwardly.

'You were excellent company.' I force a smile.

'Look, is everything okay? I know it'd been a while for you,

323

but I want you to know that I thought last night was … lovely.' He frowns. 'That's a rubbish word. It was a lot more than lovely. And so are you. Also … this is not something I tend to do either after knowing someone for so little time. So I'm slightly rattled too. But seriously, Imogen—'

'I've been sacked,' I interrupt. I don't know why my need to share that with him is so urgent, except that I can't bear listening to this any longer.

He looks shocked. 'When? And *why?*'

'I've got sixteen missed calls and a load of voice messages on my phone so I suspect I'm about to find out.' When I look at him again, my eyes land on his lips. It's followed by a wave of self-hatred. 'I need to go. Thank you, Harry.'

He steps forward. 'Imogen … I'm leaving the day after tomorrow. I'd really like to see you again. Can we get together again today?'

I hesitate and move away just enough to stop him from touching me. 'I think I'm going to have a lot on my plate. Probably best not.'

His jaw tightens and, for a moment, it appears that he doesn't know what to say or do.

I turn to leave, but he touches my hand; I hesitate, and he leans in and kisses me on the cheek. When he withdraws, my hand reaches up to my still-tingling skin.

I know I have to get out of here.

Chapter 43

The walk of shame to my room is excruciating. I avoid the lift because the prospect of getting stuck in there with someone for even twelve seconds is about as appealing as biting someone else's toenails.

So I opt for the stairs. Only, there are twelve floors to descend, meaning I can't stand too close to the rail because the possibility that someone below might glance heavenwards when I'm minus knickers is too much to risk.

The stairs are far from quiet at this time of the morning and, worse, it appears there is a certain type of person who chooses this route: families with small children; the only couple over the age of sixty I've seen in this hotel since I got here; oh, and my Italian.

'Oh! It is the beautiful Eenglish—' He stops mid-sentence and looks me up and down, deciding to quit while he's ahead.

The word 'beautiful' is so obviously tantamount to taking the piss that his mouth simply refuses to complete the sentence.

My dress couldn't be less socially acceptable breakfast attire if I'd tattooed a swastika on my face; I have brushed neither my teeth nor my hair; and, as I discover to my horror when I look down sharply, one of the false eyelashes with which I experimented last night is hanging by a precarious, gluey thread, like a caterpillar preparing to abseil down my cheek.

'Um ... hello – I can't stop, sorry!' I push past him as he pulls a curious expression: half put-outedness – he's obviously not used to women running away from him – and half relief.

I start my phone calls the second I enter my bedroom and sweep aside a note from Meredith letting me know she's at breakfast. It becomes apparent very quickly that getting hold of David is going to be near-impossible. I pace around for forty minutes and leave several messages for him before I'm forced to concede that the reception at Great Aunt Whatsherchops's caravan is defeating me.

Engaging in a conversation with David is barely necessary to work out exactly what his problem is, however. His problem is crystal clear from his messages, and I listen to them with an increasingly twisted knot in my stomach.

The first goes like this: 'Imogen. I've seen the papers, I've reviewed all the coverage and I saw your quote. Now, as you know, I always say, "Things happen. Winners make them happen the way they want." And, obviously, this has not happened the way we want. But I'm trying to stay calm. I'm trying very, very hard. Because I know you work hard and I know you're under pressure. But we need to talk about this. Urgently. So, I'm waiting on the moors right now for you to phone me back because I need there to be some sort of . . . correction, or apology or something in tomorrow's papers. I know I said I didn't care about Getreide but obviously I do and this needs to be sorted before they get wind of it. So phone me. Now. Please.'

His second message says: 'Imogen. I'm still waiting. I am relying on you. Please.' Then he adds, solemnly: 'It is now raining.'

His third message is less discernable against its background noise, which sounds as though he's watching the final scene in *The Perfect Storm* with the volume turned on high. 'IMOGEN! It is ABSOLUTELY PISSING DOWN. LIKE I'M IN AN AMAZONIAN RAINFOREST OR SOMETHING. ONLY COLDER, WINDIER AND MORE SCOTTISH.' There's a pause, followed by frantic rustling, as if he's running for cover. A few seconds later, he continues breathlessly. 'I've spoken to Charles and we both need to contact you, urgently, because I remember you saying you had some sort of alternative story that might knock this off the front pages. Well, we need it. Now. I'm counting on you, Imogen.'

Charles phones after that, demanding to know what this mystery story is. Little does he know that all David's talking about is Cosimo's press release about Grill-O-Bloo – something that's about as likely to knock anything off the front page as a scoop about grass being green.

David's fourth to seventh messages become increasingly irate, increasingly desperate, and basically illustrate that there is an acute correlation between the colder and wetter a person is and the angrier they become.

His penultimate message says: 'Imogen. I am *IN. CAND. ES. CENT.*' He takes a full breath between each syllable. 'It is one thing making this almighty fudge-up in the first place; it is quite another ignoring the urgent calls of your chief executive when this company's reputation is on the line and *you* potentially have the ability to get it out of this mess. I'm sorry I promoted you! You're clearly out of your depth!' he rants. 'And ... and ... if I don't hear from you in the next twenty minutes, I'll have no alternative but to treat this as gross misconduct and dismiss you with immediate effect.'

The next I heard from him was at exactly twelve minutes past midnight. The text that sealed my fate. The text containing words that I, Imogen Copeland, proud former school swot and workaholic never, ever thought I'd see: 'YOU'RE FIRED.'

The door opens and Meredith strolls in, back from breakfast. She's looking lovely and tanned now, simultaneously glamorous and maternal.

'What happened to you?'

I can tell from her expression that I look as though I've just crawled out of a municipal tip.

'I've just done the walk of shame,' I reply, numbly.

'YAAAAYYYY!'

'And I've been sacked,' I add.

She frowns. 'Oh, what a bugger. Why?'

'Because I screwed up,' I reply, slouching onto the bed. 'I've screwed up everything. Absolutely everything ...'

'Yeah, but at least you've *screwed*!' she whoops. She sits down next to me and holds both of my hands. 'Imogen, you've had SEX! This is the best news I've had all week. I'm proud of you,' she adds, as if I've just got my 25-metre front-crawl badge.

I look at her, bewildered. 'How can you be proud of me? It's terrible! I feel awful.'

'About your job?'

'Obviously that, but I feel very, very weird about last night, too.'

'Why? You shouldn't. Sex is a perfectly natural, perfectly human thing, Imogen.'

I sneer. 'It's overrated. Seriously, what's it got going for it?'

She thinks for a second, before offering: 'Orgasms can cure hiccups. *Fact.*' I glare at her blankly. 'That's only one benefit, obviously. Wasn't it good? Oh God, that's such a bummer when that happens. I'd hoped it'd blow your mind the first time after ... you know.'

I look despondently out of the window. 'It did blow my mind.' She says nothing. 'It blew my mind, it blew my bloody everything. I didn't know what hit me.'

'So, what's the problem?'

'The problem is—'

My phone rings and I answer it immediately. Only it isn't David, it's Roy – apparently back at work.

'Imogen, what on earth's happened? I got back from Euro Disney this morning to discover David's in hiding, we're all over the press, the office is in uproar and I've been promoted into your job.'

'What?'

'Oh, don't worry – there's no way I'm taking it. At the moment, I can't think of anything worse.'

Which, sadly, isn't much of a comfort.

Chapter 44

For the first time all holiday, my phone isn't ringing. Nobody at work wants me. Nobody in the media wants me. Even my bloody mother doesn't seem to want me.

In a bid to distract myself from dark thoughts, I spend an hour and a half twiddling with my phone attempting to solve my 3G problem, manage (miraculously) to succeed, and only then realise how little I want to make contact with the outside world anyway.

'Let's go for a wander along Las Ramblas again,' Nicola suggests decisively, clapping her hands. 'You need to take your mind off things. And off that bloody phone.'

I'm about to inform her that I'm only Googling whether orgasms really can cure hiccups (they can, according to supersexpert.com), when a text arrives on her own phone.

I pull a pot–kettle face that she decides to ignore, scrutinising the message with a frown instead.

'Everything all right?' I ask.

She looks up and shakes her head. 'Fine . . . it's nothing. Just the issue we were talking about the other night.'

'Your parents and Jess?'

She nods. 'You got me thinking about how daft the whole situation is. So I casually mentioned Jess's name in a text to my mum to see how she'd respond.'

'And?'

'She totally ignored it.' She shakes her head. 'Not a big deal in itself, I suppose. So, how about Las Ramblas?'

The prospect of returning to where my necklace was stolen fills me with unease. But I don't want to stay here while Harry's still around; lying on the beach would be too passive to take my mind off anything; and Las Ramblas at least has the benefit of proximity. So I drag on shorts and a T-shirt, trowel concealer over my black eye, and head out with my friends.

It is a disconcerting experience on every level.

The thought that I might bump into Harry has me in such a state of agitation I'm virtually twitching. Just thinking about last night makes me feel exposed, confused and, frankly, shocked. The pornographic flashbacks that persist in gate-crashing my head feature a woman very unlike me. And although there is no prospect of ever seeing Harry again after tomorrow, I do feel fairly awful about how upset he looked when it became clear that I wasn't going to suggest we break-fast on scrambled eggs and another shag for dessert.

'What did you get up to last night?' I ask Meredith.

'I went to a party at the other end of the beach with Salvatore. It was fab.'

I raise an eyebrow.

'Nothing *happened*. Although I didn't get in until 3.30.' She grins. 'I've still got it!'

I turn to Nicola. 'Has your migraine gone?'

'Just about. It wasn't my worst. They sometimes last for days,' she replies. 'But thanks for asking, especially when you've clearly got other things to worry about.' At first I think she's talking about sleeping with Harry. 'I don't think your boss can fire you, just like that. And certainly not by text,' she continues. 'I went on a management course recently and you've got to jump through hoops before you can legally sack someone. Of course, if you're determined someone needs to be given the boot, there are ways and means . . .' She glances at me uneasily. 'The point is, I don't think it's cut and dried. It'd have to be gross misconduct.'

'He says it is,' I tell her.

'Oh, well, *he* might think so. I'm not convinced what you did was that bad. Not . . . really.' We arrive at the mouth of the huge avenue that is Las Ramblas and she decides to quit while she's ahead.

It's as busy as last time, with energy and atmosphere spilling from every corner. We meander through the crowd in the direction of a market recommended by the guidebooks and I clutch my bag tightly, a reflex action that's ironic given that

I have nothing of much value this time: a cheap travel purse containing a couple of notes, a phone that's resolutely not ringing and no necklace.

'Let's put a photo on Facebook,' Nicola suggests, gathering us into a tight group. She stretches out her arm, instructs us to smile and takes the photo – before examining it with the kind of expression you'd reserve for a red-wine enthusiast vomiting on your cream carpet.

'I can't put that on Facebook. Imogen, you look as if you've . . .' Her voice trails off.

'Lost my job?' I offer. 'Or been mugged? Or slept with someone I shouldn't?'

Nicola frowns. 'You've got every right to be upset about your necklace and the job. But not the fling, Imogen. You were totally entitled to that. Overdue it, in fact.'

'And he really likes you!' Meredith pipes up. 'That *never* happens with people you meet on holiday. Normally, they're either not interested in anything beyond a one-off shag, or so ropey you want a partial lobotomy to obliterate the memory of them. Harry is *gorgeous*. I hope you're going to arrange to see him back in London.'

'If you must know, he's moving to Aberdeen as soon as this trip is over,' I mutter. 'He's not even flying back to London. And that's the only good thing I can say about this – the fact that I'll never see him again.'

Before that sentence leaves my mouth, I actually believe it.

Only as the words linger in the air, my stomach surges with disappointment. A heavy silence sits between the three of us.

'Come on, let's do your photo again,' I suggest brightly. 'I promise I'll smile enough to convince all your Facebook friends we're having a whale of a time.'

We get into position and I'm grinning like I'm about to have several molars extracted when I hear a familiar Spanish voice. I glance up to see the beautiful, ill-fated Delfina firing instructions at her group, which includes Harry. A wave of light-headedness grips me.

'Oh, Imogen, you've done it again!' Nicola protests, thrusting the photo in front of me. I'd have to admit I look like a sumo wrestler has just rollerbladed over my toe.

'Sorry, I—'

'Hello, Imogen.'

Harry's luminous eyes can hardly hold my gaze. The obvious chinks in his confidence don't suit him at all.

'Hi,' I mumble.

He forces a smile. 'Have you got a minute?'

My friends slip away instantly, refusing to give me any choice. And so I find myself face to face with the man who has profoundly shaken my world in the last twenty-four hours, watching him bite his lip in a way that's entirely disconcerting as it draws my eyes to his mouth and assaults me with a full-sensory memory of what kissing it tasted like. 'About last night.'

I'm torn between wanting the ground to swallow me up, and a raging desire to know what he wants to say about last night. But these thoughts are fleeting. Because as I stand, listening intently, something in the dim periphery of my line of sight grabs my attention and yanks my attention violently away from him.

'Oh my God.' The words snake out of my mouth in a whisper. 'OH. MY. GOD.'

'What is it?'

'That's him.' I nod as a figure cuts through the crowd, exactly as he did the last time. 'The boy who stole my necklace.'

Harry focuses on him. 'The one with the dark hair and blue T-shirt?'

I nod, fixed to the spot, incapable of removing my eyes from him as my head swells anew with thoughts about the possible destiny of my necklace. Has he sold it? Has he still got it? Has he—

'Why don't we go and have a chat with him?' It's an audacious suggestion, yet Harry looks and sounds so unfeasibly relaxed, it takes a moment to work out that he's serious.

As my heart lashes against my ribcage, a deluge of emotions sweeps through me – alarm, fear, foreboding. But then the clouds in my head suddenly clear and I experience something else entirely. I'm not sure if it's quite courage – it's closer to sheer, bloody-minded *defiance*.

336

'Yes,' I say. 'I think perhaps we should.' With Harry by my side, as we advance towards the boy I seem to grow three inches taller.

The youth is clearly on the lookout for his next target, subtly assessing who in the crowd has let down their guard. The irony that he has failed to notice *us* as we approach from behind is as terrifying as it is delicious.

Harry and I exchange glances and, despite my chest feeling as though it might explode, I reach out and tap him on the shoulder.

The boy turns round. Our eyes meet and I confirm instantly that it's him. Suddenly, every ounce of fear slips away from me. 'You stole my necklace,' I say calmly.

His mouth opens in feigned indignation as he glances at Harry. '*Que?*' He shrugs innocently.

I am about to repeat the accusation when he suddenly springs round and, before I have time to let out my breath, is darting through the crowds away from us.

'Shit!'

''Arry, we need to go,' says Delfina, grabbing Harry by the arm.

Before I can fully digest the situation, I've abandoned Harry and am going after the boy, as Harry is dragged away by Delfina.

I've never been a natural sprinter; I don't think anyone over a D cup ever is. Once I hit the age of thirteen, centrifugal forces put me at the same disadvantage in cross-country races as someone pushing a wheelbarrow full of builders' rubble. But that doesn't stop me now. With adrenalin searing through me, I race after him, pushing through the crowd. My eyes focus on my target as I dart between two elderly ladies, spring around a Vespa parked on the pavement and, as I leap over a dog tied to a bollard, feel so like I'm in a movie scene that I half expect someone to ride out of a blazing building on a motorbike and scoop me up to ride pillion.

Considering I'm dripping with sweat and wearing espadrilles, I don't do badly. My vigilante efforts might even be impressive if only my adversary wasn't quite so agile.

I've been on his trail for at least a minute, maybe more, when I realise that there's someone I recognise ahead of us.

'Mr Brayfield! STOP HIM!' I shriek as my geography teacher and his wife stop talking and look in my direction. 'HE STOLE MY NECKLACE!'

Mr Brayfield's mouth gapes.

'GET HIM, BRYAN!' thunders Mrs B as her husband panics, pulls himself together, then thrusts out one of his crutches in the path of my adversary. He stumbles ahead and falls to the floor. Hope surges through me as I realise something I'd started to doubt: I've got him. I'VE ACTUALLY GOT HIM!

He glances back and we both know he's within my reach.

Then Fate intervenes.

It's the initial wallop on my left cheek that stops me first, followed by a series of frenzied flaps that feel like a Gremlin break-dancing on my scalp. It takes a second to work out that the creature hitting me is, in fact, a pigeon, something that becomes clear only when I'm forced to snort violently to dislodge a feather stuck up my nose. No matter how vehemently I attempt to bat it away, it persists with a whirling dervish of berserk wing slaps, until I am only finally rid of it by pulling off a convincing under-arm volley with my handbag.

To my astonishment, this pantomime has momentarily stunned my target and everyone else into inaction. He snaps out of his daze and turns to sprint away just as I realise I need to do something drastic, magnificent. So I leap.

With my arms outstretched, I glide through the air, confident that justice will be mine. My adversary, however, is faster than Usain Bolt on the Japanese bullet train and consequently, I can only see empty pavement approaching. I can see it and, determined not to end up with my second black eye of the holiday, I reach out to break my fall. Sadly, I do not break my fall.

I simply break my arm.

Chapter 45

'Some VIP holiday this is,' I mutter as I sit in a cubicle, legs dangling off the side of the bed.

We've been waiting for the doctor to come and release me for four hours. I've signed the relevant paperwork, had the relevant X-rays and sat next to the relevant crack addicts, alcoholics and ne'er do wells, so by rights I should have been out of here, back by the pool and topping up the hotchpotch I call my tan ages ago.

Only they've got a rush on. And, despite the fact that I'm paying (or, rather, my travel insurance is paying, after I spent an hour on the phone to a helpline that was about as helpful as an AA meeting in an off-license), nobody seems inclined to discharge me.

'I tried to follow you,' Meredith tells me. My friends, God bless them, have refused to leave my side. 'It's bloody hard running these days though.'

'Meredith, your running days should be over until you've given birth,' I tell her.

'You said exercise was a *good* thing when you're pregnant,' she protests.

'I was talking about swimming or yoga. Not a frantic sprint through more obstacles than a Royal Marines assault course.'

'Well done for trying, anyway,' Nicola says, rubbing my good arm. 'It's a shame you didn't get to that boy. Although perhaps it was for the best – you don't know how he'd have reacted. Either way, it sounds like you were close to getting him.'

I sigh, resigning myself to one crucial matter. 'He wouldn't have had it with him anyway, so I have no idea what I'd have done if I'd caught him. But still . . .' I hesitate. 'Did you say Harry rejoined his group when I ran off?'

Nicola nods. 'I think so. That guide of theirs was quite insistent that they all head for the tour bus without delay. My attention was on you so I can't say I was concentrating on them, but he did seem to put up a bit of a fight. He clearly wasn't happy to have to leave.'

I try to hide my disappointment.

'He'd have helped if he could,' Meredith adds. 'He was obviously left with no choice.'

'It was nothing to do with him, anyway,' I point out. 'It's one thing me playing at being a vigilante – I couldn't expect anyone else to.'

I notice that Nicola is engrossed in her phone.

'Is something the matter?' I ask.

She bites her lip. 'I hate to add to your woes, Imogen, but someone's hacked your Facebook account.'

'No!'

She nods. 'It says here that you shared an article about orgasms on something called "supersexpert.com".'

'Oh God, that *was* me … but it was an accident,' I groan.

Meredith peers over Nicola's shoulder. 'I wouldn't worry too much, Imogen. You've got a record number of Likes.'

It is 6 p.m. by the time we get back to the hotel. The double doors glide open into the welcome, air-conditioned chill.

As I cross the lobby, the idea that I should fill in Harry on what happened after he left bubbles up in me. It was he who'd suggested we talk to the boy, after all.

As the others head to the bar, I make a detour to the sun deck, register his absence, then stop off at the business centre and find that he isn't there either.

I push thoughts of him out of my mind and head to the room instead, where I attempt to suppress an overwhelming desire to curl up in bed. Having dragged my friends to hospital, and thereby denied them another day of sightseeing, I think the least I owe them is dinner.

I peel off my clothes and quickly shove them in a laundry bag (which makes it sound rather grander than the reality: a Tesco carrier bag filled with unwashed pants), noting that it was a good thing I didn't see Harry after all. After an intensive sprint in 30-degree heat, I'm not exactly fragrant, not unless the term can be expanded to incorporate the rotting contents of a wheelie bin.

I attempt to shower. I say *attempt* because it quickly becomes evident that having an arm in plaster hampers even the most pedestrian of tasks. The jets of water seem magnetically attracted to my cast, despite all my efforts to undertake my ablutions with my arm raised in the air.

Then I have an idea. Dripping wet and with limb aloft, I tiptoe out of the shower and root around one-handed in my suitcase for the laundry bag I had only minutes ago. I pull it out and rip the plastic bag down one side, holding it in my teeth and feeling a little bit like in films when someone tears up their shirt to wrap around a gunshot wound.

I cover my plaster with the bag and tie it on both sides until it's near enough watertight, feeling fairly smug about my hand-iwork. I step back into the shower and carefully start to wash the day out of my hair.

I almost start to relax as water spills onto my forehead and I lose myself in its warmth. I'm not thinking about my necklace, or my tattered professional reputation or the implications of what I did last night. I'm thinking of nothing. Well, *almost* nothing. Because, slowly, gradually, before I even recognise the fact, flashbacks from last night begin to infiltrate my brain again.

I try to force them away, but they coax me, too vivid and

pleasurable to resist. So I convince myself that just *thinking* about last night does no harm. As Meredith said, it's just normal, natural, what human beings were designed for.

Warmth sweeps up my body as I look at the skin on my stomach and remember what it felt like with Harry's lips on it. I take a long inward breath and try to pull myself together but, as I massage shampoo into my hair, I'm quickly back in the pleasure zone, feeling relaxed, sensual.

And distinctly frisky if the truth be told.

Which is obviously too good to last. I'm midway through reliving the bit where Harry first lifted off his shirt, when a piercing screech comparable to the onset of a sonic boom rips through the room and I nearly slip over in shock.

It's a fire alarm. Probably a drill ...

I consider this for a moment, certain that it'll go off soon, like the ones that always go off in work: every staff member on the payroll trudges outside only to find out that all that's caused it is the office pisshead returning from a long lunch and falling through a fire door.

I calmly start to wash off the shampoo, willing the noise to go off. Because I'm *not* going outside like this. Not a chance. Besides, there's no way a building this sophisticated would have a fire. Surely—

But the longer I massage suds out of my hair, the more time I have for reflection. The vivid recollection of the article I scanned on the Internet this morning assails me: I imagine all those poor people tapping away at their keyboards, convinced the wailing sirens were a drill, while the floors below smouldered like the seventh circle of hell.

Maybe that's happening right now! Anything could be going on out there as I stand here attempting to massage high-end shampoo out of my roots with a single hand. My anxiety levels mount further.

'Oh, come *on* – just go off!' I plead to no one in particular as I set about working out the position of the kitchen in this building. I'm not saying I'd rival anyone on *CSI*, but I quickly deduce that it's perfectly feasible that, only minutes ago, an inexperienced chef's Gambas Pil Pil ignited on the bottom of a frying pan and the resulting flames are now sweeping through the entire building.

The alarm continues. 'PLEASE STOP! PLEASE—'

It doesn't stop.

I am engulfed by a feeling that I *have* to get out of here, or else I will be in hideous, mortal danger.

I turn off the shower and grab a towel, scanning the room for the bathrobe. It's nowhere. I head to my pile of washing and start rifling through it – as I hear feet running outside the room. God Almighty, I'm facing imminent death but all I can do is flick through my dirty knickers! I need to get out of here!

I wrap the towel around my dripping body and race out of the door.

Nobody's there – the only thing I'm greeted by is the now-deafening din of the alarm. I belt towards the stairs, squinting through the suds working their way into my retinas, unconcerned that the only thing covering my modesty is a bath towel. Who cares if my bum's on show when my life is at stake?

Half blinded by the shampoo, I race out of the hotel panting like an asthmatic porn star as I slip into a large crowd of people . . . at the exact moment as the alarm rings off.

I glance around. Nobody else is wearing only a bath towel, Tesco bag and enough shampoo to beautify an 18-hand race-horse. My eyes scan the vicinity for the girls, but they're nowhere to be seen – and neither, to my relief, is Harry.

'Hello!'

I look up and see my Italian friend. Having run away from him twice already I don't feel I ought to do it again.

'Hello to you too,' I reply, painfully conscious of my lack of attire. 'Listen, I'm sorry about disappearing quickly, it's just . . . is everything okay?'

He is looking me up and down, taking in my appearance, and clearly confirming that I am, as he suspected, quite unhinged.

'Everything okay yes!' he says.

'Did you have anything nice planned today?' I add politely.

He nods. 'No problem!' he replies, as he backs away, spins round, and rapidly disappears.

A hotel official comes out and tells us apologetically that it's all simply a false alarm and we can return to our rooms.

Nobody sprints up the stairs faster than I do – I cover about five stairs per stride at one point – and relief overwhelms me as I go to push open our hotel room door.

It is a momentary sensation. The door is stuck fast. I've left the key card inside.

'SHIT!'

'Is everything all right?'

I recognise Harry's voice before I spin round and look at him. 'What are you doing on this floor?' I ask in a panicked squeak.

'I came to see how you're doing after what happened in Las Ramblas. I'm sorry we got separated.'

'Oh . . . that's okay. Well, I didn't manage to retrieve the necklace, sadly.'

Harry is staring at me, aghast. 'What happened to your arm?'

I glance at my Tesco bag. 'They were two for the price of one.'

He laughs. 'Seriously, are you okay?'

'I broke it.' I shrug. 'I spent the whole day – *we* spent the whole day – in hospital.'

'You're kidding? I'm so sorry.' Harry looks at me, mortified.

'I need to go and speak to Reception and get them to open the door,' I mutter, suddenly needing to end this conversation. Despite the fact that Harry's seen every inch of me naked, I've never felt more exposed – both by the shortness of this bath towel and by the feelings stirring inside me just by being around him.

'Stay here – I'll go,' he insists.

I'm about to protest when I realise that I'm not in a position to. The prospect of going downstairs isn't one I relish.

Harry disappears down the stairs and returns a few minutes later with a woman in hotel uniform, who lets me into the room. When she's gone, he looks at me. 'Are you around tonight?' he asks, simply.

It sounds like a straightforward question. But it isn't. Of course it isn't. 'Yes. Possibly. I don't know.'

He hesitates. 'O-kay. Well, *I* should be, at least before dinner. Maybe we could meet?'

I hesitate. 'I'm not sure what time I'll be around. I don't know what our plans are,' I say noncommittally.

He scans my face, clearly wondering how to play this given my lack of inclination to set a specific time. 'Perhaps we'll say we might just bump into each other in the bar downstairs, then?'

I nod. He smiles.

'Bye, then,' I mumble.

'Bye,' he replies.

As I close the room door behind me, I wonder when my brain will stop hurting so much.

Chapter 46

The second the door closes I begin to feel a bit ill. About the fact that I am thinking about – to bring this down to the unseemly, brass-tacks truth – sex. I am literally tingling with desire. Which, in equal parts, makes me feel amazing and dreadful.

Back in the shower, I switch it onto its coldest setting and, by the time I've emerged, I've not only managed to shake the sexy feeling, but have made sure there is only one man on my mind, and that's Roberto.

I locate my soaked bath towel and attempt to dry my hair as I contemplate everything that's happened here in Spain. With my job, yes, but most importantly, myself.

There have been many times over the last five years when I've thought about when the time would be right to 'move on', but it's not something you can sit back and dispassionately *define*. Instead it is, I strongly suspect, something that simply happens, a process over which you have little or no control.

I say 'strongly suspect' because although the physical feelings I'm having for Harry represent the first time I've experienced this about another man since Roberto, they're *not* making me feel like it's time to get myself a boyfriend. They're simply making me feel guilty. Disloyal. And unworthy of a love that I always vowed would last for ever.

I sit at the desk in the room and take out a pen and paper.

Amore mio …

The simple process of beginning to write makes me feel like I've made a connection, and I submit to the fantasy that he's still here, in my life. In *real* life.

It's been a strange holiday. And not just because I've broken my arm, been mugged, thrown out of a VIP party (almost), lumbered with a black eye – oh, and lost my job after one of the worst appearances on national radio in broadcasting history.

It's also because it's prompted me to think hard about us. I know that, technically, there is no 'us' any more. I simply mean that being away, taking a break from normal life (because this trip has been a long way from anything normal), has forced me to confront the issue that everyone has been urging me to for so long: whether I'll ever get over you.

In so many ways, all it's done is confirm my doubts about

my ability to let that ever happen. And if I AM destined for
some Miss Havisham-style existence – living alone in batty
solitude – then, often, I think, 'So be it'. The reality is, amore
mio, I don't think I AM ever going to get over you ... despite
what happened

My pen hesitates over the page as the words 'with another man last night' tumble through my mind.

I pause and put down my pen as I pad over to the mini-bar to open a small bottle of water, then fill up a glass. I take a sip of it before returning to the desk. I pick up the pen again and scrub out 'despite what happened'.

I know that you can hardly need reassurance that, had things
been different – had we still been together – I'd NEVER have
looked at another man. But the bastard that is Fate decided to
throw a spanner in the works, and that fact became irrelevant.
So the question remains about whether there will ever be
'someone else'.

I must confess I like the idea of being properly happy again one
day. I know that people aren't really meant to be on their own all
the time, that the benefits of solitude are limited to little more
than not having to pay too much attention to your bikini line.

But at the same time, there's this: I love you as much as I
ever did. Not a day has gone by that's changed that. If I was
less of a rationalist, I'd say give me a message, give me a sign –

let me know what I should do. But I know that's a fairly tall order. Even if you are still the best listener I've ever known.

Goodnight, sweetheart. I love you.

Imogen xxxxxxx

Chapter 47

'So, do you want to see Harry tonight or not?' Meredith asks on the way to the bar later that night. 'Because, I've got to be honest, I'm confused.'

'Try being me for a day then. You'd be in therapy by 8.30.'

The lift reaches the lobby and the doors open as my phone springs into life. My mum's number flashes up.

I answer. 'Hi, Mum. Is Florence okay?'

'YOU'RE IN THE *EXPRESS*!'

I close my eyes and take a deep breath. 'Yes, I'd heard,' I say, hoping this is the end of the matter.

'I didn't believe it until Carol next door came round with a copy. I assured her that they must've made most of it up, because you're on holiday and would *never* use some of the language they've quoted you as saying.'

My palpitations start to augment dangerously.

'Honestly, I hope you're having a relaxing time over there because it sounds like ALL HELL is breaking loose while you're away. I dread to think what you're going to return to.'

'Can I speak to Florence now?'

'It reminds me of when I was in Tokyo, an—'

'Mum, I need to go to dinner soon. Is Florence there, please?'

She sniffs and reluctantly hands over the phone.

'Hello, Mummy.' Her little voice makes my heart contract.

'Hello, darling. I love you.'

She doesn't answer.

'I love you,' I repeat.

'Hi, Mummy.'

'What have you been up to today?'

'Grandma's been teaching me how to put on liquid eye-liner.'

I sigh. 'And how was that?'

'Good. Are you coming back soon?'

'I am, sweetheart. And I can't wait to see you.' For a split second, I long for the moment when I will have her small arms around me and feel her soft hair against my cheek. This is followed swiftly by the realisation that it's currently in doubt how I'm going to feed her and keep a roof over her head.

'Mummy, is Benjamin Hewitt going to be at my school?'

Despite her reluctance to declare her love for me, Florence has told me on several occasions that she is in love with Benjamin Hewitt, a boy at her nursery. Given that I'm very hopeful of her remaining a virgin until the age of at least twenty-four, it's not something I'm trying to encourage.

'I think he might be,' I tell her. 'Are you looking forward to school?'

She hesitates. 'Yes, but only if you're going to take me on my first day.'

I swallow, trying to hold it together. This is the one benefit of my current circumstances, I suppose. 'Okay, Florence. I'll be there.' Nothing can stop me now I'm unemployed.

She hesitates, as if she hasn't heard me right. 'Really?' She's virtually breathless with happiness and disbelief.

'Yes,' I whimper, hating myself for how overjoyed this has made her.

'You're the best mummy in the whole wide history.'

Now I want to cry. Mum grabs the phone after instructing Florence to say goodbye, and proceeds to tell me about how she bought some arnica for her bruises and it's done a magnificent job and she's bought some for me, too. Despite the fact that – broken arm and black eye notwithstanding (which she doesn't know about anyway) – I haven't actually *got* any bruises.

This is followed by the fact that she saw something on TV about a big carnival in Barcelona this week, meaning it will be overrun with people and pickpocketers and I mustn't take off my special bag, even when dining, sunbathing or indeed enjoying a vigorous session of butterfly stroke in the swimming pool.

I'm so exhausted by this conversation that by the time I manage to persuade her I *really* am going, I end the call with the words: 'Mum, you might not be able to get hold of me for the next twenty-four hours – my phone's been playing up. So try not to phone unless it's a REAL EMERGENCY.'

'I only *ever* phone in emergencies,' she objects. 'Besides, it worked fine this time.'

'Just text me, okay,' I say, which I think is a reasonable compromise.

When I finish the call I find my way to the bar, where Nicola has ordered me a drink. Never has something cold and fizzy looked so enticing.

I sit on a stool next to Meredith and glance in the mirror behind the bar to see if I can see Harry. Then I decide I'm being far too subtle, so spin round to engage in a full-scale scan of the area.

'He's not here yet,' Nicola says.

I take a sip of cava to avoid answering her. Part of me would be relieved about the idea of him standing me up. Although I do recognise that, if it was that simple, I probably wouldn't have put on the nicest of my new tops, attempted to recreate the hairdo Meredith created a few days ago and basically put in more effort to my appearance than I have in the last five years.

'Why didn't you set a time to meet him?' Meredith asks.

'I'm not sure exactly.'

'That's a cardinal dating error, Imogen.'

'I wouldn't know,' I point out, taking another uneasy sip of my drink.

It becomes evident over the course of the next two drinks that my friends are convinced Harry will arrive at some point, because they're making their cava last about six times longer than mine to play for time. I, on the other hand, am torn in two over the issue.

One minute I convince myself I don't want to see him here; then I start wondering why he's not. Which puts an entirely different perspective on things.

And, after an hour of sitting, drinking and working myself up into a neurotic wreck, eventually I just want to get out of here.

Reluctantly, my friends finish their drinks, telling me that we'll come back after dinner because he's *bound* to have meant then instead, or perhaps I misheard or . . . something.

As we're about to head through the double doors to the beach, I spot Delfina marching through the lobby. She's chatting to the guy with curly hair, who I now know is a trainee with the *Daily Mirror*.

The other members of the group are behind. There is, however, one person missing. And now I'm really wondering why.

Chapter 48

We spend our penultimate night at a harbourside restaurant devouring a paella that looks capable of catering for a modest wedding party.

It's a beautiful spot, with the scent of warm pimento and saffron in the air as the sun makes a leisurely descent behind dozens of blindingly white super-yachts. And they really are super. Huge and glitzy, the sort of thing on which Kate Moss would sunbathe with a glass of Cristal in her hand.

'Our VIP holiday doesn't look all that VIP next to those, does it?' I muse. I've been studiously avoiding the issue of Harry in any conversation. This is despite the fact that every second I'm away from the hotel, I'm wondering if he's there in the bar, wondering where I am. Then I tell myself that if I sat here all night pining after him, I'd look like a complete saddo – and therefore this, really, is the only option.

'There's always *someone* richer and flashier.' Nicola shrugs. 'I'll be honest, I've loved being away with both of you, but I'd have been just as happy on a campsite.'

Meredith looks appalled. 'A campsite? Are you serious?'

'Oh, I don't mean I'm not incredibly grateful to you for sharing your competition prize, Meredith,' Nic adds hastily. 'That was unbelievably good of you.'

Meredith shakes her head in despair, then pauses as if an idea has just popped into her head. 'I think I need to show you two a *seriously* good time tonight.'

Pregnant or not, Meredith has a nose for nightlife. She's like a wild boar hunting truffles, only her speciality is bars with opulent VIP sections, cool tunes and a nice line in out-landishly named cocktails.

After jumping in a taxi and heading to God-Knows-Wheresville, we have found ourselves in a club where the sound system has been unleashed to its full, techno potential and my breastbone is vibrating like something you'd buy at Ann Summers. It is packed, the atmosphere is electric and it's clear that Meredith feels instantly at home.

'Are you sure you don't want to go somewhere you can find a seat?' I ask.

'No way! I'm going to dance,' she insists, dragging Nic away by the hand as I head to the bar.

I spend twenty minutes waiting to be served two G&Ts, and a cranberry juice for Meredith. Having got them, I weave back through people far cooler than I am, towards the spot where I left my friends.

I see Nicola first, and then I realise that Meredith is deep in conversation with another woman. Although 'conversation' isn't quite the word: Meredith appears to be getting a mouthful from her. I arrive with the drinks only to catch the end of it.

'Diz is not a place for a woman carrying a baby,' the woman is saying, anger etched on her face.

'That's enough,' interrupts Nicola furiously. 'She was only dancing.'

The woman throws her a look of disdain as Meredith gazes at her hands silently. 'You don't deserve to be a mother,' the woman adds venomously, before spinning on her heel and leaving.

'What's going on?' I ask.

When Meredith looks up, her eyes are clouded by a film of tears. 'Do you mind if we just go?'

'Of course not.' I follow her through the crowd until we step into the fresh air outside. We pick up a taxi with merciful ease.

'What an absolute bitch,' Nicola spits, as we head back to the hotel. 'Does she think pregnant women are supposed to sit at home all day knitting booties and counting their varicose veins? Meredith was only dancing. It's not as if she'd popped a couple of Es and started lap-dancing on the tables.'

Meredith looks out of the window.

'I should've told her to sling her hook at the beginning.

How ignorant. I'm fuming.' Nicola has always had a defiantly protective streak when it comes to her friends. 'I mean, God Almighty, you've been drinking orange juice all week, Meredith. I know you haven't been studying every line of *What To Expect When You're Expecting*, but so what? This is one of your last big nights out for a long time and that bloody woman's gone and ruined it.'

I add nothing to this conversation, partly because I agree with everything Nicola's saying, but also because, as I reach over and clutch Meredith's hand, I can't help studying her expression.

She's trying to pretend she's not upset. And she's failing miserably.

When we arrive back at the B Hotel, I ask her if she'd like a cranberry juice now instead, as Nicola heads for the Ladies.

'One for the road, eh?' Meredith shrugs as I find a sofa to sink in to.

'Are you okay, Meredith?'

'Yeah,' she says too insistently. 'Of course.'

I frown. 'Only . . . you don't look it, if you don't mind me saying so.'

She sighs and looks up. 'Do you want the honest answer?'

'Only if you want to tell me.'

Her jaw clenches and she hesitates, before confessing something that's obviously been on her mind for some time. 'I'm not ready to be a mother, Imogen.'

I shake my head. 'All pregnant women have moments when they doubt themselves, Meredith. Especially the first time, and especially when it's been a surprise.'

She looks at me with blazing eyes. 'This is not just last-minute cold feet, Imogen. This is a *mistake*. It was from the beginning. I never, *ever* felt broody. I never even wanted kids.'

I swallow. 'Well, you know what ... me neither. I'd never wanted them before I found out I was pregnant with Florence.'

'Seriously?' Meredith's eyes now search mine.

I nod. 'I suppose I never knew how much I wanted a daughter until I had her.'

'But you were over the moon when you found out you were pregnant – I remember it. It was totally different from the meltdown I went into.'

I'm suddenly unable to deny it.

'I felt ... *feel* terrified,' she continues. 'That's literally the only word I can use to describe it.' She takes a sip of her drink. 'I've never told you this, but I was booked in for an abortion. Not once, but twice.'

Shock grips my throat. 'You're kidding?' I whisper. 'Why didn't you tell me?'

'I planned to tell everyone that I'd miscarried. It was early days, before twelve weeks the first time and then at sixteen weeks the second time.'

'So what happened?'

She takes a deep breath. 'I got in there and, for some utterly

362

unfathomable reason, I couldn't do it. I have no idea why, but I couldn't. And, the fact is, Imogen, I *should* have done it. But now it's too late.'

'Why do you think that?'

She looks at me as if it's obvious, as if there's simply no need for her to spell this out. 'Because I know I don't have it in me to be a good mother to this child. I'm the least organised person I know. My passions in life have been' – her voice takes on a sarcastic tone – 'hmm, let me think . . . going out and getting off my face a lot. Nothing I do or have done has equipped me for this. And, worse than all that is this – I keep hearing about how women fall in love with their babies every time they feel a kick in their tummy, or the second they've given birth and are in their arms. But I'm not the falling-instantly-in-love kind, Imogen. Nathan is the only man I've ever felt anything for, and a lot of the time I'd happily throttle him.'

I put my arm around her, squeezing her into me reassuringly. But if I'm entirely honest, what Meredith is saying has got me worried. She's doing herself down, of that there's no doubt, but the fact that she's not bonding at all with this baby has been nagging at me for ages, and I'm not naïve enough to think that things will instantly turn into a fairytale the second he or she is in her arms.

I press my hand into hers. It feels small and slightly swollen. 'Meredith, there's no point in me trying to tell you being a mum is easy or no big deal. It *is* a big deal and, as you've already seen from my life, it can make everything extremely hectic, complicated and difficult. But I say this with total sincerity and it's all I really can say to you – becoming a parent was the best thing that ever happened to me. It's worth every minute.'

We look up and see Nicola approaching.

'To *you*, perhaps,' Meredith whispers, as Nic sits down, unaware of the conversation.

'I'm still incensed about that woman,' she harrumphs.

Meredith forces a smile. 'Forget about it, honestly.' She pats her on the hand. 'Listen, I hope you don't mind, but I'm suddenly not feeling too good. I'm going to head up to bed.'

'Is everything all right?' Nicola asks, concerned.

'Yeah. I think something I ate disagreed with me,' Meredith replies, running her hands unconvincingly over her stomach. But before anyone can argue, she's heading towards the lift.

'She'll feel better after a good night's sleep,' Nicola says. 'Do you want to swap again? You haven't had an undisturbed few hours since you got here.'

'Oh, what's another night?' I shrug. 'Thanks, but I've given up on the idea of sleep.'

She smiles. 'Hmm … what's that lovely smell? Whatever they're cooking in the restaurant tonight smells amazing.'

I breathe in and freeze as I recognise it instantly. 'It's sage.'

She raises her eyebrows. 'Blimey, you're good. I'd never have guessed that.'

'Roberto pointed it out once. They use a lot of it in Italy. It apparently symbolises lifelong happiness . . .'

My voice trails off as the scent transports me vividly back to that evening in San Gimignano. Every element of the night fills my senses: the sweet, chestnut biscotti crumbling in my mouth; the gentle coo of turtledoves on the roof; Roberto's smile when he told me about the old man who'd found happiness with a new love and his insistence that he'd want me to do the same.

Neither of us had any idea how prophetic that conversation would prove to be. I am fleetingly reminded about my wish that Roberto would send me a sign, but push the thought out of my head immediately. I find myself surreptitiously scanning the bar area.

'Perhaps he came while we were out at dinner,' Nicola offers. 'There's still time for him to turn up,' she adds.

'It's not a big deal anyway,' I reply, to convince myself more than her. 'I've got a lot on my plate at the moment.'

Nicola suddenly looks serious. 'Can I say something, Imogen?'

'Of course.'

'I understand about why you'd feel awkward being with another man. But it's not a betrayal of Roberto. He'd *want* that.'

My jaw tightens, despite my recollection of that conversation with him in Tuscany all those years ago. 'Do you *know* that?'

'I'm certain of it. Roberto was a good man and he would not have wanted you to be by yourself.' She pauses, looking at me carefully. 'Life is precious, Imogen. You've got to live it. Be true to yourself. Otherwise you'll wake up one day full of regrets.' She hesitates, as if letting her own words filter into her brain. Then she looks at her hands. 'You don't need to say anything. I'm in no position to lecture you when I've totally failed to be true to myself. Or Jess, for that matter.'

'I know how hard it must be for you to address this thing with your parents.'

'But that's not much of an excuse really, is it?' She takes a deep breath, clearly wanting to change the subject. 'Anyway, you and Harry . . .'

'I don't even know if Harry really likes me. He'd be here if he was keen.'

Nicola looks at me. 'I don't know why he's not here, but I'm one hundred per cent certain that he likes you. And whether he's moving to Aberdeen or not, most women wouldn't be avoiding his attention.'

'I'm not most people.'

'I know. But,' she hesitates, 'you can't waste the rest of your life mourning a man who isn't coming back, Imogen.'

The words feel like knives in my stomach. 'I . . . I . . .'

'Live your life, Imogen. Suck every bit of happiness out of it. You deserve it. We all do.'

Chapter 49

There are some nights when you've spent so long analysing things that all that's left to do is get drunk. Paralytically, inhumanly drunk.

'We're going to be so hung over we won't be able to see straight tomorrow. You do realise that, don't you?' Nicola asks.

'I don't care,' I insist through an inebriated slur. 'I've got no job to go to any more, so I can get *banjaxed* every day of the week if I want. I could start swigging WKD before I got up, with nothing more to tax me than wondering how the guy on Jeremy Kyle eats solid food with so few front teeth.'

She sniggers. 'Somehow it's impossible to imagine it. I don't think you'd manage a day of being dysfunctional, Imogen.' She hiccups. 'You're far too uptight.'

I nearly spit out my drink. 'I'd *thought* that sentence was going too well.'

She laughs again now, throwing back her head, which oscillates so violently I'm briefly concerned about its ability to stay put. 'Oh, don't worry, it's one of the many qualities I love about you.'

'Being neurotic?'

'Nobody does it better,' she replies with a giggle.

I shake my head. 'The only possible response to that news ...' – I pause to hiccup this time – '... is to order two more glasses of cava.'

'Good idea,' she concurs, almost falling off her chair.

I order the drinks from a waiter. 'Anyway,' I continue, 'you wouldn't call me uptight if you knew what I got up to last night.'

'I *know* what you got up to last night,' she splutters.

'I was a *demon* in bed,' I assure her.

'That good?' She raises an eyebrow.

I pause to think for a second. 'Well, I *hope* so. Though that might be wishful thinking. And the fact that he's not exactly pursuing me would tend to indicate the opposite.' Drunken paranoia sweeps through me. 'Shit!' I turn to her, wide eyed. 'Maybe I was rubbish.'

'I'm sure you weren't.'

'I hope I was passable at least. Although I just don't know. I'm very rusty.'

'Did you enjoy it?'

I think about a polite way to put this. 'It was very pleasant. Distinctly agreeable.'

'So it was basically amazing?'

'YES!' I shriek.

'Maybe you could try and do it again, just to make sure?' Nic says, looking up and smirking.

'I don't think so.'

She nods to the door. 'Well, you're going to have to do something. Harry's heading this way.'

Chapter 50

Harry approaches looking so heartbreakingly sexy that my body tingles just at the sight of him.

'I'm going to leave you to it,' Nicola whispers.

I grab her by the arm. '*Don't.*'

'Why?'

But before I can answer he's there in front of me, with his chest undulating as if he's slightly out of breath and a film of moisture on his forehead. Every bit of him vies for my attention – the way his shirt falls open at the collar; the slight part of his lips before he speaks. 'I'm sorry I've only just got here.'

My mouth suddenly feels very dry. 'That's okay. Why don't you join Nicola and me for a drink?'

She's clearly itching to leave but for a reason I can't pinpoint, I want her to stay. As back up. To stop me saying or doing something I might regret.

'How's your day been, Nicola?' he asks. If he's bothered by her presence, he doesn't look it.

'Great, thanks,' she replies, suddenly looking far more sober than me. 'I hope you don't think I'm being rude, but I need to hit the sack. I haven't got the stamina to keep up with this woman.' She grins. 'She's got me horribly drunk.'

I stiffen as I become aware that I'll be on my own. With my own decisions. And indecisions. And *fear*. 'Are you sure you're okay?' I ask, as she kisses me on the cheek. 'Are you sure you don't want to stay? Are you sure—'

'Quite sure.' She looks into my eyes meaningfully, the way you do when warning a small child to behave itself in public, as she backs away. 'Just remember what I said, okay?'

A shot of heat inflames my cheeks and I pretend I haven't heard her as I turn back to Harry, zooming in involuntarily on his mouth as I'm hijacked by a vivid flashback of him kissing me in bed only twenty-four hours ago. The thought exhilarates and horrifies me. Does he expect the same to happen tonight? Do *I* want that?

Yes. *YES!*

Oh God, no . . .

'Have you been running?' is all I can think to blurt out, desperately trying to drown out my thoughts.

As Harry sits next to me, his smell stirs every one of my senses – a clean, warm scent of sandalwood and zingy top notes that makes my insides swirl.

'It's been an eventful evening.'

'Oh?'

He hesitates, as if about to tell me something important, then simply says, 'Have you heard any more about your job, yet?'

I shake my head. 'The last official message I had from my boss was two words long and effectively indicated that my P45 was in the post.' The reminder makes my throat clench.

'I'm really sorry, Imogen. I feel terrible about telling you to switch your phone off. I genuinely believed that everyone needs a break on holiday. Your company obviously thinks otherwise.'

'Well, it was my decision. Besides, you were one hundred per cent right in principle. They *should* all be able to get on with things themselves and give me five minutes' peace. Unfortunately, the timing wasn't great – that's what made the ramifications of this so difficult.'

I catch his eye and, as if he can't bring himself not to do it, he reaches out and touches my arm. I stiffen at first, but as my adrenalin subsides, I realise he's inviting me into his arms.

I don't even think about whether or not to do it; I simply slide into him, a sensation that feels in equal parts gorgeous and exhilarating, to the point of discomfort.

It's only as my cheek presses against his that I realise this is not a romantic gesture – more a friendly, supportive squeeze. The thought sends an anxious ripple through me. I look up drunkenly at his lips, feeling an urgent need to reach up and kiss him, but fairly certain I won't dare. Then he says something that makes me jerk back.

'I wonder if I could help?'

My thoughts are yanked back down to earth. 'I don't know how you could. I don't know how *anyone* could.'

He releases me from his arms and turns to face me. 'I've been racking my brains about how to make it up to you. I feel honour-bound to do something.'

'You don't need to—'

'The thing is, these stories tend to run for a few days, sometimes weeks.'

I let out a spontaneous groan and run my fingers through my hair. I might no longer be in the employ of Peebles, but I will be far happier when I've seen the back of those articles completely.

'It's the same with any scandal story, whether it's about a new vaccine – the type of thing I cover – or some boss caught with his pants down.'

'That's one item of clothing that stayed on,' I mutter, 'as far as I know.'

He pulls his leg underneath him as he concentrates, and the distance between us suddenly seems more than physical.

'I'd make the world's worst PR man,' he continues, 'but I *do* know people in the media.'

I frown, wondering where this conversation is going. 'I'm not sure what you're suggesting—'

'We can't re-write history – those stories are out there now. But, I suppose what I'm wondering is, would some positive press make a difference?'

I think for a second. 'I'm certain it would. But how's that possible? Every journalist who's mentioned us in the last two days is fixated on David and the overactive contents of his trousers.'

He suppresses a laugh and we catch each other's eye. 'It might've been a misunderstanding.' He winks.

'What, the woman wanted something to go with her G&T and he got the wrong idea when she ordered nuts?'

We both collapse into giggles.

'Perhaps she was just practising the brace position under that blanket?' he muses.

I nearly spit out my drink. 'Or the air con broke so she had to remove her top? I do it all the time myself.'

Delirium takes over as innuendo after innuendo is trotted out, becoming more and more outlandish with each one. Eventually, as I'm wiping a tear away, Harry manages to pull himself together. 'The thing is, I can't guarantee anything. Nothing at all. But if you wanted to get something more palatable out there about your company, I *can* make sure you get heard by the right people. Whether they'll print it is a different matter.'

My mind starts whirring. The fact is, I'm in this odd limbo where I can't *entirely* define my employment status. As Nic pointed out, terminating my contract would surely involve something significantly more than a stroppy text message from David – even if, as Roy's rapid promotion would indicate, that turns out to be the catalyst to the inevitable. And even if he *has* instructed the HR department to instigate dismissal proceedings, the fact that neither he nor I are actually there at the moment *might* mean they haven't started yet. I know I'm clutching at straws. But if there's even a chance of saving my job – a job that might have given me significant grief in the last few days but that, fundamentally, I love – then I want to grasp it with both hands.

'Are you sure you wouldn't mind doing this for me?' I ask, tentatively.

'Of course not. I wouldn't be doing much – just putting you in touch with some contacts. No promises though, honestly. At the end of the day, it's up to you to come up with something sufficiently newsworthy to end up in the paper. I can't do that bit.'

I nod. 'I understand.'

'Why don't you think about it overnight?' he suggests.

'As long as you mean it, I'll get on to my boss first thing in the morning.'

He holds my gaze and my insides turn to marshmallows again. 'Of course I mean it.'

For a moment I think he's going to kiss me. I feel almost – almost – sure he's thinking about it too, from the way he's looking at me: silently, expressively. Yet he doesn't move. He doesn't do anything except allow this pressure-cooker moment to build until it becomes too much to bear.

'I'd better go,' I announce, standing up.

The second I'm on my feet, I regret it. I hesitate and turn back, wondering if I could just do the deed myself – lean down and kiss him. I was intimately acquainted with this man's inner thighs only a day ago, so the fact that I'm not grown up enough to do this is ridiculous. So I decide I'm going to do it.

I AM!

The problem is, my surge of confidence coincides with *him* standing up . . . and kissing me politely on the cheek. I have no other option but to slink away.

'Imogen, wait.'

'What is it?'

He puts his hand in his pocket and looks strangely apprehensive. 'I've . . . I've got something for you.'

'What is it?'

He swallows. He withdraws his hand from his pocket and pulls something out. As he unfolds his fingers, my knees slacken.

He's holding my necklace.

'I don't understand,' I stammer, clutching it between my fingers as I prop myself clumsily on the nearest bar stool.

'When you stumbled and fell, I hadn't even realised we'd lost you. I just carried on running,' he explains. 'I was only focused on chasing that boy.'

'Nicola said you'd gone off for the tour with the rest of the group. She thought Delfina insisted.'

'Hmm, she tried to and that's what initially held me back. I was about to catch up with you just as you fell over. Sorry I didn't stop – I had no idea you'd hurt yourself so badly. I thought you'd want me to keep going.'

'So you caught up with him?'

'Eventually, although he didn't know it. I was completely lost by the time he stopped running – obviously convinced he'd managed to shake us. We ended up in a maze of back streets, and I caught up with him as he was about to enter this doorway. It must have been miles from where we'd started by then. It was only when he had a key in the door that I tapped him on the shoulder.'

My eyes widen. 'What did he say?'

'Nothing – he tried to smack me in the jaw instead.'

'Oh God, are you all right?' Then I remember about him practising judo and almost feel sorry for the boy.

'I'm fine, although he was pretty determined.'

'You didn't kill him, did you?'

'No!' He laughs. 'I managed to pin him down long enough to have a conversation with him. He tried to deny the whole thing at first and say you'd got the wrong person, but it was obvious he was lying. He was hysterical that I'd found where he lived.'

'So what happened?'

'I said I was going to tell the police where he was – and give them his address – unless he gave me back the necklace. In which case I'd leave him alone.'

377

'So he gave it to you?'

He shrugs awkwardly. 'It wasn't quite that simple. He said his aunt had it and was in the process of selling it. I got the impression they thought it was worth quite a lot.'

I look down at the necklace. I've never thought of it in terms of its monetary value – that has never been relevant. But I have no doubt that they were right.

'I was in two minds about whether to just go to the police, but they've been so uninterested that I became convinced, rightly or wrongly, that I'd have more of a chance of getting it back my own way,' he continues.

'Which was?'

'I arranged to meet him tonight. I said that both he and his aunt would have to explain themselves to the law unless he kept his side of the bargain. I didn't know whether or not he was going to come, which was why I didn't say anything. I didn't want you to get your hopes up.'

'That's where you were tonight?'

'I was due to meet him at eight. He turned up half an hour late, saying his aunt still had the necklace and couldn't get there until later. I thought it'd never happen but she finally turned up at eleven, and only then after I'd started dialling the police station's number. The whole thing was a charade, but at least I got it back.'

I clutch the necklace between my fingers before lifting it up and, with trembling fingers, returning it to its rightful place around my neck. 'Harry, I don't know what to say. I'm so grateful.'

An easy smile appears on his lips. 'I'm glad.'

Suddenly, all I can hear above the clink of glasses as the barman cleans up is my pulse, thundering in my ears. There seems to be nothing else to do but walk back to him, take his face in my hands and press my lips against his. And that is what is running through my head as I push myself tentatively off the stool and take a small step forwards.

It's as I become aware of his hand reaching for mine that the barman clears his throat, loudly. We both look up, startled, as he says something to Harry in Spanish.

'He'd like to close,' Harry tells me.

'Of course!' I grab my bag. 'Of course.' I smooth down my dress and smile awkwardly as we head out to the lobby towards the lift.

Harry's arm is brushing against mine as we walk side by side, firing electricity through me as we wait for the lift and step into it when it arrives. I press the button for the sixth floor.

He hesitates and looks at me, taking in the significance of this gesture. I might as well have said: 'No sex for you tonight, m'laddo!' Yet, what do I say? 'Whoops, my mistake . . . let's go to your place and get naked!'

I touch the necklace and curse myself. What the hell do I want? Perhaps the answer is to be *persuaded*. I want Harry to make it impossible for me to resist, to take this decision out of my hands.

The six flights up to my floor are, in turn, both excruciatingly slow and way too fast.

As the lift door opens, I'm aware that somebody needs to say something.

'I'll see you in the morning, shall I?' It's him. 'Let me know if you want me to put you in touch with those journalists.'

'I will.' I hesitate, then step out and force a smile. The lift doors start to close. The movement sends me into a panic and I respond by shoving my foot between them, which has a similar effect on my outside metatarsal as a walnut cracker would. 'Um . . . Harry?'

'Yes?'

'Thanks,' is the only thing I can manage. 'For . . . just about everything.'

Day Seven

Chapter 51

When my eyes flutter open the next morning, I feel hung over but curiously well rested. I reach up to my throat and idly roll the delicate chain of my necklace between my fingertips, refamiliarising myself with the feel of it against my skin.

My phone beeps and I reach over to it to find a text from Harry:

> Morning, sleepy head. I took the liberty of speaking to a friend on The Economic Times. He can give you ten minutes on the phone later. Entirely up to you – ? H x

I sit up and compose a response, grinning spontaneously.

> You really are my knight in shining armour, aren't you?

Then I remember the just-good-friends squeeze and bin it instantly.

Will try and get hold of my (ex) boss now and give you a
shout asap. THANK YOU! x

I pull up David's number and am about to dial it, when the
phone rings and 'MUM' flashes up. I cut her off and quickly
dial David's number instead, surprised when he actually
answers.

'My life is in tatters!' he cries, through a self-pitying snivel.

'Hello, David. It's Imogen.'

'I know.' If I didn't know any better, I'd say he sounds
relieved to hear from me. 'What the Bill Barnacles do I do,
Imogen? My children won't talk to me. My wife won't talk to
me. And the board of Getreide want me to Skype them
tomorrow to explain myself. But how *can* I explain myself?
There IS no explanation except I was drunk, stupid and as
randy as two Jack Russells in a Swedish sauna. *What am I going
to say?*'

The sustained whine in his voice prompts me to sit up
straighter. 'Are you asking me that in a professional capacity?'
I ask curtly.

'I'm asking you in *any* capacity!'

'Only, you did sack me . . .'

He sighs theatrically. 'I know.'

'And told me you'd started proceedings against me, to boot
me out.'

'I know, I know.'

'When I spoke to Roy, he said he'd been offered my job.'

'Oh, he's exaggerating. Look, you know what I always say, Imogen – "Go big, or go home." Well, I can't flaming well go home. And look where going big has got me.'

I roll my eyes. 'Am I still fired, David, or not? That is a fairly fundamental question.'

'Imogen, I'm ... *sorry*,' he wheezes. 'I was angry. And you did make a Horlicks of things.'

'Yes, I did,' I concede. 'But do I really need to point out we wouldn't have been in this mess in the first place if—'

'PLEASE DON'T FINISH THAT SENTENCE!' he yelps. 'I know whose fault this is. I know I've only got myself to blame.'

'So can I have my job back? I might have a plan that could make it worth your while,' I add cryptically.

'I didn't really start the proceedings,' he whimpers. 'HR wouldn't be interested in anything right now except my flight, that woman and her bosoms.'

'I don't think I've got long left with this company, Imogen,' he continues. 'I'm thinking of resigning.'

'Don't do that just yet, David,' I reply, sitting on the edge of the bed as I start to explain what I have up my sleeve.

The morning is chaotic but productive. I'm never off the phone, but at least this time I feel like we're getting some-where. It's a whirlwind of talks between board members,

David, Charles and the team at Getreide, all of which requires 300 per cent of my attention. And, for once, I'm proud to say I manage to avoid Mum's constant attempts to distract me with her nonsense.

The business centre becomes the command hub for me and Harry. He's a revelation: calm, supportive, the voice of reason when all are flapping like lost homing pigeons. And almost as determined as I am to make sure I get this right.

The prospect of speaking to the journalist from *The Economic Times* makes me feel like I'm about to share a Jacuzzi with a shoal of hungry piranha. After my previous experiences with the media, I'm just waiting to be tripped up. Equally, I'm aware that I have little to lose at this stage.

I persuade Harry to go down for lunch while I dial the number, dread in the pit of my stomach, feeling too self-conscious to conduct the interview with him there.

As it turns out, the experience is rather different from what I was expecting.

'So tell me,' Montgomery Smith, the journalist, begins in a voice is so plummy his tonsils could have their own personal set of bell-ringers. 'This assignment of Harry's – it sounds like hell!'

I laugh nervously. 'From what I can see it's involved a lot of hard investigation . . . into the mini-bar.'

He guffaws. 'And if I know Harry, he'll have women throwing themselves at him. Lucky sod. Some men were born with sex appeal. In my case, it was just jaundice.' He hesitates. 'You and he *are* just friends, aren't you? That's what he told me.'

'Er . . . yes.'

'Not that you've got anything to worry about. Decent chap by all accounts.'

'I was getting that impression.'

'Anyway, we need to get down to business. Peebles. That boss of yours has got himself into a pickle, hasn't he?'

I hesitate, wondering if we're 'on the record' yet. I try to conjure up a politician's answer, but decide that's only going to get me into more trouble. 'You could say that.'

'Well, that's not really the angle we go big on at *The Economic Times*. We'll have to mention it, of course, but I'm more interested in his share price than private life – not that he kept things all that private, of course!' he hoots. 'The only way that would change was if he was given the boot, or some such thing.'

My lungs inflate at the idea. 'There's no suggestion of that at the moment. I do have a half-decent business story for you, though, if you'd like it?'

'I'm all ears!'

Chapter 52

As I emerge from the hotel into dazzling sunlight and approach Harry's table, I realise he's ordered me some lunch. The sky is a blistering, cobalt blue but he looks unfeasibly cool in his sunglasses and one of those effortlessly hip T-shirts. His tanned legs provide the best view in the place and I get a peculiar pang of pride that I've run my fingertips along them.

He glances up as I sit down. 'Is this for me?' I ask.

'I took the liberty. It's only just arrived.'

I arrange a napkin on my lap as a text arrives on his phone. He glances at it and rolls his eyes.

'Everything okay?' I ask.

He grins. 'I told my mum I'd take her out for a celebratory dinner on my first evening back in Aberdeen and she's responded by saying she's got a prior engagement. Which, I can only presume, means she's going to bingo.'

I laugh.

'How did the interview go?' he asks.

I pick up my fork. 'I take nothing for granted these days but ... okay, I think. Thank you so much. Again.'

'I didn't do anything,' he insists, tearing a piece of bread.

With the knowledge that there are now less than twenty-four hours left of this holiday, I am overcome by the need to say something to him about matters that go beyond my press campaign.

I clear my throat. 'Listen ... about what happened. Between you and me.'

He opens his mouth to say something, but forces himself to stop.

'What is it? I ask.

He puts down the bread. 'I was going to say that you didn't need to explain. But my curiosity got the better of me.' He smiles.

I laugh, feeling heat rise up my neck. 'Okay. Well, the issue, really, is this—' My mobile rings.

I cut off the call and put the phone on silent while I prepare for the terrifying and liberating prospect of being honest with him.

'I think, Harry, that ... I think you're absolutely amazing, actually,' I say, barely able to believe those words have come out of my mouth. 'I've only known you six days but I've worked out that much. And' – I take a deep breath – 'I loved sleeping with you.'

He looks torn between delight and embarrassment, but I'm still glad I said it.

'You already know it was a big deal for me given that it was the first time since Roberto died. So the fact that I enjoyed it so much . . . well, I've got a lot to thank you for.'

He smiles.

'But . . .' I begin cagily.

'How did I know there was a "but"?'

'As much as I loved it, I was also a little scared by what that step represents.'

'That's understandable. You're not sure you were ready.'

'I suppose that's it. In a nutshell.'

'That's okay, Imogen.'

I suddenly feel very stupid – and presumptuous – for even having this conversation.

'I don't know why I'm telling you all this,' I mumble. 'It's not as though you're proposing a relationship or anything like that. I mean, to all intents and purposes this was nothing more than a fling. By definition. You're moving to Aberdeen, so it couldn't be.'

He takes a sip of beer. 'You're right. Technically, at least. *By definition*, as you say. Only . . .' His voice trails off, and I can't bear to not hear his thoughts on this matter.

'What?'

He puts down his fork and looks at his hands. 'You know I told you I had that . . . problem?'

I smile at the word. 'You want a thunderbolt, but you can't find anyone to have one with.'

He laughs self-consciously. 'Precisely.'

'What about it?'

He shakes his head and looks into the distance, over the balcony and across to the far end of the beach. 'Well, I don't want to scare you off or anything' – he looks back at me briefly – 'and I feel an absolute idiot for saying this to someone I met six days ago ... But if I don't say something then I'll wave goodbye to you tomorrow and wish I had, for no other reason than this doesn't feel like something I ought to keep to myself.' He stops talking, clearly having a change of heart.

'So don't keep it to yourself,' I urge.

He rubs his thumb against his chin, troubled. 'Well, it's just this ... ' He finally looks in my eyes and swallows. 'I can't stop thinking about you, Imogen.'

I can feel my mouth dropping wider and wider without any ability to stop the process. Because, frankly, the idea that this man, this beautiful, kind, charismatic man, would even give me the time of day is revelation enough. My head begins spinning with the implications of it all, and I suddenly don't know what to say, do, or where to even look.

It's therefore entirely by chance that my eyes land on my silent mobile phone at the exact moment that a call rings off, followed by a list of the calls I've missed. There are nine. And most of them are not from my mum, but Dad.

'Oh God,' I mutter, all other thoughts gone in an instant as I begin flicking through my phone. I have a very bad feeling.

'Is everything okay?' Harry asks.

'Can you excuse me a minute?' I dial the number as the sickly sensation swirls through my insides. 'Dad, what is it?'

He hesitates, before the sentence froths from his mouth in a cold panic. 'It's Florence, sweetheart. She's been in an accident.'

Chapter 53

Five years ago I awoke in hospital and my dad was forced to tell me that Roberto had been killed.

The ominous nausea that engulfed me in the seconds before that now return to haunt me. Unlike then, when I knew immediately that the person I loved most in the world had been snatched away from me, Florence's fate is terrifying in its lack of clarity.

The blood in my veins seems to freeze over as I listen to what Dad has to say, noting how he's trying to sound calm and how badly he is failing.

His knowledge is patchy. He's in his car on the way to hospital and only has a mishmash of hysterical messages from Mum, left on his phone, to go on. But he knows this much: they were at the zebra crossing near the park. Florence saw the swings and ran ahead. A car came out of nowhere and, seeing Mum at the side of the road, didn't register a small child four feet away from her. The car braked. Mum dived to grab her out of the way.

It was too late.

'Is she conscious?' Nicola asks, as I frantically stuff clothes into my suitcase.

She and Meredith spent the morning relaxing in the spa. The air of tranquillity with which it left them disintegrated the second they heard my news.

'I don't know,' I manage through trembling lips, zipping up the case. Nicola has had a look online and discovered that there isn't a flight from Barcelona to the north-west of England for four and a half hours, but I want to get to the airport as soon as I can, even if it'll mean hanging around. 'Dad's trying to play it down, but he knows little until he gets to the hospital. He said he nearly didn't phone me at all until he knew more, but I'm glad he did.' I pick up my passport and slump on the end of the bed, looking at the clock anxiously as the second hand moves inordinately slowly. 'This is torture.'

Emotion prickles through me and, despite my attempts to hold it together, tears flood down my face.

'I'm going to phone the airline and try and get you onto that flight,' Nicola tells me.

'In the meantime, let's get you downstairs,' says Meredith, putting her arm round me. 'You should go and have a stiff drink – there's no point going to the airport yet, the flight's not for ages.'

I shake my head. 'I just want to get there.'

I drag my bag out of the hotel room and Meredith and I take the lift to the lobby, while Nicola stays in the room on hold to the airline.

Harry is waiting downstairs for me. 'There's a taxi outside – I've spoken to the driver for you, and he's all geared up to take you to the airport.'

I nod, still trying to hold it together but failing miserably. And, suddenly, Harry's arms are around me, squeezing me into him. I close my eyes and for a brief, quiet moment, allow the tension gripping me to float away. Then I fill my lungs with air and pull away, rubbing my hand across the wet skin on my cheek.

'Don't you think you'd be better off waiting to see what the deal is?' he asks. 'You should speak to your dad, once he knows exactly what's happened, before you do anything hasty. She might be okay . . . '

He has a way of saying things that makes it impossible not to feel optimistic, despite evidence to the contrary. 'She might, mightn't she?' I mutter. 'I mean, I don't know she's badly injured. It might just be a scrape.' But as soon as I've said it, I am overcome by the notion that I'm being complacent.

'You should wait here and try to stay calm until you've got news. That plane's not taking off any earlier, whether you're here or sitting in some crap café in the terminal.'

'He's right,' insists Meredith.

Knowing full well that I'm not thinking straight at the

moment, I defer to the judgment of those around me and follow Harry to a sofa by the bar, while Meredith goes to the loo.

'Have you got a picture of Florence?' he asks, clearly trying to distract me from my own hysteria.

I nod and pull up my favourite of dozens of choices stored on my phone. She's wearing a pink Hello Kitty bobble hat, the apple of her cheek pressed hard against mine as we grin like lunatics. 'That was at Christmas when we went ice-skating at the Tower of London. Have you ever been?'

He shakes his head. 'I'd break my neck.'

I manage a smile. 'She was surprisingly good at it, considering her age. They have these special little skates with two blades. I could've done with them myself, to be honest.'

'So she's a natural?'

'Definitely, although she's got this terribly independent streak – which is good, obviously, and I'm glad she has – but when it comes to things like that she absolutely refuses to do something as babyish as hold someone's hand. It resulted in quite a few falls. It's the same when she's crossing the road ...'

My voice trails off as a horrifying thought occurs to me that I may never be able to take her ice-skating again.

''Arry Pfeiffer!' All of a sudden, Delfina is marching towards us, fury imprinted on her face. 'This is 'ow you say ... *beyond a joke*. No wonder I am getting the sack with you not turning up on our excursions!'

'I'm sorry, it's my fault,' I tell her. She looks me up and down, before turning back to Harry.

'It's not her fault,' he insists. 'It's nobody's fault. Let me explain . . .' He takes her to one side and I suddenly feel very alone.

I stand up and walk towards the big glass doors, where I gaze across to the beach with a hideous, numb feeling of time slowing down. I need to know what's going on. Now.

As if answering my prayers, my phone rings. I nearly break my arm trying to answer it.

'Dad!'

'It's Mum. I'm on your father's phone as mine's run out of battery.'

'Mum, is she alive?'

Mum starts to cough. 'Florence? Of course she's alive!'

My body goes limp with relief and it takes a moment for me to gather my thoughts. 'Dad said she was hit by a car.'

'Not Florence. Me.' Her voice is trembling. 'I'm afraid your dad got his wires crossed when I left him a message. I was in a bit of a state so I mightn't have been as clear as I could've.'

'Mum . . . what happened? Are you okay?'

'I'm fine, just about. My nerves are in tatters and I've got a leg full of cuts and bruises, but apart from that it's nothing serious. I'm walking out of the hospital now, or at least limping.'

'Oh, thank God,' I breathe, holding my hand over my mouth.

'Imogen, it was my fault. I dread to think what might have happened.' Her next sentences are delivered in a frenzied stream. 'I couldn't get Florence to hold my hand. She slipped away and the car appeared out of nowhere. I managed to push her out of the way, but tumbled to the ground myself. It was a miracle nobody was really hurt . . . if Florence had been a foot closer . . . oh God!'

'Mum.' I've never heard her so upset.

'I'm so sorry, Imogen. I nearly . . . she nearly . . .'

I sit down on the nearest sofa, my knees are shaking so hard. 'Mum, you've got nothing to be sorry for. I know more than anyone else that four-year-olds are not like robots. Trying to keep them under control can be a nightmare. Sometimes, accidents happen. All I care about is that both of you are okay.'

'We are,' she whimpers.

'I think I should still come home now,' I say. 'There's a flight in four hours.'

Nicola taps me on the shoulder and I look up. 'Sorry, Imogen, but it's full,' she mouths.

I groan and go back to the phone. 'I can't get on that flight, but I'm going to see if there's another one today.'

'Imogen, don't,' argues Mum. 'You're flying back tomorrow and that's soon enough. We're all fine. I'm so sorry we scared you. You must've been out of your mind. Would you like to speak to Florence?'

'Yes, please.'

'I'll put her on. And ... Imogen?'

'Yes?'

'I don't say it often enough, but you're the best daughter anyone could hope for.'

The phone crackles as she hands the phone to Florence. As usual, she dispenses with any pleasantries and starts talking as if the conversation has been going on already for several minutes.

'I've been helping out the doctors, Mummy,' she tells me. 'I stuck a plaster on Grandma's leg. They said I can do an operation next.'

'Wow.' I laugh. 'You must be a natural.'

'Mummy?'

'Yes?'

'Have you got a boyfriend?'

I pause, wondering where on earth this has come from. Then I glance at Harry, who is watching me make the call. He smiles, totally unaware of the question. 'What makes you ask that?'

'I heard Grandma saying last night she wished you'd get one.'

I'm suddenly lost for words, and I can hear my mum trying to wrestle the phone off Florence. She loses.

'Um ... well, what would you think if I had one?' I feel compelled to ask.

'Good,' Florence says simply. 'I've got to go now.'

'Okay, sweetheart. I love you.'

But she's already gone. My living, breathing, well and truly okay daughter.

Chapter 54

A hot, early evening breeze dances across the beach as I emerge from the hotel under a vivid pink sky. This stretch of sand has been largely deserted for the day, except for a group of teenagers playing volleyball and three game, elderly men – mercifully all wearing trunks – bracing themselves for a swim.

The waves are stronger than usual, fizzing against the shore like spilled champagne and splashing against the boardwalk, where rollerbladers whiz past kissing couples and ladies walk overgroomed dogs.

I bypass the hotel sun loungers and remove my flip-flops, my toes sinking into hot sand as I head for the beach side of the boardwalk. There, I perch on the edge, dangling my feet as I take my notepad and pen from my bag.

Despite there being no future with Harry, there's one thing that this week – and today – has taught me. And that's that being on my own for the rest of my life probably isn't a good idea. That I'm missing out on a whole bundle of stuff: support, companionship, fun and, although my feelings for Harry won't have the opportunity to blossom into anything so grand ... love. Something that even my four-year-old daughter recognises.

Tomorrow, I go home and Harry flies to Aberdeen. We are destined never to see each other again: a thought that makes my stomach turn inside out when I dwell on it too long.

But there is tonight. And there is the rest of my life. And there are some things I need to say to the man I loved more than any other.

Amore mio,

This is the last letter I will be writing to you. Not because I don't love you, and I won't always love you. But because I think I'm finally starting to came round to the idea that my friends probably have a point. That it's time.

That little piece of you that meant so much to me, your necklace, is back where it belongs. I will wear it every day of my life, and think of you, and of the wonderful thing that we had together that nothing will ever change, even death.

I've spent the last few years fundamentally unable to accept that you're gone and that I'm facing a future without you. But, as impossible as it is to stomach, I have no choice.

And, if there's one thing of which I've reluctantly become convinced, it's that you wouldn't have wanted me to be like this. You wouldn't have wanted me not to live the rest of my

*life. You were too kind for that, too generous, too good; and you
loved me too much to want to see me as anything other than
happy.*

*So, as difficult as it is, I'm going to let go, Roberto, just
enough to live again.*

Goodnight, my darling. I love you. Sleep tight.

Imogen

xxxxxxxxx

I pause to look up at the clouds, which are tumbling across the
sky in a kaleidoscope of light. Then I tear out the page from
my notepad and carefully fold up the letter, before getting up
and continuing my way along the boardwalk.

It takes about five minutes before I reach the end. I stand
with the wind billowing through my hair as I gaze over the sea.
As the breeze dies down, I clutch the letter tightly, feeling
Roberto in my heart stronger than ever. I kiss the page softly
and slowly, before withdrawing it from my lips. Then I let go.
And watch with stinging eyes as it drifts out to sea.

Chapter 55

As this is our last night, we're booked in for a luxurious dinner at the hotel's opulent Michelin-starred restaurant, before flying home in the early hours of the morning. With Harry leaving tomorrow too, tonight is his final, must-attend-on-pain-of-death media dinner with the boss of the hotel.

We've arranged to have an aperitif together before dinner in the only free half-hour either of us have. And, despite the fact that nothing can happen between us now – we've effectively run out of time – there's a firestorm behind my ribcage as I walk into the bar.

I'm in my one little black dress, a slinky number with chiffon sleeves that I brought from home and which has the unique quality of affording Meredith's approval. She even declared I looked like Audrey Hepburn in it, though I suspect *Breakfast at Tiffany's* might not have been quite so iconic had Audrey Hepburn sported a black eye and plaster cast.

Harry is sitting on a stool at the vast, gleaming bar with his back to me. I can see from the reflection in the mirror behind that he's texting. I'm steps away, contemplating how to announce my presence when, almost instinctively, he turns and lowers his phone to the bar. For that small moment as I stand, our eyes locked, I'm not trembling with nerves, or terror, or anything other than an indefinable quality that brings a smile of pure joy to my lips.

He responds with a shimmering smile that confirms to me that he's thinking the same thing as me: that, if circumstances had been different, we could've been good together, him and me. Really good.

'You look beautiful,' he whispers, as I sit next to him.

'You're exaggerating,' I whisper back.

'I'm absolutely not. You're making this whole thing very hard to swallow for me.'

'What – your olives?'

He smiles, then lowers his eyes. 'Saying goodbye.'

Although it's exactly what's on my mind, the words make my stomach twist. 'If it means anything, it's hard for me to swallow, too.'

He looks up. 'Well, it does mean something. Because I know you had regrets about the other night. I understand them, even if my ego is struggling to come to terms with the fact that you didn't come back begging for more.'

'It wasn't due to a shortage of enjoyment, I assure you.'

He laughs. 'Well, that's a relief. I was about to go home and order a self-help book.'

I become aware of someone approaching us. It's Darren, the junior reporter from the *Daily Mirror*. 'Apologies for interrupting.' He turns to Harry. 'Here's the thirty euros I owe you. Sorry it's taken a couple of days – you can't have been flush after forking out for that necklace.'

Harry shifts uncomfortably. 'Oh. It's fine. No problem.'

'Right, I'll leave you to it. See you at the dinner, Harry. And have a nice night.' He nods to me politely.

'I will, thanks,' I mutter.

As soon as he's out of earshot, I turn to Harry. 'What did he mean about the necklace? Did he mean *my* necklace?'

'Um ... no,' Harry says, entirely unconvincingly. I glare at him and he crumples. 'I've always been a crap liar.'

'You're a journalist!' I point out.

'How did you get such a low opinion of us all?' he says, in an obvious attempt to deflect attention from the real issue.

'Harry, what did he mean about the necklace?'

He sighs. 'I shouldn't have even mentioned it to Darren – it was only because he was quizzing me about getting a load of money out of the cash machine when all our expenses were paid.'

'I'm lost.'

'Okay.' He hesitates. 'It wasn't *just* my magnificent powers of persuasion that got the necklace back. I had to ... to buy it back. It was a rash decision, I know, but I'd never have got it otherwise.'

I open my mouth to say something but am suddenly speechless. 'But that's so unfair,' I eventually manage.

'I'm sorry. I'd have loved to be able to tell you justice had been done and he was firmly locked up behind bars or something, but my main priority was getting it back. I could see how much it meant to you. And that was the only way.'

'How much did you pay for it?'

'Not much,' he says unconvincingly.

I narrow my eyes.

'You're scary when you do that.'

'Good. Because you've got to tell me. I insist on paying you back.'

He throws the warning look back at me. 'And I insist you drink that drink and let me enjoy the limited time I have left with you. The clock's ticking.'

I'm about to argue but those last three words stop me in my tracks. 'Harry, I know we're going our separate ways. And I know that things never quite worked out as they were meant to. We didn't even manage a proper holiday fling.'

He laughs. 'No. Half a fling, maybe. A bloody good half, I might add.'

I hesitate. 'I want you to know this. I think you're one of the most fantastic men I've ever met. And if things had been different . . . well, who knows what would've happened if things had been different? It hardly matters in some ways. But I need you to know that . . . saying goodbye suddenly feels horrible.'

He leans in and puts his arm around me, kissing me on the head. 'I know.'

I pull back and look at him. 'I still find it impossible to stomach the fact that things ended before they began. That I'm never going to see you again.'

He squirms in his seat and is about to say something, but takes a sip of his drink instead.

'What were you going to say?' I ask.

He shakes his head. 'Nothing.'

'Come on, say it.'

He turns and his jaw clenches. 'It was nothing . . . just . . .'

'Harry?'

'Why do I want to kiss you every time I see you?'

There's suddenly only one thing to say to that. 'So kiss me.'

He hesitates, looking at me through those big, inky eyes as he takes me by the hand.

As his mouth touches mine, I'm lost in the soundtrack of my dancing heartbeat, and all I can think of is how desperate I am to be alone with him.

I pull away and decide that for the first time in a while *I* need to be the one to suggest something reckless. 'How bad would it be if you missed your media night?' I whisper.

He looks at me and ponders the question. 'Well, Delfina's lost her job already so I don't suppose I'd be getting her in trouble. However, I can't imagine the hotel owners will be impressed.' He looks up at me. 'So I'd have to say: It'd be bad.'

I nod.

'How bad would it be if you missed your competition prize dinner?' he asks me.

I bite the side of my mouth. 'That's be bad too.'

We utter one sentence in perfect unison.

'I'm sure they'll understand . . .'

Chapter 56

There are no distractions. The phone isn't ringing. My daughter is safe. If I stopped to think about my work worries – or any worries – I'd no doubt whip myself up into another cyclone of anxiety. But I'm not stopping to think any more.

I'd almost forgotten how vast and resplendently cool Harry's suite was. Yet it's not the champagne bar or plunge pool that I can't keep my eyes off. It's him.

I gaze at him with a single thought dominating my head. A wish. That this could be more than a holiday romance. If we knew each other better, then the fact that he's moving somewhere a ten-hour drive away wouldn't be insurmountable. But it's not like we've been lovers for a year. I can't start a long-distance romance with a man who I hardly know – when I think about the implications of that, it makes my head spin and not just from my vertigo. He doesn't know that I grind my teeth in my sleep. He's never met my daughter . . . or, God help us, my mother. He doesn't know that most of my underwear isn't fit to wash the dishes with. He doesn't know that I weep every time I watch *Top Gun* or that the one and only time I tried marijuana I fell asleep in the corner of a party and snored like someone was using my nostrils as bagpipes.

But, considering it's only been seven days, he knows some of the big stuff. He knows about me and Roberto, me and my job, me and Florence. He's seen me at my most vulnerable and hopeless (because there's no other word for someone who buys denture cream for their feet), and it still hasn't put him off.

I wish, to an indescribable extent that, after I fly into Heathrow tomorrow, Harry and I could continue what we started this week with a relaxed drink after work one night, or lunch on a Saturday afternoon. Then just see what happens. That's all.

As soon as this thought filters through my head, another one crashes in behind it. This isn't simply about me feeling ready for a romance on a general level, because the only romance I feel ready for is with him. I want us to go on our first, proper date in London. I want to invite him to dinner and to meet Florence. I want to stroll along the Thames and let this thing between us unfold at a nice, leisurely pace.

But, given that we're never going to get the chance, I push the thought away, determined not to dwell on something that isn't a possibility and, instead, live for the moment. Tonight, for one night, I won't plan and I won't worry. I won't think about anything beyond what's happening in this room, right now.

I push away my trepidation about heights and take a small, cautious step onto the balcony, gazing at the vast, twinkling sky. There I slip into Harry's arms, submitting to his kiss, melting as his fingers sweep around my neck. As music drifts across the room I feel drunk on the moment, pressing my nose into his neck and kissing him gently as I breathe in the scent of his skin.

I take a step back into the room and, without a shred of embarrassment, reach round to the zip on my dress. Lust rushes through me as I prepare to slip out of my clothes, unashamed for the first time in a long time of my body; a body I know that, for some odd and unfathomable reason, this man seems to appreciate every inch of.

My zip is a quarter of the way down when it refuses to budge. I tug at it gently, imagining that seductive scene in *Nine ½ Weeks*, where Kim Basinger coolly strips and never stops pouting.

I try not to stop pouting. But, unfortunately, decisive action is required and, as I yank at the zip, it's stuck fast.

'Okay, I'll never get a job at Spearmint Rhino,' I mutter.

Harry struggles to contain his laughter. 'Do you need some help?'

'Would you mind awfully?' I turn round and lift up my hair.

He starts out gently, before realising that *gently* isn't going to move this zip. 'I don't want to damage your dress,' he says.

But as I feel his hands against my skin, something takes over and I spin around, grab the zip and thrust it downwards, causing an almighty rip. 'Shit! Oh well.' I shrug.

'I'm *so* glad I didn't do that.'

'I wouldn't care,' I declare, flinging the dress to the floor as I slide my half-naked body into his arms.

I can't tell you how satisfying it is to feel, against my stomach, exactly how much he wants me. In a burst of brazenness, I rub my hand against his crotch as he sighs with pleasure.

I feel empowered, I feel wonderful; I feel like a goddess, ready to have the sex that, until this week, I haven't had for five years. And, given the circumstances, may well not have for another five.

This thought seems to spur me on as I unzip his trousers and he . . . freezes.

I look up, trying to work out what's gone wrong. I step back and study at his face. He's clearly unnerved by something.

'What is it?' A moment of panic sweeps through me. 'I'm sorry . . .' I grab my dress and pull it around my chest.

'Don't be silly. I just thought I heard—'

His sentence is stunted by an insistent *rat-a-tat-tat* on the door.

'Did anyone order room service?' he jokes.

'Not me,' I reply.

He shakes his head. 'Maybe they'll go away.' He falls into my arms once more, pushing away the dress and brushing his hands over my breasts as my body floods with desire.

It's only then that I hear the voice from the other side of the door.

'Imogen!'

I step back. 'Oh, no. Please, no.'

'You could always ignore it,' he says, kissing my neck as I close my eyes.

'IMOGEN!'

I take a deep breath. 'Not after what happened last time. I'm sorry.' I step back and throw on my dress, holding it together like a defective hospital gown as I hobble to the door.

The second I open it, I can tell from Nicola's expression that something is wrong.

'It's Meredith,' she manages breathlessly.

'What about her?'

'I think she's in labour.'

Chapter 57

When I arrive at the room, Meredith is leaning against the mini-bar. 'Ow,' she says, as if someone's just pulled an Elastoplast off her arm really fast.

Which reassures me. Having been in labour myself, I know that if she was close to delivering the baby it'd feel like she was trying to squeeze a breeze block through her cervix. She's clearly a long way from that. She just doesn't know it yet.

'This *hurts*.' She frowns.

'Well, labour does hurt, but … a little more than this. What makes you think this is it?'

'I *think* my waters broke. But I'm not sure if it was just a … you know, bladder malfunction. Which never used to happen before I got pregnant, for the record.'

'Are you getting contractions?' I ask, rolling up my sleeves. I don't know why exactly, as it's not as though I'm going to have a root around in there, but it feels strangely reassuring.

'Well, it does hurt every so often.'

'Meredith, you're not due to give birth for weeks. They'll be Braxton Hicks,' I say.

'I've heard of those!' she says proudly. 'They're practice contractions, aren't they?'

'Yes. The key questions are whether they're regular and, if so, how far apart are they?'

She looks at me as if I've lost my mind. 'I don't know. Isn't it the midwife's job to time them?'

'Well, it tends to be yours, first.' I look at her. 'I really doubt you're in labour. But if, for argument's sake, you were . . . well, the timing of the contractions is just to work out if we need a taxi because we've got twenty hours to go, or an ambulance because we've got twenty minutes.'

Nicola inhales emphatically and steadies herself against the bureau. 'That has got to be a joke.'

'I *honestly* don't think it's imminent,' I reassure them. 'Like I say, she's not due for weeks. Even if it was, labours take ages. At the stage when I felt like you do, Meredith, there were still another fifteen hours to go.'

Meredith's eyes widen and her face goes slightly red. '*Erugghh.*'

I frown. 'This is probably wind, you know. Everything feels uncomfortable at this stage in pregnancy. But maybe we should go to hospital just to be on the safe side.'

I pick up the phone to the 'Whatever your whim' service to ask them to call the nearest maternity ward and warn them we're on our way. It's very apparent from the reaction of the young telephone operator that this is the first client whim of this nature he's ever had to deal with.

Meredith's in pain again, just under five minutes later.

'There's really nothing to panic about,' I tell her. 'I'm going to time this now, but they don't seem regular. I suspect the hospital will check you out and send you away again.'

'But premature labours do happen. And I'm only thirty-four weeks pregnant, not forty, like you're supposed to be. God, I'm really worried now . . .' Meredith looks at me, as if seeking re-assurance in my face.

I take her hands. 'Even if this was the big day, babies are fairly well developed by thirty-four weeks,' I say. 'You're in the final stretch, so please don't worry. Besides, I was born at thirty-one weeks, and look at me!'

'Let's just get to hospital, shall we?' Nicola says failing to marvel at this miracle as much as I'd like.

'What if they don't speak English?' Meredith says plaintively. 'It's bad enough giving birth early without it being abroad. I've already checked in the travel dictionary, and they don't list the word for "epidural".'

'Meredith, you won't be giving birth today, I'm certain,' I repeat. 'I'm happy to come with you to translate . . . if you want.'

I spin around to notice Harry, who's been holding my zip together to cover my modesty since we got here.

417

'Would you mind?' Meredith pleads.

'Of course not. I'm not sure how much obstetrics I know in Spanish, but I'll do my best.'

We're in the hotel lift when Meredith suddenly emits a squealing noise, like a wild pig that's being threatened with a barbeque. I must admit it throws me slightly, despite being convinced that this *isn't* labour. The sooner we get her to hospital to confirm that, the better.

The lift opens on the fourth floor and my young Italian wanker steps in, holding hands with a gorgeous brunette in her late teens.

'Ah, hello! It is the ... Eeenglish lady.' I note that I'm no longer 'beautiful', but realise I'm hardly in a position to complain, under the circumstances.

'Hello, how are you?' I smile.

Meredith starts panting exuberantly and he glances at her, alarmed.

'Your friend's ass – it seems very bad.'

'My ass?' Meredith frowns, touching her backside.

'She wees ...'

Meredith's eyes widen as if trying to work out if she's had another 'bladder malfunction'.

'Wees?' I ask. A chord of recognition chimes in my head. 'She wheezes! Ah, no, it's not *asthma* – she's having a baby.'

'You really think this is it, then?' Nicola asks nervously.

'No, I'm sure this is a false alarm,' I reply.

'Ah, congratulations!' The Italian grins as the door opens on the second floor and the Russian guy and Yellow Bikini Lady get in. I shift nervously into the corner of the lift, hoping he doesn't recognise me as the woman who disturbed him while his wife was dyeing her upper lip.

'Owwww!' says Meredith.

'You must be orgasmic!' Italian guy adds.

'I might be in labour,' Meredith explains to the Russians, apparently unconcerned about their Mafia connections. 'It's my first time.'

When we step out into the lobby, I can only describe the reception we receive from the staff as being comparable to the arrival of royalty. As Nicola phones Nathan to let him know what's happening, they are all over us, rushing to provide Meredith with cold towels, then hot towels, then help her down the steps like she's a geriatric. 'Is there anything at all we can get you?' asks the concierge.

Meredith thinks for a second. 'Ooh, champagne would be nice.'

'Madam' – a young female staff member with cropped black hair and an air of organisational efficiency that would rival Alexander the Great takes me to one side – 'we have phoned the maternity hospital and they're expecting you imminently. I have ordered you a car, but if time is of the essence, there is an alternative.'

'Oh?'

'Mr Venedictov heard about your plight and has offered that you take his personal limousine and driver.'

'Really?' I answer anxiously. What exactly is the protocol when one of the world's most infamous crime lords invites you to use his personal car when your heavily pregnant best friend needs to be seen by a doctor? Clearly, offending him is something I'd rather avoid, although we've got enough to worry about without thinking we might need to divert somewhere on the way to go and chop off someone's fingers one by one.

'The hotel's car should be here soon, but Mr Venedictov's limousine does have the benefit of being outside now. It's entirely up to you.'

I grab the assistant by the elbow and pull her to a quiet corner. 'Is it . . . safe?'

She looks perplexed. 'Is what safe?'

I twitch awkwardly. 'You know, the car. Given that it's owned by . . . Alexander Venedictov.'

She looks at me blankly. 'Alexei.'

'What?'

'Alexei Venedictov. The well-known Russian businessman and philanthropist.'

I blink. 'Not . . . mafia boss?' I hiss.

She stiffens, looking like I've just accused her mother of working the streets. 'Absolutely not. We are not that kind of establishment. Mr Venedictov is a highly reputable and successful businessman, a deeply religious man who is totally devoted to his wife, Iarena. And their nine children.'

I glance over at Yellow Bikini Lady and what I'm convinced is her fourteen-inch waist. 'Nine . . .?'

She nods. 'He's entirely respectable,' she reassures me. 'But the choice is yours.'

'Thanks,' I mutter, and go to put this proposition to Meredith.

'It wasn't the red-carpet treatment I'd imagined,' she pants, 'but why the hell not?'

Mr Venedictov's limo is insane. In some ways, it looks like something out of a very bad porn film, but I can see how you could get into the swing of things in different circumstances. I'm scrutinising the mini-bar when Meredith's next pain arrives and she lets out a shriek that threatens to shatter the champagne glasses.

'I will take to hospital,' announces the driver, a short, rotund man with cheeks like Cox's Orange Pippins and sideburns that look capable of sweeping out a garage. 'I have driven Mr and Mrs Venedicktov around Barcelona many times so I know all the best routes. You will have good, smooth journey.'

'Thank you,' I say, as he hits the pedal and Harry clutches my hand.

'I've never been in one of these before,' Nicola muses, picking up a remote control. She pushes a button and, like something out of *Thunderbirds*, a flap lifts up to display a flat-screen television.

'Please, help yourself,' says Meredith, gesturing to the mini-bar, in all seriousness.

'Meredith, we're not going to sit here and get pissed when you could be in the throes of labour,' Nicola points out.

'Oh, I don't min—*ARRRGHHHH!*'

As her eyes bulge, I look at my watch and start timing. It's only as the stopwatch on my phone passes the 30-second mark and she's still clearly in a lot of pain that I realise something: Meredith really is in labour.

The next two contractions seem to be suddenly and significantly closer together, a discovery I make at the exact moment we pull up at traffic lights and hit the sort of jam you'd expect on the M25 during rush hour.

'Is everything okay?' Harry whispers.

I flash him an uneasy a look. 'Maybe we should've phoned for an ambulance. Could you ask the driver how far away the hospital is?'

His eyes widen as he silently comprehends the implication of my question. The implication being: I hope he's going to say two minutes. And not a second longer.

Because while I know most first-time mums spend hours in labour before the baby actually arrives, Meredith's contractions have become alarmingly close, alarmingly quickly. That's on top of the fact that, despite my earlier reassurances, she *is* weeks away from what is her due date and, therefore, I won't relax until she's in the safe hands a of a medical professional.

Harry says something to the driver in Spanish and turns back to me.

'Usually no more than ten minutes.'

'Usually?'

'There's a festival on tonight so the traffic's bad.'

My eyes jerk to Meredith as she shrieks, 'Oh God, here's another one!'

The driver spins round looking mildly aghast.

'Shall I tell him he needs to put his foot down?' Harry asks.

Meredith lets out a scream capable of curdling the haemoglobin of a vampire bat. 'Yes. YESSSSSSSSSS!'

Harry and the driver proceed to have a frantic exchange in Spanish which culminates in the latter's face turning a peculiarly inhuman colour, which I can only describe as pistachio. He then clobbers the accelerator and, before any of us can register what's going on, we're screaming along the pavement like a tank fashioned out of oil drums and a chainsaw in a final scene from an episode of *The A-Team*.

'Shit! What's happening?' Meredith asks, and it seems obvious to everyone but her.

'Let me phone ahead,' decides Harry. 'I think we should ask for an ambulance to come and get us.'

'Good idea,' I say, wiping sweat from my forehead as it

becomes evident that Meredith's contractions are blending into one big, giant ball of pain.

I glance out of the window and witness pedestrians of all ages and persuasions diving out of the way as our limo ploughs along the pavement, before plopping down on the other side of the kerb.

'How far away is ... *ARGGHHHHHHHH!*'

I pick up my phone and start dialling a number. 'Who are you phoning?' Nicola asks, panic written all over her face.

'Carmel, my boss's wife,' I reply.

'Why?' demands Nicola.

'She's a midwife,' I explain, as Carmel answers the phone, clearly expecting a discussion similar to our previous ones.

'I have nothing more to say to that dickwad,' she announces.

'It's not about David,' I blurt out. 'My friend is in labour, I really think she's close to giving birth but we're in a limo stuck in traffic.'

'Oh God.'

'Carmel, I need you to help.'

I can sense her panic before she even speaks. 'It's more than thirty years since I've even looked at another woman's vagina, Imogen.'

'I'm sure it's like riding a bike. Besides, you're all we've got.'

I can hear her take a deep breath. 'Okay. Right. Let me think. Have you phoned an ambulance?'

'My other friend is phoning to try and get one, but I'm worried that she's going to have the baby before it gets here.'

At this, Meredith glares at me. 'Jesus H. Christ – ARE you? You never mentioned that before!'

I ignore her. 'And I'll be honest,' I whisper into my phone, 'I don't know what to do.'

'YOU DON'T KNOW WHAT TO DO?' Meredith shrieks. 'BUT YOU KNOW *EVERYTHING*, IMOGEN! YOU KNOW … ARGGHHHHHHHH!'

'Has the driver pulled over?' Carmel asks. She suddenly sounds incredibly, mercifully, calm.

I look up and realise that he's taken a diversion through a pedestrian part of the city and we're currently driving through a dense parade of Flamenco dancers. The car is engulfed in a rainbow-coloured array of bodies, as if we've crash-landed the set of *Strictly Come Dancing*.

'No.'

'Then get him to.'

'STOP!' I yell, banging on the driver's window with my good arm. He slams on the breaks and Meredith – mid-contraction – goes flying into the mini-bar.

'Remind the mother to pant and not push until she's absolutely ready,' continues Carmel – an instruction I repeat to Meredith – before she adds, 'Have you had a look?'

I squirm. 'No.'

'You need to. Let me know if you can see the baby's head.'

She says this so matter of factly, you'd think we were camped in woodland and she was asking if I could see a great spotted woodpecker.

I wedge the phone into my shoulder and instruct Harry and the driver to avert their eyes, an entirely unnecessary request as that's clearly the last place they want to look: Harry continues talking on the phone in frantic Spanish, breaking only to tell me that an ambulance knows where we are and is on its way. Then I try to manoeuvre Meredith into a position so I can get a good look as Nicola holds her hand and tells her she's doing brilliantly. I lift up her skirt and take a deep breath, hoping that I'm not going to see what I think I might about to.

'Is the baby's head visible?' Carmel repeats.

I open my eyes and there it is – the bulge of the head of the baby, its soft, distinctive hair showing clearly.

'Yes,' I croak.

'FUCKKKKKKKKK!' Meredith screams, and I don't know whether that's prompted more by that revelation, the sheer pain, or the fact that several dancers dressed like large, green parakeets are now involved in a furious altercation with the driver about his choice of parking spot, oblivious to what's going on behind the blacked-out windows.

'Place your hand on the head and provide it with support to stop it from popping out,' Carmel tells me. 'Remind mother to try and pant at this stage – we don't want her to tear.'

I try my very best to summon up some inner strength and to appear matronly. 'Meredith, don't push – just pant,' I instruct her.

'I can't help it! I need to push. Something's *making* me push! It's happening on its own.'

'She needs to push!' I tell Carmel.

'Okay, in that case you need to guide the baby out then. Just guide, don't pull.'

I decide not to bore her with the small matter of me only having one non-broken arm to play with and instead place my hand gently on the warm hair of the baby's head.

'Let me help,' says Nicola, 'I've got two working hands.'

She squeezes in next to me and places her hands underneath mine so there's absolutely no chance of the baby falling to the floor. Slowly, but probably not as slowly as I'd like, it begins to emerge. Meredith has a break in contractions and looks at me with eyes like tennis balls.

'Is it happening, Imogen? Nicola? Is my baby being born?'

I swallow and force myself to nod as my chest feels like it's about to burst open. Another contraction arrives and Meredith lets out a guttural roar loud enough to be heard in France, the sheer force of Mother Nature pushing this baby more than she is.

Before I can take anything in, the baby's head is out.

With adrenalin coursing through my body, I'm torn between terror and a strange but very clear surge of optimism.

'You can do this, Meredith,' I say, as her face twists with pain. '*We* can do this. It's going to be okay. It's nearly here. You've done the hard part.'

I don't know why I'm convinced this emphatic speech would be enough to get her through it . . .

'No-I-fucking-well-can't-Imogen-Copeland,' she growls.

I hate to disagree with a woman in this position, but there's no other option. 'You can, Meredith. You *are* . . .'

My words emerge as she launches into another vociferous push and I am only dimly aware of the door opening, Spanish-accented voices instructing everyone to get out, and someone dressed in a reassuringly medical-looking outfit appearing at my side.

I slip back along with Nicola as the contraction reaches its height and I'm outside when I hear the first, raw cries of a tiny newborn human.

I dip my head back into the limo to see Meredith in a state of catastrophic dishevelment. The floor of the car looks like it's in a Quentin Tarantino movie.

But it's not the shock or the gore or anything else that I focus on. It's the sight of the beautiful baby curling into its mother's arms for the first time.

There's only room for one of us in the ambulance and Meredith, clearly convinced that I am some sort of obstetrics guru, wants it to be me. It means I'll miss my flight – we're meant to be leaving in less than four hours – but she's the immediate priority, so I don't hesitate.

I go to step into the ambulance, but pause and turn round. Because, in the chaos of the last hour, one unpalatable fact has been pushed to the corner of my mind and it now hits me now like a freight train.

This is the last time I'll ever see Harry.

It's just gone 11 p.m. and his flight leaves at 6 a.m., meaning he'll only have time to go back, pack and perhaps catch a couple of hours' sleep before heading to the airport.

This rushed farewell isn't the one I'd imagined, yet the speed of it isn't the main problem.

The main problem is that I don't want to be saying goodbye at all.

'I need to go with Meredith,' I tell him.

'This is it then.' He nods, taking a step towards the ambulance doors and reaching out for me.

Our fingers touch as a paramedic ushers me in and I become acutely aware that there is a woman and tiny, premature baby inside who probably need urgent medical attention.

'Goodbye Harry.'

He drifts backwards, his face bathed in the warm glow of the streetlights as music blares out from the carnival. 'Goodbye, Imogen.'

The door shuts and he is gone.

Chapter 58

It's a baby boy. Such was the shock of the whole thing, I only thought to ask when we were in the ambulance and on our way to hospital. Given that he was born at thirty-four weeks, he's tiny – only 5lb 6oz – but not so tiny that he seems anything other than healthy.

His size meant that as soon as we got to hospital, doctors and nurses were all over him, before he was moved to a special care unit. But, according to the English-speaking midwife who visits Meredith immediately to check her over, it's a precautionary measure. Reassuringly, he's the biggest baby in there.

'How are you feeling, or is that a silly question?' Nicola asks Meredith as we sit next to her bed on a bright maternity ward. Nic ended up returning to the hotel in the limo with Harry, before making her way straight back here once the carnival had died down.

Meredith looks shocked and exhausted, overcome with emotion. 'I feel like ... like ...'

'Yes?'

'I'm a mummy.' She shakes her head incredulously.

I grin. 'I told you that you could do it.'

'You two delivered my baby,' she breathes.

'I did nothing, thank God,' Nicola protests. 'It was Imogen really.'

'YOU delivered your baby, Meredith. I was just there to catch him. Although I'm very glad it didn't quite come to that. Thank God that ambulance arrived when it did.'

'You were brilliant,' she continues. 'Who gives a toss if your radio-interview skills leave something to be desired? You've just brought a new life into the world.'

When she puts it like that, it's hard not to feel a whole lot better about things.

Nicola and I find a spot to sleep in a waiting room just outside the maternity ward. By and large, I'm happy to report the place has a significantly pleasanter class of clientele than the last Barcelona hospital I found myself in.

I'm attempting to settle into a position suitable for snoozing when Nicola says something that makes me suddenly less sleepy: 'Imogen, something weird happened when I went back to the hotel.'

I frown and sit up. 'Oh – what?'

'I thought I'd better let Elegant Vacations know what had happened and that we weren't going to be catching the flight, only I didn't have any numbers for the woman Meredith has been dealing with. So I went to Reception and asked if they could put me in touch with her or, indeed, anyone from Elegant Vacations.'

'And?'

'It turns out Elegant Vacations has nothing to do with our booking. They didn't know what I was talking about. We're not on an Elegant Vacations holiday.'

I frown. 'They must've just made a mistake. Maybe the person you spoke to didn't know about the competition.'

'Hmm. That's what I said. In fact, I was so insistent they ended up calling the general manager, thinking he was bound to know about the competition.'

'And?'

'It turns out there wasn't a competition.'

This development filters into my brain, followed by the next fact, which Nicola repeats almost simultaneously to me thinking it. 'The booking was in Meredith's name. Along with the bill.'

Day Eight

Chapter 59

I nap fitfully, my dreams interspersed with thoughts of Florence, and Harry, and colourful flashbacks of the unforgettable experience we've all been through. I'm woken by a vivid morning sun ascending over Barcelona as I realise Nicola is on the phone, pacing up and down the corridor.

'Mum, this isn't an ultimatum,' she says. 'It's simpler than that. It's about me telling you that I love you and that I'm sorry I couldn't be the person you wanted me to be. I'm sorry I couldn't marry a nice man, or provide you with the grandchildren I know you'd have loved. But I love you and Dad more than anything. And if you love me, then I'm asking – from the bottom of my heart – for you to do this thing for me. It's not too late. It'll never be too late.'

She continues the call for another ten minutes or so. When it finally ends, she sits down next to me looking drained.

'You okay?' I ask.

She nods. 'Maybe I'm delirious from lack of sleep, or my

head is wrecked from everything that's happened ... but I woke up with an urgent need to address some of the issues I've failed to address lately.'

'About you and Jess, you mean?'

She nods.

'And?'

She shrugs. 'It wasn't a total dead loss. But I've thought that before ...'

We're approached by the midwife who's been in and out of Meredith's room all night and she gestures to Nicola and me to follow her. As we pad along the corridor to the special-care unit, we see Meredith standing by the door to it in a hospital gown, gazing through its large pane of glass. Her smile when she turns to us is no less sparkling for the fatigue.

I clutch her hand and we quietly enter the room, watching in a bubble of emotion as the midwife lifts up the baby and gently puts him in his mother's arms.

His eyes flicker open and he starts to stir, bleating like a newborn lamb. Meredith rocks him gently and, with an instinctive shush, presses her lips against his head until he quietens.

'Have you decided on a name?' I ask.

'Adam,' she tells me. 'It's Nathan's middle name.'

I grin. 'I bet his dad's looking forward to seeing him.'

'He managed to get a flight last night. I think he'd have waterskied here if there had been no alternative.'

'When's he due to get here?' I ask.

'In the next couple of hours. And my mother should be here by early evening. Have you two tried to get another flight yet? I'm so sorry you missed the one that was booked for you.'

Nicola looks at me. I look at Meredith. There's a loaded silence, as Meredith bites her lip.

'Bugger. You know, don't you?'

'What on earth are you doing paying all this money for us to come on this trip with you, Meredith?' I say, with gentle exasperation.

She rolls her eyes. 'Never let me commit a bank robbery, I'm clearly rubbish at subterfuge.' She sighs. 'I just wanted us all to have a brilliant holiday together. You know, before everything changed for me. I just thought, I've got this money that Dad has passed on to me. I *could* invest it or do something sensible and dreary with it, like my mum wants me to, or I could do something that *I* really want. I knew you'd never be able to afford somewhere like this yourselves, and that it'd take something really special for you to agree to leave Florence, Imogen. I also knew you'd never come if I told you I wanted to pay.'

'Well I'm paying you back,' I insist.

'Me too,' Nicola says.

Meredith reaches over and clutches both of our hands. 'No, you're bloody not.'

I go to open my mouth when she interrupts. 'Do not argue

with a woman who's just been through what I've been through. I haven't got the energy.'

I lean in and give her a hug, deciding to leave this matter for a more appropriate time. 'Thank you, Meredith. It was unbelievably generous of you.'

'It was, you daft thing,' adds Nicola.

A smile flickers to Meredith's lips. 'Now, what about those alternative flights – have you managed to sort one?'

'I spoke to the airline,' replies Nicola. 'There's a flight direct to Manchester at 5 p.m. if we want it. You'd have to get the train back to London with Florence though, Imogen, from your mum's—'

I nod. 'That'd be fine by me. But, Meredith—'

'Take it,' Meredith insists. 'My back-up will be here by then. They'll stay with me until Adam and I are allowed home. Besides, you need to get back to Florence, Imogen. She needs you more than I do.'

I bend down to move my face closer to Adam and breathe in his delicate newborn scent, one of the best smells in the world. It takes me back to that spellbinding moment when I first held Florence in my arms, how frightening and wonderful it felt. It's followed by an overwhelming pang of yearning to feel her four-year-old hand in mine.

'She does,' I nod. But the truth is, it's me who needs her the most.

*

Nic and I stay for only an hour after that, once we've walked Meredith back to her ward. It's long enough to see Nathan gallop through the door, so breathless you'd think he'd run all the way here.

In contrast to the usual attention he pays to grooming, his hair is mussed up beyond any designer look and his T-shirt so creased you'd think it'd been rolled up in his pocket for the last month. He's carrying a humungous box of chocolates, a leather holdall and has a duty-free bag containing what looks like a bottle of champagne. As he tentatively enters the room, Meredith's face illuminates with relief and happiness, emotions I doubt she'd have predicted.

'Hello, sweetheart,' she whispers with a wobbly smile. I stand and take the bags from him as he throws his arms round her, squeezing her face tight into his neck.

When eventually he pulls away, it's with an unmistakable look in his eyes – one that confirms something that probably never occurred to me before now.

He really does love her, God help him.

'I think I've got everything you need,' he says, pointing to the bag. 'For the baby, I mean – clothes and nappies and things. And I brought you some stuff – slippers and some nice smelly stuff and Lucozade and—'

She interrupts him by reaching over and clutching his hand. 'Thank you for getting here so quickly. I'm sorry you missed it.'

'I wish I'd been here for you. But nobody could've predicted this. And I'm just glad he's okay.' He swallows. 'I can't wait to see him.'

'I'll ask the nurse if we can go now, shall I?' She grins.

He stiffens in apprehension, before a wide smile breaks across his face.

I'm about to announce that, now Nathan's here, we'll leave them to get to know their new little boy while we go back to the hotel to pack. Then Meredith whispers something so softly that I barely hear it.

'I love you, Nathan.'

I wonder for a moment if she's delirious from all the drugs. Then I remember – she hasn't had any.

Chapter 60

Nicola and I bypass the business-class lounge in Barcelona airport, head to a shop where we can spend our last euros on a sandwich, and settle into the cheap seats overlooking the runway.

I can't pretend I'm overly enthusiastic about keeping it real by forgoing free Buck's Fizz and croissants, but that's not the only reason things suddenly seem less colourful than on the way here. Everything's unnaturally quiet without Meredith around, and strangely dull without a handsome, bespectacled stranger in front of whom I'm guaranteed to show myself up.

As I'm heading for the gate, a text arrives from Meredith:

You were amazing last night, thanks for everything, Imogen. Baby Adam is AWESOME (tho it took me 2 nappy changes to work out I was doing them backwards. Thank Christ Nathan's here – all those bloody books he read are coming in handy!) x

I grin and hit 'Reply':

> You are totally right about Adam – you've got the
> scrummiest baby ever. Take care of yourself and see you
> back on home turf x

I hit 'Send' at the exact moment that the phone beeps again.
My pulse ripples when I register the name that comes with it:

> Wish we'd said goodbye properly, but I wanted to tell you
> how much I enjoyed this week. You were excellent
> company ;-) Harry xxxx P.S. I've attached a scan of the
> piece in today's Economic Times. Hope it's more
> palatable than the previous coverage.

I download the attachment and read the piece, headlined:
'Peebles poised to announce merger with mystery conglomerate.'

The article teases with our news about the merger with
Getreide without giving so much away that it would spoil the
formal announcement on 2 September. It talks about how
Peebles is 'believed to be in talks' and goes on to describe
'exciting rumours about the creation of a company, the scale
of which Europe has never seen before'.

It will, of course, prompt a flurry of phone calls from other
media trying to get the scoop on who the company is, but
Charles is prepared for that – and confident that a carefully

worded quote or two in a publication as prestigious as *The Economic Times* will help deflect attention from David and remind the stock market that Peebles is a company that's going places.

Under the circumstances, it couldn't be more positive.

I am about to forward it to my boss when Nicola points out that the Departures screen is instructing us to go to our boarding gate. My phone beeps again. It's another message from Harry:

> Scrap what I just said. I miss you already and hate the
> idea of not seeing you again. Please move to Aberdeen
> immediately! xxx

I swallow back the raw feeling in my throat and compose a text back.

> I miss you too, badly. Please stay in London –
> immediately! xxx

It's only as I'm hitting 'Send' that I realise how much I wish that was possible. I jostle the thought to the very back of my mind and instead force myself to open my book.

'*Here is a small fact . . .*'

Chapter 61

Florence's little legs gallop towards me as I emerge into Arrivals at Manchester airport. She flings her arms round my neck and squeezes me like she's trying to deflate a set of armbands.

I laugh, taken aback, and close my eyes as I breathe her in: the strawberry shampoo that infuses her hair and biscuity scent of her warm skin. 'Gosh, I missed you,' I whisper, kissing her on the head. 'So, so much.' I pull back and look at her. 'What's that?'

'My steposcope. I want to be a doctor.'

'Really?'

'Yes, I want to do brain operations.'

My eyes widen. 'Really?'

'Yes. But I'm going to be a princess doctor. So I can wear pretty dresses and have nice hair and do brain operations at the same time.'

'I think that sounds like a fantastic idea. You'll be the most glamorous doctor around – good for you.' I grin. 'Perhaps we could get a medical kit for your birthday.'

She scrunches up her nose. 'No. I still want the pink hoover.'

You can't win 'em all I suppose.

I stand up and hold her hand, as Mum walks towards us. I notice the limp immediately. She looks suddenly and dramatically frail: not the powerhouse of a woman I left behind, but a broken bird.

'Your dad's just parking the car,' she begins. 'What happened to you?' Her eyes widen, focusing on the cast on my arm, before switching to my dodgy eye.

'It's nothing, worse than it looks. How are you, Mum?' I step forwards to put my arms around her.

'Oh, I'm all right,' she says, stoically.

'Thank you so much for looking after Florence. I'm incredibly grateful. The bits and bobs I picked up at the duty-free hardly seem sufficient under the circumstances.' I step back from her and look her full in the face. 'You didn't need to come and meet me. You look as though you should be resting.'

'That good?'

'I didn't mean . . .'

'I know,' she smiles softly. 'Welcome home, sweetheart.'

Dad strides towards us, clutching a parking ticket. 'Good break?' he asks before doing a double take, directed at my arm. 'What happened to you?'

'Nothing, worse than it looks,' I say.

'Well, Florence has been as good as gold,' Dad continues, ruffling her hair, like he did to me when I was a little girl. 'Apart from nearly killing herself, obviously. We're going to miss her. Can't we keep her?' He grins.

'No! I want to be with Mummy!' Florence leaps in. I raise my eyebrows and kneel down to give her another squeeze, before she whispers that she has a secret to tell me.

'What is it?' I ask.

She cups her hand over my ear and says: 'I love you, Mummy.'

A second later, she's tugging at her granddad's hand to ask if she can have one of his mints and the moment is gone.

'Where's Nicola?' asks Dad.

I glance around before spotting her, about twenty feet away, in the midst of an emotional reunion with Jessica. 'Will you give me a minute to say goodbye to Nic? I'll be back in a sec.'

Florence slips her hand in mine again and skips along with me, crunching Polos noisily.

'Hello, Titch!' Jessica grins at her when we reach them. 'And Imogen. You look . . . what happened to you?'

I can see I'm going to have to get used to this. 'I thought it was a shame not to put my medical insurance to good use.'

'It's been an eventful holiday, there's no doubt,' Nicola says with a smile. Then she looks up and freezes.

As I follow her gaze I realise what's caught her attention.

Nicola's parents are walking cautiously towards us, her mum two steps ahead, her dad following obligingly behind.

They're wearing the same tentative expressions, their faces etched with emotion and a clear understanding that not being here today – at their daughter's request – wasn't an option. And not because she forced them into it, or blackmailed or cajoled them. But because they love her, and she needs them to be on her side.

When Nic's mum is in front of her daughter, they stand silently for a moment or two. Then she smiles. 'Nicola. Do you still need that lift? And Jessica, too. It's nice to meet you. Perhaps you could both pop home for a cup of tea?'

Nicola's jaw drops. Jess struggles to hide her incredulity.

If Nic's parents notice, they don't let on. 'I'm Marion,' Nicola's mum continues, holding out her hand.

Jess shakes it enthusiastically as her face breaks into a beaming smile. 'It's LOVELY to meet you,' she replies, before abandoning her hand and sweeping her into a hug instead.

Chapter 62

I knew Stacey would deliver on the homemade cake she promised, but I hadn't quite anticipated the scale that would be involved: the mountain of sponge and icing waiting on my desk when I arrive back at work would cater for a modest wedding party. Next to it is a scrawled note: 'The size of cake is directly proportional to the amount of shit you've had to put up with this week! In a meeting until 11 but will catch up afterwards. S xx'

Apart from that, the only notable thing about my first morning back at work is how little has changed, on the surface, since the last time I was at my desk, overlooking the comings and goings of Southampton Street.

A glance at my inbox reveals that it contains 342 unopened emails, and so many exclamation marks that looking at the screen makes me feel like I'm being shouted at.

Over the course of the next twenty-five minutes, I discover that if I sit still enough, sipping coffee and gazing with a lobotomised expression out of the window, I can muster up a curious if entirely improper sense of calm. Everything is so peaceful in fact, that you could be forgiven for thinking that I'd hallucinated the last week, although frankly I doubt I could imagine anything so fantastical even if I'd eaten four bowls of magic mushroom soup, garnished with a generous swirl of LSD.

The silence is, however, deceptive. Outside my office, up a marble staircase, past a machine selling some of Peebles's best-loved confectionary and through a set of austere rosewood doors, sit the men and women who hold the future of the company, my boss, and me, in their hands: our board members.

They are discussing the lot: the scandal, the publicity and the aftermath. To my alarm, I appear to have become known as 'David's right-hand woman' in the last eight days, a soubriquet that now makes my blood curdle, but from which it's hard to distance myself without putting the kybosh on my employment prospects in the event that he clings on to his job. Besides, given that my name was on all that bad publicity, there's no doubt that my own future here is inextricably linked to David's. In short, I might be sitting here, but my job, yet again, is on the line. It's little wonder I'm savouring the superficial peace.

As I'm thinking all this, I hear David storming up towards the door of my office, before it bursts open. I'd recognise his rampaging footsteps anywhere. In those few seconds, I know it could go either way.

This fact has less of an effect on my anxiety levels than I'd imagined, a phenomenon I can only attribute to the fact that this week has inoculated me against stress.

'IMOGEN!'

The door is closed and David is striding towards me. I can tell in the moment just before he leaps around the desk that his job is safe, at least for now. He might have sweat marks under his armpits, but this is a man with relief written so vividly over his face it's as if the firing squad have put down their weapons and invited him in for a couple of Martinis.

'Imogen . . . come here!' he shouts, opening his arms wide and apparently expecting me to leap into them like a loyal puppy, albeit one who's been kicked in the arse several times over the last week.

When I don't move, he bends down and hugs me anyway, nearly smothering me with his weight. I resist the temptation to add 'inappropriate physical contact' to the list of misdemeanours he's committed and, instead, as he stands up, push myself away in my chair with the intention of precipitating my detachment from him.

In the event, the chair castors propel me further than I'd imagined, and I end up speeding off like a Dodgem as David stumbles and comes very close to ending up with his face plastered on the carpet.

'Sorry,' I mutter, with rather less conviction than he seems to be expecting.

He frowns, straightens and brushes himself down as he takes

in my expression. And I can tell that it's only now, for the very first time, that it's occurred to him that I'm a little pissed off.

He looks torn between indignation and fear.

'Don't worry, Imogen,' he says, and heads to the chair on the other side of my desk.

I suddenly feel safer with him there. Safer, and a little bit dangerous.

'Imogen, our jobs are saved!' he declares, grinning as he opens his arms wide, as if launching into a number in *Jesus Christ Superstar*.

'That's very good news, David.'

'It is, isn't it? I got a rollocking, of course. I expected nothing less. But it's nothing I haven't had before.' I raise an eyebrow as David continues, oblivious. 'Barely a week went by without me getting a couple of sharp slaps on the backside with a ruler when I was at school. Thankfully, it didn't come to that this time. And, even better, the police have dropped the indecent-exposure charge against me – it should never have been brought, given how discreet I was with the in-flight blanket. So that means I've only got drunk and disorderly to deal with, which carries a maximum sentence of a fine. It means I won't be able to get the conservatory replaced until next year, but I can live with that.'

'I'm glad to hear it. What about Carmel?'

'Oh, she'll come around. Carmel and I have been together for thirty-one years, you know.'

'She told me it was thirty-four.'

He frowns. 'Maybe it is. Hmm. The point is, I know Carmel better than she knows herself. And she might be angry with me now – hairy McMary, she's got every right to be! – but we're made for each other.'

I'm about to ask him if he's heard about the heroic part she played in Meredith's labour when he looks me up and down. 'Have you . . . done something to yourself?'

'Yes, I broke my arm, and fell over and gave myself a black eye.'

'Oh. Sorry to hear that. But I was talking about' – he waves his arm around in front of me – 'you know . . . your frock. And the lipstick and whatnot.'

I look down at my clothes. I don't know why I felt the need to put on one of the dresses we bought on my *Pretty Woman* day in Barcelona, and throw on some make-up Meredith donated to me, but it just made me feel good knowing I look half decent. I might even do it again tomorrow.

'Nothing important.' I shrug.

'Well, you look . . . fantastic!' He grins. 'You'd better watch yourself, or Gaz Silverman will come onto you.'

In fact, Gaz has already invited me to lunch, which I obviously declined. But he wasn't too upset; the woman who cleans the phones is due in again next week.

'Anyway,' he continues, 'the point I wanted to make was that that article in *The Economic Times* went a *long* way towards making amends. And I've told the board – both here and at Getreide – that, with your contacts, there's plenty more where that came from when the merger is announced in September.'

'I'll certainly see what I can do.'

'That's the next big thing for you and me, Imogen. The merger. We need to prepare for the announcement on September the 2nd like we've never prepared in our lives.' He pauses and rubs his hands together. 'If you can imagine something in between Rocky Balboa getting in shape for a big fight and a ground squirrel in the run-up to winter – that'll be you and me. The press conference is scheduled for 9 a.m. and I want you right by my side so that—'

'I'm not attending the press conference, David.' He looks like I've kneed him in the solar plexus. 'I can't attend. I have a more important engagement.'

He can barely get the next word out. '*What?*'

'I can't attend the press conference. I'm sorry, but I need to book the morning off.'

'You *have* to be there, Imogen. It's simply not an option to not be.'

'David, it's my daughter's first day at school.'

'I'm sure little Fiona—'

'It's Florence. And I *have* to be there.'

He looks as though a small explosion is going off in his cerebral cortex. 'Imogen, this is the most important day of your year, the most important day of your *career*. The idea that you couldn't be there, well, it's—'

'David, let me stop you there,' I say, lowering my voice slightly. I read once that it was a technique for commanding authority favoured by Margaret Thatcher and it's blisteringly effective. 'I have given this company my blood, sweat and tears for the last seven years. You were very good to me during my maternity leave, and you've been an excellent boss.'

'Why are you saying that as if you're resigning?' he whimpers. 'It'll look terrible if you go off with stress too, Imogen.'

'I'm simply saying, David, that I think I've been good too – at least, I've tried to be. I've *tried* to do everything I possibly can for this company. Because I love working here, David – I've loved working here since the day I started. But I *haven't* loved this week.'

'Nobody could dispute—'

'I have just been on what was supposedly my first holiday in more years than I can remember. And, instead of being allowed to relax, I have returned feeling as though I've spent the week crawling through the Burmese jungle attempting to fight off snipers.'

He opens his mouth to argue, but I cut him short. 'The phone has not stopped. I've had meetings, I've done interviews, I've spent every waking minute devoting this week to *trying to save your arse*. This is despite the fact that I still haven't officially been given this job, let alone the salary to go with it.'

He sticks out his bottom lip.

'And, yes, it didn't all go as smoothly as I might have wanted. But I *tried*,' I continue, impassioned. 'And that's why I'm asking this of you. In fact, I'm not asking – I'm telling. My only daughter wants me to take her to her first day at school on the morning of September of 2nd. And I am going to be there.'

We gaze at each other as if we've both got a pistol in our pocket and can't decide who's going to draw it out first. I'm so determined not to back down, I'm prepared to develop eyeballs like sandpaper.

Eventually, he sniffs and looks at his fingernails. 'Could you come in afterwards, maybe join us for the debrief?'

I try not to smile. 'Of course.'

'That's settled then.'

It's only then that I realise how shocked I am. And how glad I am that I don't have to start job-hunting. Because, as much of a knob-head that David can be, he's not *all* bad. And I love this job; I *need* this job. Imperfect and demanding as it is, it's mine.

He stands up and straightens the sleeves on his Savile Row suit. 'I'm glad we cleared all that up.'

'Me too.'

'And I'm sure we can sort out the job title, you know –

make it official. The pay rise might have to wait until next month but, again, it's all do-able.'

I bite my lip as the hangover of adrenalin kicks in. 'Thank you, David.'

He nods. 'No, Imogen. Thank *you*.'

Sometimes, that's all you need to hear.

Chapter 63

We don't get as much post as we used to. Like every other office in the world, most things are done electronically these days, from the delivery of invoices to asking a colleague two desks away if she'd like you to pick up a cheese sandwich for her on lunch. But today, Laura enters with a stack of documents for my in-tray and alerts me to the fact that the letter on the top is distinctly out of kilter with the rest.

'Morning . . . um, Imogen. Quite a bit of mail this morning. Including this . . .'

She smiles as I take it from her. It's the colour of Amaretto, tied around with a plush, dark-chocolate-coloured ribbon. 'Private And Confidential' is handwritten in half-cursive letters in the corner. There's no postmark and no stamp.

'Did this come in another envelope?' I ask.

'It did, now you mention it. Why?' she replies, clearly overcome with curiosity.

I consider asking if there was an Aberdeen postmark, but

decide it's easier to find out for myself. 'Probably someone trying to sell me something,' I say, hoping that this isn't the case. I twirl it round between my fingers. 'Thank you.'

'Oh ... a few of us are going to Punch & Judy after work on Friday. I know you've got Florence so it must be difficult, but Elsa and Stacey said you used to go quite a lot. I just thought it'd be nice if you could make it, maybe for half an hour or so.'

'Oh, I couldn't ...' I hesitate. 'Actually ... maybe I could. For half an hour, anyway. As long as I leave on time, of course. Which I'm going to.'

'Fab,' she says, before disappearing out of the door.

A smile flickers over my lips as I open the thick, crisp paper, and I stand and walk across the room.

July 28th

Dear Imogen,

I've made a rash decision. I'm writing this having stepped on the plane only minutes ago, partly because you said you missed letters and partly because there are no decent in-flight movies. (I'm joking of course. They've got Miss Congeniality.)

Actually, neither is the whole truth. I wanted to write to you, really, to underline something at which I've hinted already but feel honour- bound to spell out, while trying my best not to sound like a lunatic. Which will be quite some feat given that this time two weeks ago, I didn't even know you.

Still, if I've been gripped by a temporary madness, at least I can say it's the best kind.

Imogen, in the last eight days you've entered my world like a blaze of fireworks. It's something I've not ever experienced before and, after thirty-four years, I'm not overly optimistic about experiencing it again. You might argue differently and it's a moot point, of course. But it's also not a chance I relish taking.

In case it isn't obvious, this is a love letter. A bona-fide, bells-and-whistles love letter, the kind that is supposed to have been obliterated by modern technology. Although I'd never be so hasty/tacky/plain daft as to use that word – the L word – after just eight days (because we both know that's JUST NOT POSSIBLE), I am prepared to believe this:

You are the most incredible, funny, gorgeous and amazing woman I've ever encountered. And, yes, we barely know each other. You don't know my bad habits (of which there are obviously none ;-)) and I don't know yours. But I am certain about something: I think you and I need to be given a chance. My hunch might be wrong, but I couldn't live with myself without at least trying to find out.

So I have one big question for you and it's this—

I am holding my breath as I turn the page.

Would you like to go for lunch?
  Harry X

With my heart racing I grab my mobile out of my bag and pull up Harry's number before sending a text:

What do you mean: 'Would you like to go for lunch?!' x

A response arrives a second later:

I *mean*: would you like to go for lunch?

I scroll down, holding my breath, as I read his explanation: the smallest of sentences that bursts into my head like sherbet on my tongue:

I'm downstairs.

Chapter 64

I walk out of my office in a near daze, only briefly acknowledging Stacey waving at the other end of the room, ignoring the Minnie Mouse ears Roy tries to foist on me (his gift to say sorry), and dodging David's PA's attempts to book me in for a meeting. I glide past Accounts until I reach the lift, step in and press the down button, feeling my stomach whirl as it sinks to the first-floor balcony overlooking the lobby.

I inhale deeply, my legs tingling as I step onto the short escalator that leads down to the ground floor, and descend, fixing my gaze on the man by the door in the geometric T-shirt with the shimmering midnight blue eyes.

He is pacing next to the window, watching the taxis jostle for space outside, or perhaps watching nothing at all. Then he turns. I step off the escalator and stand, convinced as he looks at me that I've never seen a more beautiful man in my life. I am momentarily immobile, certainly speechless. He smiles.

Then I do too, not knowing what to do except walk towards him with wonder and elation running through my veins.

'This is a long way to come for lunch,' I say.

He laughs. 'I know. I'm hoping it'll be worth my while.'

We walk towards one of my favourite Covent Garden cafés on one of those grey, leaden days you sometimes get in the UK, the ones in defiance of the fact that it's supposed to be summer. It's a world away from the blinding sunshine of Barcelona, yet as heat spreads through me, I've never felt warmer.

'Did you get in trouble for not attending your media dinner on the last night in Spain?' I ask.

He looks sheepish. 'I hope I've made up for it.'

'Oh?'

'I wrote an email to the owner of the hotel as soon as I got home, thanking him for his hospitality and praising Delfina for her superb work in promoting them. My travel piece is going in next week, and I couldn't have been more glowing about them if they'd offered guests a complimentary wank every morning.'

I burst out laughing. 'Shame it's too late to save her job.'

'Yes and no. She emailed me this morning to let me know she's got another PR role – for Calandria Benevente.'

'The film star at the hotel?'

He nods. 'So you don't need to feel too sorry for her.'

There's a momentary silence as we approach the café, until

I turn to Harry, unable to stop myself from grinning. 'Thank you for your letter.'

The brush of his arm against mine provokes an urgent need to reach out and touch his fingertips, but I restrain myself.

He stiffens and takes a deep breath. 'I don't know whether to be embarrassed about it or not.'

'Why would you be embarrassed?'

'Because I hardly know you. Yet here I am making all these grand declarations like a complete . . . plonker.'

I stifle a laugh. 'I don't think you're a plonker. Besides, there's a lot to be said for grand declarations.'

At that, he takes my hand gently and we stop and turn to each other. He looks into my eyes and I swear the rest of the world has disappeared as my heart races in anticipation for just one more kiss from him . . .

Only he doesn't kiss me. Instead, he says something that makes my legs momentarily incapable of supporting the weight of my body.

'I'm not moving to Aberdeen.'

I shake my head, feeling my chest rise. 'What? But why? What about your mum?'

He thrusts his hands in his pockets in a way that makes him look sweetly vulnerable. 'Turns out she didn't say no to dinner because she was going to bingo.'

'Oh?'

He suppresses a smile. 'She's got a boyfriend.'

'What?' I laugh. 'What happened to "she'll never find someone"?'

'I guess I've been proved wrong. Which I'm very happy about, incidentally. He's called Frank. He's owns a landscape-gardening company, and likes cooking and jazz. And they're in love. At the age of fifty-nine, my mother has fallen in love.'

'Wow. So there's time for you yet,' I tease.

He goes to say something, then stops himself. We both carry on walking.

'So with this boyfriend on the scene, do you feel like you're no longer needed?' I ask.

'She didn't put it quite so bluntly, but that seems to be the upshot.'

'And how do you feel about that?'

'Obviously, part of me feels a bit odd about reversing the whole plan and staying in London just because some new bloke is on the scene. But, as you'd probably guessed, I never wanted to leave London anyway, and she's absolutely determined that life's just grand back home without the benefit of me around the corner.' He stops walking and turns to me again. 'Imogen, I don't want anything from you that you're not ready for. Except perhaps this.' I realise I'm holding my breath. 'I'd like to get to know you.'

A smile twitches to my lips. 'You would?'

He nods. 'What do you think?'

I can barely process the implications of all this; I simply

blurt out what instinctively I know to be the case. 'I think I'd like to get to know you too. Very much.'

At that, he reaches round my neck and draws his face closer to mine. As our lips touch, happiness races through me.

I have no idea where this thing between him and me might go – it feels horribly and beautifully risky, and I'm completely out of my comfort zone. But there's one thing I do know: for the first time in as long as I can remember, I'm ready to find out.

Epilogue

Sunday, 1 September 2012

I'm laying out Florence's school uniform in her room and trying to stop Spud from leaping onto her bed when David phones.

'Are we all fired up and ready to go?'

'Absolutely. Parents have to stay for an hour after the official school start tomorrow, then I've got a cab booked to bring me straight to the door of the office. If my timing's right, I should be there ten or twelve minutes into your presentation.'

'I didn't mean the presentation. I meant Florence's first day at school. Big day for anyone – I remember it myself. Golly McMolly, I was nervous. Near-enough incontinent for a week as I recall ...'

David and I run through the final details of his presentation, as well as the schedule for tomorrow. He manages to hold it together, at least enough to keep up appearances.

'It sounds like we're all on top of things,' he concludes. 'So I'll see you tomorrow, shall I?'

'Yes, see you then. And, David . . . are you okay?'

For the first week after Carmen officially kicked him out, David slept on an old school friend's sofa, until his wife, quite reasonably, decided she wanted the sofa back. So he checked into a hotel round the corner from work, where he lives an Alan Partridgesque existence in which his only distractions are collecting miniature soaps and pressing his trousers in the Corby 3000.

The tremble in his voice says more than his words. 'Been better, I'll be honest.'

'Is Carmen still not returning your calls?'

'Not one. The only person who's phoned is Lydia.'

'Oh, well, that's something.'

'It was to tell me she hates me.'

'Oh.'

'And that Carmen slept with a paparazzo.'

'Oh, dear.'

'It was one of the ones camped outside our house. According to Lydia, she gave him an exclusive – and then carried on giving. They all blame me. And they're obviously right.'

When I've finished on the phone, I pack a picnic and Florence and I jump on the Tube. We emerge from Hyde Park Corner into brilliant sunshine and walk towards the Serpentine with her hand in mine.

467

I've deliberately arrived an hour before everyone else to do something with my daughter that I've been meaning to do for ages.

I'm aware that the pedalos on offer would be more practical for a woman with as little nautical expertise as me, but I want to do this properly. So I opt for a little blue rowing boat, one bigger than we really need but which is perfect for our purposes.

I pay the man at the side of the lake and he helps Florence in, leaving me to an ungainly boarding in which I almost capsize the lot of us.

It takes about forty of our allocated sixty minutes before I'm significantly proficient with the oars to propel us further than six feet, but Florence doesn't seem to mind: every time I come close to dropping the oar or crashing into a pedalo, she collapses into fits of giggles. Eventually I rest the oars in the boat and allow my shoulders to absorb the sunshine.

'This is what your daddy used to do with his granddad when he was a little boy,' I tell her.

'On this lake?'

'No, in Italy. Your daddy loved it. He wanted to do it with you.'

She smiles. 'Then he'll be happy up in heaven that I'm having a go.' She says this entirely matter of factly, but the thought makes my eyes hot.

'There's no doubt about it,' I reply. 'He'll be extremely

proud of you. And he'll be watching over you tomorrow when you go to school for the first time. His big girl.'

When we've finished in the boat, we lay out our picnic blanket at the edge of the lake as we wait for the others to arrive, my stomach rippling with nerves.

It's Nathan I spot first, with Adam in one of those baby rucksacks as he swings Meredith's hand, a beaming smile on his face. As they approach, it strikes me how unfeasibly glamorous she looks considering Adam is apparently awake for half the night.

'Oh, the night time thing's fine,' she tells me. 'I just wake up to breastfeed him then go back to sleep while Nathan does his nappy and burps him. We're a pretty good team, aren't we?' She grins as Nathan kisses her on the cheek looking, I can't help but notice, significantly more exhausted than his girlfriend.

Nathan carefully removes Adam's pudgy pink legs from the rucksack and the baby's eyes briefly flutter open. It strikes me how much he's grown in the seven weeks since he was born. He didn't stay in hospital for long; he thrived right from the beginning, and the doctors seem confident that his prematurity won't affect him in the long term.

'How's your mum after the accident?' asks Nathan.

'A lot better, thanks. And Florence has promised *never* to run across the road again, haven't you?' I throw her a meaningful look, which she tries to ignore.

'When's your friend getting here, Mummy?' she asks instead.

Meredith suppresses a smile.

'Soon,' I reply. 'He had to work today but he's finishing early to come and meet you.'

'He's your boyfriend, isn't he?' Florence says, clearly fancying herself as a junior sleuth. 'Do you think you'll get married?'

I rustle around in the picnic bag and find a sausage roll to put in her mouth.

'What a shame Nicola isn't here too,' Meredith says. 'It'd be like a Barcelona reunion.'

Nathan turns to me. 'Did you manage to enjoy your holiday? It sounded quite eventful – for all of you.'

'Well, yes. We still had the time of our lives, though,' I reassure Meredith. 'I've no doubt Nicola will say the same when I go and see her next week. We're going over to her mum's for a barbeque on the Saturday. And so's Jess, apparently.'

She clears her throat with zero subtlety and I look up to see Harry approaching us.

He has a present for Florence under his arm. I'd told him he didn't need to buy her something, but he insisted that he was prepared to try every cheap trick in the book to make sure this went smoothly. I was happy to concur, although I drew the line at the pink hoover.

My pulse quickens as I glance from him to Florence and a series of anxious questions flutter across my brain.

Will she like him?

Will he like her?

Should I have left this introduction a little while longer?

It's the last thought that's thudding in my head when Meredith leaps up and removes her sunglasses. 'Well, look who it is!' she says, grinning as she gives him a flamboyant hug. She then introduces him to Nathan and Adam who, technically, she says, Harry's already met after, as she delicately puts it, she'd 'squeezed him out in the back of the limo'.

Eventually, Harry turns to look at me and Florence, who's been scrutinising him silently. He smiles and kneels down, kissing me on the cheek self-consciously enough to make me realise he's nervous too. As he pulls back, he turns to my daughter. 'You must be Florence. I'm Harry. And this is for you.'

He hands her the present and she gasps. 'THANK YOU!' Then, 'You know what,' she continues, ripping off paper and barely pausing for breath. 'I think my mummy loves you.'

He catches my eye and I stifle a smile.

Because I think she might be right.

CBS●drama

Whether you love the glamour of Dallas, the feisty exploits of Bad Girls, the courtroom drama of Boston Legal or the forensic challenges of the world's most watched drama CSI: Crime Scene Investigation, CBS Drama is bursting with colourful characters, compelling cliff-hangers, love stories, break-ups and happy endings.

Autumn's line-up includes Patricia Arquette in supernatural series Medium, big hair and bitch fights in Dallas and new Happy Hour strand daily from 6pm with a doublemeasure from everyone's favourite Boston bar Cheers.

Also at CBS Drama you're just one 'like' closer to your on screen heroes. Regular exclusive celebrity interviews and behind the scenes news is hosted on Facebook and Twitter page. Recent contributors include Dallas' Bobby Ewing (Patrick Duffy), CSI's Catherine Willows (Marg Helgenberger) and Cheers' Sam Malone (Ted Danson).

www.cbsdrama.co.uk

f facebook.com/cbsdrama

🐦 twitter.com/cbsdrama